EMERGENCE

T0095320

EMERGENCE

The Novawynd Odysseys- Book 2

Amia Kettier

iUniverse, Inc.
New York   Bloomington

Emergence

The Novawynd Odysseys- Book 2

iUniverse books may be ordered through booksellers or by contacting:

iUniverse
1663 Liberty Drive
Bloomington, IN 47403
www.iuniverse.com
1-800-Authors (1-800-288-4677)

ISBN: 978-1-4401-0406-0 (pbk)
ISBN: 978-1-4401-0408-4 (cloth)
ISBN: 978-1-4401-0407-7 (ebk)

Printed in the United States of America

iUniverse rev. date: 1/29/2009

To Mom, thank you for nurturing our creativity.

Prologue

As I mentioned in Awakening, the first book in the Novawynd series, this series of stories started as a result as my adolescent imaginings at bed-time. As I grew up, I went through a series of personal experiences that first shook my faith in God, and then restored my belief that there is another ethereal realm we humans don't have the capability to fathom at this point in our evolutionary journey.

During my college years, I had an encounter with what I believe to be a super-natural entity, while living in a house dating back to the 1800's. I had been a skeptic about such things as ghosts, but after seeing an apparition with my own eyes on cool summer night, I knew I couldn't deny that there was something else. I attempted to apply all the logic I could muster to explain what I saw, as well as the other various unexplainable phenomenon that occurred in that house, but all events defied rational explanations.

The experience changed my perception and I became curious about super-natural occurrences of all kinds. I had a theory, which I would later come to find others shared: if we are beings made of atoms and atoms are energy, then why couldn't that energy exist after our death. I started to believe that the Universe was permeated with energy, and there are packets of energy imprinted with memory and even intelligence, floating around within that great ethereal realm. I explained this a bit in Awakening: Novawynd Odysseys- Book 1, but in the next volumes, I delve deeper into the concepts of how this translates into space travel and psychic abilities as well as how they are all interrelated.

Years later I was to learn about concepts in Quantum Physics, such as the String Theory, which may explain this energy field I had theorized to exist. Besides that, physicists have been studying the Zero Point Field (ZPF), which is a factual field of energy that does surround us. It not only surrounds us, but we are part of it…basically one with it. From what these scientists describe, we are less like individual, separate entities, and more like jelly-fish swimming in the ocean. We are less individualistic than we think and we are more like the substance that surrounds us (energy). It doesn't take a stretch of the imagination to realize, that on the sub-atomic level, we are the same as all other matter in the universe. I am no different from you, and we are not even any different from the book you are reading now. We are, and everything else is energy.

Physiologists are making leaps in discovering how the human body works on a sub-atomic level. It has long been thought that our actions and reactions are so instantaneous, that it can't be driven by chemicals alone. It is our molecules ability to communicate instantaneously that drives us. Furthermore, these scientists discovered quite by accident that our own molecules retain memory and that memory and intelligence is transmuted to the ZPF that surrounds us. This creates a personal energy bubble, or what some new-agers call an aura. (So far it is only conjecture, but it is hypothesized that our memory may actually exist outside of our brain, contained in this aura.) Apparently, other scientists working in the areas of parapsychology have proven, with study after study, that we are capable of connecting our aura with other people's auras and influencing them, healing them, sharing dreams and even remote-viewing their location. The United States Government was instrumental in performing studies on remote-viewing. During these studies, it was determined that not only is it possible, anyone can do it. You don't have to be "gifted". These remote viewers were able to connect with their subjects over great distance instantaneously.

There are a lot of theories floating around about why something like that may be possible. There are camps that rally for the theory of the non-existence of time or space. Some physicists theorize that everything is occurring in the here and now and there is no linear time. This is how sub-atomic particles called Tachyons can communicate across the universe instantaneously. Imagine if we could transmit ourselves or other objects like that. Considering we are beings of energy, we may one day be able to. However, we live in this hologram called "reality" and we are stuck on the concept of our individual, physical being. We are so caught up in our own emotion, physical feeling and well-being, not-to-mention, self-preservation; we fail to see we are all part of a collective psyche. Jesus knew what he was talking about when he said "Love thy neighbor" and "Do unto others as you would have done unto you". The eastern philosophers knew this concept hundreds of years before Jesus. They called it (and still call it) Karma. In essence, every negative thing you may have done to someone or something will come back around on you. Conversely, any positive thing done will come back to you too. We are all part of one great field of energy. Call it God or Heaven, Nirvana, the Zero Point Field, the Great Spirit, the Ethereal Plane or the Omniaural, it is all the same. The more we come to understand the science behind it, the greater our strides in evolution will be.

CHAPTER 1

Novawynd asked the central computer what its name was. "Michael" was its response. She thought it was unusual that all the central computers were given Earth names, angel names no less. Perhaps the original people who had the names Michael, Gabriel, etc. were Xaxons that the ancient Earthlings had known and mistaken for angels. They had probably been great Xaxons, if central computers were named after them. She would ask someone about the names another time. Right now, she wanted to find her classmate from the Analida Academy, Ameda.

"Michael, where would I find the Leluminalia Ameda… I mean Black Claw?" She had almost forgotten he was to be called by his Leluminali name.

"He is residing on level 452, section H tier 2, unit 560."

"Thank you Michael."

"It is my honor to serve you, Your Supremacy."

"What do you mean by 'Your Supremacy'?" Novawynd was thrown by that term.

1

"It is said that you are the most supreme one, the one being who achieved self-flux, the Lajiachine."

"I know what the Lajiachine is, Michael. I meant, why are you addressing me as 'Your Supremacy'?"

"The Lajiachine is to be referred to as 'Your Supremacy'. It is common knowledge."

"Well, that knowledge was obviously not common to me, besides it's just a rumor, so please don't call me that. Okay?" But, people *were* recognizing her, they may or may not have known about the Lajiachine rumor, but they stepped aside and regarded her with the same intimidation factor she had seen them treat Zefram with. If Lilil made eye contact with someone, they would bow low to her. It was a little weird.

After taking three different elevators, and six different shuttles and trans-carts, she finally arrived at Ameda, a.k.a. Black Claw's quarters. "Hi!" she chirped and waved as his door opened. She was thrilled to see her lion-like friend again. He was pleasantly surprised to see her. He immediately embraced her in his black, furry arms.

"I'm glad you did come to see me. Tomorrow the bidding will begin on my services and I may leave here as soon as my loyalty is sold. At least we'll see each other one last time."

"Can we go get a drink somewhere around here?" Novawynd hadn't had a drink in an anio. They weren't allowed to consume alcohol at the Analida Academy. She needed to unwind a little. The thing about a Leluminalia and alcohol is that one needed to drink a lot and keep drinking to keep a buzz going, because the Leluminali bodies healed so fast, the effects of alcohol did not last long. The beauty of this was that the hang-over was an experience never to be felt again by Novawynd, and she was okay with that.

"Yeah a few sections over, but you can't be seen drinking with me, I'm an inferior." Black Claw seemed nervous that he might even be seen talking to her outside his door.

"Nonsense! The Superior Council itself told me they wanted me to be myself. They valued the person I am. And, the person I *am*, would have a drink with a friend. Besides, what are they gonna do about it?"

"They could scrap you." he warned.

"They won't." she put her hands on his shoulders and gave him a little shake. "Come on." She turned and he reluctantly followed her, then he caught up and joined her at her side as she walked.

When they reached the bar, like the last time Novawynd entered a bar, the din fell silent when they entered. This time, unlike the last time Novawynd entered a bar on a Xaxon, it was because they were Leluminali, and she was Novawynd to be precise. As Novawynd and Black Claw got their liquor and sat down together, some people left because they didn't quite know how to handle being in the same bar as the now illustrious Novawynd; rumored Lajiachine. Others were too drunk to care.

"You know, they have stories all over the telebulletins about you. Everybody knows you graduated with the highest scores *ever* and a lot of debate has begun over whether you are the Lajiachine or not."

"I hope I disappoint them. I don't want to be this *Lajiachine*. Do you realize the pressure behind that expectation?"

"No, I doubt that I can even guess."

"Besides, it's ridiculous to speculate on that. No one will be sure who the Lajiachine is until he or she fulfills the Prophesy anyway. As long as I'm here working for the Xaxony. I can't be the Lajiachine. The Lajiachine is against the Xaxony, not with it."

They drank, heavily and got louder and sang and laughed and generally had a great time, until an Eron came over and pulled up a chair to join them, interrupting their reverie. This Eron was pale, light-blue skinned and had shoulder-length, violet hair with long bangs sweeping over and nearly covering his dark purple eyes.

"Hi!" Novawynd cheerily and drunkenly greeted the stranger. "I'm Novawynd and this is Black Claw."

The Eron smiled at her, "I'm Stunner." he introduced himself.

Novawynd tittered, "Yes, you are." because he actually was quite stunning. She was aware that Erons did not take Ephilderone, the libido blocking drug. There was no need because they were only attracted to females of their own species. Because of their particular mating habits, the females weren't allowed on Xaxons or Xaxon ships. If it seemed sexist, it was, but their society was actually matriarchal. The men were seen as not much use except for heavy labor and fighting, so they were sent off to fight while the women ran everything else. The Eron women managed Eron.

He ignored the comment and continued, "It's funny that I should run into you here of all places. I came here to Xaxon 2, because I was commissioned to be the commander of the space-guard on your ship; when it's ready. In the mean time, I'm supposed to whip together the finest space-guard I can muster for your elite guard."

"How come you're talking to me like I'm a normal person?" Novawynd slurred a little.

"I could see you were acting like you want to be treated like a normal person, so I'm just treating you the way I thought you wanted to be treated." he seemed semi-apologetic, as if his boldness was going to get him in trouble.

"You're very perceptive, for a drunken person." Novawynd pointed at him.

"You're very drunk for a perceptive person." He countered.

"What!" suddenly seeming angry, she stood up, knocking her chair over in the action. "You want to fight about it?" she yelled. Some people quickly exited, fearing annihilation if there should be a fight. Stunner just shrugged his shoulders. He didn't understand. He hadn't said anything inflammatory. Novawynd began giggling. "Just kidding. Just wanted to see if you'd start sweating purple sweat or something." Novawynd tried to sit back down, but her chair had been tipped, so she fell over onto her butt. She laughed hysterically. Black Claw started laughing heartily and he bent down to help her up.

"I think you've had enough tonight, if I may say so." Stunner noted, and then offered, "Shall I escort you home?"

"Oh okay." Novawynd finally submitted. Outside the bar they parted company with Black Claw. She hugged him one more time. "Good luck. I hope your home-world buys you tomorrow. We'll see each other again, hopefully sooner than later." He waved to her as she rode away on the trans-cart, which Stunner had commandeered. She didn't remember much about the ride, except she was happy, then sad, then happy again. Stunner had to help her to her bed. Not because she was incapacitated, but because she didn't want to go. Stunner took his leave of her and Novawynd passed out soon after from shear exhaustion.

*   *   *

Zefram approached his new mission with the same ambition he would any mission. Leluminalia are trained to suppress physical responses and needs. Some physical responses that were typically suppressed were reactions to situations, such as horror or disgust. Other physical responses suppressed were emotions. More difficult to suppress than the others were the body's necessary functions, such as hunger, or thermal regulation or the need to excrete waste. But, the most difficult physical responses to suppress were those derived from one's own personal prejudices. In other words, if a Leluminalia didn't like the Cornithons, he had to put those feelings behind him to do a job that involved the Cornithons.

In Zefram's case, being a clone, he hadn't developed many prejudices. However one of his aversions was to sex. Although he was educated as to the various mating habits of beings across the universe, his only interest had always been nothing more than scientific. The Superior Council had given him the mission to learn the courting and mating habits of the Earthling male, so he could woo a uterine born being, or UB. That UB was Novawynd, and ironically, his only other prejudice. He used his Lelumin training to put his disgust of the physical act of intercourse aside and think of what he had to do as "only a mission".

Zefram knew Novawynd would be suspicious of him not being on Ephilderone. His greatest challenge in wooing her would be to get her to accept that. She would wonder why he suddenly wasn't on it. Ephilderone was a shot given once every three aera (an aera was approximately equivalent to an Earth month). The dosage was usually administered by Xaxon doctors so each Xaxonite's use of the libido blocker could be regulated and verified.

Sometimes a Xaxonite was not near a Xaxon Ephilderone administrator when the shot was needed. Zefram had heard about the cases of men and women that were caught in the wrong place at the wrong time, and unable to get their dosage. The detoxification process sounded horrible, resulting in black-outs, erotic-dreams that occurred while awake, and physical reactions that could not be controlled. The sexual arousal that occurred was said to be so intense as to be excruciating. These reactions were not something that went away on their own, given time. The only relief was sexual release or another dose. That was the part that concerned Zefram. What if his dosage wore off and he wasn't in a place where Novawynd would accept him? It had already been nearly an aera since his last dose and he hadn't even commenced with his primary mission, which was to be Novawynd's mentor. He had a plan, but could he carry it out in only two aera?

*   *   *

It had been an aera since Novawynd had last seen Black Claw. She had heard his home planet of Brekka had been able to buy him after all. She was glad for him, because it was what he had wanted. He must be so proud to be the first Leluminalia from his home world of Brekka, not-to-mention the first Leluminalia to serve Brekka. Novawynd looked forward to the time when she could visit her felinesque, alien friend on his home-world.

Over the last aera, she had grown less attached to her Earthling roots. Having become somewhat of an instant celebrity, the fame perhaps was going to her head a little. She enjoyed the attention, the respect and the perks she was given as a result of her position. Because of this, she was constantly reminded that she had an important role to play, on a universal level, no less. There was nothing for her on Earth now. Of course, she still missed her family. She had thought about having them upgraded, that is, brought aboard a Xaxon and genetically altered to be as perfect as they could be. She did not go through with it because she knew they wouldn't take to the Xaxon society.

Also, in the aera Novawynd needed to wait until her ship was ready, she shadowed Stunner to keep tabs on how his mission to develop her space-guard was coming. He was far more amiable than Zefram, so she sought out his company whenever she could. He always acted inferior to her when other people were around. She thought this was funny, because she felt inferior to him. In fact, she felt inferior to most people around the Xaxon. Stunner, at least treated her as an equal when they were alone together. She understood why he felt he had to act otherwise in the presence of others.

He had no qualms about bringing her to the Xaxon's docking bay and opening a shuttle's engine compartment to show her the inner workings. Novawynd sensed he was thrilled that she showed an interest in the things that interested him. He showed her the simulator that trained the space guard in how to remotely control the flying battle-droids. These droids were called battleots. She had not learned how to control these battleots during her Lelumin training, because the "powers that be" believed such a duty was beneath a Leluminalia. However, Novawynd thought it was great fun, and now she could do it if she had to.

Novawynd could not help but to be attracted to Stunner, even though he was an alien. His name was apropos for his appearance. Aside from his azure skin and violet hair and eyes, he was quite tall and well built for his height, but not bulky, like Black Claw had been. This was common for Eron males. Although he was not subjected to Ephilderone, Stunner was not attracted to Novawynd. As an Eron, he was only attracted to Eron females, because they exuded the appropriate pheromones. Novawynd liked that she could spend time with him, and there was no concern about him putting the moves on her.

On the other hand, Novawynd had done some research on Erons after having met Stunner. She learned that there had been some couplings between Erons and non-Erons from time to time, so she flirted with the fantasy that something could happen between them. Novawynd entertained this fantasy because of the other thing she learned about Eron males. That was their unique physical endowments, the kind of endowments that most women, not prohibited by Ephilderone, are curious about.

None-the-less, she never picked up on any mutual feelings on his part. She was able to get close to him and even to touch him, somewhat inappropriately at times, without him realizing what she was up to. This was as far as she took it, even though she knew he liked her physical contact. Of course she couldn't read his mind, so she didn't know why, but perhaps it reminded him of some latent pleasure he used to get from his mother doting affection on him when he was a child. Who knew? He wasn't accustomed to women who acted that way, but he didn't dissuade her. Before Novawynd's ship was even completed, she and Stunner had developed a close friendship in this way.

Novawynd would often accompany Stunner and some of the other space-guard to public events such as Lightning Cycle (or li-cy) races. Or rather, they would accompany her, as she received preferential treatment. Novawynd knew it probably unnerved Zefram, because she should not be seen cavorting with the common people, but she did it anyway. She kept tabs on her approval level through Michael, the Xaxon's computer, and knew the people liked the fact that she was not pretentious. Her approval level was the highest of any Leluminali, ever.

*　　　*　　　*

One dialo (approximately equivalent to an Earth day), Novawynd's door chimed and it was Zefram standing outside. At first she was sure he'd come to chide her for her unwarranted cavorting with lesser beings, but she sensed his intentions were pleasant, so she allowed him access.

"Good dialo Novawynd." he said sweetly.

"As it is to you." was the typical Xaxon response to that greeting.

"Will you accompany me to the Superior Council chambers? I need to show you how to summon them." he informed.

"I suppose I'm free?" she thought it a little strange that he hadn't just blipped her to ask her to meet him there.

As they journeyed to the council chambers Zefram told Novawynd how he was glad to see that she was adjusting to their society so well and it was great that she was becoming a Leluminali of the people. This was not what she had expected him to think. She was ever so suspicious that he was still just kissing her ass. But then he said, "Being a genetically engineered being, you know I have a stereotypical disdain for nature-born beings. Obviously, in the beginning I didn't hold back my disdain for you, because you were nature-born. The Superior Council told me to take some time to reflect on your special ability and to come to terms with it before we go on our mission together. I hope you appreciate that I've taken a page from you, when I say that I think it is more important for us to work together as friends than as rivals." he paused and looked at her, as if he was looking for her approval. Novawynd just slowly nodded as she looked away.

Still looking at her he continued, "The aera that you didn't see me around, I came to realize that you are a spectacular creature of nature's creation and the influence of the Omniaural. How can I hate something like that? Perhaps you are the Lajiachine and perhaps not; none-the-less, you are special, and I want you to know that I am your right hand." He smiled at her.

She was beginning to believe he had come around, but she was still a little suspicious that he was saying what she wanted to hear. Over a hundred anios of ingrained hatred can't be erased in an aera. However, she would accept that he was at least acting human.

"When you summon the Superior Council, you should ask them about going back to see your family." He suggested. That was a good idea. She would ask, and hopefully they would tell her she could.

At the council chambers, Zefram led Novawynd to the center. "Okay, remember how you were taught at the Analida to meditate to connect with the Omniaural? This is the same thing, only you look for the energy, which the Superior Council has. You've felt their energy every other time you've been in their presence, so you should be able to easily find it in the Omniaural again and draw it out. Once you've made the connection, they will come." Zefram instructed. Novawynd closed her eyes and almost instantly the Superior Council appeared.

"Novawynd, you have successfully summoned us for the first time. However, from here-on-in, please do not summon us unless it is extraordinarily important. We sense you have a question."

"Yes, Your Excellencies. I would like to go to Earth, just to pay a visit to my family. I want to know they're alright, and let them know I'm okay. I'm asking for your permission."

"You may go." Their response was immediate. They were not about to deny the potential Lajiachine a request. Novawynd bowed to them in thanks, and they disappeared.

Outside the chambers Zefram suppressed a pang of jealousy. When Novawynd summoned the Superior Council, they came immediately. They hadn't hesitated in granting her request for even a second. It was obvious they didn't even have to think about it. When Zefram told Novawynd he had come to accept her for what she was, he was telling only fifty percent the truth. Every time Novawynd displayed unusual abilities, he came closer to being completely acceptant that she might be the Lajiachine.

On the trans-cart ride back to her unit, Novawynd had to ask a question that had been on her mind. "Zefram, I know about the Omniaural and the enti, and I accept that it works; however, I still don't know the actual science behind it?"

"Hmph!" Zefram gave a short chuckle. "Well, there are two types of energy in this universe. E1 and E2. E1 is an inert energy and E2 is a supernatural energy. The non-physical plane in which both E1 and E2 exist is called the Omniaural. Both forms of energy permeate everything, because as all matter is made up of atoms and atoms are just energy. So, atoms can be manipulated by extraneous forms of energy, but specifically E2. E2 is unique because it was once E1, but had intelligence imprinted on it. This is possible because energy remains constant throughout the universe, it merely changes from one state to another. Energy that courses through an intelligent being's nervous system changes from inert to active and intelligent. In essence, it evolves. Once a being dies, but particularly if the being dies suddenly, that evolved energy remains imprinted with intelligence, to a point, but it is no longer bound to the physical shell it once was in.

This is what the enti are; packets of disembodied, intelligent energy floating around in the Omniaural. When we speak of the Omniaural as a great omnipotent entity that allows all the abilities we have, we are loosely referring to all the collective enti within the Omniaural as if they make up one entity. Those of us who emit brainwaves on the appropriate frequency attract the enti and that allows us to communicate with and manipulate the E2. That's what gives us our psychic abilities. It is also thanks to E2 and the cooperation of psychics who can manipulate E2 that we have been able to develop the technologies that we currently have, including the flux engines. The flux engines somehow, and don't ask me how, use E2 to move our ships from one point in space to another, inter-dimensionally. You obviously have the ability to manipulate E2 to accomplish the same result."

The trans-cart stopped in front of Novawynd's door, but Zefram had one more thing to say. It was on a different subject. "Once you get your ship, we will make our first mission to Earth. I suggest, besides seeing your family, you should gather anything you might want from Earth, such as entertainment or food. We will fit the ship to accommodate whatever your needs are. If you have some Earthling things around you, you will feel less lost." He turned to face her, "Additionally, you should upgrade an Earthling male to be your companion. I'm sure that would be of great comfort to you, as no Xaxon males will be able to meet your needs." Zefram sort of smirked as he finished this last sentence.

As Zefram moved away on the trans-cart, Novawynd paused a mecron before she entered her unit. She couldn't help but think that Zefram's last comment seemed almost flirty. She couldn't wait to see Stunner again, so she could tell him of Zefram's sudden about-face.

*   *   *

The Xaxony had already chosen a name for Novawynd's new ship. They called it the Zenith. Novawynd could live with that. It was a good name. The day had come for her to leave on her first mission on her first ship, but Novawynd didn't actually get to command the ship. There was a captain enlisted to fulfill that duty. She hadn't met him yet. His name was Djynk (pronounced "jink"), and he was a Wol. The Wol had red skin and blue eyes. They were hairless and had a unique deeply furrowed pattern in their skin beginning at the bridge of the nose and continuing all the way over the head and down the back. They had severely pointed ears and sharp teeth. They reminded Novawynd of demons, but they were nice enough people and highly intelligent.

It was written in the annals, that a Wol could live up to three hundred years, if left to age naturally. One would not likely see a Wol that old, since they were beings engineered by the Xaxony, and the Xaxony stopped the Wol's aging at approximately twenty-eight anios, like everyone else. The Xaxony specifically engineered the Wols to be capable of fitting the Xaxon ships with the unique fluxing engines. These engines emitted intense electro-magnetic forces, or EMF. Droids and Artificial Intelligence workers could not do the work, because the emissions wreaked havoc on their delicate electronic systems. Other beings could not get near the engine without a suit and an oxygen supply, because the engine was immersed in a gas that served as the fuel. The regulators on such protective suits would frequently go crazy from exposure to the EMF and the beings wearing the suits would risk suffocation. However, the Wol were not affected by the EMF and they could breathe the gas without ill effect. They had been engineered to be able to breathe the gas and it was believed that their nearly glowing blue eyes were a result of the gas inhalation and not an actual genetic anomaly.

Wols were rarely seen outside Xaxon 3, the city where Xaxon ships were built, but from time to time a Wol would emerge as having a skill other than an engine fitter. In Djynk's case, he was a tactical genius, and there was no one better to command Novawynd's ship. Captain Djynk was not actually a captain and Commander Stunner was not actually a commander. Those were Earthling military ranks. In the Xaxony the commanding officers were called by the Xaxon number which denoted what level they were. Djynk's rank, which was equivalent to a captain, was *zelo*, that being the Xaxon word for "one". Stunner's rank was *intin*, Xaxon for "two". He had three *atas*, which were like majors, under his command. They were Ata Aleph, Ata Bet, and Ata Cef. Ata was the Xaxon word for "three". Aleph was "A", bet was "B" and cef was "C". There were thirty space-guards on Novawynd's ship rotating in three shifts of ten "on duty" space-guard per shift. Each of the atas were also space-guards as well as the team leaders in command of their shift.

There was also a sub-zelo. Her name was Kananga and she was in control only when Zelo Djynk was not. When commanding officers were not on duty, their rank did not exist. The only time Zelo Djynk was not on duty was while asleep or on leave. Intin Stunner, on the other hand, was always on duty, even while asleep. If the space-guard had to go into action while he was sleeping, he had to wake up and take command.

Novawynd had been trained to command ships in a battle during her training at the Leluminali Analida Academy and so she had thought she would get to do so. That training, it seemed, was only so she could take command if necessary. She was the right hand of the Superior Council now and she did not need to concern herself with commanding ships. She was the eyes and ears of the Superior Council, but more importantly, she was their mouthpiece in negotiations. Most important of all, she was their figurehead.

As the alleged Lajiachine, she was flaunted, so all who might oppose the Xaxony would shrink with fear. Ironically, Novawynd had wanted to use her abilities to be a negotiator of some sort when she was still on Earth. "Professional persuader", she had called it. Now she was getting to fulfill that position and she hated it. She wanted more action. Perhaps the time would come.

Novawynd was ceremoniously introduced to Zelo Djynk, Sub-Zelo Kananga, Intin Stunner and the space-guard. She was a little nervous about her zelo's name sounding like the word "jinx". She'd met some of the space-guard already. Novawynd had participated in activities with a few of them and liked the ones she had met so far. However, upon being "officially" introduced to them, she had to act professional and completely devoid of any familiarity with any of them. They understood this protocol and responded with the same professionalism a space-guard should demonstrate under the circumstances. She was proud and honored to be in the capable hands of these people.

After the virgin voyage ceremony, the Zenith was off to Earth. Novawynd had put a lot of thought into who she would choose to upgrade as her male companion. She considered Will Warner, the actor she had played with in dreams, and Matt McClellan, the rock-star she visited while astral projecting. But she didn't feel either of them would be a good fit for her. Novawynd had to focus on celebrities because she hadn't personally known any men she would upgrade, other than her former physical therapist, Rodney, and he had a little boy. She didn't want to take Rodney away from his son.

Finally she settled on a model named Trevor Eams. She had read an article about him once when he was at the height of his career, and he stuck in her brain because he had a few things in common with her. Like Novawynd, he had come from a farm and his mother had been a nurse. Also like Novawynd, he liked ale. Novawynd had a yearning for some dark Irish ale. That was first on her list of Earthling foods to take with her. She imagined it would be fun spending time chatting with him as they tipped a few back.

Trevor was gorgeous. People all over the world had websites devoted to worshiping him. He was six-feet tall and muscular. Blue eyes sparkled from underneath his shoulder-length sandy blond hair. His smile could knock any woman or gay man out. He obviously made a lot of money off his looks, but in all his photos, he gave off a playful, down-to-Earth, even slightly naive quality. It made him seem, to one looking at his picture, as though he was just a regular guy who just happened to have his picture taken. These qualities were a large part of his appeal.

Although a beautiful man, Trevor was not a super pretty-boy. He had some scars and got his body by lifting calves and bails of hay, rather than working out for hours in the gym. Because they had a few things in common and he was more normal than the usual celebrity,

Novawynd figured they might get along. She supposed he might be arrogant, as most people who make careers out of their looks tend to be; but she didn't have to love him, or vice versa.

The icing on the cake for Novawynd was that Trevor was Australian. She had always had a soft spot for Aussies. She loved their accent and colloquialisms. Plus, every Aussie she'd met in her previous life seemed to have a care-free, adventurous attitude. Trevor also gave off that vibe in every article and interview. Novawynd hoped Trevor was adventuresome, because he might be more willing to accept being upgraded if he was. The one thing on which she insisted was that she wasn't going to upgrade him if he wasn't willing. She would show him around the ship, tell him what would be expected of him, and about the history of the Xaxony. She would let him make his own decision. If he said "no", she would use her telehypnotic abilities, referred to as *Junatiel* by the Leluminali, to suppress his memories. He would return to Earth having no memory of her, the ship or the Xaxony.

The Zenith was already approaching Earth and ready to position itself in a fixed orbit above North America. Novawynd was in the command center, also referred to as commcen or CC, as they came out of the flux. Earth appeared on the four-dimensional display and grew larger as they drew closer. Her heart filled with joy seeing her home planet like this. Earth would never know there was a massive alien craft hovering just above the stratosphere, because the Xaxon ships had a stealth device that caused light and sound waves to distort. Radar, Lasers, visual devices and the naked eye couldn't see the ship. These devices merely picked up on the distortion. A well trained zelo could determine where a ship was by keying in on the distortion, so stealth mode worked best when sneaking up on another ship or planet, such as the Zenith's current situation. Also, Earth would not detect the Zenith's communications. Novawynd didn't know, in fact, no one but the people who developed the system knew, how the Xaxony was able to communicate instantaneously across the universe. The only thing Novawynd could learn on the subject was that communications were achieved by means other than radio or light waves. The Earth had no way to pick up these transmissions.

The central computer on the Zenith had been named Zacharieth, and the male voice chosen for it was deep and soothing. Zacharieth's voice blipped in Novawynd's ear, notifying her that her shuttle was ready and Zefram awaited her in the shuttle bay. Novawynd hurried out of the CC, eager to be reunited with her family. As for her list of Earth supplies, a ship-to-ground or S2G team comprised of space-guard was given the duty to procure it. A second S2G team was assembled for procuring Trevor Eams.

Zefram was already preparing the shuttle for the trip when Novawynd hopped aboard. Zefram didn't need to chauffer Novawynd, act as her body guard or be her personal assistant; however, he *had* said he was her right hand and that meant he was at her service. She had decided she liked this situation, and took advantage of it as much as she could. If nothing else, just to push him to see how much he would take. So far, he was handling it well.

*   *   *

Kat, Novawynd's mother, had moved since her daughter had gone missing. She didn't want the memories associated with the cottage. She used the lottery winnings to buy a nice home in the hills overlooking a river. She now had the gardener that Lilil, now known as Novawynd, had dreamed up for her. She didn't care to do the gardening anymore. She didn't care to raise the animals and she didn't ever care to mold another glob of clay. She spent a lot of time on the deck overlooking the valley, watching the boats go by. Far below, a houseboat was tethered to Kat's dock. Lilil had always wanted one. If she came home, it would be there for her.

Ana, Novawynd's sister, had also relocated closer to Kat. She was only a few minutes away and had another house on the bluffs up river from Kat. Both Kat and Ana could have spent the lottery money more freely, but couldn't bear to. Every time they used the money, they felt tremendous guilt. It was Lilil's money. They spent a lot of the money on private investigators who were out trying to find Lilil. No one, not even the police, could find a trace beyond Lilil's old bedroom.

It had been quite a news story. "Woman that wins lottery disappears within a day of winning". The majority of Kat's stress came from the fact that so many people suspected her. She felt that sometimes even Ana suspected her. Kat had always led an active life, trying to stay young in mind and body. She previously looked and felt a decade younger than other women her age. But over the last year and a half, those ten years had caught up. There were times she thought about just crawling over the railing of the deck and taking a plunge off the steep cliff. But, she was plagued by these dreams of Lilil telling her, "I'm okay mom. Don't worry. I'll see you soon." Kat always woke up feeling oddly reassured, but then immediately melancholy. It had just been a dream, after all.

The evening Kat got a knock at her door, she got a bad feeling. Immediately, she thought it would be the police telling her they found Lilil's body. She hesitated at opening the door. She almost wanted them to go away, if that was what they would tell her. But, she was driven to open the door anyway. She almost couldn't believe that it was Lilil standing there in front of her. Kat gasped and her hand went to her mouth by reflex. She fell forward to embrace her daughter. Like when Lilil woke up in the hospital, Kat cried and shook. She stepped back to take a look at Lilil, almost as if she needed to make sure it was her.

Kat didn't immediately realize that Lilil was dressed oddly, she was just overjoyed that her daughter was here and unharmed.

"Oh god Lilil! Come in." She pulled Lilil in and shut the door.

"I'm glad you're happy to see me. You can't imagine how happy I am to see you." Lilil didn't even need to say it. Her smile was so wide, her face hurt. Tears of happiness streamed down her cheeks. "Call Ana and get her over here right away." Lilil commanded. Kat shuffled into the kitchen to find her cell phone. Lilil loitered around the new house's living room. She chuckled to herself at the shrine that Kat had created for her over the fireplace mantle. But, then she became sad that her mother had to endure the distress of loosing her daughter a second time.

"She's on her way. She's only a few minutes up the road." Kat informed as she shuffled back into the living room. She stopped for a moment just to take in the sight of her daughter again. "You look good. Real good."

"I've been telling you I'm okay and not to worry about me mom. You know, in your dreams." Lilil pointed to her head to emphasize the point. Then she laughed. Kat laughed and began to cry again when she realized those dreams were real.

"I always thought your disappearing had something to do with those psychic abilities you developed, but I could never tell anyone about that." Kat looked questioningly at Lilil. "Was that what happened?"

"Yes, a new psychic ability I developed was responsible, but I'd like to wait until Ana gets here before I explain. I can't stay, and I don't have long. Why don't you show me around this nice house you bought with the lottery money? I'm glad you are living well anyway." Lilil admired.

Sooner than Lilil expected, Ana arrived with her daughter Maris. Maris, Lilil's niece, was five-and-a half-years-old. She almost didn't recognize Lilil at first, but then she and Ana embraced her and wouldn't let go. Eventually Lilil calmed everyone down. She explained what happened and what she'd been doing. "I thought I'd ask you if you wanted to be upgraded too, but I did a lot of thinking about it and I really believe you would be so unhappy there. They're too civilized to *physically* spit on you, but they would do the emotional equivalent of it. If not for my ability to learn things supernaturally fast, I don't think I could've assimilated to the Xaxon society. But, I want you to choose. If, after all I told you, you would want that life, I would grant it to you." Lilil paused.

Kat was the first to respond. "It sounds exciting, but I would miss the wind in the leaves, the sun on my face, and the feel of the dirt in my hands. Besides, I can hardly work the ice maker on my refrigerator; I'd never get along with that technology thrust on me."

"I agree" Ana conceded. "I feel the same way, but I think Maris could benefit. Could you take her with you?"

"She's too young Ana. But, the Superior Council said the Earth will be upgraded in twenty years. She'll definitely be upgraded into the Xaxony, if I have anything to say about it."

"Twenty years is a long time. By then we could all be ready to get off this planet." Ana joked.

"Is that a uniform?" Maris asked in reference to Lilil's outfit. She had always been intelligent beyond her years.

"Yes, this is my Leluminali uniform." Lilil educated.

"Leluminali" Maris repeated. "Can I be a Leluminali like you when I grow up?" They all laughed. Maris' innocence was adorable.

"You probably will be." Lilil assured. Zefram blipped in her ear that their departure time was nearing in ten mecrons. "Well, unfortunately I have to go." Lilil informed. "Walk me out to my shuttle."

"You have a space shuttle here?" Ana seemed surprised.

"Of course. How'd you think I got here? They didn't beam me down. That only happens in *Star Trek*." Lilil laughed.

"What if we change our minds about the upgrading thing? How do we reach you?" Kat wanted clarification.

"I'll still visit you in your dreams from time to time, like always. You can let me know then, if you change your mind."

They walked to the shuttle, but were silent. Kat, Ana and Maris had never seen a Xaxon ship and were just as in awe of its appearance as Novawynd had been the first time she saw one. As they approached, Zefram stepped out onto the lawn. Ironically, one of Kat's Peacocks strutted by at that moment. Novawynd almost laughed out loud at the symbolism.

"This is my counterpart, Zefram," Novawynd introduced. "Zefram, this is my mom, Kat, my sister, Ana and my niece, Maris." She could tell they were smitten with this stunning man. They had probably not seen someone so beautiful in their lives. She knew Zefram sensed it too.

"It's an honor to meet the mother, sister and niece of Novawynd." Zefram affirmed. He crouched down to Maris and gently brushed her cheek with his thumb. Then he smiled at her and she grabbed her mom's leg and hid her blushing face. Novawynd rolled her eyes. He could act so charming when he had to. She still wasn't sure if it was only an act. Novawynd felt the confusion in her family about her name.

"Oh, Novawynd is the name they gave me when I graduated from the Analida. Everyone out there knows me as Novawynd." She explained. They seemed to understand. Zefram sprung back up into the shuttle and began to prepare for take-off. "That's my cue. I have to go, but I'll be back from time to time." She reached out to hug her mother and Ana and Maris joined in a group hug. "And, don't ever forget that I love all of you, very much." Then Novawynd took her leave. She was reluctant to leave them there, but knew it was for the best. At least she had gotten the chance to see them again and let them know she was alright.

CHAPTER 2

When Novawynd returned to the ship, she was told Trevor Eams was aboard and being held in solitaire unit twelve. Solitaire units were small rooms that had a single bed, a tiny closet, a vanity with a sink and a small compartment housing a toilet. They were only used for temporary guests, and usually the guests were guards or servants of more important guests. Novawynd took a trans-cart down to SolU12.

When she entered the unit, Novawynd found Trevor inspecting the amenities of the unit. He recoiled when the door first opened, but relaxed when he saw the person entering was a woman.

"Hello Trevor. I'm Novawynd. I'm sorry about all this, but I want to assure you, you are a guest here, not a prisoner. You aren't going to be held against your will. To prove it to you, I'd like you to take a walk with me." She motioned to the door and it opened again for her. He tentatively moved toward the door.

"You're American?" he ascertained, his Australian accent barely detectable.

"Yes, I'm from Earth like you." Novawynd confirmed.

"From Earth? Aren't we still on Earth?" he was obviously confused. Just then, a Napojan space-guard passed them in the hall, saying something to Novawynd in Xaxon. Trevor stared in disbelief until the Napojan was gone. "Okay, I guess I'm not in the Land of Oz anymore after all." He conceded.

"This is a space ship called Zenith. It's an ambassadorial ship built just for me. We are currently in geosynchronous orbit above Earth. You are, in fact, very far from the land of Oz." She laughed, and then continued, "An ancient and superior space race called the Xaxony owns this ship. They have been genetically engineering beings and placing them on viable planets for many thousands of years. Earth was one of those planets. When a civilization reaches a certain stage of advancement, the Xaxony brings them into the space race. This is called upgrading, but Earth is not ready for upgrading yet. I'm actually the first Earthling to have been upgraded." She sensed he was bursting to say something, so she paused.

He stopped. "This is a dream right." he asked as he looked around.

"This is definitely not a dream." Novawynd assured, somewhat apologetically. She continued, "I was upgraded because I have a very special psychic ability. So, the Xaxony put me through a school where I learned to become a special kind of psychic warrior known as a Leluminalia. This uniform is a Leluminali uniform." Trevor was silent as they walked. He was just trying to get his head around this reality. Novawynd went on, "We Leluminali are like Clint Eastwood, Bruce Lee, James Bond all rolled into one." This reference to Earthling iconography got Trevor's attention again.

"So, you said we were put on Earth by this Xaxony?" Trevor was trying to comprehend, but things were apparently sinking in slower than Novawynd had hoped.

"That's right. I was upgraded and now I work for the Xaxony, which makes me a Xaxon as well as an Earthling. However, technically we Earthlings are all Xaxons. There has been a long history of Xaxon emergence on Earth, but I'll explain more about all of that later, if you want me to."

Trevor just nodded. They were at the cargo bay, where her Earth supplies were currently stowed. Novawynd asked Zacharieth to show her where her favorite ale, the one with the undertone of chocolate was. She sensed Trevor was confused by the fact she was speaking to him in a different language. He couldn't have known she was speaking to the computer and not him. A four-dimensional image of the crates appeared before them, and the crate that contained what she was looking for, glowed red. Trevor walked around the display, obviously amazed that he could see the detail of the crates from all sides, not just the front. He passed his hand through it to test if it was solid. It appeared solid, but it wasn't there. It was just an image.

"That's the four-dimensional imaging they use here instead of flat screens like Earth."

"Where is that coming from?" Trevor looked around to see if he could find the source.

"There are projectors everywhere. You can ask the main, ship's computer to show you something wherever you are, and it just appears." The image disappeared and Novawynd summoned Trevor into the bay. She found the containers of Earth food she had requested. She crawled up onto the totes searching for the one Zacharieth had indicated. "Aha! Here it is." She pulled out a six-pack of the ale she'd been craving. "Is this okay or do you prefer something else?" She showed the package to him and his face lit up.

"I wouldn't turn my nose up at that." Suddenly his Aussie accent returned.

"We'll go back to my unit and I'll explain why you are here over a pint or two."

"I'm sorry, what's your name again?" he needed reminding.

"Novawynd."

"Novawynd, I think you're a woman after my heart." He flashed that spectacular smile at her. She couldn't help but blush. Novawynd could sense he was beginning to feel comfortable, but she knew some alcohol would smooth things over a bit more. They left the cargo bay and Novawynd hopped on a trans-cart that was waiting outside. She urged him to climb aboard also. He did so cautiously, and then they were off.

"We need to make a couple of stops on the way, if you don't mind." Novawynd asked for approval. Trevor shook his head and pursed his lips. She asked the trans-cart to bring them to battleot operations, and then she continued to explain, "This ship is equipped with an elite fighting force, but we don't attack anyone. The Xaxony is a neutral governmental body in the universe, so our space-guard, like the warriors who picked you up, is primarily used for defense purposes. Rather than flying space jets, the space-guard remotely control drone fighters." They were at the battleot operations center by that time, and Novawynd got off the trans-cart and Trevor followed as if in a trance. They entered a room with a line of ergonomic chairs imbued with various complex controls. "This is where the space-guards remotely control the drones, which we call battleots." Trevor nodded in numb acceptance.

Once she was done explaining the concept of the space-guard and the battleots, Novawynd asked Zacharieth to show them a 4D display of the engine. She explained the Xaxon ship's fluxing abilities and the concept of fluxing in general. When she felt he had a basic understanding of these things, they left the battleot operations center and moved on to the entertainment facilities, which only needed a brief explanation. She hoped the facilities were sufficient to meet his need for entertainment. Then, they finally ended up back at her unit. He was impressed by the size of the unit and how technologically advanced everything was. She set down a couple of glasses for the ale and cracked open the cans. While expertly pouring the substance, she continued.

"I said I would get to why you're here. You see, this ship was built just for me and this is its maiden voyage. I will primarily be providing negotiation and ambassadorial work, but I'll be out in space a long time. They suggested I choose a companion from Earth to keep me company, so I chose you." She could feel the concern flooding into Trevor's mind, so she quickly added, "But, I want you to know, I won't hold you here against your will. After all I tell you and show you, after I make it clear what would be expected of you, and what you can expect; if then you still want to go back to Earth, I will let you go. Before you decide, just hear what I have to say. There is still so much more to know, good and bad. You should know it all before deciding." Novawynd sensed that he was feeling excited about the possibilities, not frightened, and this gave her hope.

"How could I go back to living a normal life, after what I've seen and what I know? I mean there's life out here. I'd want to yell it from the roof tops." He dramatically threw his arms out wide to mock the action of yelling something out to the whole world.

"You don't have to worry about that. If you choose to go back, I'll suppress any memories you have of me, this place or anything you learned about the Xaxony. You will never be the wiser, and if any memories do come back to you, you'll only think they were a dream." Trevor looked contemplative. "Let me finish telling you what you should know…"

Novawynd explained the fact that aging and illness had been eliminated, and about how naturally conceived, uterine born UBs and genetically engineered, tubal born 2Bs didn't get along. She also explained about the libido vanquishing Ephilderone and why it was used. She explained, because of the Ephilderone, the women on the Zenith would not be sexually available. "But there are zillions of alien women 'out there' that would like to know an Earth man. You could be the first Earth man to get some alien poontang; you know what I'm saying?" She laughed. The liquor was obviously loosening her inhibition now. Trevor also laughed, not believing she just said that, but liking that she had.

"But what about you?" he wondered. "Aren't I going to basically be your kept man? Shouldn't I be doing that for you?"

"I'm not on Ephilderone, but I wouldn't be upgrading you so you can be my sex slave. If you never touched me in that way, I wouldn't care. I wanted to upgrade you so I can have someone fun to relate to on an Earthling level, and I thought you might be a fun person. I thought you would be adventurous enough to grab this opportunity and run with it." She paused, looking into his eyes to prove her sincerity. "But, I also chose you, because if you did want to touch me in that way, I couldn't say 'no'." Novawynd gave him a naughty smile and winked.

"Mmmmm." He purred.

"Let me show you the room you would get if you stay." She led him out of her unit again and into the unit next door. It wasn't as expansive as Novawynd's, but still quite spacious and nice. There were two droids present, fitting the giant screen TV she had requested for Trevor's quarters. "You wouldn't need to work. Your finances would be unlimited. But, if you felt listless, we would find some way for you to contribute that would befit you." Trevor walked around the unit trying to decide if he could handle this. Novawynd felt that he was positive.

She let him have a look around before ushering him back to her own quarters. In the hallway they ran into Zefram. After being introduced to Zefram, Trevor made the observation, "You're wearing the same uniform. Are you the same type of warrior as Novawynd?"

"I am a Leluminalia, yes." There was an awkward silence and then Zefram said, "I have to move on, but it was a pleasure meeting you Trevor. If you choose to stay, we'll have a chat over Cirrilean brandy sometime."

Back in Novawynd's quarters, Trevor laughed. "That guy totally wants you." He teased Novawynd.

"Zefram is on Ephilderone, he isn't capable of thinking like that." Novawynd denied.

"As a guy, I know when I get *the look* from another guy. The 'you're my competition, huh? I'm gonna stomp on you.' look."

"He may want to stomp on you, but it would be for another reason, you see, he's a 2B and he considers himself quite superior to our kind. Zefram would squash us if I wasn't his superior."

"You're his superior?" A surprised tone came from Trevor.

"Yes." She affirmed. Trevor laughed whole-heartedly and Novawynd joined in. It *was* funny when she took a step outside of herself and looked at it through someone else's eyes.

"Who's your superior then?"

"When it comes to Leluminali, there is no one superior. I'm the top dog, but I answer to the Superior Council. They are the eight ancient, ethereal beings that are the sovereigns of the universe, including Earth. I exist to do their bidding."

"Wow, an Earth woman is at the top of the top? Go Earth!" He pumped his fist in the air. Novawynd smiled.

"Yeah, every day I learn something new about myself and I'm still astounded. I was just an average woman from Earth, and now I'm this super, universal, psych warrior. I've become desensitized to it all, but only because I'm still waiting to wake up."

"You said you had psychic abilities. Can you read my mind right now? What am I thinking?" he tested.

"It's not like that." Novawynd continued to explain about some of the commonly known Leluminali abilities, but she also explained her self-fluxing ability and the importance of that. Leluminali each had their unique abilities, which they were never to disclose; not even to other Leluminali. These abilities were called, *hidden* abilities for a reason. If others knew of a Leluminalia's hidden abilities, he or she would have an advantage. Everyone knew about Leluminali empathic abilities and the telehypnotic Junatiel. Also, the whole universe knew of Novawynd's self-fluxing ability, so she was free to talk about those things. But, she had many more abilities only she knew of.

"That is astounding. I'm… astounded." Trevor smirked again. He was so cute when he did that.

"Trevor?" Novawynd was serious suddenly. "It's getting to be time for me to leave you to think this over before making a decision. I want you make an informed decision. Do you have any questions for me?"

"Will I get to see my family ever again?"

"Yes. I'll be back from time to time to visit my family. You can visit your's then. I'll even give you a chance to say good-bye initially. But, all you should tell them is that you're going away and assure them not to worry. Don't say anything about this." Novawynd indicated to their surroundings.

"What if I say no, but change my mind later?"

"You won't have any memory of what transpired here. If you say 'no' tonight, you'll wake up back in your bed in the morning and you'll never remember. So, you won't be able to change your mind. Likewise, if you say yes, you will be processed, which means you will undergo gene manipulation therapy. You will never grow old or get sick again. You will also become sterile, so you'll never produce children of your own. You could never return to Earth then, because everyone you know would grow old and die, and you will not. That would be weird, don't you think?" Trevor contemplated what Novawynd had just said.

"Can I have a pet?" That question seemed to come out of the blue.

"Do you have a pet?" Novawynd needed clarification before she answered.

"I have a little female border collie. Her name is Swizel."

"Swizel? That's a funny name for a dog. Where did that name come from?"

"Well my mum had a dog she named Olive. So as a joke on my mum, my brothers and I decided it would be fun to name all our dogs after things you put in drinks. At first it was Cherry and Worm and Peel. It went on from there so then it was Brandy, Tequila and Shooter. The litter Swizel came from also had Snifter and Shaker."

"I think a border collie would be too confined here. But, what we could do is bring Swizel along, and have an artificial version done of her. You would never know the difference. The real Swizel can go back to Earth and run free, and the artificial Swizel will be content to hang out on the ship."

"I don't think I can feel anything for a robot dog." Trevor struggled with that.

"You'd be surprised. You might like an artificial dog better." Novawynd reasoned. "Think about it. It shows genuine affection when appropriate. It behaves. It never poops, barfs or farts in your house, and it outperforms a real dog. You could tell the real Swizel to go get a beer for you out of the fridge and she would look at you funny because you haven't taught her that trick. But, an artificial dog would know just what you're talking about, and do it for you, and without having to be trained. Plus it will never grow old or die, so you don't have to deal with the emotional stress of its passing. If you got tired of it, however, you could just have it scrapped and get a new one."

"Well… I'll have to think about it."

"Do you have any other questions?" Novawynd asked again.

"I can't think of any right now, but can I bother you later if any come up while I'm thinking this through."

"Absolutely. It's no bother at all." Novawynd assured. Novawynd brought Trevor back to his potential quarters. She gave him a quick tutorial on how to utilize Zacharieth to blip her, and to research anything he wished to know. Before she left him to ponder his options, she had one last thing to say. "You are being offered an opportunity of a lifetime. You can be the second Earthling ever upgraded; the first Earth man to be upgraded into a superior civilization. There are so many fascinating alien worlds and people to experience and so many adventures to be had. It would just be a shame if you said 'no'. But, whatever your choice, I said I would honor it, and I will." With that, she left him to think things through.

Novawynd headed off to the CC. When she arrived, Djynk was there. "Zelo Djynk, I need a shuttle ready to return to Earth ASAP. The Earthling has been given two tecrons to think things through, but the shuttle should be ready in case it doesn't take him that long." Novawynd was always careful to speak to Xaxons about her own people, as if she was not one of them. This helped them accept her better.

The Command Center was not a very large room; only about twelve-foot by twelve-foot. The captain could command the ship from anywhere, but the room served as a central meeting place for the officers to congregate and confer if they should need to. Typically, Zacharieth took care of all navigation and communications functions, as well as all engineering and mechanical maintenance. Zelo Djynk hung out in the CC, as zelo's often did, just to have a place where others would know he was always available.

There were no windows in the ship. The ships were designed to accommodate magnetic drivers that created magnetic fields, which allowed the ships to have gravity. This did not allow for windows. Windows weren't necessary anyway, since Zacharieth could project a view from any direction requested. One of the things typically viewed in the CC was the primary view of interest. Some other displays typically viewed by the commanding officers in the CC were ship's system status, as well as crew status and locations. Zelo Djynk requested a display of the shuttle bay and gave the command to have Novawynd's shuttle readied.

The zelo rank, although the highest on the Xaxon stellar armada, was not the highest rank there was. The rank of *tekla*, equivalent to Earth "zero", was reserved for VIPs, such as political leaders, sovereigns, and Leluminali. A tekla had the right to give the commanding officers orders, including the Zelos. Political figures didn't care to stick their nose in the commanding officers' business, instead leaving the commanding of ships to the officers, except if absolutely necessary. The Leluminali, on the other hand, were actually expected to give orders. And so it was, that when Novawynd ordered Zelo Djynk to do something, he did it unflinchingly.

Only fifteen mecrons passed before Trevor blipped Novawynd. "Yes, Trevor?" she acknowledged.

"I've decided…I want to stay." he informed.

"Trevor, you took less than twenty minutes to make your decision. Are you certain?" she wanted him to be sure.

"I don't need any more time. The way I see it, I'd be an idiot to turn this opportunity down. Whatever difficulties there might be, I'll adapt. I'm determined."

"Very well, meet me at the shuttle bay. I'll take you to say good-bye to your mother and father. We'll have to make it quick, I'm expected to get moving on my mission soon."

"Fine. How do I find the shuttle bay?"

"Ask Zacharieth. He'll guide you."

"Okay. Thanks…um, over and out?" Trevor didn't know how to end the transmission. It wasn't like pressing a button on a cell phone.

Novawynd chuckled to herself, "Zacharieth, end transmission." she commanded. She turned to Djynk then, "We won't be long, but as soon as we're back, we need to get to Xaxon 2. We'll leave him there for processing while we head off to Uinalon." When Novawynd was finished laying out his orders, Zelo Djynk just nodded in understanding. He was a man of few words.

Trevor met Novawynd at the shuttle with that smile of his. "What did you decide about Swizel?" she asked.

"I want to take her with, but only to get an artificial version made. Then I want to put her back on Earth to live out her days."

"That's a wise choice."

*   *   *

Trevor's parents were sleeping soundly when he entered their bedroom. He crouched down by his mother's side of the bed and touched her shoulder gently. When she didn't wake he shook her a little, "Mum" he said aloud. She woke up and blinked the sleep out of her eyes.

"Trevor? What're you doin?" she asked sleepily.

"Trevor?" came his father's voice from the other side of his mother. His father sat up.

"I wanted to tell you guys I'm going away for a while. I'll be back, so don't worry about me." Trevor made his explanation quick.

"What are you talking about? Are you in trouble?" His father grilled him.

Trevor snorted, "No. I'm just going on a long trip. I've discovered something fantastic and I can't tell you about it right now. But, I've never been less in trouble and I'm happiest I've ever been. Besides, I'm telling you, I'll be back. I have to go. I love you. Tell Troy and Trent I love em too, okay?"

"But Trevor, If you're in some sort of trouble son, we can help." his mother tried desperately to get to the root of what he was talking about.

Trevor was already nearly out the door, but he turned back, "No worries eh?" he assured and left. He was down the stairs, out the front door and in the shuttle in seconds flat. He and Novawynd took off to pick up his dog. His parents got up and walked out onto the front porch, thinking they would catch him getting into a car or on a motorbike. But, there was nothing there. Not even dust or tail-lights in the distance. It was such a strange visit, and so ghostly the way he came and went.

At Trevor's flat in the city, Swizel was waiting and so happy to see him when he returned home. He crouched down and rubbed her while she licked his face. This was the usual greeting they shared.

Novawynd made a suggestion, "If you have a couple of large suitcases, I suggest you fill them with any personal items you want to bring along. I'll help you pack if you tell me what you need." she offered.

Trevor went in the hall closet and pulled out a large suitcase and a large duffel-bag. "I want pictures, movies and CDs. Also, Swizel will need her food. I suppose I don't have enough to get her through." He stopped to contemplate that.

"Don't worry about that. The ship's sustenance replicator will make a reproduction food for her. You won't need CDs or DVD's. I just picked up every movie that's ever been manufactured on DVD and we have every movie and every song ever digitally recorded on Earth. Zacharieth is working on uploading everything, and you'll be able to access whatever you want, when you want it." She started putting his photo albums in his bag. Trevor went into his bedroom. "You won't need clothes." she called after him. "They will make whatever you need on Xaxon 2 while you're in processing. Then you'll be in the latest Xaxon fashion." Novawynd giggled a little. He had been a professional male model after all. The thought of him mugging in his new Xaxon clothing started to get her hot. "You can put on a show for me." She yelled to him. He came back out of the bedroom with a pillow and some framed pictures.

"I wasn't a runway model. I was an under-ware model, there's a difference." He informed.

"It doesn't matter. I would still like a show. It would amuse me." Novawynd joked and gave him a flirty smile and a wink.

When they were finished packing, all Trevor had was pictures, some Australian foot-ball trophies ("footie trophies" he had called them), and a box of magazines and printouts from Internet pages which had various interviews with him. When he picked up the box of magazines, he hesitated and looked sad for a moment.

"I was saving all this for my kids and gran-kids. But, I won't have kids, will I? Should I leave it here?"

"Bring it along. You won't have kids, but you could have clone Trevors and Trevorettes running around. Perfectly engineered children, made to order." she commented sarcastically.

Novawynd and Trevor took off and arrived at the Zenith, which immediately left Earth's orbit and cruised out into space a few thousand miles, before fluxing back to Xaxon 2.

*   *   *

As soon as they stepped out of the Zenith's docking tube, Novawynd was blipped by Xaxon 2's main-frame computer, Gabriel.

"Welcome back Novawynd. Let me say congratulations on your status." Gabriel greeted her.

"Thank you Gabriel. Is genetics central ready for us?" she inquired, cutting short the formalities. Trevor looked at her perplexed, and then remembered what she told him about the communication devices. He would have one of his own soon.

"Yes, they are awaiting Trevor's arrival."

"Tell them we will be there in twenty mecrons." She commanded.

Novawynd hopped on the first available trans-cart that passed by. They would switch trans-carts on this level once. Take an express elevator up 800 levels, take two more trans-carts and ride the trolley for quite a great distance, before they were at central genetics. This was just one of eight genetics labs in Xaxon 2. This was also the lab Novawynd herself was processed in. The lab tech, Zella, who also processed Novawynd, was still working in the lab. Tren, Zella's counterpart, had been given a promotion to a different lab.

As was the habit of any being that had just been upgraded into Xaxon 2, Trevor stared in disbelief at all the unusual beings surrounding him. Novawynd whispered to him, "Don't stare. Many aliens consider staring a form of aggression. Some consider it more aggressive than others. You can look, but if you don't want to get blasted, avert your eyes and act nonchalant if anyone sees you looking at them." Novawynd laughed to herself, because Zefram had given her the same advice when she first arrived there.

Novawynd hung around, translating to Trevor the explanations of what was to be expected in this process. She gave Zella strict instructions not to alter Trevor in any way. She liked his flaws, such as the scars he had here and there, including one on his face. None of them were horrible, just character marks. She would always know the real Trevor because of these marks.

Soon Trevor was sedated, just as she had been a year-and-a-half before, or anio-and-a-half, as the Xaxonites would say. She took her leave, as Trevor would not be released from stasis for another aera. It was time for her to concentrate on her duty, and so she returned to the Zenith.

CHAPTER 3

After leaving Trevor on Xaxon 2 for processing, Novawynd's first real mission was to visit the planet Uinalon, and then the planet Vilijian. The tension between these long-time rival planets was escalating again. The Superior Council needed Novawynd and Zefram to keep tabs on the status.

The Vilijians were humanoid, but with onyx black skin and eyes as black as pools of ink. Their noses reminded Novawynd of a bat's nose. Wide, wrinkled and set with two giant nostrils. There was a bit of a flap of skin at the very tip of the nose, which it was said was super sensitive to vibrations. The Vilijians had incredibly acute senses of smell. Their scent memory was as advanced as a dog. If they couldn't see anything, they could get along fine by sense of smell alone.

Vilijia was a volcanic planet with a porous rock mantle. The planet was basically an Earth-sized pumice stone. There were no oceans, but the planet's mantle flowed with subterranean rivers and lakes, basically all interconnected by intricate tunnels. Like Earth, the planet had forests and prairies and savannas and deserts on its surface, but no water was visible from space. Unlike Earth's ethereal blue, this planet appeared green when viewed from space.

The Vilijians were initially placed on the planet by the Xaxony. They had not been genetically engineered for the Vilijia environment, they had just been genetically engineered and the Xaxony needed to put them somewhere. Vilijia won that lottery. The new Vilijians quickly learned that it was easier to subsist if they lived close to the water; therefore, they built their cities underground. They evolved and adapted over hundreds of thousands of anios. This is how they developed their super-sense-of-smell and keen night-vision.

The Vilijian civilization was many centuries more advanced than that of Earth. They had developed an advanced robotics industry built on their search for water. They needed robots that could go down holes they themselves could not. Eventually, one nation began using the robots to wage war upon the other nations of their own planet. The war robots became quite elaborate in their design and function. Once the Xaxony upgraded the Vilijians, the planet of Vilijia found peace. Their robotics programs were adopted by the Xaxony and its allies and Vilijia became quite prosperous on their robotics industry.

The planet Uinalon was also seeded by the Xaxony. The planet itself was much like Earth and really unremarkable. The people were remarkable, however. In appearance, they were ultra tall and fine limbed with elegant facial features. They were nearly hairless, with the exception of a striped mane on the head, which covered the shoulders and extended part-way down the back. Their most unusual features were their stripes. The naturally occurring, dark markings on their deep golden-brown skin looked as though someone had burned-in the reflection of water ripples on the skin. The Uinalons evolved with this feature as camouflage.

The Uinalons had developed artificial intelligence. Many other races developed AI as well, but they were driven out of business by the superiority of the Uinalon product. The Uinalons focused on the most appropriate uses for the artificial people, or AP, and prospered while its competition floundered and fell away. Over the course of a couple thousand years, the Uinalons became the only manufacturers of artificial people in the universe.

The Xaxony and its allies used the AP for many reasons, but primarily where a replica of a living-being was needed. Other purposes for AP were to fill positions that required a being to retain massive amounts of information and perform tasks perfectly. They made excellent instructors, therapists and service workers where a more "human touch", than a robot could provide was necessary. For instance, the beautician onboard the Zenith was AP. She could do manicures, pedicures, facials, any hairstyle ever done or that could be imagined. She would relate to her clients as if she was human, No one could tell she was AP if they didn't already know, except she could perform all her tasks flawlessly and more quickly than any human ever could.

Strangely enough, the Uinalon's greatest market was in pleasure AP. Despite the fact that most citizens residing in a Xaxon, serving on a Xaxon ship or an allied Xaxon ship were subject to the sexually repressive results of Ephilderone, the majority of the universe was not. Prior to Uinalon's AP, the slave trade was extensive and the majority of slaves became sex slaves. After AP, the slave trade become nearly extinct, only existing because a living-being slave was cheap and the AP servant or sex toy was very expensive. However, to those who had the AP, it was well worth it. The Uinalon AP was unmatched for realistic quality.

The friction between Uinalon and Vilijia started when Uinalon entered the warfare arena. Certain civilizations began commissioning

AP soldiers. It had been determined that an artificial soldier was more cost effective than a living-being soldier because it could do the work of ten men, it was nearly impossible to destroy and it was accurate, so less ammunition was wasted. The AP soldiers did not require sleep, nor did they need to eat, bathe, have sex, defecate or urinate. They only required simple, routine maintenance. AP soldiers had no emotional problems relating to warfare. They would do whatever was ordered of them and they had no fear, nor did they have regret.

The Vilijians contended that a robot soldier could do all that and more, because it was not limited by the constraints of being a replication of a living-being. On the contrary, the AP soldiers were necessary where a replication was needed, in order to fool other living-beings. This wasn't needed often, but the Vilijian's were still concerned. They had the warfare robotics market sewn up before the Uinalon's interfered. It was a hot-button issue. Whenever one planet encroached on the other's market foothold, sparks usually flew.

The Xaxony needed both planets' products, so it kept Uinalon and Vilijia from destroying each other physically or financially by supporting both planets. This was good for the Xaxony and its allies because it fueled competition and thereby created better products. It was a delicate balance, and the pendulum had begun to swing too far to one side. It was now Novawynd's mission to determine the problem and restore the balance.

*   *   *

A lot of time was spent floating in dead space during missions. The reason was because, one needed appointments to visit planetary leaders, but the ship couldn't stay docked at a Xaxon when the docks were needed by other ships. So, if it wasn't time to arrive at the appointed place and the Xaxon needed the port, a ship would simply flux out to some point in space, and wait. This state where a ship was waiting to go on to its next appointed destination was called *caesura interval*. The Zenith would hold its caesura interval for two dialo.

Because she had not seen Stunner for nearly a dialo-and-a-half, Novawynd found herself oddly needing some of his company. She went to his door and Zacharieth announced her presence. It was odd to find Stunner in his unit. He was enjoying some down-time, because now that they were officially on a mission, he was officially always on duty. When he slept, he kept his uniform at the ready if he should be summoned. When not sleeping, he almost always wore his uniform. At this moment, however, Novawynd found him without his boots and jacket on.

"Novawynd!" he was pleasantly surprised by her unannounced visit. He dropped his tone down to a more casual level. "What brings you by?"

"Just a friendly visit. Needed to chat. Do you have some time?" Novawynd asked considerately, but hoped he's say *yes*.

"Of course." He jerked his head towards his unit as a signal for her to enter. "What's on your mind?" he probed. Novawynd noticed his jacket was hung at the ready by the door. The Xaxon space force's uniforms were grey with red trim. They reminded Novawynd of a motocross rider's outfit; sporty but flexible. They were padded in some areas and vented in others and made of the same insulating material the Leluminali uniforms were made of.

Novawynd plopped down on his sofa with one leg tucked underneath her. "I guess I'm a little nervous about this mission, considering it's my first. I just don't want to mess it up."

Stunner sat down on the same sofa, facing her in the same position; one leg tucked under him. "You have nothing to worry about. All you have to do is go ask each of the planets' rulers what's up and give the info to the Superior Council. They'll tell you how to proceed from there. I'm surprised Zefram hasn't gone over that with you yet."

"He probably will, but he'll wait until last minute, just to let me sweat it out a bit. Or, he hasn't had a chance to tell me. I haven't been hanging around with him, which is odd, because you know how much I love him." she reminded him sarcastically. Stunner snorted.

"Even so, you're Novawynd, the Lajiachine." Stunner meant that in a teasing way, because he knew how much she rejected that notion. "If you asked the leaders of Uinalon and Vilijia to dance and sing, they'd do it for you. Nothing you could say would be wrong in their eyes." He put his hand on her knee and squeezed it in reassurance.

"That's what I'm worried about." Novawynd admitted. "I'm worried about what kind of damage I can do with that kind of power." She thought about his hand on her knee just then and she knew it was just a friendly gesture, but it was getting her aroused. "Zacharieth finished uploading all the Earth entertainment I collected." she changed the subject. "You should come over to my unit tonight and watch this movie with me. You'd love it." she was thinking of a Clint Eastwood western. She thought he would like that genre of film.

"Sure. I'd love to. You've told me so much about Earth movies, I'm looking forward to seeing them all."

With that Novawynd got up to leave. "Be at my unit in three tecrons." she commanded. Stunner nodded.

*   *   *

Novawynd really liked Stunner. He was a just a great guy and he was genuinely a good friend to her. He would bend over backwards for her, and not just because she was a Leluminalia or the alleged Lajiachine. That was just the kind of guy he was. There was a reason he was the intin of Novawynd's space-guard. He had gotten there because of his abilities, but also because people just respected him. He had been around a while and had gained quite a bit of wisdom. He was tough when he needed to be and soft when he needed to be. Novawynd looked to him for guidance more than she looked to Zefram, even though Zefram was supposed to be her tutor.

Novawynd regularly found herself lusting after Stunner's body. Not just because he was very nice to look at, but because of the well known Eron male attributes which she had become very curious about. Novawynd had learned about the fact that Eron males had two penises: the *penis majora* and the *penis minora*. The penis majora was the organ the Eron male used for breeding, and it was large. This was because the Erons in general were large, which meant the females were large and their vaginas were therefore, accommodating. But, the penis minora was small; only the size of a man's pinky. It was used for urination only. The majora was attached to the testes and the minora was attached to the bladder. Both organs retracted into the Eron male's pelvic cavity, but both became erect when the Eron male was aroused. The minora worked during sexual intercourse as an additional stimulator. It stimulated the clitoris from the front or the rectum from the rear.

Additionally, the Eron males, when aroused, exuded a lubricant. This liquid was nothing more than lubricant to an Eron female, but to other females with dissimilar body chemistry, it was said to cause a tingly sensation, which heightened arousal for several tecrons after intercourse. It was noted that this sensation caused orgasms in certain subjects up to twenty tecrons after coupling.

Erons were pheromone driven, as mentioned before, but their mating practices were unusual because of this. Men and women did not have relationships on Eron. If a female gave off the right pheromones to attract a certain male, he was instantly aroused and had to mate with her right then. Earthlings would see this as rape, but the Eron females were more than accepting of this practice. On Eron, this was the way it had always been; they knew no other way. Their society had been built around accommodating such acts. Alongside public restrooms, there were public breeding rooms everywhere on Eron.

Once an Eron female was impregnated, the Eron male would not be a nurturer to the child. In most cases, an Eron female needed to be bred several times before she would conceive, so it was never known who the father truly was anyway. But, the Eron females were quite adept at being single mothers. It was a matriarchal society, so the women and children were quite well cared for by society in general. The Eron males, being raised solely by women, were quite respectful of women and were capable of having emotional bonds with them, such as they had with their mothers and sisters. But, they just couldn't help the physical reaction that occurred when a female giving off the right pheromones came into their midst. Therefore, monogamy was something that just wasn't for their kind.

It was not clear to how a non-Eron female ever had intercourse with an Eron male. Many alien species throughout the universe have pheromones, and it was thought that some women had some similar scents to that of Eron females. It was also thought that women who experienced Eron males, may have used Eron pheromones to entice the men.

Although Novawynd entertained the fantasy of possibly discovering these wonders, she didn't have Eron pheromones. She might have been able to use her Junatiel powers to fool Stunner into believing she had the scent, but she was afraid to try it because things would change between them if they ever became sexually involved. If sexual intercourse ever occurred between them, their friendship would become a sexual relationship. It would become more complex than Novawynd cared to have her relationship with Stunner. However, Novawynd did intend to take their relationship to another level. She needed some physical affection, but without the sex.

That evening when Stunner showed up to watch the movie, he was in uniform, as always, but he wasn't wearing his jacket. Instead he had it slung over his shoulder, hooked with one finger. Novawynd took his jacket and hung it by the door. She asked him to take off his boots. He did so, but kept them near the sofa, in case he would need to get into them quickly. They settled on the sofa and began watching the movie. Stunner was transfixed. Novawynd found it easy to snuggle up next to him without him noticing. She wrapped his strong arms around her, and he didn't seem to mind, in fact he seemed to like it. He smelled nice and his strong, warm embrace comforted Novawynd. This was exactly what she needed.

Once the movie ended, Stunner mentioned he wanted to see all of the Earth movies. The Xaxony didn't have entertainment like that. "I can't believe such a huge industry grew up around beings needing to be entertained." He shook his head as he pulled on his boots. "This was nice. What are we going to watch tomorrow?" he asked as he stood up.

"I'll surprise you." Novawynd winked. Then he did something unexpected. He bent down quickly and gave her a peck on the cheek. It was completely innocent. The kind of peck he would have given his sister. But, it meant something that he felt close enough to Novawynd to share that with her. He turned and left. Once the door closed behind Stunner, Novawynd squealed with delight.

*   *   *

The next morning, Novawynd was awakened by Zefram blipping her. "Novawynd, I need to brief you. Can you meet me in my quarters in twenty mecrons?"

"Sure. I could be there sooner if you like." she offered.

"If it pleases you; I'm ready now."

"Okay. I'll be there in five."

When Novawynd arrived at Zefram's unit, she found him in a way she had never seen him before. He was reclining casually on his sofa without his uniform jacket or boots on. He was going over schematics of the Uinalon factories, and he seemed quite relaxed. A one-hundred-percent turnaround from the way Novawynd usually saw him. The day before when she had seen Stunner out of uniform, it struck her as odd, and now Zefram was also out of uniform, which she didn't think she'd ever see. Then she realized, now that they were off on missions, she would see them relaxing more in their own environments. That was acceptable.

"Have a seat, if it pleases you." he offered.

Novawynd unfastened her jacket's buckles and took it off as well. If this was to be a casual meeting, then she intended to relax too. She threw her uniform jacket over the back of the sofa and sat on the edge of the seat in anticipation of what Zefram had to say. "Why are you going over schematics? If you need them, can't you have the Zenith transmit them to you on your metaband?" she was truly curious.

"I'm comparing schematics we had in our system from an anio ago to current schematics. I'm looking for discrepancies." Zefram explained.

"I see. So, we'll know about any anomalies, before we even talk to them. But, this isn't the first time a Leluminalia has come to inspect their operations. They would expect this." Novawynd had studied the logs from all previous visits to Uinalon to learn how other Leluminali handled the negotiations. Novawynd shouldn't have been surprised to find that two of the Leluminali that previously visited Uinalon for similar negotiations were the first Zefram, or Z1, and Danalian.

Zefram 1 had logs that read nearly the same way the second Zefram's did. Danalian's logs, on the other hand, were embellished with more mutual respect between him and the Uinalon politicians. Novawynd decided to play this the way Danalian had.

Novawynd felt more comfortable knowing she could read from an unwritten script. But, the research Zefram was doing now, prepared them, should they need to improvise. Zefram began to quiz Novawynd about the Uinalon political leader's titles and status and how to refer to them. She passed the test on all the formalities, so he made her role play with him. He acted as the Uinalon premier and went through the motions the premier would likely go through. But, after only a few minutes into their scenario, Novawynd stopped Zefram.

"Zefram, this is the way the Premier would act toward me if I were just a Leluminalia, but because to them I am the Lajiachine, he'll act differently. I need to know how to act in the event of his kowtowing and genuflecting, etc."

"You're right. I was testing you yet again to see if you realized that. Of course, you are too perceptive to have let that get by you." Zefram conceded, so he changed his demeanor and remodeled himself as a greatly humbled and sycophantic premier. They acted that scene out for a while and Novawynd thought she was doing quite well, but Zefram scolded Novawynd.

"You are treating the Premier with far too much respect. You have to command their respect, and if you don't get it, you can discipline whoever doesn't give it." But then he paused and softened his tone a bit before continuing, "I know you don't accept that you are the Lajiachine, but you just have to play the part. I know you don't want to discipline anyone for not showing you the level of respect the Lajiachine should be shown, so leave that to me." he assured.

"Zefram, I don't want to be the Lajiachine that commands respect by intimidation and fear tactics. I want people to respect me because of my skill, intelligence, mutual respect, honesty and fairness. You attract more flies with honey than with vinegar." This last phrase was lost on Zefram because flies, honey and vinegar were all completely foreign to him, but he got the point. He was silent for a moment.

"Novawynd, I know you think I'm a cold, emotionless killing machine. You've made that clear to me. Just because I'm a product of the Xaxon designers, doesn't mean I don't feel. When I have to kill someone or something, I do it because it's my duty. But, I have a connection to the Omniaural and when I take a life I feel it. You haven't had a chance to experience that yet, but you will.

Look around you. You've never been in my unit before. You didn't know that I have a passion. It's art. Come over here." he coaxed Novawynd. Reluctantly she followed, deciding to allow him to get this off his chest. "The art I like to collect is art that depicts history of civilizations and evolution. This piece I got from your planet." It was a cave drawing of a buffalo and men hunting it. "I collect these things because I don't have a past or a lineage like this. I can't say I evolved... I was just created. The only thing I have to hold onto is that the Xaxony created me to be the most perfect male being in the universe. That's the only thing I have. My ancestors didn't fight for freedom, or design motorcars or computers. Most of us who are what you call 2Bs envy you who are nature born. We resent that you have so much rich history to be proud of and we have nothing, so we act proud, because all we have is to be proud of who we are. As Leluminali we are trained not to show our feelings or our reactions to things that affect us. But you, Novawynd, can turn that training on and off. You don't know how lucky you are. You can show feelings and the people love you for it. I show feelings and the people think I'm weak." he bit his tongue then.

He was beginning to say too much. Again, he would not let Novawynd in and so she could only wonder if his feelings were true, or if this was only an act.

"If you have these feelings, then why do you continue to block me? There's no reason for you to fear what you feel. Not with me." she reasoned. Then it occurred to her, maybe there was a reason he was blocking her. Maybe it wasn't revulsion he felt towards her. He acted very much the way a little boy acts on the playground when he likes a girl, but doesn't want anyone to know. He torments her, to make it clear to everyone that he has no interest in her, but in private, he might give her something special. Zefram's showing Novawynd his art collection was as close as he could come to showing her something special.

"It's better for both of us if we just continue to block each other. Trust me in this." was all he could say. Novawynd was beginning to think she was wrong about him. Maybe her supernatural attraction was taking its toll on him too. The Omniaural forbid that she should have to deal with his advances too.

*   *   *

The Zenith had taken position above the planet Uinalon and the time had come for Novawynd to make her first ambassadorial mission to an alien planet. Besides her usual Leluminali uniform, she had to wear her official "state" shroud. It was a long black velvet cape with a large hood, fastened with a silver clasp, which was the well known Leluminali symbol of interlocking infinity triangles; the same symbol tattooed on their necks.

They took the shuttle down to the planet. Novawynd was calm. She felt confident that she was in control of this situation. The premier, although seventy anios her senior, would respect her because of who he thought she was. When they arrived, they were greeted by the premier and some of his attendants.

The premier was not the ruler of Uinalon, but was only the ambassador who dealt with all business between Uinalon and other planets, or with the Xaxony. His position was a very high position, but the ruler of Uinalon was called the *hijk* (pronounced shek). The hjik was more of a figure-head of the planet and didn't deal with business transactions, so as politicians went, the premier was the highest ranking official that could deal with Novawynd and her entourage. She would meet the hijk later, as a formality.

Novawynd, Zefram and their attendant space-guard walked down the gang-plank to the waiting reception party, which was made up of about fifteen to twenty Uinalons of varying ranks. Novawynd could see there was thousands upon thousands of Uinalons flanking the pathway that lead to the building they were to enter. They had apparently all come to see the Lajiachine. The Uinalons, except for the reception party, were all prostrate and waited patiently. Once Novawynd stepped off the gang-plank, the Uinalon reception party knelt on one knee and bowed their heads. Their dark striped skin shining in the Uinalon sun. They were adorned richly in various lavish materials and golden jewelry. The striped golden fur on their heads, necks and backs were also adorned with various golden clips. The premier was alone, out ahead of everyone else, and he was the most lavishly adorned of all the Uinalons.

"Your display of respect is noted. Thank you all, now please rise." she persuaded.

The Uinalons slowly rose, starting with the premier.

"It is our greatest honor to have you with us, Your Supremacy." the premier greeted her. "This day will go down in our history annals as the day the Lajiachine graced us with her presence on her first mission.

This day will forever be a global holiday known as 'Novawynd Day'."
the premier informed.

"I'm honored." Novawynd conceded and bowed her head.

"It is our way to show our unflinching loyalty to Your Supremacy."
the premier assured. Novawynd realized the calculated choice of words
on the premier's part. He had stressed their loyalty was to her— not
to the Xaxony. She understood why most civilizations would take
that stance. In the event that she did fulfill her destiny, which was to
destroy the Xaxony's control of the universe, they would still want to
be in her favor.

After some more formalities between the premier and Zefram, the
premier showed the Xaxon entourage along and as they walked the
several paces to the door of the building they were to enter, drums
pounded out a powerful rhythm. The crowds chanted "Nova-wynd!
Nova-wynd!" It was heart-wrenching to Novawynd, the faith they had
in her. The same faith she didn't have in herself.

Once the group was away from the raucous outside, Novawynd
spoke to the premier more casually. "Premier Ghunta, I have another
favor to ask."

"Anything that you ask." Premier Ghunta appeased.

She uncovered Swizel, who had been sedated and lying on a levi-
palate, which one of her space-guard attendants had been pushing
along. "This animal here, we'll need an AI version made of it."

"It will be a pleasure." The premier made a gesture toward some of
his attendants. They came over to retrieve the levi-palate.

"I *do* need the original animal back alive, however," Novawynd
added.

"Of course." the premier assured and nodded to the attendants.
They nodded back and proceeded to push the levi-palate away to some
unknown lab in the bowels of their production facility. "We know you

will only be here for two dialos, so I hope you don't mind that we've prepared an agenda."

"I'm glad you did." she agreed.

"First, we will bring you to your quarters. There you will find your agenda."

After Novawynd got used to her quarters and read over the agenda, the premier was already back at her quarters with Zefram in tow. They were given an extensive tour of all the production facilities. They had arrived early in the morning, but it was already late afternoon by the time they finished their sightseeing trip of the replication labs, the intelligence servers, the research offices and the many different facilities that produced the intricate unique pieces that made up the AI creations. Novawynd was even able to see Swizel's replication as it was in process. It would be some time before the actual AI version of the dog was complete, but the process of measuring, sample taking, patterning and intelligence gathering would be done before they left the next day.

Everywhere they went, everything seemed so sanitary. The walls were not made from Isotarin, as the Xaxon constructs were. It was some sort of resin, pre-molded and hinged together. In most cases it was smooth and painted in light, sanitary colors. However, in the personal quarters, the walls were sculpted into quite interesting, almost primitive, tribal patterns. There was brilliant painting of the details, including gold leaf in many cases, which gave the personal quarters an opulent feel.

The tour ended in a non-descript room with an exam chair of some sort in the middle. It reminded Novawynd of the dentist's office. There was a woman sitting in the chair and she was an exact replica of Novawynd. This was the AP replication that was to be used as a decoy, or to stand in for Novawynd in other situations, not yet determined. Novawynd approached the AP.

"Novawynd, I presume?" the AP addressed her.

"That's right." Novawynd was studying the AP in amazement.

"I don't have a name yet. You should give me a name." The AP suggested. Even her voice, inflection, dialect and manner of speaking were identical to Novawynd's.

"I want to call you Bianca. That means 'white'." Novawynd decided.

"An excellent name, Your Supremacy." Premier Ghunta pronounced. "Bianca belongs to you. She will do as you wish."

Novawynd and Zefram were escorted back to their quarters to prepare for the banquet, at which they would meet the hjyk. Novawynd had not discussed any business thus far. It was on the agenda to discuss business after dinner with the hjyk in his council chambers. Neither she nor Zefram felt the Uinalons were hiding anything. The schematics that Zefram had gone over were all accurate. Nothing too unusual, and what few anomalies there were, the premier was shrewd enough to cover with explanations during their tour.

Bianca followed Novawynd into her unit, of course, where else would she go? "What am I going to do with her?" Novawynd thought to herself. "Bianca?" she addressed the AP.

"Yes, Novawynd?"

"You need to stay here in these quarters for the duration of our stay here. Then you will come with us back to my ship. Can you shut yourself down, or something?" Novawynd was concerned about Bianca sitting around with nothing to occupy her.

"Yes. I can go into hibernation mode." Bianca informed.

"You'll probably want to do that until I need you to come onboard the ship. I really don't have any use for you here." In fact Novawynd felt a little guilty that the Xaxony had Bianca made at all. She really didn't foresee needing the AP version of herself, but Bianca was a tool, and nothing more. Novawynd felt like Bianca should be more, because she was so life-like.

"I understand. Where would you like me to do that?" Bianca inquired.

"The chair?" Novawynd suggested.

"Very well. I will be over there hibernating. Just move me in some way if you need me to reinitialize." she instructed. Novawynd nodded.

After preparing for dinner, which pretty much meant putting her formal cloak on over her uniform and fastening it with the Lelumin symbol brooch, she met Zefram in the hallway. He accompanied her to the official dining hall.

"Zefram, do you have an AP version of yourself?" she was curious.

"Yes."

"Where do you keep him?"

"In a niche in my quarters."

"Is he anatomically correct?" Novawynd asked, tongue in cheek, but she knew the question would annoy him.

"Do you find me attractive?" came Zefram's question, and it was not the response she had expected. She stopped.

"You are the universe's most perfect male specimen. I would be insane, not to find you attractive." she affirmed.

"I thought you hated me." He sounded almost as if he was hurt by the notion that she did.

"I can still hate someone I find attractive. It's your personality I hate, but your body…" she just smiled and turned to keep on walking.

"I don't really know if he is anatomically correct. I've never checked, but even if he was, I'm afraid he'd be as useless in that area as I am. He's not a pleasure model." Zefram clarified.

Novawynd laughed. "I was only joking anyway Zefram."

*   *   *

Before dinner, the premier introduced Novawynd to a Vilijian. He was introduced as Sia Donata, (Sia was the Vilijian word equivalent to Mister.) the Vilijian scientist the Uinalons were accused of having kidnapped, as well as the real reason Novawynd and Zefram were there.

"But, you can see he is here of his own free will, and quite happy I might add." Premier Ghunta assured.

"That I am." Sia Donata added his opinion.

Then Novawynd was ceremoniously introduced to the hjyk and his wives. The hjyk wore a tall, golden, domed crown, a wide golden collar and golden bracers; all enameled with bright colors. It reminded her of what the Egyptian Pharos used to wear. The hjyk and all ten of his wives bowed low to her.

"My people and I are honored to have you with us, Your Supremacy." He said while still bowing, then he stood up. His wives also followed suit.

"I consider it a great privilege to be honored by you and your people. And, I don't know about you, but I'm hungry. I'm looking forward to this feast you've prepared for us." Novawynd chuckled and everyone else also laughed. They were seated and they were served several courses. A lot of the dishes were unusually flavored, but not unpleasant. Just unlike anything Novawynd had ever tasted before. Dancers and musicians entertained them with the artistic, traditional dance of their people as they ate. After dinner, as was outlined in the agenda, Novawynd and Zefram were escorted into the hjyk's council chambers.

"Did you enjoy your meal, Your Supremacy?" the hjyk inquired.

"Yes, quite so. I just love to partake of other cultures' cuisine. I'm thrilled that I was able to experience yours. Not-to-mention the music and dancing was quite a pleasure as well."

"Oh, you're too kind, Your Supremacy." He gave a deep chuckle then motioned to two chairs set out for her and Zefram. He made a little motion with his hand. They sat. "Shall we get down to business?"

"Yes, please."

Sia Donata, who was not present at this meeting, was the topic. It was explained that although the Vilijians accused the Uinalons of having forcibly kidnapped Donata, they had actually lured him away with an extravagant offer. He was an expert in micro-robotics and the Uinalons needed his expertise to build micro AI. Micro AI would resemble creatures such as insects, that could literally be used as "bugs" or other vermin that could sneak, unnoticed into a rival's establishment with a tiny, but destructive amount of explosive material. Their need for the micro-technology came about as demand for it became too great to ignore.

The Uinalons efforts at micro-robotics were pathetic. They had many aspects to consider when creating an AI and robotics was only one. Their robotics experts, although genius, were stumped by creating a tiny, self-propelled, energy recycling droid. The Vilijians, on the other hand, had mastered the micro-technology and were already venturing into nano-bot technology. The work that Donata had done was old-hat to the Vilijians, so he simply took an offer where his old concepts would be new again and he would be treated like a king.

"I don't mean to insinuate that you haven't thought of this, but I have to say," Novawynd spoke up after listening to the story, "that the

Vilijians are far too upset about the loss of a scientist who was the head of last anio's technology."

"You mean, of course, that they are putting up a front. To make us think they're truly upset, when they truly mean for him to be here?" The premier laughed. "We don't trust Sia Donata for one mecron. We feel very sure that he will give information back to the Vilijians, if given an opportunity, so he has limited access and is monitored. So far, he hasn't had a chance to get his hands on anything, or to transfer anything to an outside source."

Novawynd used her empathic abilities to probe the premier and the Hjyk. They felt sincere. "I don't see the problem then." she assured. "At least the true problem doesn't seem to be their's." Novawynd added in a tone of warning. There was an awkward silence among the group then.

"Well," the hjyk broke the silence, "I think it's been a long dialo for all of us. We should perhaps find our nesting spots for the night." Novawynd smiled at that quaint statement, considering they all knew where they were going to sleep. She was always amused by alien phraseology and the origins of such. The Uinalon's language obviously evolved with archaic phrases still imbued into their lingo, much the same as Earth had. "I agree." she concurred.

*   *   *

At the very first light, the next morning, Novawynd went for a run. She had been genetically altered to resist aging and illness, and her body healed abnormally fast as a result of the effects of the Milk of Fillatrofia. None-the-less, she could still get out-of-shape if she didn't watch herself, so she worked out anytime she could fit it in.

She ran along the pre-fab, resin sidewalks that interlaced through the waking city. From time to time she came across a Uinalon going about his or her business. The Uinalons she came across were alarmed at first to se a non-Uinalon running along. She kindly greeted each person she came across, and their concern subsided when they came to realize the non-Uinalon was not being chased, but running as some sort of ritual.

After a while, she came to the wide open area where she and her entourage had been welcomed to the planet. She was surprised to see a large cargo shuttle of an unusual design sitting on the pad and seemingly unloading massive containers of something. There were two men supervising the unloading of the containers, and Novawynd knew they were not AP, because she sensed their emotions. APs gave off nothing for her to pick up on. If Novawynd didn't know better, the two men could have been Earthling. They were average in height, weight, and looks. Not the typical picture of perfection the Xaxons usually had. She took a turn towards the two supervisors. They noticed her approaching and turned with their weapons readied. Novawynd sensed their alarm at her running toward them, so she stopped. She was not out of breath, but pretended to need to catch her breath. This way, the supervisors who were scrutinizing her, would ascertain she was not a threat.

She looked up at them and met their gazes. She could see the glint of orange in their eyes. It reminded her of Eridia, her teacher at the Analida. "Talosians!" she realized. She was excited that she had this encounter. She had wanted to know more about them, but was unable to get any information from the Xaxon central computers. Talosians were considered reluctant allies and most knowledge of their civilization was erased. It was in Novawynd's nature to want to know more about that which she was not supposed to know.

She lifted her hand in greeting and slowly approached them. It was clear that she was not armed, so they relaxed as she approached. The long-sleeved, thermal semi-turtleneck she was wearing nearly covered her Lelumin tattoo; therefore, they would not immediately realize she was a threat, even without weapons. She had no intent to harm, only to see what they were up to. "Jalida!" she called out. This was the Talosian greeting equivalent to an Earthling "hello".

When she got close enough for them to see what small portion of the tattoo was not covered. "Novawynd!" one of the men cried out in realization and went down on one knee, bowing his head low. The other man realized her identity more slowly, but he also fell to one knee and bowed his head. Obviously they had heard about her.

"Your Supremacy; we didn't know who you were at first. Please forgive our insolence." The first man almost begged as Novawynd drew close to them.

"I thought nothing of it." she laughed. "Please rise." she asked. The two men slowly stood, but kept their eyes down. "Do either of you have the capability of getting a message to Lord Danalian?" Novawynd probed. They nodded. "Good. Tell him a new age is coming and the time for a new alliance has come. I'd like to have a discussion with him some time." She chose her words carefully. She did not mention the alliance would be with the Xaxony. She knew he would not be receptive to that. Novawynd knew Danalian and the Talosians pledged their loyalty to the Lajiachine, not the Xaxony, so she hoped he would see her invitation as an opportunity to meet his needs. She would use it as an opportunity to draw him back to the Xaxony.

The men nodded in affirmation after she made her statement, so she turned and walked away. She read the words clearly stenciled across the containers, Isotarin. Of course, the Talosians still shipped Isotarin to Uinalons for the skeletal structures and many other components that went into the make-up of the AI creations. In fact, the Talosians shipped Isotarin to many of the Xaxon allies. This was not a secret, nor was it forbidden, but they kept their business dealings low-key none-the-less. Novawynd determined there was nothing untoward going on here. Her curiosity being satisfied, she began running again and headed back to her room.

*   *   *

After cleaning herself up and packing her things, her door chimed. It was Zefram and the other two space-guards that had accompanied them on this trip. It was time to leave Uinalon for Vilijia already, and he had come to escort her to their ship. On the long ride back to the landing area where their ship awaited, she hardly recalled the ride. She was excited about how Danalian would respond, if at all. She hadn't been given the mission to patch things up between Talos and the Xaxony, but she didn't think the Superior Council would mind her taking the initiative.

As they walked down the path between the throngs of Uinalons that had come to see the Lajiachine depart, Novawynd looked for the Talosian ship. It was gone. Of course they would have unloaded their shipment and gotten out of there before the Uinalon people started to come. She breathed a sigh of relief, although she wasn't sure why.

Again, there were traditional Uinalon dancers moving in choreographed sets to the Uinalon drums as the boarding party walked along. The premier waited by the gang-plank and this time, the hjyk waited with him. Both the hjyk and the premier were fully adorned in their official dress. Novawynd hadn't seen them in anything else in her time there, but she was sure they didn't always dress like that. Novawynd formally said her goodbyes, as did Zefram, and then they were on their way.

CHAPTER 4

The Zenith would not need to hold in a caesura interval. It would flux immediately to Vilijia. Novawynd had only enough time to bring Bianca to her unit and put her into hibernation mode before heading back to the shuttle that would bring them to the sub-surface of Vilijia. As she was rushing down the hallway to the bay, Stunner met up with her "Hey Novawynd." he greeted.

"Hey Stunner." she reciprocated. "I don't have time to talk now. I have to get to the shuttle." she informed.

"I know. I get to go with this time."

Novawynd regarded him as she kept her swift pace. "How did you get Zelo Djynk to allow that?" she smiled.

"I convinced him the probability of the space-guard being needed while in orbit around Vilijia was minimal and he agreed. Or…it was more like I begged him. I haven't set foot on a planet other than my own in…I don't remember how long." Stunner seemed almost giddy. It was a side of him Novawynd hadn't seen yet, and she liked it. She suddenly felt as giddy, knowing that he would be near her most of the time.

They were at the shuttle by the end of Stunner's explanation, so they hopped on board and took their seats. Zefram was sitting directly across the shuttle from Novawynd. As she settled in, she saw what she thought was annoyance on his face. She couldn't tell if he was annoyed because she kept them waiting, or if it was something else. His eyes shifted between her and Stunner, indicating he was wondering if something was going on between the two. When Zefram realized she was regarding him, trying to read him, he straightened up and any semblance of human emotion dissolved from his face.

The shuttle needed to hover down into a deep fissure to reach its landing pad. Whereas most planets had cities that built structures reaching to the sky, the Vilijian cities penetrated deep into the planet within the multitudinous cavities winding their way endlessly though the planet's mantle. The shuttle then moved forward again into another orifice, in which its landing pad waited. The opening to the landing pad was just large enough to accommodate the shuttle. Inside the large cavern, the primitive, porous, gray rock juxtaposed against the smooth, Isotarin structures and robots.

There was no crowd here like there had been on Uinalon. Novawynd was aware that the Vilijians did not accept her as the Lajiachine. To them, she was just another Leluminalia. To say that the Vilijian society was strongly patriarchal, was putting it mildly. The truth was the Vilijian women were no better than slaves. They were bought and sold between the men and one Vilijian man would have several female mates. The females were never allowed outside, so one would never see them out and about for any reason. One certainly never saw them on Xaxon starships.

The Vilijian men that were upgraded to work for the Xaxony adopted the Xaxon ideals that males, females and "its" were equal. Vilijians that had been upgraded into the Xaxony acted civil towards beings of all sexes; much the same way Sia Donata acted so cordially to Novawynd on Uinalon. However, if you took those same males and put them back in their own society on their own planet, they would go back to treating females like nothing more than animals. The Vilijians rejected the notion that Novawynd might be the Lajiachine, because they could not believe a woman could be. Novawynd knew, if Zefram's advice about putting someone in their place, in order to garner respect was needed, this would be the place. She really hoped she wouldn't have to put anyone in their place.

Once the shuttle was settled and the doors opened, the diplomatic party exited. Stunner and his other space-guard counterpart were first, followed by Novawynd and Zefram, side-by-side. There were only three Vilijian men waiting to meet the landing party. Quite a difference from the outstanding welcome they received on Uinalon. On Vilijia, the rule of the planet was split equally three ways. There was a king-like figure called a *gian* and he was the ruler of the people. A second man was ruler of the military. He was called a *lian* and was basically a dictator. The third man ruled over the universal business end of things. This man was called a *ruan* and was the CEO of all business and commerce on and off the planet.

One man wore a suit with a metal chain, imbedded with some sort of stones, draped across his shoulders. He also wore a wide, chunky metallic band around his head. He was obviously Gian M'Osuto. The next man wore a uniform-like suit with some metallic adornments. He would be Lian Mar'Ipos. The last man was not particularly adorned, but wore a simple suit that seemed quite elegant. This man, Novawynd surmised, was Ruan It'Akal. All these men gained their status by the merits of their efforts. Any man could become the next gian, lian or ruan, if he had the knowledge, skills, connections, resources and money to achieve that status. No woman would ever achieve those positions.

No woman would likely even acquire the right to step outside of her father's or husband's house, without risking certain death.

This is why when the gian greeted them, he addressed Zefram first. "Lord Zefram, we welcome you." he acknowledged with arms spread wide. It looked as though he intended to embrace Zefram, but he would not. This stance was merely the Vilijian way of greeting others. Zefram stopped short and without saying anything to the gian, turned aside to face Novawynd. He gazed intently at her. This action was a subtle sign of disrespect to the gian and announced loud and clear that Novawynd was the one they needed to be addressing. Novawynd, getting this cue immediately, spoke to the gian, as well as the other two dignitaries.

"Gian M'Osuto, I hear the voices of your ancestors who have passed into the Omniaural and they tell me a man named Sia Vexian Ital'Akta is in succession to take your position today if I should happen to kill you. Is this true?" This question caught Gian M'Osuto off guard. Novawynd could sense he resisted answering her question, but thought better of it.

"Yes, but why would you kill me? I've done nothing." the gian defended with a nervous laugh.

"You may not believe I am the Lajiachine, but the Superior Council of the Xaxony does. I have the ultimate authority to use any means necessary to make it clear how serious they are, including killing the gian of Vilijia for his insolence. But, I know your society's ways, and I will forgive your show of disrespect just now, as long as you address me as primary from now on. Just to make it clear, I am primary and Zefram is secondary. He will defer to me any time you mistakenly address him." Novawynd regarded them silently and the gian bowed, so the other two also bowed to her.

Mar'Ipos spoke up, "We certainly respect the wishes of the Superior Council Your Supremacy." he appeased. "If either of these men disrespects you, I'll kill them myself." he really meant it too. Obviously they worked together, but only because they had to; not because they actually got along. Novawynd sensed the lian would welcome an excuse to off one of the other two. Gian M'Osuto and Ruan It'Akal glared at Mar'Ipos, but said nothing when they saw Novawynd had completely ignored Mar'Ipos's offer.

"Your Supremacy, as women are not allowed to be seen in public on our planet, we have brought a ginzhu for you to ride in while we give you the tour." Ruan It'Akal informed. A ginzhu was a small, enclosed electric cart. The domed window was tinted such that you could not see into the vehicle. Women obviously needed to be transported from place to place when they were sold and bought. The ginzhu were used only for the temporary transport of women, so they could be brought from one place to the next, without being in the public eye.

Novawynd knew their law forbade women to be out in public, but she was a diplomat and not to be held to any laws except those of the Xaxony. So, as much as they would like her to keep herself hidden, she rebelled. There was no way she could show submission by giving in to that request. "No thank you, I think I'll walk." The three heads of state gasped in protest, but they knew there was nothing they could do about it. "We shouldn't waste any time in getting through our tour. I think we've wasted quite enough time here." Novawynd suggested. The Vilijians grumbled and turned to lead them on. Zefram smirked and nodded at Novawynd, and then turned to follow.

As Novawynd began to follow, she heard another starship entering the main crater. She looked over her shoulder and saw yet another Talosian transport ship. Probably more Isotarin to construct the robot parts, but she got a compelling curiosity that overwhelmed her. She lingered for only a moment before deciding she'd better move along.

Aside from a highly acute sense of smell, the Vilijians also had infra-red vision, so they could see quite well in the dark. The streets, which were really just the naturally occurring tunnels and caves, were lined with luminescent tubing that helped visiting non-Vilijians see. It was a type of light that was easy on the Vilijian eyes. In the deeper areas of Vilijia, where outsiders never went, there was no light-source at all. On the Xaxons and the Xaxon ships, the Vilijians wore contacts or goggles that protected their eyes from the light.

The group walked along following the Vilijians. The greenish light cast a sickly glow on the black pockmarked walls of the caverns that were their streets and sidewalks; quite a dismal difference from the sanitary walls of Uinalon. As was suspected, the Vilijian men that passed by were startled to see Novawynd, at first; but then they realized who she was, and hastened away from her. Novawynd could feel their condemnation, but she dismissed it.

They spent the next several tecrons touring the production facilities where robots built robots. The group saw everything from where the lowliest floor sweeping robots were created to where the amazing battleots were conceived. They saw the micro-technology labs where Sia Donata had worked, and finally, they moved on to the nano-technology labs. The Vilijians had been working on nano-technology for hundreds of anios. They could build nano-parts for nano-bots, but hadn't been able to find a way to program the bitty creatures or power them long enough to perform useful functions. Novawynd and the others were allowed to look at the nano-bots through a high-powered microscope. They looked like bacteria. In a sense, that's what they were; robotic bacteria, or possibly robotic penicillin.

The purpose for the nano-bots was to get them into miniscule crevasses of machinery, infiltrate the inner mechanics and spread a virus in computer functions. So far, the nano-bots couldn't even move, much less perform that complex of a function. Novawynd was always amazed when she learned that civilizations like the Vilijians and the Uinalons had difficulty developing technology. They had thousands of years of advancements on the Earthlings and still faced shortcomings from time to time. Somewhere in the universe, some mathematician was solving the problem that would allow other scientists to develop the technology that would drive the nano-bots.

Novawynd wondered to herself if the nano-bots could be powered by E2, the energy Zefram had told her about, funneled from the Omniaural. If E2 could be manipulated to achieve certain powerful, yet controlled bursts that achieved varied effects, then why couldn't these nano-bots be imbued with that energy? She had heard about civilizations that could imbue weapons and armor with Omniaural energy. This gave the objects seemingly magical powers. Because E2 was both powerful and intelligent, it could both power the nano-bots, and perform an intelligent function, such as penetrating a mechanism and finding a link to its computerized functions. Only people, like Novawynd, who could manipulate the Omniaural's energy, could channel the power to the nano-bots, and it would probably be temporary. Novawynd kept her thought to herself. It struck her as a good idea, but something just told her to keep that ace up her sleeve for now.

The robots ran the gamut of varied shapes, sizes and body styles. They were each created for a specific purpose, so each design was meant to be the most practical and efficient for the type of work to be performed. There were robots with tentacles, or multi-segmented bodies, or numerous legs and arms. Some robots hovered or flew.

Some rolled along the floor and still others crawled along the walls and ceilings, but none walked on two legs. There was simply no logical reason for a robot to emulate a bipedal creature. That was left to the AP. The difference between the AP and robots was robots didn't need to look like anything specific, whereas the AP were created to fool the eye.

After the tour, the group went directly to a private dining room; where Gian M'Osuto, Ruan It'Akal and Lian Mar'Ipos would sit down to eat with Novawynd and Zefram without anyone else present. Stunner and the other space-guard attendant, who was called Sonic, would stand by the door outside and keep an eye open for trouble, but they would have to take dinner later.

As was the custom, the Vilijians sat on cushions on the floor, forming a circle, with trays set in front of them. Servants came in and set down other trays of various types of food in the midst of the circle. The Vilijians immediately attacked and began consuming the offerings. The primary food source for the Vilijians was cave dwelling creatures such as: cave lizards, praxis larvae, miggum fish and something that looked like steamed moss. Novawynd could handle the lizard, fish and moss, but she still couldn't stomach the idea of eating insects, even though she'd heard praxis larvae were delicious.

Novawynd reached over to help herself to a roasted cave lizard carcass and the Vilijians stopped eating abruptly. It was customary on Vilijia that the women did not eat until the men had taken their fill. Afterward, the women would divvy up the leftovers amongst themselves. The men realized Novawynd could not be held to that standard either, so they went back to devouring their nosh.

They ritualistically washed their hands and faces after everyone had their fill. It didn't take long for Novawynd to have gotten her fill. Her appetite had been dampened by the crunching and slurping of the

Vilijians. Once they had cleaned up and the servants had taken away all remnants of dinner, it was time to get down to business. Novawynd decided to be the first to speak.

"So, what action do you intend to take against the Uinalons?" She knew she could be direct, because everyone knew a Leluminalia would know if one was lying or not. Most people didn't dare lie to a Leluminalia. She also could use Junatiel to loosen their tongues if she felt it was necessary.

Ruan It'Akal was the one to answer this time. "We were hoping the Xaxony would see things our way and impose an embargo." He laughed nervously, as did the other two Vilijians. This was a joke, because they knew the Xaxony would never take sides. Novawynd had to be careful to seem impartial. She did not laugh at his joke.

"You're wasting my time ruan." she stated flatly. "Really, I want to know why you care about losing Sia Donata when there are other scientists who are as bright taking over his position. Besides, you're more focused on your nano-tech at this time anyway. I spoke to Sia Donata on Uinalon and he was well treated and seemingly happy with his position. I don't see an abduction. I see a man leaving of his own free will to take a generous offer. I'm waiting for you to convince me otherwise."

Gian M'Osuto spoke up this time, "He was in fact abducted. You see, he was lured away from his home planet with promises the Uinalons don't intent to keep. Then, once they get the information from him that they need, they will kill him. If he doesn't give him the information they need, they will kill him. Either way, he's doomed. For a hundred anios, they have lured our scientists away, never to be seen again. We take issue with this and it has to stop. We intend to stop it now."

"Why would they kill a scientist that would be more useful to them alive?" Novawynd countered.

"Because, regardless of what wealth or status the scientists are promised, Uinalon is simply no place for a Vilijian anymore than Vilijia is a place for Uinalons. Eventually, they want to leave. The Uinalons can't allow that, for they fear their secrets will get into our hands."

It seemed odd to Novawynd that they would be so concerned about the human rights of a scientist, when they had no concern for the human rights of their own females. But, their world was not like Earth, so she could not project her expectations on to them. "Are you concerned that the technology that Sia Donata is working on might compete with your market-share?"

The men laughed genuinely. Ruan It'Akal answered, "Nothing they can make with Donata's technology would compete with our product. We see no reason why a microbot loaded with explosives, needs to look like a real insect. If it's so small no one sees it, what does it matter what it looks like?"

Since they didn't claim they wanted Sia Donata back because he was indispensable, Novawynd knew he could not have been working on something big. They also were not concerned about the Uinalon product destroying the Vilijian foothold in that market. That could only mean that Donata was in fact a spy. Their over-the-top posturing made it obvious to everyone that Donata was more-than-likely a plant. She opted to come right out and ask. "So Sia Donata is a spy then?" They didn't need to answer that question. She could feel their unrest at her having seen through their deception, but it was fake unrest. They were doing a poor job of acting surprised that she'd figured it out, and this reaction to her question made her uneasy. They were playing some sort of game. They wanted people to know he was a plant, but why?

The Xaxony expected Uinalon and Vilijia to coexist and to breed healthy competition. Therefore, the two planets did coexist. If one planet attempted to take over the other planet, it would not be tolerated by the Xaxony or any of its allies. The only way any action might be acceptable, is if one planet provoked the other. Novawynd could see the Vilijians had set up a scenario in which they would have the right to attack Uinalon, thereby enslaving its people and taking over its commodities.

Of course, that was it. Vilijia had never aimed any propaganda at its scientists, warning them of the danger of taking a Uinalon bribe. Over the many anios that the Uinalons had lured Vilijian scientists away, they were building up to this. Novawynd kicked herself for not having seen it sooner. She wondered if the Uinalons had figured it out. She knew what she needed to do.

Zefram turned to look intently at her. He was curious what she was thinking, because she had been quiet for so long. She snapped back to reality. "Well, the Uinalons have always suspected he is a spy, and they are keeping close tabs on him. If they gave him back to you now, he couldn't have gleaned much from them." Novawynd rationalized.

"It's not really about what they are working on, but more about what they aren't." Lian Mar'Ipos decided to fess up. "We just want to make sure they aren't working on something we should be concerned about and he should have been there long enough to ascertain that." He explained, but Novawynd could sense the half-truth in his comment and it only confirmed her fears.

"Very well," Novawynd put on a pleasant tone, "I will convince the Uinalons to give up your scientist and I hope you get the information you need." She smiled. "Now please, if you will excuse me, I would like to retire."

"Thank you, Your Supremacy, for helping." Gian M'Osuto offered cordially, but with an undercurrent of displeasure, because they really didn't want Donata back. Novawynd rose, as did Zefram. They left the room with Stunner and Sonic following behind.

"Do you really think the Uinalons will just give back Donata?" Zefram condescended.

"I'm sure I can persuade them." Novawynd assured.

"I sense an underlying motive." Zefram continued.

"As do I. I'll brief you as soon as we get off this planet."

They were at Novawynd's door then and she entered her room. She breathed a sigh of relief. The tension that had been so present all day was finally off her shoulders.

*   *   *

Novawynd had lain down for only a moment, but apparently she fell straight to sleep. She was awakened with a start when her door chimed. She got up and crossed the room to the door. She could see on the monitor that it was Stunner. He was looking over his shoulder nervously. Novawynd opened the door and he quickly slid in. He bent down to kiss her cheek.

"I don't have any entertainment in here for you Stunner." she informed.

"On the contrary, I believe it will be far more entertaining to snuggle with you and talk until we fall asleep, then to hang in my room alone." he gave her a wink. If it was any other man, she would sense he was trying to get into her pants, but this was Stunner, and she knew he was completely plutonic in his feelings for her. "Oh," he added, "a Talosian gave me this in the hallway and asked me to give it to you." He was holding a small Isotarin cylinder. Novawynd backed away.

"Stunner, you don't just bring a strange cylinder from a stranger into my presence! That could be a bomb! You're my guard, you're supposed to protect me not bring the weapon straight to me!" she exclaimed.

"Relax, I checked it out, it's just a cylinder that is holding a rolled up piece of parchment with symbols written on it. Completely harmless." he assured.

Novawynd took the cylinder, and as soon as she did, she got a vision. She saw a tall, young man with golden brown hair and the gleaming orange eyes of a Talosian glinting beneath a hood. Then the scene changed and she saw her angel, the man who called himself Star. It was a replay of the last thing he said to her when he came to her in her Milk of Fillatrofia induced hallucination. "Find me and you'll find the truth." he had prognosticated. Was the piece of parchment really the message or was the cylinder itself imbued with a psychic message for her?

The vision ended and she was alert again. Stunner was looking at her oddly. She knew the Talosian in the vision was the man who had handed Stunner the message, but why Star. She had all but forgotten about him. At first, she was driven by Star's message. She thought he might have been an enti, so she tried to reach out to him in the Omniaural during Analida training, but she couldn't draw on him. Deciding he was a real person, she had tried to reach him in her dreams to no avail. She couldn't seem to catch him when he was sleeping. After a while she just stopped trying. Novawynd felt these two men were tied together by destiny in some way. Perhaps by finding this Talosian, she would find Star.

Novawynd opened the cylinder. As Stunner had mentioned, it had a roll of parchment with English words written on it. It said:

"Do not read this aloud, it is written so your CI can't record it. Lord Danalian has information for you at the docking bay 56. Use discretion."

Novawynd quickly rolled up the paper and carelessly stuffed it back in the cylinder. It was time to use Junatiel. "Stunner, stay here and wait for me, I'll be right back." she could see the persuasive powers kick in as he blankly nodded. She turned and left the room. She would use Junatiel to make anyone who came in contact with her, believe there was no one there. In this way she would be invisible to everyone she passed. Junatiel didn't work on everyone. Some beings had the ability to block the telehypnosis. A Leluminalia never knew when he would cross a being like this, so they were trained not to depend on it too much. The Talosians were known to be able to block the telehypnosis that Junatiel was based on, but the Vilijians were of no concern.

She ran to the docking bay the note indicated. The Talosian cargo ship was still there. It appeared that the ship was undergoing some minor repairs. The gangplank extended and the hatch opened for her. The Talosians, or at least one Talosian, could see her coming. She quickly climbed the gangplank and entered the ship. The hatch closed behind her and she was met by the tall Talosian she had seen in the vision. He was cute, but he had an air of maturity, importance or aristocracy someone of his apparent age wouldn't normally have. He dropped to one knee and bowed his head, as the Talosians she had seen previously had also done. He stood up again and he held his forefinger to his lips, shushing her, but not making the "shhh" noise. He held up another piece of paper with more writing. She took it from him.

It read:

"My allegiance and the allegiance of Talos is with you, Your Supremacy. I will create bonds with you, but as for the Xaxony, those bonds are irreparable. I have many reasons for this; reasons that are kept from you, by the Xaxony, and you know this. I would like to explain it all to you, but can't speak to you of such things without risk to you, so I have written it all down for you to read".

When she was through reading she looked searchingly at the young man in front of her. Because he was able to block her, Novawynd was certain he was Leluminali. Could this possibly be Danalian himself? He handed over a thick packet of papers. She cautiously took it and flipped through it. Clever, Lord Danalian had done his homework. He knew Earthlings could read, and he painstakingly wrote the history of Talos' separation from the Xaxony, in English. This way she could get the story from his point of view without anyone being able to retrieve it from her ear-bud later. The Talosian bowed to her and turned on his heel to leave. The hatch reopened behind her queuing her to leave. She wanted to ask so many questions, primarily, who was he? Was he Danalian or just a messenger? She sensed he was Danalian, but couldn't believe he would risk coming here.

*   *   *

Back in Novawynd's unit, she maintained her Junatiel shroud to keep Stunner from seeing her as she entered the room with the packet of papers the Talosian had given her. It was funny to her how people under the influence of Junatiel were oblivious to things that were obviously occurring, such as the way Stunner lay silent, in a trance without noticing the door to Novawynd's unit was opening and closing. She crossed the room and put her new acquisition in her bag, then exited the room again. She unveiled herself from the Junatiel invisibility and re-entered the room. This time Stunner noticed her.

"Novawynd! Where have you been? I must have fallen asleep." He sat up groggily.

"Don't worry about it." she persuaded with Junatiel.

"Okay." he affirmed robotically.

Novawynd took off her jacket and boots and climbed onto the bed. She lay down and Stunner curled up next to her, spooning her. She couldn't believe that an Eron like Stunner would need this physical contact and affection, but it didn't matter. She loved the way she felt when he embraced her by wrapping his strong body around her. She felt so safe. She caressed the fine violet hairs on his blue arm.

"Novawynd, do you know how you are able to flux on your own?" he was curious.

"You know about E2, right?"

"Yes."

"Well, E2 occupies a dimension that is enmeshed with our own physical dimension, but it isn't held by the constraints of time and space like physical matter is. E2 moves freely throughout the universe, inter-dimensionally. That is why an enti can be one place in the universe one zecron, and a split-zecron later, somewhere across the universe. Physical beings are energy too. Their atoms form a different pattern that makes up matter. If you can reconfigure your atoms to the pattern of energy, thereby becoming an enti, you can become free of the constraints of the physical world and move anywhere without moving through space and time. Then you re-configure your atoms back to the same physical shell you were before, on the other side. You can't do this unless you have a strong connection to the Omniaural, however.

I hypothesize that I died when I had my accident, and a powerful enti possessed me, saving my life, causing me to recover quickly and develop my abilities. This gave me my strong connection to the Omniaural. My enti knows how to move through the Omniaural, and so it passes that knowledge on to me, as if it were instinctual. I don't really know how I do it, I just do it." Novawynd finished.

"Why did the enti choose you?" Stunner pondered.

"I was just in the right place at the right time. It could have been anyone." she theorized.

"I disagree. I think you were chosen because anyone else wouldn't have been strong enough to handle it." he complimented. They were silent then and something suddenly occurred to Novawynd. How was it possible that Danalian was able to write that thick packet, in her language, in the short couple of tecrons from the time he must have gotten the message she sent, to the time she noticed the Talosian ship on Vilijia? Unless, man on the ship was Danalian. He would have had more time to work it out if he had been here the whole time she had. Or, was it possible that he had written it as soon as he learned of her existence, in anticipation of meeting her one day?

The other odd thing was that he knew she was curious to learn his side of the Talosian separation story. How could he have known that she would care to know? She could have succumbed to the brainwashing of the Lelumin conditioning, and blindly followed the position of the Xaxony, which was that the Talosians were in the wrong and Danalian had gone rotten. In that case, she wouldn't care less what his side of the story was, but she *did* want to know and he knew it.

Then there was the mystery that was Star. She had also hoped to meet Danalian, because she wanted to ask him who this Star person was. She had so many questions and felt sure Danalian's age and wisdom could be an excellent resource. She wondered if his writings would shed light on her questions, as if he could know in advance what her questions would be. She ached to read the manuscript, but knew it would have to wait, for now.

*   *   *

Back in her quarters on the Zenith, after having briefed Zefram on her fears about the Vilijians intentions, Novawynd hailed Premier Ghunta. "Premier Ghunta, you need to return Sia Donata immediately if you want to avoid being invaded by the Vilijians. They are looking for a reason to take aggressive, offensive action against you, and they feel they can't be blamed by the Xaxony if it is in the name of human rights. They have been setting you up since you bribed the first scientist over one hundred anios ago. They have waited patiently, as one by one you continued to lure their scientists away, only to execute them. They feel that at this point, no one can blame them if they took action. Sia Donata was sent in to be sacrificed for the cause. That's why my ship is sitting above Uinalon right now and I intend to personally escort Sia Donata from your plant, back to Vilijia. This way I can be sure he was safely delivered to the gian, lian and ruan."

"Your Supremacy," the premier calmly acknowledged, "you are welcome to take him. We have what we need anyway. You see, it was never really about the micro-tech anyway. We were more concerned about a different technology, and Sia Donata was our test subject. This technology is AI that is capable of problem solving and rational, independent thought. We took all of Sia Donata's knowledge and put it into an AP that will be capable of not just thinking like Sia Donata, but more brilliant. Sia Donata is no longer useful to us. The Vilijians can have him back, none the worse for it."

"So when the Vilijians said they put him there to make sure you weren't working on something they should be concerned about, they knew you were working on something they should be concerned about, but they didn't know what?"

"We leaked some information to pique their interest, so they would willingly allow a scientist to come to us. Ironically, Sia Donata will not be able to tell them anything, when he was in fact a very integral part of the project." the premier chuckled. "The information we extracted from his memory database will allow us to create replications of other scientists he knew on Vilijia. We can send those AP to Vilijia to pose as those scientists, just long enough to download data, and transmit it back to us."

"I have two concerns. The first is, if they should discover any of your AP, what kind of back-lash will occur? My second concern is AI of the advanced level you're talking about could be dangerous for all bio-life-forms in the universe."

"We knew, before we even began to develop the AI, that if allowed independent thought, one might determine itself superior to all bio-life-forms and begin a genocide. We made sure all AP only performed the specific functions they were designed for to circumvent this from the start, but we have also been experimenting all these anios, with ways to get around that. We have now developed an AP capable of rational thought and problem-solving skills, and yet is still confined by the parameters it is programmed to remain confined to. Any attempt by the AP to go outside of these set parameters, results in total systems failure." The premier finished his explanation. Novawynd could feel he was sincere. But, naiveté like this coupled with hubris made a dangerous mixture.

"I have serious doubts premier." She warned.

"I understand Your Supremacy. We have only created the one, so it would be easier to put it down if it goes psychotic. Anyone owning an AP with this new super-AI would have a significant advantage over his rivals and competitors, and so we would not allow just anyone to acquire the super AP. We would charge a very hefty price, if anyone wanted one, to keep the super AP minimal. The Xaxony would be the first to get one, if they wanted one, of course. Before any of that happens, however, the prototype will be thoroughly tested."

"Even so, the Superior Council will have the final say in this matter." Novawynd assured. "For now, I will escort Sia Donata back to Vilijia."

CHAPTER 5

Novawynd and Zefram had successfully escorted Sia Donata to Vilijia. If anything happened to him after that, it wouldn't matter. The Vilijians couldn't blame the Uinalons. After the delivery of Donata, the Zenith returned to a caesura interval while they awaited their orders for their next mission. There was a lot of activity going on in the universe for a Leluminalia to keep busy with, but not for Novawynd. Her status kept her delegated to high status missions, which were really few and far between.

Novawynd needed to apprise the Superior Council on the situation between the Uinalons and the Vilijians. She went to the council chambers and reached out with her mind to summon them. They appeared almost instantaneously. "What were you able to learn?" They asked. Novawynd explained the situation to them and how she handled it. "Very good." was all they had to say.

"Council members, I implore you to require them to destroy this *super* AI they've created." She felt passionately that it was a danger.

"We recognize your concern, but we will allow this one to exist, no more than that. We feel that it is important for them to develop this technology. You will monitor the situation. If it gets out of hand, we charge you with personally scrapping it."

"It will be done." Novawynd confirmed.

"As for your next mission; we have an interesting one for you. We have sensed the presence of an intelligent life-form on a planet in the Acropol system." The Acropol system was within a region Earthlings call the Pleiades. "It is a water planet and the life forms are marine-life. You and will observe and collect data on the planet first, and then you and Zefram make first contact with the inhabitants." Novawynd was thrilled; finally a job that required some risk. They knew nothing about this planet, or what kind of dangers it may hold.

"Sounds fascinating; I'll look forward to it." she honestly confirmed.

"Our faith is with you Novawynd." The Superior Council added, and then they were gone in a flash.

*   *   *

After Novawynd explained to Zefram what their new mission was, she blipped Zelo Djynk. She gave him the coordinates they were to flux to. Apparently the Zenith fluxed as she made her way down to the CC. The four-dimensional blue globe that was the planet they were to study was already fixed on the display. The Zenith's sensors had begun to scan the orb. Overhead, Zacharieth read off audibly the various statistics about the planet. These statistics included: the name of its sun, distance from its sun, rotation period, sidereal rotation period, mean atmospheric temperature, atmospheric pressure, gravity, mass, density, diameter, and percent water verses percent of solid matter.

Finally, the sensors began scanning the life forms. Even with Zacharieth's technological might, it would still take several tecrons to complete. The next step would be to drop probes, which would get down close to the water surface to do the observational scanning. This data gathering process would then be reviewed by Novawynd, Zefram and the other CO's. This was the least invasive way to observe the behavior of the indigenous life-forms. From the data gathered, determinations could be made about the danger, or intelligence level of the various beings.

There was nothing more Novawynd could learn until the life-form data returned, so she went to find Stunner. She would have to bring him up to speed, because he was to prepare the emersion vehicles and suits for her and Zefram's excursion. Most of the shuttles were capable of submerging, but didn't need to go sub-surface for very deep. There was a special shuttle onboard each ship for that purpose. These submarine shuttles were equipped to also fill with water inside, and still remain completely functional. The purpose for this was to reduce sub-surface pressure. Novawynd hoped they wouldn't be going too deep. The Isotarin aqualungs would never be crushed under the weight of the water molecules, but their bodies could be. Zacharieth would have information on the location of the intelligent beings' dwellings, and how deep they lived under the ocean, soon enough.

Stunner was in the bay control room. He was pulling out the submarine shuttle already even though it wouldn't be needed for some time. Novawynd sensed Stunner was nervous. "Why are you nervous? You're not worried about me are you?" she prodded, but she actually was a little nervous herself. It wasn't that she was concerned about making contact with a completely alien civilization that might just as soon kill them. Or, possibly being devoured by a mega-shark; it was the scuba-diving. She had never done it before, except in hypothetical situations. During her training at the Analida Academy, Master Malica had put her through such situations in the sensory suit. Novawynd knew she could expect the submarine shuttle to be completely automated and bring them down and up at a pace their bodies could adjust to, but she dreaded the cold, the darkness and the pressure. She shuddered in an attempt to shake off the thought.

"I've never dealt with a mission of this magnitude before." he started to explain, "I want to make sure everything is perfect. You're depending on me."

"I am depending on you, but you're the best. I trust you." Novawynd nudged his shoulder with her fist in an effort to get him to loosen up a bit. He got serious suddenly and looked her squarely in the eyes.

"I've lost a lot of friends in my life-time, but none were as close to me as you are. I couldn't go on if I lost you Novawynd." This was the moment it hit her that he was in love with her, but it was a love that was purely platonic and that was difficult for her to fathom. She had feelings for him too. She didn't know if it was love, but she definitely felt very strongly toward him. However, she did want him sexually. It was so disappointing that he would never be able to get to that level with her. She was suddenly flustered and horny.

"I have to go." she said abruptly and rushed out of the control room. Stunner let out a small, dismayed grunt in protest, but she was out of the room before he could utter any words. Novawynd had no intention of turning back. She went straight to her unit and took some time to masturbate. Every time she thought about Stunner in that way, she compulsively needed to pleasure herself. After this mission was over, she could retrieve Trevor. She had promised him he would not be expected to be her sex-slave, but she hoped he would need her as much as she knew she would need him. That helped her get through moments of desire such as those.

*   *   *

The time had come for Novawynd and Zefram to descend. The marine shuttle flew down to the coordinates on the planet's surface, just above the alien city. It set down gently on the water and began filling with water. The liquid flowed in slowly, so the temperature of the water could be adjusted to match Novawynd's and Zefram's body temperatures. They were strapped into their seats and didn't have their masks on yet, but would wait until those parts of their bodies were almost under water. They couldn't waste good oxygen waiting for their submergence.

Once the shuttle was completely submerged, Novawynd and Zefram could communicate with each other via a microphone and headset contained in their masks. Their suits were made of a shiny, metallic, ultra-thin, but ultra-tough material, which was woven with a heat netting. In the event that they needed to leave the protection of the shuttle, they may be exposed to sub-zero temperatures and the heat net would keep them warm. Novawynd had been nervous about being submerged, but it wasn't actually that bad. She had meditated before coming to join Zefram on this mission, and she had resolved to be positively minded during this trip.

"Zefram, I've been wondering about why all the computers are given names that are the same as the celestial beings we had legends about on Earth. We called those beings angels. Do you know how that could be?"

"Of course. The Xaxony's computers are given names of previous Leluminalia who were legendary. They perished, unfortunately, in time, and as an homage, the computers were and still are named after them. Between three and four thousand years ago, I'm not sure of the exact date, some of these Leluminalia were sent to Earth. It was an experiment. The point was to engage the inhabitants and determine if there was any residual memory of the Xaxony left from the Earth's initial seeding. There was a little residual memory and from that sprang the dominant religion on Earth. From those encounters, your ancestors came to know the names of the heavenly beings. The inhabitants, your predecessors, marveled in the Leluminalia technology and their abilities, which they thought was magic. I think the iconographic depiction of an angel having wings evolved from the idea that the Leluminalia flew. They didn't actually fly, they used li-cy, of course, but this was an unfathomable concept to the primitive minds."

"Hmm. That makes more sense." she conceded, and then she changed the subject. "I hope these aliens are friendly."

"That's why you are the perfect Leluminali for this job. If they aren't, you can always flux out of the situation." Zefram responded.

"But what about you Zefram?"

"I am expendable. Only you matter." He blankly stated.

Novawynd turned her attention to the depth gauge as it ticked away. Zefram added, "That's a useful ability you have. It would be nice if I had it too."

Novawynd turned her attention back to Zefram. "You say that as if I have the capability to bestow that on anyone. I don't know how to do that." She lied, because she didn't know the Superior Council had told Zefram she might be able to.

"You should learn how to."

"Zefram, I may or may not be the Lajiachine. Either way, if I bestow that ability to everyone, then anyone who has that ability could become the Lajiachine. It's maybe better if I don't help anyone else achieve it."

"The actual prophesy states, word for word, 'the Lajiachine will be the one who brings about the down-fall of the Superior Council and will diminish the might of the Xaxony by revealing the truth and bestowing the gift to all beings to self-flux'. Therefore, you are the Lajiachine, because you are the first to achieve the self-fluxing ability and your very existence changes things." Novawynd snorted. "The thing about prophesies is that they all seem to repeat themselves. We had a similar prophesy on Earth." Novawynd added.

"Exactly, going back to what we were talking about before; your prophesies all originated from the Xaxony. They just changed over the thousands of years your ancestors had to bastardize the stories."

"So, the names changed, but the story remains the same." Just as Novawynd finished that statement, an odd sensation struck her and Zefram like a chilling gust of wind. "Whoo!" Novawynd cried gleefully, as it was a bit titillating. "I guess our friends know we're here." she stated in a more subdued manner.

Captain Djynk's voice popped in their ears, "That was a sonar wave. We detect there are more moving towards the shuttle." Just then, the two shuttle passengers were agitated again as they felt themselves scanned, this time by multiple sound-waves.

"I don't sense any hostility in this, do you Zefram?" Novawynd asked for affirmation.

"No. Not yet, anyway." Zefram concurred.

Djynk blipped in their ears again. "We are picking up on a strong pulse of electron particles moving straight for you." He sounded stressed.

"Again, I don't sense that this is an attack, just information gathering. They are curious about us." Novawynd tried to console the captain. The shuttle was jolted as if it had hit a bump.

Stunner had been in the CC also, watching as all of this was happening. Zacharieth cluelessly counted off the depth as Zefram and Novawynd underwent the probing by the alien hosts. Stunner couldn't take it any longer. He was starting to feel faint, so he left to get some air. Once he stepped outside the room, he took a deep breath and felt immediately restored. He realized he had been holding his breath in anticipation. He didn't understand why he felt this way about Novawynd. If she was in trouble, she could just flux out of it anyway, so there should be no worries. He felt a little better having come to that realization. He collected himself and returned to the CC. He was still able to hear Novawynd and Zefram responding and that was a relief.

"What's happening?" Novawynd asked Djynk. "Something hit us, but I don't think it had any effect."

"It's some sort of shield that has enveloped the shuttle. It seems to be expanding…like…a bubble. It's filling with air." Djynk seemed amazed. The shuttle's passengers were jerked about in their seats as the shuttle seemed to tilt over to one side. "Wait, your rate of descent has just doubled." the captain added.

"I still don't sense hostility." Novawynd assured.

"We're reading, that despite your doubled rate of descent, your pressure is not changing. Is that correct, what are your readings down there?"

Zefram answered this time, "No change in pressure."

Novawynd looked out the window and could see a wall of water and beyond it a great expanse of blurry light. Soon they were completely enveloped by the light. Then not long after, they seemed to come to a stop and set down gently on some hard surface. Novawynd and Zefram both felt that they were obviously being watched, and the curiosity of those watching was almost overwhelming. "Well, we seem to have landed at our destination safely." Novawynd confirmed. Djynk, but especially Stunner, breathed sighs of relief.

Novawynd continued, "I suppose we need to go meet our hosts"

"Allow me to go first, Novawynd." Zefram insisted.

"Be my guest." she said, imagining he would get incinerated the minute he stepped off the ship, then instantly feeling sorry she had thought such a terrible thing.

Zefram released the water and it flowed out faster than it came in. They unfastened themselves and Zefram got up to open the door. He felt alarm coming from the aliens outside, as they saw the door open and anticipated what would emerge. Zefram was the first to exit the shuttle and he had a scanner. This device could remotely scan a creature or structure in several ways, including x-ray. The image of one of the beings was sent back to the Zenith. Djynk and Stunner were able to see the aliens clearly.

The creatures were twice the length of a man, long and serpentine. They looked like long, slim squid. At their posterior, they had four short, thick tentacles, each having wavering fins that propelled them in any direction nimbly. At the front of their cylindrical, slender body, they had what seemed to be ten tentacles. Six long octopus-like tentacles that served as arms and four shorter tentacles that ended with bulbs. The bulbs were in fact eyes and the tentacles were retractable ocular shafts that could look in any direction, even around corners. Although only ten tentacles were usually visible, there were in fact fourteen tentacles at the head portion of the beings. The six tentacles and four eyes on the exterior protected four interior tentacles. These interior tentacles looked more like the feathery fans of a sea-anemone. They served several purposes, the two most important were breathing and communication. When unfurled these intricate fans sent and received sonar emissions, and that was how they spoke to each other over great distances, or saw things too far away to see with their eyes. In addition to all those features, they were semi-transparent. The surface of their bodies seemed to emit light that changed color in different patterns, much like a squid. It was somewhat mesmerizing to look at them.

Novawynd and Zefram were standing on a white, slick surface. It was slick, because it had recently been wet. The whole city they were in seemed to be comprised of this material. Novawynd took off her mask and when Zefram saw she could breath fine without it, he did the same. Novawynd had a remote analyzer, which could determine the atomic structure of things. She pointed the gadget at the white floor. The reading came back and Novawynd had to laugh. "Salt." she said in near disbelief. "They constructed everything out of salt." There were some unique characters carved into the salt floor. These beings did have a written language after all. She held her mask back up to her face. "Uh, Captain Djynk, have the cameras on the shuttle scan all the characters on the floor." She heard his response faintly as she let her mask down again.

Novawynd looked around and realized she had overlooked the indigenous being's obvious ability to bend water to their whim as well. She and Zefram should not be standing in this pocket of air they were standing in at the moment. There were no supports or barriers to hold the water back. It was as though the air itself was the barrier. Perhaps they were actually manipulating the air instead.

There were three creatures present on the outside, observing Novawynd and Zefram. The one in the middle approached the wall and opened up its fronds. Novawynd and Zefram were then bombarded by more sonar emissions, which was apparently this being's effort to communicate. Novawynd listened and tried to understand its meaning. It always took a little time to acclimate to new languages, but this one was particularly difficult, since their environment and their perception of reality was completely upside-down from Novawynd's, having lived under water their entire existence.

"They are curious, but I think they are asking something specific. That is, if we come from a specific place. I get 'top-land'. I think they are asking if we are from the land up top." Novawynd conveyed. She wanted to answer, but felt immediately frustrated. She didn't have the capability to speak in sonar waves. How could she answer?

She reached out to the enti in the Omniaural. "Please give me the ability to speak to these beings. If I could project my answers to their minds, from mine, I could communicate." Just then, the answer came to her. She walked forward, right up to the water wall. She put her hand up to the wall. It felt soft and pliable, just as it usually feels to submerge your hand.

"Don't Novawynd!" Zefram cried out in concern.

"I know what I'm doing." she flatly responded, as if in a trance.

Her hand went through the wall, into the water on the other side. The being on the other side, reached out with one of its fronds and wrapped it around Novawynd's forearm. They both felt a rush. It was a temporary, psychic connection in which mutual understanding was implanted in each being's mind. The creature and Novawynd released each other and then Novawynd could converse with it in its language and showed it pictures telepathically. Novawynd understood she would only be allowed this ability for a short time.

Novawynd began to explain, "We are from beyond the sea of air that surrounds your sea. Beyond the sea of air, there is a sea that has no water or air, in fact it has nothing. This sea of nothing is so vast that there may not be an end to it at all. We call this sea of nothing 'space'. Within space there are spheres of life, like this one, on which you live. We call these spheres of life 'planets'. Our lords built a ship that traverses space and we go around looking for the planets. We try to make friends with those who live on those planets. If those beings that live on the planets are advanced, they are invited to join us in our search for other planets."

"Amazing!" The creature responded. "We would like to see other beings and other worlds. Do you think your lords will invite us to join you in finding planets?"

"Perhaps. You seem to have a very advanced technology I think they would be interested in." Novawynd suggested.

"And what is that?"

"This ability you have to manipulate water, salt and air; we can't do that" Novawynd admitted. "Our lords may see your abilities as proof that you are sufficiently advanced to upgrade, but they would need to know how you do it. You would need to share your knowledge with us."

"I don't know how we do it. We just do. We tell the molecules of air to do what they do, or the water to do what it does or the salt to form structure."

"But, how do you tell the molecules to do it?"

"We are able to use electron particles to form the molecules into shapes. But, that is all we do."

"What emits the electron particles?"

"We emit the particles from our srwersh." The word *srwersh* was not translatable to Novawynd, but it was their word for their frond-like tentacles.

"I see." Novawynd was disappointed. She had been excited by this new technology, and almost as quickly let down when she realized it was created by an amazing physical attribute given to these creatures by nature. That ability probably wouldn't be reproduced by a machine. Not that the Xaxony wouldn't try. "Our lords will send others down here to get to know you. They will bring equipment that will tell us all sorts of things about you and they may even want to take one of you back with them. So, you should decide who you would send away with the aliens. You will want to choose someone that you won't miss if he or she should not survive."

"Not survive?" There was alarm emanating from the creature.

"Well, all the ships that traverse space are filled with air inside, because as you see, we are air breathers. If we were to bring one of your people with us, we would need to encapsulate him in water, the same as we are encapsulated in this air bubble right now. How long can one of your people survive being isolated like that? If he is too delicate, he may not survive. It wouldn't be because of any neglect on our part. To the contrary, we would only wish to keep him alive, and return him to you. I venture to guess that one of our people would not survive for long contained in a bubble like this." She suddenly realized this must be how the dolphins at the zoo must feel.

"Will you tell us more of space and the planets you have found?" The sub-marine natives were so curious.

"I will, but I should tell you that I will only be able to communicate with you for a short time, and I don't know how much longer we can talk. We need to name your planet. What do you call this city you live in?" Novawynd made a broad sweeping motion with her right arm.

"Ngu."

"Then your planet will also be called Ngu." she declared. Novawynd regaled the aqua-beings with stories of other beings in space and their civilizations. The whole time, Zefram said nothing. He just sat down, cross-legged on the wet, salty floor and meditated. He could not hear Novawynd talking, but he could see her making hand movements and gestures. It was somewhat boring, so he zoned out.

Finally, after about a tecron, Novawynd could not communicate anymore. It was like a steel curtain slammed down in her mind. The Ngu realized what had happened and they sent Novawynd a final communication. She sensed it was a bid of farewell. They swam out of the room. The air bubble Novawynd and Zefram were contained in, began to shrink slowly. Zefram jumped up. The two of them retreated into the shuttle. The shuttle remained contained in an air bubble that was only slightly larger than the shuttle itself. They were not completely strapped in when the shuttle began moving. They were off in a flash; a giant air bubble floating to the surface. They reached the surface twice as fast as the shuttle would have brought them there, but their pressure was miraculously equalized and there was no need for them to decompress. At the surface of the ocean, the bubble burst, leaving the shuttle floating on the surface. Zefram engaged the air drive and they returned to the Zenith.

*   *   *

Novawynd was relieved to be back on the ship and out of water. When the doors of the submarine shuttle opened, Stunner was waiting in the bay control room to greet her. Novawynd had to strongly fight the urge to run to him and jump into his arms. She could sense he was fighting back overwhelming pleasure at seeing her too. However, before they could have any contact with others onboard, she and Zefram would need to go into the decontamination showers.

A drone robot led Novawynd and Zefram to the showers. They stripped down to the nude. Novawynd didn't mind Zefram seeing her in the buff. She knew he would have no reaction to her while under the influence of Ephilderone. But, she was thoroughly enjoying the show she was getting, watching Zefram as he unwittingly bathed in the ionic rinse. The way his muscles gleamed in the mist accentuated his already perfect physique. If she didn't know better, Novawynd would swear he was trying to entice her. She tried not to let him catch her looking at him and she blocked him from feeling her current attraction to him. This last mission had them working very closely together. The jerk that Zefram had been when Novawynd first met him was a distant memory. He had begun acting decent toward Novawynd and he had used this last mission to develop trust bonds with Novawynd. She was beginning to think she had judged him too harshly, but perhaps she was just thinking with another part of her anatomy at that moment.

After standing in the dryers, they put on disposable jumpsuits and slippers. They would have to pass through the bay control to leave the area. There Stunner waited. A wide smile crossed his face.

"Another successful mission Novawynd." he approved, trying to be nonchalant. Obviously, he wasn't able to hide his feelings from Novawynd, or Zefram for that matter.

"You say that as if you had a doubt."

"Not even one doubt." he lied. Novawynd adored the fact that he worried about her. The common thread all humanoids shared, regardless of what planet they were from or the color of their skin was emotions. Even if the Xaxony could suppress emotions by training or chemical methods, this commonality of emotions could bond beings of completely different types. At the same time, it could sever relationships just as easily.

Zefram, sensing the obvious connection between Novawynd and Stunner, rolled his eyes. Initially, he was just going to ignore it and walk away, but he decided to say what he was thinking. Keeping his gaze trained on the door, instead of addressing them directly, he spoke, "You two do know the rules. Novawynd is not to pursue relationships with crew members. I don't care what kind of relationship you have with each other. I won't report you, but if I can see it, others can. Just make sure you keep a low profile." He paused for a moment, and then exited the bay control center. Novawynd and Stunner looked at each other.

"If I didn't know better, I'd think he was jealous." Novawynd joked, but she was beginning to wonder. "I suppose he's right. If he picked up on it, we probably should spend less time with each other in plain sight of others. The last thing I want is for you to get transferred." she tried to explain.

"I guess I never had a relationship like this with anyone else before." Stunner mused. "I hadn't even given any thought to how I was acting towards you in public. I'll take care to be more discrete and professional." They exited the bay control room.

"I have to give Zefram some credit where it's due." Novawynd thought out loud as they strolled down the hallway. "I used to think he was the type who would turn you in without question. After this last mission though, I'm starting to see him in a different light."

"Well," Stunner seemed to want to change the subject, "I do have to get back to my duties." He smiled softly and gave a slight nod. Then he slid past her and headed down the hall. Novawynd watched him go. She couldn't help but stare at his perfectly formed rear-end. She was really beginning to feel desperate. She really wanted Stunner to feel more for her. She wanted more than platonic. Then she remembered Trevor. The Zenith was to head back to Uinalon to pick up the AI version of Swizel, and then off to Xaxon 2 to pick up Trevor. It had already been nearly an aera. The Zenith crew would take a brief leave at Xaxon 2 while Trevor's processing completed.

CHAPTER 6

On Xaxon 2, finally, Novawynd had an opportunity to read the composition the Talosian had given to her. She pulled it out of the protective wrapping she had hidden it in. After leaving Vilijia, she had put it in a safe place and nearly forgot about it with all the tumult that occurred with Sia Donata, and then going straight into another mission. She sat back on her bed and laid it across her lap carefully and started to read.

"I know that you are curious as to how I broke my conditioning and why I forced my people to break away from the alliance..."

The manuscript went on to describe the history of Talos' relationship with the Xaxony, and how Talos was one of the first seeded planets. Being one of the most ancient of the Xaxony's creations, the inhabitants of Talos developed a close bond with the Omniaural and their psychic abilities came as a result of a natural evolution. Because of that, the Xaxony upgraded many of the most gifted Talosian psychics into the Xaxons; specifically Xaxon 2. However, the upgraded Talosians coincidentally ended up disappearing completely, more often than not.

Four Talosians became high level Leluminali and they were Danalian, Eridia, Jenata and Kiliam. Novawynd had not heard of the last two, but they were still alive. He had been able to break their conditioning and they still worked with Danalian. As Danalian had been a Leluminalia of the highest order, he was privy to sensitive information while he worked for the Xaxony. However, since he had been classmate to the original Zefram, and Zefram scored higher, it was Danalian that had to be sold. The Planetary Confederation of Talos bought him, of course, and he became their Commander-in-chief. He was second only to the planet's president. Danalian's primary purpose as Commander-in-chief was to handle business, political and military dealings with the Xaxony and its allies. The president of Talos was responsible for running the planet. But, in all matters, Danalian always deferred to the Talosian presidents to make the final decisions on anything. Because of Danalian's influence in the universe and after he had served so many presidents, people began to believe he was more powerful than any of the presidents. In fact it was thought that the Talosian presidents were merely his puppets. (At this point in the manuscript, Danalian made sure to set it straight that he always considered himself a servant to his president's whim. He advised, but never manipulated the president of Talos.)

Besides psychics, the other commodity Talos had was *Isotarin*, a substance that could only be found on their planet. The planet was huge and rich with the substance. Isotarin was like a hybrid of titanium and silicon, but it was an element in itself. Because it was lightweight, incredibly strong and created an impervious shell, Isotarin began to be used for everything. Talos grew rich on providing Isotarin to the universe, but the planet began to show the scars. Rebel groups formed all over Talos protesting the destructive effects the Isotarin mining had on the planet.

A little over one-hundred-anios into his service as a Leluminalia, Danalian discovered what had been happening to the Talosian psychics. The Xaxony had been scrapping them and using their genetics for their twisted pursuit of creating and controlling the Lajiachine. The Talosians didn't need to be scrapped. Once their DNA was logged, the geneticists could have just used the data, but it was an excuse for the Xaxony to systematically eliminate powerful psychics. Slowly but surely, the most powerful psychics on Talos were being terminated. This was done because the Superior Council feared the Lajiachine might develop naturally on Talos, and then he or she might not be controllable.

This realization was part of what broke Danalian's Lelumin conditioning. That was also when he realized what a mess the Isotarin mining was causing on the planet as well. It was like he had been shrouded by a cloud the Xaxony kept over him so he would be their puppet. When his conditioning failed, it was like the cloud dissipated and he could see everything clearly. That was the one time he did use his influence to manipulate the president of Talos. Together, they refused to allow any more Talosians to be upgraded. Then they declared Talos a "reluctant" ally. They imposed an embargo of Isotarin to the Xaxony. The allies could get it, but only exactly the amount they needed. It could not be stockpiled. Planets in need of Isotarin had to provide proof of what the Isotarin was to be used for, before Talos would supply it.

The Xaxony had to resort to recycling Isotarin, which was a good thing anyway. This made the Isotarin that much more valuable, and it became one of the favorite substances for pirates to obtain. Being neutral, the Xaxony could not retaliate. They couldn't do anything offensive towards Talos without making the allies angry. Not to mention that the "Lozian Catastrophe" had just occurred and the allies were very angry about that.

The *Lozian catastrophe* was an unfortunate incident that occurred at almost the same time Danalian discovered the truth about the Xaxony's systematic extermination of powerful Talosian psychics. If not for that coincidence, his conditioning might not have been broken. The Lozian incident was loathsome enough to break the *first* Zefram's conditioning. He had been in charge of that operation, but not directly responsible for the results. None-the-less, the result was horrifying enough to force even the hardened Zefram number-one to choose exile.

Lozia was a beautiful planet, just on the cusp of an industrial revolution. The people were deeply spiritual and had an amazing connection with the Omniaural and the enti. It was said some people had the ability to manipulate the Omniaural energy and draw out enti to do their bidding. At least twenty percent of the fifty million people on the fairly undeveloped planet were basically "magic-users".

Lozia was fraught with warlords constantly vying for territory. Those who had the bond with the Omniaural were trained as the superior soldiers for the warlords' use. They honed their magical skills and developed a fighting technique that rivaled the Leluminali. They imbued jewelry, weapons and clothing with magical abilities.

The Superior Council perceived the Lajiachine might evolve on this planet. Although the people were not developed enough to upgrade, the Superior Council dictated that they be upgraded anyway. The Lozians were still primitive and superstitious, so when the Xaxons came to them with the offer to upgrade, they refused. The Leluminalia responsible for the upgrade attempt went to each warlord to make the offer; and to his surprise, each warlord refused. This Leluminalia

was a far lower level than Zefram, and made one fatal error. He told
the Lozians about the legend of the Lajiachine and how the Xaxony
believed he would evolve on their planet. This story only made the
warlords arrogant; each believing he was this Lajiachine, and so why
join the Xaxony?

The Superior Council was not at all pleased with this result. They
commanded Zefram do a scouring of the planet. A super virus was
made and released on the planet, it was only supposed to kill those
who had the DNA that allowed them to have the super connection
with and manipulate the Omniaural and enti. Only twenty percent of
the population would have been eradicated. However, the geneticists
that developed the virus got something wrong. They didn't isolate the
right gene, and after the scouring, only 500,000 people of the original
population survived. The irony was that most of those who did not
survive were not magic-users, the intended targets.

If a normal man had unleashed this *accident* on a planet and
killed off the majority of the population, he would have been driven
to suicide. Zefram number one was trained to not be bothered by
such glitches. However, the incident *did* affect him enough that his
Lelumin conditioning switched off, and he defected. He was personally
responsible for spreading the truth of the near genocide of the innocent
and defenseless people of Lozia. There was an outcry amongst the allies
and the Xaxony left Lozia alone in an effort to restore their image. The
Xaxony has never gone back to Lozia and has wiped memory of the
incident out of archives. No one was supposed to speak of it. As far as
the Xaxony was concerned, Lozia didn't exist.

As for Zefram number one, or Z1 as Danalian referred to him,
he became a pirate, but also had people on the inside of the Xaxony
who would rescue beings that were Xaxon experiments gone wrong.
He became a self-imposed captain of a huge, outdated freighter

where these misfits were brought to find refuge. Together they work to undermine the Xaxony anyway they can. That is why the Xaxony disallowed anyone to speak of Z1.

Because the Lozian catastrophe occurred concurrently with Danalian discovering the truth about the Talosian psychics, his Lelumin conditioning also broke. He rebelled and that is when the infamous Isotarin embargo was imposed. In addition to that, he made it clear that if the Lajiachine should arise, he and his people would pledge allegiance to him or her. (Novawynd already knew that part.) All of this occurred 400 anios prior and Z1 was still floating around the universe pirating and taking stabs at the Xaxony, while successfully eluding any capture attempts. Also, Talos still had the embargo in place against the Xaxony. That was where Danalian's lengthy explanation ended.

There was a part of Novawynd that struggled against believing any of this was true, but that was the Lelumin conditioning; what little was left in her. She just knew in her soul that it was *all true*. The Xaxony was like any other government and the Superior Council was like any other governing body. They made mistakes from time to time, but always in the *best interest* of the Xaxon people and its allies. The Superior Council was ethereal, but not all-knowing. They were in tune with any spiritual ripples in the Omniaural, but anything else, they were oblivious to and relied heavily on information being fed to them.

Novawynd was relieved to have at least some of her questions answered, but it left her with new questions. She had never heard the Lozian story before, and now she wanted to know what happened to the planet in the last 425 anios. Did they survive? She started to feel a strange, new fascination about Z1 and Lozia developing. She wanted to know more.

*　　　*　　　*

When Novawynd entered the lab, Trevor was sitting on the lab table. He was cleaned up and in a white, ergonomic jump-suit. He looked a little groggy, but his face lit up when he saw Novawynd. She couldn't help but smile at his reaction.

"Novawynd!" he called out to her.

"Hey, Trevor." she answered sweetly. She moved up next to him and put her hand on his back. She stroked him consolingly. "How're you feeling?"

"Not bad." his Aussie accent evident. "How long has it been?" he rubbed his own shoulder as if it was stiff.

"About an Earth month." Novawynd informed.

"Wow! That long? Seems like I just went to bed."

"Yeah, I know what you mean." she assured.

"It's odd that I know the language here now. Did they implant that too?"

"No. While you're in stasis, they insert contact lenses that pipe images into your eyes. Images are fed into your visual receptors and sound is fed into your audio receptors, via the CI, in the form of lessons on basic Xaxon language, as well as time and other units of measure. It's basically like educational video played in your mind every mecron of the dialo. But, your body and the areas of your brain that don't deal with learning and memory remain in stasis. This way, by the time you are released, you're basically ready to go out into the Xaxon universe. You still will have to do some learning of course, but you should be able to grasp things quickly now with the knowledge you've been given."

"One thing I do know…I'm really horny. It's been a month without relief."

"Aww, poor you, a whole aera." Novawynd was facetious, just to poke fun at him a little. She realized a man like Trevor would be used to getting some action more than once an aera, but she was willing to accommodate. "I brought you an outfit that was custom made for you." she motioned to the stack of clothes she had brought in with her. "Why don't you get dressed and meet me outside. Then I'll take you to the unit that will be your's until we leave on the next mission."

Trevor hopped down off the lab table and sidled up next to Novawynd. He looked down into her eyes, "You mean you aren't going to take me back to your quarters until we leave on the mission?" he asked seductively. Novawynd could sense that he was in fact horny, but not one hundred percent behind what he was implying.

"You know Trevor. I realize this is still all really strange to you. You were upgraded to be my kept-man in a way, but you're not a monkey on a leash. If you're really not in the mood, don't put on an act because you think it's what I expect. If you're not attracted to me, I'm okay with that."

Trevor gasped in frustration. He put his hands up to either side of his head and made a twisting motion. "What's going on up here is private! I don't want you in here. It's not fair, and it's really not cool. I want to keep my thoughts and feelings to myself. Is that too much to ask?" He scolded her. Novawynd felt ashamed. He was right. She could block it, so why use the sense when it wasn't necessary. Besides, she had grown bored with never being surprised by anything.

"For the record, it's just your feelings I sense. I only guess at your thoughts based on your feelings; but you're right." she admitted. "So, I'll make this promise, not just to you, but to everyone. I will block my empathic abilities from this day forward, unless something really sinister pushes through. I don't always need to know. I don't always want to know."

"I'm sorry. I shouldn't have gone off on you like that. It's just very annoying. And for your record, I do find you very attractive. You're hot. Smokin' hot. I'm just not sure I'm in the mood to perform, but I do know I want to try and find out." Trevor caressed Novawynd's cheek.

"No pressure Trevor. When the time is right, you'll know." She turned to leave him to dress.

When they got to Trevor's unit, he was unimpressed as he surveyed the surroundings. The three-room unit was small compared to his quarters on the Zenith, but it was temporary anyway. He gave Novawynd a sultry look. "So, if I need to find you, where are your quarters?" He smirked.

"It's easy to find my quarters. I'll show you. Follow me." Novawynd said as she led Trevor out of his unit. She walked a few paces to the right of his door, where she stopped and leaned up against the wall next to another door, folding her arms as she did so. "Your quarters will always be right next to mine, usually on this side of you. She motioned to the door and it opened for her. She rolled off the wall into the open doorway. She sauntered into the room and began to take off her uniform jacket. Trevor hesitated only a moment before he followed. Novawynd laid her jacket over the a-morphic blob of tech-foam that served as the sofa. She was practicing blocking Trevor's emotions, but she could feel him following her like an animal on the prowl. Suddenly he was close behind her. He ran his hands over her shoulders and down her arms as he buried his face in her neck and took in a deep breath of her scent.

Trevor bit gently into the flesh at the apex of Novawynd's shoulder and neck. She sucked in her breath. It had been so long since she was subject to the skills of an experienced lover like Trevor. She was aching to be taken. Novawynd's heart raced and she began to breathe faster. She became flushed all over and especially between her legs. She felt as though the moisture was pouring out of her. His hands were everywhere;

pulling at her shirt to get his hands under it. He spun her around to face him. They kissed for the first time, deeply. Novawynd felt as though she was melting into him. He picked her up and she wrapped her legs around him. Still kissing, he walked, carrying Novawynd into her bed chambers. He laid her down on the bed and continued to kiss her and press the hard bulge beneath his pants against her. The feeling of that object, familiar and yet still unknown to Novawynd, made her delirious to reveal it. They tore at each other's clothes and their own until they were completely nude. Kissing, licking and biting as they entwined.

Suddenly Trevor stopped and sat back on his haunches, his erection standing at full attention. Novawynd was relieved, because it was an impressive staff. Exactly the way she liked them. She wanted it inside her with the weight of his body holding her down. He slowly spread her legs wide as he began to crouch over her. She reached out and took the rod in her hand to stroke it. Trevor pushed her legs back so her hips were tilted up towards him at a better angle. She guided his member to the opening of her vagina. He leaned over her and braced himself. He let out a moan as he felt the head of his cock at the mouth of her juicy center. He looked into her eyes with those dreamy, ice-blue eyes and smiled as he pushed. Novawynd arched her back in ecstasy and met each of his thrusts with a thrust of her hips.

This love making session lasted quite some time. Trevor's endurance impressed Novawynd. She came several times during the course as Trevor held out. Finally, he began to come to his climax. Novawynd had blocked his emotions up to that point, but as he began to come, she let down her guard and the intense feeling she felt in him overwhelmed her. The intensity of the rush was better than she remembered from the last time with Viv. The two lovers cried out their pleasure as they mutually climaxed and lay back exhausted, panting.

They made love like that, into the night, finally falling into a deep sleep when sheer exhaustion overtook them. They slept for some tecrons before Trevor woke Novawynd. "Good morning beautiful." he said as he kissed her affectionately and caressed her hair.

"How long have we been holed up in here?" Novawynd inquired.

"Why? Do you have somewhere to go?" Trevor joked.

"No. But I'm hungry, aren't you?"

"Ahh yeah, I could go for some bacon and eggs."

"Well, you're out of luck then, because there is no such thing as bacon or eggs. Instead, how about some sort of solid matter that looks like tofu and tastes like, well…tofu?"

"Is that my only option? Because, I'm thinking I may have made too hasty a decision in coming here."

"Well, there aren't many products manufactured here that aren't ergonomic or practical, including the food. As long as it provides the necessary nutrients, and it all comes out the same anyway, why worry about minor things like aesthetics or flavor."

"Just because you are saying that, I'm craving a nice juicy steak right now."

"Oh, I have steak on the Zenith, but not much. All my special food is rationed. I need it to last. I'll share my steak with you, but only on special occasions."

"This is a special occasion. It's my re-birthday and the first time you and I got to bangin'."

"That is pretty special." Novawynd answered sarcastically. "But even so, we can't get on the Zenith right now, so we'll have to wait. Then the first thing we can do is have a steak and Earth vegetable dinner. In the mean time, I can order out for some alien libations. That means real meat and real fruit and vegetables of some sort, only not Earthling. It tastes different, but still pretty good."

"Why didn't you say so?" Trevor tickled Novawynd and she squirmed and giggled. She couldn't remember the last time she squirmed and giggled, but she liked it.

Novawynd and Trevor had their alien take-out. Then they made love again in the shower. Once they were dressed and Novawynd put on her make-up and did her hair, she got back to work. Trevor sat and watched her but quickly got bored. "I think I'm going to go for a walk and learn something about the people around here." he notified Novawynd.

She tore her attention away from her work long enough to say "Okay." before turning her attention back to her work.

Trevor pulled on his boots, which had recently been custom made for him and fit perfectly. He grabbed his jacket, which went with his boots. It had a very sporty, yet utilitarian style. The jacket was yellow, with white mesh vents, outlined with thin blue piping. There was a grey, hive-patterned material inside as a liner and also inside the flaps. This jacket sported several pockets. It was fairly form fitting, but not too snug, and the material was thin despite its insulating qualities. Any shirt or pants Trevor wore would match his boots and jacket so his outfits would be coordinated. Of course, here everyone's clothing seemed to be coordinated. As a former model, he noticed those things. Odd, however, that these advanced beings didn't put much effort into the aesthetic principles of their surroundings. Design of items seemed to be driven more by practical and ergonomic principles than whether it looked cool or not. For instance: chairs automatically adjusted to a being's height and lumbar structure to provide perfect posture despite the being's physical attributes.

Trevor pulled on his jacket and went out. He had, as part of the processing, been subliminally implanted with basic knowledge of how the transportation system in the Xaxons works. Also, he could read the signs he needed to know to get around and he understood how the currency worked. The Xaxon written language reminded Trevor of a digital clock that had been broken. Combinations of short vertical, horizontal and diagonal dashes configured letters and numbers that looked similar to Earth letters and numbers. Trevor noticed that this written language was used scarcely, however. Novawynd had already told Trevor about how communications were audio or video, so the written word was nearly archaic. The most frequently written characters were numbers, since math was indispensable. Novawynd had explained that it was simpler, when so many life-forms were being brought together, to learn a spoken language, but not have to worry about reading or writing it.

There weren't a lot of beings around, so Trevor blipped Gabriel. "Gabriel?"

"Yes, Trevor?" Gabriel's voice sounded in Trevor's CI.

"Is there a place where I could find a greater concentration of beings to observe?"

"There is a li-cy race going on at the arena. You will find everyone there." Gabriel informed.

"Thanks." Trevor hopped on a trans-cart which took him to the main corridor. He referenced his metaband to figure out which "centipede", as Novawynd called them, to take. He managed to get to the arena. Trevor was thinking as he journeyed along, "Maybe there are some females here that aren't on that Ephilderone stuff." He had just made love to Novawynd, but he just wanted to scope; to keep his options open. He noticed it was true what Novawynd had told him about people looking down their noses at him. He had never felt so ugly. The further away from Novawynd Trevor got, the more he wanted to go back to her.

He arrived at the arena without any incident. He wandered though the crowd, scanning; trying not to stare, as Novawynd had instructed. He was trying to figure out if one needed to purchase a ticket, or how did one get into the event? He heard his name called. It was a man's voice, which he didn't recognize, but what was the likelihood that there was another Trevor in this crowd? He whirled around trying to find the man who called out to him. A few paces away he saw a light-blue-skinned man with purple hair motioning towards him. The man was in fact, calling his name and beckoning to him.

Trevor moved toward the man, who seemed friendly enough. As Trevor got closer, the azure-skinned man asked "Is Novawynd here?"

"No. I came alone. She's working back in her unit."

"Oh well." The blue guy responded, trying to seem nonchalant, but he seemed genuinely disappointed. "I'm Stunner." He decided to change the subject. "I'm the intin of the space-guard on the Zenith, and a good friend of Novawynd's. If she was here, we could get better seats, but oh well…" That wasn't really why Stunner was disappointed, but Trevor wouldn't ascertain the truth. "Why don't you come sit with us?" Stunner was accompanied by some other people in similar gray uniforms. Trevor determined they must also be Zenith crew members. He thought a couple of them looked familiar, but couldn't figure out where he'd seen them; probably on the Zenith at some time.

Trevor followed the others and they found a row of seats together. Stunner sat next to Trevor. He felt he had to keep an eye on Trevor for Novawynd, to make sure he didn't end up in a trash receptacle somewhere. Also, he really wanted to get to know Trevor. He didn't realize why, but it was a latent desire to live vicariously through Trevor. If Stunner couldn't make love to Novawynd, perhaps Trevor would talk about what it was like, and Stunner would be able to find some pleasure in that.

"So, Trevor, I understand you like ale."

"Yeah."

"You should try some Timmian ale. Novawynd likes it a lot. The first time I met her, she was getting quite sloppy on the stuff." The Xaxons were generally reserved about drinking. They weren't really that into it, because it wasn't a healthy habit unless taken in moderation. But, at the li-cy races, alcohol flowed freely. The crowds got quite rowdy as they cheered for the racers. Levitating beverage dispensers floated up and down the aisles and across the rows when someone flagged one down. The alcohol dispensers were metallic blue. Stunner hailed one and it floated over to him. He poured a cup of the ale for himself and one for Trevor.

Trevor took it gratefully and took a swig. It was good. Just the right amount of sweet and bitter combined, with a good head and dark color. But, it had a flavor that was not quite like Earth beer. He realized it was because it was made of something alien, but it wasn't unpleasant, just different. "Not bad." he commended. Stunner nodded happily as he swallowed his own beer.

"I can't believe Novawynd let you go wandering around by yourself so soon after your processing." Stunner mused. "But, I often forget she's more in tune with the undercurrents of the Omniaural than I can ever comprehend, so she obviously didn't see any danger in it."

"Danger? Is this a dangerous place?" Trevor was concerned suddenly. "I thought the Xaxon's were peaceful."

"People go missing all the time. They cross the wrong being at the wrong time. There are conflicts going on all the time between races, and just because these beings are upgraded, it doesn't mean they automatically lay their differences aside. But yes, the 2B Xaxons are peaceful. As a UB, you're probably safer than a 2B, because certain UBs don't like 2B attitudes, and that can be a problem. However, these tiffs and the way they are handled are generally accepted. Call it population control in a society that doesn't age or get sick." Stunner explained a little. "On the other hand, you could still meet up with that one alien who takes an extreme dislike to you for no reason at all."

"How do I know I can trust you?" Trevor rationalized.

"You don't." Stunner grinned and was silent for a moment to allow Trevor to start sweating a little. "I do know that you are special to Novawynd, and she's my boss. Because of that, you can be assured I'd lay down my life for you if she wanted me to."

"That's cool." Trevor nodded. Then he decided to shift gears. "Novawynd was telling me about the space-guard. That sounds great. What do I have to do to become a space-guard?"

Stunner was silent again. This was a delicate subject. Trevor's occupation was designated as "companion to Novawynd", and here he was talking like he had a choice. "You would first be subject to a battery of tests to see if you could handle it physically and mentally. If you pass, you would go through a couple of anios of training, and then you would be assigned to a ship. It takes several years of service and proving yourself to get good commissions, so you'd have to be very lucky to get a commission on Novawynd's ship. I think she would be very upset if the man she carefully selected to be her companion were to go off and become a space-guard. But, maybe we can find a way to get around that on the Zenith. I'll see what I can do."

The Zenith group watched the races and got quite riled up. Once he got the idea of how the races worked, Trevor got into it too. By the time they left the races, they were singing Xaxon fighting songs, which Trevor learned as he went. Stunner kindly escorted Trevor home since was drunk; and being new to the Xaxon life, left to his own, he wouldn't have found his way back. Besides, Stunner would be able to use the opportunity to visit Novawynd. Stunner ushered Trevor unto his unit and after the door closed, he turned to Novawynd's unit. He paused for a moment, but decided to blip her anyway.

Novawynd was sleeping at that moment, but when Gabriel announced Stunner was at her door, she groggily gave permission for Stunner to enter. She dragged herself out of her bed and pulled on a robe. She met Stunner in her living area. "So, what brings you here at this hour?" she was slightly annoyed.

"I ran into Trevor at the li-cy races and he got a little drunk. I made sure he got home alright." Stunner explained.

"Oh…thanks for that." Novawynd turned away to go back to bed. She dropped her robe and crawled into bed. Stunner paused for a moment. He turned to go, and then he decided to stay instead. He took off his jacket and boots as he moved towards Novawynd's bed. She lifted her head. "What are you doing?"

"I'm too tired to go all the way back to my unit, can I just stay here?" Stunner had cuddled with Novawynd before, so she didn't see the harm in it.

"Okay." she approved. He stripped down to his under-ware and slid under the covers to snuggle up next to her. They slept, cuddling together until some time later when Gabriel blipped in that the Superior Council wanted to speak to Novawynd. Stunner dressed quickly and said his goodbye, wishing her luck with the Superior Council. She took a little longer to get ready, because she needed to get her hair and make-up in order.

Make-up was still used, not because it was needed to hide flaws, but it was an integral part of Xaxon life. It was worn as decoration more than anything. Novawynd went for the natural look back on Earth, but here anything went, so she played with it a bit more. She liked to draw red lines under her eyes to the corners of her face and outline her eyes in black. She added red streaks to her white hair to compliment the Leluminali uniform.

*   *   *

Trevor was awakened early by the wet nose of his dog, the *real* Swizel. She had crept onto his bed in the middle of the night, which was something she had never done before. Trevor had almost forgotten about her. She hadn't been in his unit when Novawynd first showed it to him. Apparently, the dog hadn't been brought over from the ship yet at that time. When he felt her tongue affectionately brush his face, he sat up, hugging and scratching her all over. Swizel excitedly wriggled around licking his arms as he did so. Then he saw it, the copy Swizel. It lay quietly on the floor, its head perked up and tail gently wagged as if it was amused by the scene, but nervous about joining in. It hadn't been asked to join, so it would wait for a command.

"Come here Swizel!" Trevor exuberantly coaxed. The faux dog ran over to the bed and leapt onto it. The *real* Swizel growled and snapped at the copy Swizel with a vicious bark. The replica canine recoiled. "Okay! Get down off the bed." Trevor commanded the faux dog. It did as it was told. Trevor then realized why the real animal was on his bed. She was vying for the dominant position with the master. Either that or she was protecting her master form the thing that looked like a dog, but didn't smell right. "This is very interesting." Trevor thought to himself. He hadn't had a chance to play with the new improved version of Swizel. He got out of bed and stretched. Both Swizels watched him. He turned his attention to the fake dog. He made a motion with his hand to it as if he was signing the symbol for number one. This was the signal for her to pay attention to him. It stood at attention. He looked around for something to have it fetch, but the room was devoid of anything. He pointed to the floor at his side, which was the signal for it to heel by his side. The replica dog immediately jumped into position. "Very nice." he thought. He walked over to the dresser and it followed. He pulled out a pair of socks and tied them together. It acted excited when it saw the old stand-by for playing fetch. The real Swizel also displayed anticipation at the sight of the tool used in her favorite game.

Trevor threw the socks for the faux canine, but it did not run. Instead it crouched by his side ready to fetch, waiting for the command. The real Swizel knew what to do, so she leapt off the bed and sprinted to retrieve the socks. "Well this is going to be impossible with the two of you here." he said to the old Swizel as he took the socks from her. He found it interesting that the mock Swizel didn't run after the socks. It was programmed with the real Swizel's memory impressions. It was to know what certain things were and it was to respond with the same reaction a regular dog would, but it was also programmed to do only what it was asked to do.

Trevor ended this experiment when he had to release the liquids he imbibed the night before. As he stood over the human waste receptacle, he thought about Novawynd. Perhaps she would be available for an early morning "roll-in-the-hay". He decided to drop by her unit to see if she was awake. Trevor noticed as he was leaving his unit, Stunner happened to be leaving Novawynd's, and he was taken aback. Stunner noticed Trevor and his odd reaction and stopped.

"Good friends, huh?" Trevor called out as he sauntered towards Stunner. "I guess I know now what kind of friends you are." Trevor was teasing Stunner. He wasn't upset about the prospect of Novawynd being with another man. He was just annoyed that his opportunity to get back into bed with her had just been ruined.

"It's not like that." Stunner defended, not realizing Trevor was being facetious. "I'm an Eron. E-R-O-N. If you do some research about us Erons, you'll understand. I have to run." Stunner turned to go, and then partially turned back to Trevor. "Novawynd is on her way out to the Superior Council chambers, so I'm afraid you're out of luck." Stunner said, assuming he knew what Trevor's intentions were. A trans-cart came near Stunner, so he hopped on and rode away.

Trevor stood there wondering if he should go back to his unit or not. Just then the door opened and Novawynd stepped out, as she adjusted her jacket. Trevor gave her a knowing smile. Novawynd was curious, "What kind of 'no good' are you up to now?" she interrogated.

"I just ran into Stunner coming out of your unit." He explained and crossed his arms.

"It's not what you think, Trevor. He didn't feel like going all the way back to his unit after dragging your drunk ass home, so he crashed at my place." she explained.

"Fine." he said mock-tersely.

"I'm on my way to the Superior Council Cham…"

"I know." Trevor interrupted, "Stunner told me. Mind if I ride along?"

"Come on." she motioned him to join her as she caught the next trans-cart that came along.

"Basically, Stunner told me the same thing. But, he said something about him being an Eron. What did he mean by that?"

"I'm sure he meant that Erons don't feel attraction to females that aren't of their own species. They are pheromone driven, you see."

"Oh, like dogs?"

"Yeah, like that."

"Speaking of dogs. I was messing around with the new Swizel before I came by. I went to throw tied-up socks for her to fetch and she just crouched down. She didn't seem to know that she should retrieve them."

"The AI Swizel knows how to act like a dog, and she knows about playing fetch, but she's also trained *not* do anything you don't tell her. If you tell her, 'Swizel, when I throw this, you will immediately run to pick it up and return it to me. Don't wait for my command, just do it and you should do that every time I throw it.', and then she will do it every time, or until you tell her otherwise. Basically, you need to program her to your liking. She's meant to be like Swizel, but a version of Swizel that will do everything you ask her to do, and nothing you don't."

"Well, she is really life-like. I wouldn't have known the difference, except the old Swizel acted like Swizel, and the new Swizel, just didn't."

*   *   *

Novawynd exited the Superior Council chambers in a serious mood. Trevor had been waiting outside, but it hadn't been long. "I just got my next mission, so it looks like we're off again." She turned to Trevor. "We will need to return Swizel to Earth right away. You remember that was part of the deal, right?"

"Yeah." he affirmed in a disappointed tone. "You should have just put her back while I was still in the tank."

"I thought about it, but I wanted you to be able to say goodbye to her, and make sure she was in a safe place. Where should we put her?"

"My parent's farm."

"Gabriel?"

"Yes, Novawynd?"

"Blip Zelo Djynk for me."

"Yes, Novawynd."

A moment later it was Djynk's voice in her ear. "Yes, Your Supremacy."

"Recall everyone to the Zenith; we are embarking on our next mission immediately. I will brief you, the other COs and Zefram once we've all boarded."

"As you command." he simply stated.

Novawynd and Trevor cruised back to their respective units to pack up their belongings. They were ready to go about the same time and converged in the hallway outside her unit. Trevor had the two dogs in tow; the real Swizel on a leash and the fake Swizel heeling on its own. There was no chance it would bolt.

After many trans-cart transfers and elevator rides, they finally arrived at docking port eighteen. Other members of the crew were arriving and Trevor thought he recognized some of them. As they entered the Zenith, there were several alien beings milling about. Stunner was one of them. Zelo Djynk, Sub-zelo Kananga and Zefram were also there. They were present to make sure all crew-members were accounted for. They greeted Novawynd and Trevor respectfully.

"Zelo, when everyone is accounted for, take the Zenith to Earth again. Once we get there, we will meet in the CC, and I will apprise you all on our new mission." The others bowed their heads in acknowledgement. Novawynd lead Trevor back to his unit onboard. "Trevor, to get to your unit, remember section three, elevator down to level two. We are in units one and three. You're in three, I'm in one. But of course, when in doubt as to where you're going, Zacharieth will show you on your metaband. You won't be able to access any areas you don't have authorization for."

They were at Trevor's unit now. The door opened and he brought the dogs in. He took off the original Swizel's leash, and then he came over to Novawynd. He got very close to her and reached out to hook his finger in one of the fasteners of her jacket. "Do I have authorization to access any of these parts?" He coyly asked and closed in for a kiss. She met it willingly.

"Anytime, anywhere." She responded. "Zacharieth... let me know when we get to Earth. End." She started to unfasten her jacket. "We may not have a lot of time, so a quickie if you don't mind."

"My pleasure." He took off his jacket quickly. She led him to the sofa where she pulled down her pants and bent over the sofa for him. He was stiff already and his erection sprung from his pants as he closed in on her poised and juicy passion flower. He thrust into her from behind and felt instant relief and pleasure all at once. He realized he really liked being there, inside her. None-the-less, it was over quickly. Trevor usually held out longer, but not that time since they were in danger of having to cut it off. Since getting out of the processing, he could swear his penis was slightly larger, and sex felt more pleasurable than he remembered. Plus, Novawynd's pussy was the tightest he'd experienced, and he'd experienced many. But, it wasn't just the physical pleasure, there was something else he couldn't put his finger on. Making love to her was like feeding an addiction, because when he wasn't doing it, he needed it.

Trevor was clueless as to how powerful Novawynd really was. To him, she was just a woman in a powerful position, who needed release every once and a while. Novawynd didn't care if he ever learnt about her psychic abilities. He had been told about some of them, but just knowing the abilities existed, was far different from experiencing them first-hand.

Zacharieth blipped Novawynd as she re-dressed herself, and with a quick peck on Trevor's lips, she departed. Trevor fell back on the sofa, relieved.

*   *   *

Trevor headed down to the lounge to have a drink, or three. When he got there he set himself up with some Timmian ale, which had become one of his favorites since he first experienced it at the li-cy races. He sat down and watched a 4D projection about what was going on in the Xaxony. It was like the news-channel of the universe, but that was always the only thing on. There was no mindless entertainment, the likes of which they had back on Earth. The people of the Xaxony and all its allies watched this and regarded the beings making the news channel like celebrities. A lot of times, Trevor had to laugh at the stories, because they were so banal. But, there just was nothing else to report out in the universe. Sometimes certain stories didn't make sense to him, but they were intriguing none-the-less. It gave him something he would go back to his unit and do research on.

As he sat watching the display, someone came up behind him. "I had promised to buy you a Cirrilean brandy. Is now a good time?" It was Zefram. Trevor turned to look at Zefram with surprised apprehension. Then he relaxed.

"Sure. Belly up." He waved Zefram to the chair next to him. Zefram set a glass of brandy down in front of Trevor and took the seat while holding onto his own glass of the caramel colored liquid. Zefram toasted Trevor and took a sip.

"I'm surprised you're talking to me. Novawynd had me under the impression you wouldn't lower yourself to speak to a lower life-form like me."

"If Novawynd treats you as an equal, then I can't say you're inferior to me."

"I see…and you wouldn't want to imply that Novawynd is inferior to you, would you?" Trevor understood. "But, I'm not equal to Novawynd. I'm more like her dog, really."

"That would make two of us then." Zefram related, and then changed the subject. "I wanted to talk to you because I have been pursuing a side project, and I need some info." Zefram leaned back. "You see, the Xaxon database has information on the mating habits of Earthlings. It's not that different from other similar humanoids and really quite clinical. However, I've noticed with Earthlings, there is a courtship involved that is deeply buried in many psychological layers. It almost seems like a game of complex, opposing strategies. For the sake of our annals, I've been trying to gather data on this subject and submit it. I need to know what goes on inside a man's head when he pursues a woman. So, I'm looking for your help in this. Do you mind?"

Maybe it was the Cirrilean brandy, but Trevor's tongue was loosened and he actually felt privileged to be sought after for his input on something. His knowledge on the wooing skills of the Earthling male would be the go-to source for all beings in the universe for the rest of eternity. He liked that idea. "Well, the most important thing to either a man or a woman, in any relationship, is that both just want to be appreciated. But, that is where their commonality ends. A man feels appreciated when his woman allows him to have sex with her as often as he feels the need. A woman feels appreciated when a man caters to her emotional needs. That's where it gets complicated. First of all, emotions, there are so many of them, especially when it comes to women. Then you attach the various needs to those emotions and the fact that each woman has unique 'emotional needs' and the possibilities for the emotional needs become infinite. A man has to learn what these emotional needs are and how to meet them, or he doesn't get the sex he desires." Trevor paused. This left an opportunity for Zefram to ask a question.

"So, let's pretend I have the ability and the desire to woo an Earth woman…well, let's use Novawynd as a hypothetical example, since we both know her. How would I learn her needs and go about meeting them?" This was rather sly of Zefram. He knew Trevor would never suspect he really was trying to woo Novawynd, and Trevor's arrogance would give him all the ammunition he needed.

"Well, Novawynd is a good example of a very strong and independent woman. She doesn't need a man for much of anything, but I know she needs me to listen to her when she needs to talk about things that are bothering her. She doesn't want my advice, per se. She really just wants me to tell her she's doing the right thing and everything will be okay. That's just an example of how most women have insecurities and how they look to their man to build them up. If you're pursuing a woman, a sure way to get her panties off, is if you key in on her insecurity and erase it with flattery. But, there is a fine line. Most confident women can tell the difference between sincere flattery and blatant obsequiousness. However, insecure women will believe just about any flattery, because they so badly need to hear it."

Zefram interrupted at this point to clarify something he'd been wondering about. "I get this feeling, from the way you describe this courtship process, that you are only acting like you care about these women's emotional needs in order to get your own needs met. Are you never truly concerned about her feelings?"

"If by her, you were referring to Novawynd, then yes. Each woman is different. I know my *purpose* here is to be Novawynd's companion. I know I only need to perform and I don't need to be sincere at all, but I admire her, so my empathy toward her feelings is very real. There have been other women in my life that I have felt that way about too. But, there have been far more women that I pretended with, just to get sexual gratification. There were even women that I pretended with for a very long time, because the sex was so good, even though my respect for them wasn't there."

"How many women have you had sex with?"

"Well, I started when I was fifteen-years-old. I maybe had one girlfriend a year until I became a model when I was twenty, then the women came easy. That was when I really started messing around. Now I'm only twenty-six and I've been with over a hundred. But, I can only estimate, because who's counting?" Trevor smirked.

"So, you're telling me that you did *that* with all those women, just to have the pleasurable experience of sex with them, but not for the purposes of finding a mate to procreate with?"

"Not always." Trevor felt a little defensive against Zefram's judgmental tone. "A lot of times, in the beginning especially, I did it to keep the woman happy so I could have a comfortable place to sleep, a warm meal in my belly and to be able to pursue my other interests without interference." Trevor thought about what he had just said. "Well, you make it seem like I'm a monster, but I assure you they were okay with it."

"Why would a woman put up with a man who was using her like that?"

"Like I said…a man *like me*, doting affection on a woman, makes her feel like a goddess. It makes all those insecurities I mentioned, go away."

"In Novawynd's case, I don't get that sense from her. She seems very self-confident."

"Novawynd draws her strength from within, not from others. She is truly self-assured. Most men are afraid of women who are self-assured, because they can't get what they want from a woman like that. They can't emotionally control a woman like that. But, there are a few brave souls who are drawn to women like that. A woman like that presents a challenge. A woman like that is never boring. I find Novawynd's power and confidence very alluring. Basically, I'd do anything she asked. I've never been that way with any woman before."

This interaction was encouraging to Zefram. He was on the right track. So far, he had consistently made an effort to assist Novawynd. He had supported and encouraged her. He had done all this instinctively. It just seemed the right thing to do, but perhaps he was picking up some feedback from the Omniaural that she was emitting. Zefram pushed himself back from the table. "I think I have all that I need." He stood up and bowed to Trevor. "Thank you, Trevor."

"Glad to help." Trevor responded proudly.

CHAPTER 7

"Well everyone," Novawynd addressed the commanding officers as she entered the comcen. "We are here on Earth because we need to release Trevor's dog. She obviously was never meant to live aboard. But, that isn't the mission. As soon as we drop off the dog, we need to go directly to Galtrain 5. The Terrans have been tampering with the seeds."

"Seeds" was the term the Xaxons used for the beings that the Xaxony genetically engineered and placed on a planet. Such planted beings were referred to as seeds until they were upgraded. Earthlings were seeds also. The "Terrans" were an ancient alien race, possibly older than the original Xaxons. Of all the hostile "found" civilizations, they were the worst, in the eyes of the Superior Council.

The Terrans came from the planet Terra, which failed to sustain life many thousands of years before. They escaped to take up a life in space like the Xaxons. The Terrans were the first found civilization the Xaxony upgraded. Unlike the Xaxon's planet, which was destroyed by a catastrophic, natural disaster, the Terrans had destroyed their own planet by polluting it. They never learned from their own mistakes, however. They polluted their own ships, lived in their own filth and even evolved to become dependent on it.

The Xaxons hoped the Terrans could be upgraded from this obsessive polluting, but couldn't de-program them from thousands of years of ingrained, evolutionary behavioral patterns. When the Xaxons gave the Terrans a new ship, they would pollute it in no time. The Xaxons became disgusted by the Terran's complete disregard for cleanliness and hygiene.

The Terrans were small and sapient-like, but seemed as though they may have evolved from creatures that were more like lemurs, than apes. They were night creatures and their skin was pasty and grey with large black eyes. They had small mouths and no nose, only two nostrils in the middle of their face. Their arms were longer than their legs and they had eight long fingers and eight long toes. They had no hair on their bodies at all. When Novawynd first saw the image of a Terran, she was shocked. It reminded her of the pictures Earth people used to draw of their alleged "alien abductors". Terrans looked just like that, and there was a good reason.

The Xaxony worked with the Terrans for thousands of years and became disgruntled when they couldn't curb the Terrans of their bad habits. Ultimately, the Xaxons turned their backs on the Terrans, so the Terrans set out to get even. They intended to undo the Xaxony's seeding, by finding planets that had been seeded, and polluting the genetic make-up of the beings with their own genetics. The Terrans had developed their own ships that moved at light speed. Although the Terran ship's engines did not function as efficiently as the Xaxon engines, they could get around. More importantly, they didn't need the Xaxon fuel, which made them virtually untraceable.

When the Xaxony learned the Terran's plan, they outlawed the Terrans. All Terrans were to be executed on sight. The Xaxony kept tabs on their seeded planets to make sure they hadn't been tampered with by the Terrans. If it was discovered that the Terrans had altered the genetics of a seeded planet, the Xaxony would infect the seeds with a virus designed to kill only those with Terran DNA, much like what was done on Lozia, but with more effective results.

When Novawynd was studying the Terrans at the Analida, she realized the Terrans must have been secretly polluting the genetics of Earthlings for nearly one hundred years; thus, the various reports of these aliens being sighted on Earth and the alleged abductions. However, The Xaxons were not aware, since they hadn't been back to Earth for over three-thousand-years. The last time they were there, the people were still so primitive, that they believed the Xaxons to be gods and angels. Novawynd was not about to offer information about Terrans on Earth to the Superior Council.

"As I'm sure you've surmised, Galtrain 5 will need to be scoured. The viral capsules have been loaded onboard and are currently contained in the cargo hold."

"Scouring" was the rather sterile term used for the process of releasing the virus on the planet. The virus was transmutable via air and fluids, bodily or otherwise. It could live outside a body for two dialos, but it only killed those who were carrying the Terran DNA. The capsules, which were like basket-ball-sized bombs, would be jettisoned into the atmosphere of the target planet. They were preprogrammed to explode over specific, concentrated areas of civilization, sending alien, virus-laden vapor out into the atmosphere. Beings didn't show symptoms until a corona after being infected. Meanwhile, they would be transmitting the virus via breath and exchanging body fluids with others.

Once the virus began to work, the body of the host would begin to undergo necrobiosis at an alarming rate. Cellular structure of the body would break down and liquefy. This includes the skin, hair, organs, even the bones. The only things left, after another seventy-two tecrons of the virus running its course, are the teeth. The gelatinous puddle left behind, typically dried up into a flaky substance like ash. It would take approximately a corona-and-a-half for all the beings carrying the appropriate DNA to basically turn to dust.

The process of "scouring" was not done often, but when it was, the most superior Leluminalia had to carry out the mission. The reason was because the allies, although fearful of the Terrans, generally balked at the idea of this practice. (Novawynd had only recently learned that this was because of the Lozian catastrophe.) The Superior Council kept these missions ultra-top-secret and trusted only their highest Leluminalia and his or her crew for security purposes. Otherwise, anyone could carry out this mission.

*   *   *

In the middle of the night, the smallest shuttle left the Zenith to the continent of Australia. The shuttle set down a quarter mile from the house. Trevor could see the house from the shuttle door as it opened. He took the leash off Swizel's neck and she ran out the door. She realized Trevor was not following her so she stopped. With tail tucked between her legs, she turned to look at him. The shuttle door was closing and Trevor took one last look at his favorite old dog. He fought back the moisture welling up in his eyes when he realized the dog was symbolic of his old life.

*   *   *

The Zenith approached Galtrain 5 and set itself in geosynchronous orbit. Novawynd ordered the pods to be loaded. There were twenty-five thousand pods that needed to be loaded into their chutes continuously as they were launched. The robots made quick work of the loading, and they were flawless in their timing. The pods were programmed to target specified coordinates within the globe's troposphere. In this way, they created a net that covered the entire globe. Once they released the virus, the virus would be carried on the wind currents over a hundred mile area. No one would escape contamination.

Novawynd was not thrilled to be bringing a mini-genocide down on a planet, in light of what happened to Lozia. However, this particular virus had been used on several Terran-tampered planets and proved to work quite effectively. It targeted only those beings meant to be affected. Zacharieth had done the calculations and had pre-determined that approximately one million people would fall victim on this planet. Galtrain 5 was populated by one billion people. A loss of one million lives was hardly enough to devastate the population.

The process would take a corona to begin to take effect, so the Zenith would wait in orbit around the planet for a corona and a half, until the virus had run its course. Once the scanner probes confirmed the Terran genetic presence was at an untraceable level, it would be reason enough to declare the mission was successful.

Novawynd was given notification that the pod chutes were at capacity. She gave the order to begin the launch. Everything went as planned. The viral pods took up positions and released their lethal concoction. The only thing left to do was wait for the results, so Novawynd went back to her unit. She had been deciphering the characters from Ngu. Back on Xaxon 2, during the meeting in which she received her orders to scour Galtrain 5, she also informed the Superior Council of the Ngu technology. They were interested, but didn't see how the technology would be useful. A being with powerful telekinesis could manipulate matter in the same way. There was no reason to upgrade the Ngu. But, Novawynd was instructed to keep tabs and translate their language for the Xaxon libraries.

Because she couldn't verbalize the Ngu words, Novawynd had to use retinatrodes to imagine the sounds. Retinatrodes were reverse retinal imaging devices that were electrodes put directly into the eyes like contacts. If a person could imagine something, the computer could render it. It was quite a useful gadget. This way, Novawynd could translate and catalog the Ngu sonar sounds. Trevor was in Novawynd's unit at the time she was doing this. He liked to hang around with her as she was working in her unit. This way, he caught up on a lot of universal events. Not-to-mention, Novawynd confided in him about her other co-workers, but specifically she liked to vent about how much Zefram rubbed her the wrong way. The sounds of the Ngu were coming out from the overhead speakers and the sound was like fingernails on a chalkboard to Trevor. It was enough to drive him out of Novawynd's unit. He didn't come back that evening, or that night.

Novawynd wondered where Trevor had gone. He had probably fallen asleep in his own unit, which was fine with her. She would take advantage of her "alone time" to explore something she had been wondering about. She took the opportunity to attempt to visit Stunner in his dreams. She thought if she couldn't have him in real-life, perhaps things could be different in his dreams. She had never talked to Stunner about dreams and didn't know if he even had them. But, he was likely asleep, so she was going to try to reach him.

She succeeded in getting into his dream almost immediately. In his dream, Novawynd found him sitting on a bank of a large pond. He was not wearing his uniform; instead, he was clothed in some classic Eron attire. He looked out over the pond serenely. Novawynd looked down at herself and realized she was naked. "Stunner?" she called out to him. He turned to her and a look swept across his face as though he was very pleased to see her naked. She approached him. "Take off your clothes." she suggested. He looked down, he hadn't taken off his clothes, but they were just suddenly gone. He was still reclining on the bank, so Novawynd approached him and knelt down beside him. She took in the sight of his body. His chiseled muscles rippled under his azure skin and were a similar structure to an Earth man. She looked at his face. His violet eyes were wide with anticipation and his lavender hair wisped about his face in the dream-wind.

She leaned over and kissed him. He met her kiss eagerly and brought one large hand up to her head. He pressed his lips against hers passionately. He guided her hand to his penis majora so she could feel his endowment. She turned to get a good look at his peculiarities. He was blessed, as Eron men were rumored to be, with a substantial penis majora. Oddly, to Novawynd, the penis minora, which was about the size of her thumb, was also standing quite erect.

A milky fluid was dripping from the tip of his shaft, and he stroked it, seemingly milking the majora and smearing the monster liberally with the Eron lubricant. Novawynd looked at his face again and an odd feeling came over her. "I've wanted this for so long, but I don't know. Something doesn't seem right. I shouldn't be messing with you like this." She began to get up, and as she did, she was unexpectedly tackled from behind by Stunner. He obviously had no intention of letting her get away. Stunner had her pinned down on her stomach and chest. This was not rape. It was not exactly how Novawynd would have wanted their first coupling to be, but she *had* wanted it. Now she was getting it. Besides, this was the way Erons practiced intercourse. They mated; they did not make love. It was Stunner's dream too, and this was completely natural to him.

Stunner rubbed the tip of his engorged majora through Novawynd's love valley, from her anus to her vulva. She could feel the lubricant smearing across her skin. Without warning, he pushed his hugeness into her. This was all so exciting to Novawynd that she came immediately in the dream and woke up, ending the episode abruptly. She still felt residual waves of pleasure, but they subsided. She lay awake wondering if he had come as well.

Throughout the corona, while the Zenith waited for the results of the scouring probes to come back, Novawynd visited Stunner in his dreams this way. Even if Trevor was asleep in the bed next to her, she would still be able to have her trysts with Stunner. She often woke up in silent orgasm with Trevor still snoring away, completely unaware. Novawynd even coached Stunner, through his dreams, to make love like an Earth man, and there were some interesting scenarios played out that way. Leluminali were not to talk to anyone about their hidden psychic abilities, otherwise they wouldn't remain hidden for long. Stunner and Trevor did not know about Novawynd's dream walking abilities. Stunner would never know Novawynd had been instigating the dreams the whole time.

The virus had begun to take effect on Galtrain 5, and so Novawynd went to the comcen to watch the results. She watched for a while and grew bored. "Let me know when the virus has run its course." she commanded Zacharieth. Two dialos later, she got confirmation from Zacharieth that the virus seemed to have died. "Release the scanner probes and let me know when they've returned." she ordered and went back to her work.

*   *   *

Trevor had been shadowing Stunner since he came aboard the Zenith, in an effort to learn as much about being a space-guard as possible. Something like that would not normally be allowed, but Trevor received special consideration in many areas because of his relationship to Novawynd. While the Zenith was waiting for the results of the scouring, Stunner had the space-guard going through routine practice sessions with the battleots. Trevor had been shown how to work a control station and had shown promise. It reminded him of video games, so it wasn't a stretch for him to grasp it. He wasn't obligated to go through any of the other rigueur the space-guard were, so when he was done fooling around with his battleot, he got up to leave. Stunner was watching his people and keeping tabs on the statistics as Trevor passed by.

"I've had enough for today. I think I'm going to find Novawynd and see if she's in the mood for a quickie." Trevor announced. He and Stunner had gotten to know each other well enough, and because of Stunner's apparent (albeit false) disinterest in Novawynd, Trevor felt he could say such things to Stunner. Trevor left the battleot command center. Once he was gone, Stunner slapped a bottle of water that had been sitting next to him on a desk, across the room. Some space-guard noticed his fit of anger and felt immediately nervous because they had never seen Stunner loose his cool and had no idea what evoked it. Stunner bit his fist, attempting to ward off a violent urge. He noticed people looking at him.

"Sorry." he said as he waved them off. He went back to dutifully gauging the space-guard, but he felt clamped in a vice of anxiety. As soon as the exercises were over and the last space-guard left battleot command, Stunner was alone. He didn't know what had come over him. He just felt so jealous of Trevor at that moment. He suddenly couldn't bear the thought of that guy touching Novawynd. Stunner blipped Zacharieth. "Is Novawynd with Trevor right now?" he inquired.

"No, she is alone now." Zacharieth responded.

"Will you blip her for me?"

"Communicating now, please wait."

"Yes, Stunner?" came Novawynd's voice in his ear.

"It's been a while since we watched a movie together. I'm kind of missing your company. Would you like to come over to my place to watch one with me?" Stunner schemed.

"Yeah, actually I'd love to." Her response was quick and assured.

"How about in half a tecron?"

"Sounds good."

Once Novawynd arrived at Stunner's unit, she took off her Leluminalia jacket and boots. She was planning on getting real comfortable. They curled up together on the sofa. The movie was an older rated "R" movie that was both romantic, but racy. Novawynd hadn't seen the movie for a long time, but as it got to the first steamy part, she remembered this was the type of movie, to which an Earthling man would take a date, if he wanted to get lucky. She knew she had nothing to worry about with Stunner though.

Just then, she felt something she had never felt in all the times she cuddled with Stunner. The hard bulge growing in his groin area was too obvious. She was shocked, but tried to pretend like she didn't notice. Perhaps it was a fluke. However, she couldn't ignore his hand as it gingerly began to explore beneath her shirt.

"Stunner!" she stopped his hand. "What is going on with you?"

"I don't know. I've never felt like this before. The last couple of dialos, I've been having dreams about you and me together. Then I started getting erections whenever you were near me. If that were to happen on my planet with an Eron woman, I wouldn't be able to control myself, but with you, it's different. I can control it, but it's driving me crazy having to control it. I want you." he nuzzled her neck.

Novawynd thought she was safe just fooling around with him in his dreams, but it obviously caused Stunner to become attracted to her without needing pheromones to turn him on. Her supernatural attraction was more powerful than she thought, after all. But, this was happening in real-life and she wasn't sure she wanted to go down this road with Stunner, in real life. Everything would change. She considered the situation as he continued to kiss her neck. She had also just had sex with Trevor less than two tecrons prior, and she felt a little odd about allowing another man between her legs so soon after. She had taken a shower, but she knew Trevor's juices still lingered. However, this was Stunner and she had coveted him for so long, how could she say "no" to him?

Novawynd turned to Stunner and met his kisses. She felt like she was melting under his crushing weight. This wasn't just sex, this was special. She had developed strong feelings for Stunner bordering on love. She had wanted this so badly. Stunner was excitedly passionate, but not animalistic like he had been in her first dream. They eagerly pulled each other's garments off, kissing, licking and biting each other as they went until they were completely bare. Stunner knelt upright between Novawynd's legs, so she could take in the sight. His endowments were just as they had been in the dreams. And, like in the dreams, the penis majora exuded creamy lubricant, which Stunner stroked onto his shaft.

He then squeezed some of the fluid out onto Novawynd's eager pussy. She spread it around her clit. Stunner moaned at the glorious sight of her enjoying his juices. Novawynd pushed herself forward to a kneeling position and began to straddle him as he was sitting back on his haunches. He helped position his member at the mouth of her vagina. When she felt it was positioned correctly, she moved down on it. It was large enough that she had to move up and down a little at a time, until the lube had her moist enough to take him all the way inside her. This time she would not wake up, but the pleasure was as intense as the dreams.

The mythical tingling sensation was beginning. This, she had not felt in her dreams. Her clit was so ultra sensitized by the Eron lube, that she felt like she could achieve an orgasm without any other stimulation, but the minora slid against her erect clitoris, stimulating it.

Stunner was so strong that he easily lifted her hips and helped her pump up and down on him. She arched her back so the tip of his engorgement hit her G-spot, and she became so weak in the knees from the pleasure, that she couldn't continue in that position. Stunner bent over forward, wrapping her legs around him as he did so. He wanted to lie on top of her. He wanted as much of his flesh to press up against hers as possible. In this way, he felt he was completely dominating her.

Stunner began to feel his climax coming. They hadn't been at it for very long at all, but Erons were quick about getting their business done, and this was a very different experience for Stunner altogether. Novawynd decided she was going to use her empathic abilities this time to sense Stunner's pleasure. That way, the two of them could come together.

Stunner began to thrust harder and let out powerful, rhythmic groans with each thrust. At last, the couple became enveloped in a moment of joy and sheer physical bliss that was so incredible, they both cried with happiness when the final orgasmic firework went off. They collapsed panting and laughing. They fell asleep entwined, smiling.

*   *   *

Novawynd and Stunner's first coupling was short lived, because as they lay sleeping a Kirkazet pirate ship was bearing down on the Zenith. Novawynd sensed them as soon as they came out of flux. She woke up Stunner and the two of them threw their clothes on as the ship's alarms began to sound. That sound meant they were already in the grip of a flux inhibitor. A flux inhibitor was a beam that retarded a ship's capability to engage a flux. Pirates used it often on ships they intended to commandeer. Xaxons used it on illegal ships they intended to seize. The Zenith bore the mark of an ambassadorial ship. This told pirates that there was nothing of value on board. Some brazen pirates would still attempt an invasion if they thought it was meant to detract them, and there really was some sort of booty on board. Generally, however, pirates did not board ambassadorial ships, because there was usually a Leluminalia on board. No pirates, save for Zefram 1, would attempt to go up against Leluminali.

Normally, if a pirate ship unwittingly locked onto an ambassadorial ship, they would release the ship and high-tail it out of sight. But, this was a Kirkazet ship. The Kirkazet were another race that originally were seeded by the Xaxony, but suffered a global virus. This virus was not a natural virus, but a supernatural virus. It caused those who became infected, to develop an allergy to sunlight, and to have a lust for blood so strong, they could only consume pure, raw blood from other creatures.

Basically, the Kirkazet were vampiric, but they weren't like the vampires of Earth lore. These vampires were not deterred by crucifixes or holy water. They did not shape-shift or turn into mist. They did not lack a soul. They had reflections and were not dead. In fact they were more likely ultra-alive, being infected, or rather possessed, by a powerful negative enti. On the other hand, they were similar to the legendary Earthling creatures in that they were normal people, not monsters, except when the blood-lust overpowered them. They were ten times stronger and faster than a normal man and had intensely superior sight, hearing and smell. Unless decapitated, incinerated, or completely obliterated, they could virtually not be killed, but especially not with a wooden stake. Besides, an average being would never get near enough to a Kirkazet to wound one so.

Xaxon scientists believed Kirkazet needed to drink blood, because it was the purest way to imbibe another being's life-force. It wasn't the blood they were after as much as the life-force, which fueled the enti-virus. When the virus overtook planet Kirkazet, those infected began to farm non infected beings, purely for their blood. The Superior Council, having learned of this atrocity, ordered the planet scoured, but it was too late. Some Kirkazet had already found means to space travel through a wayward alien craft. This craft was a Kaersling ship. The Kaerslings felt the fairly unadvanced planet, without the technology to detect their presence, would be a safe haven for minor repairs. Much to their dismay, the Kaerslings stood no chance against the vampires. The vampires were highly attuned to the electromagnetic fields the Kaersling ship gave off, and were drawn straight to it.

From that point, the Kirkazet entered the space race of their own accord, and continued to hunt their prey across the universe. Even though the scouring of Kirkazet was successful, the Kirkazet vampires still infected others, thereby increasing in numbers. It was difficult to pin down where they were in the universe, as pirates often are. In the event of crossing paths with the Kirkazet, each Xaxon ship, and Xaxon ally's ship was equipped with scouring agent to use against the vampiric marauders.

The trick with this was getting the viral pod onboard the Kirkazet ship. The tactic most zelo's used to deploy the pod was to draw the Kirkazet onboard the Xaxon ship, then release the virus. This was very effective, but it also caused casualties amongst the Xaxon crews as well, as some of them would undoubtedly be infected by the Kirkazet during the skirmish. Novawynd did not intend to allow this to happen to any of her crew.

"It's Kirkazet, Stunner." she informed him. "Don't let any of them get near the ship. I'll take care of the rest."

Stunner nodded but surprised her with a quick kiss followed by "I love you.", and then he ran with all his power to the space-guard command center.

Novawynd stood stunned for a moment, unsure of how to respond, but he was gone. She shook her head to snap herself back to the moment. "Zacharieth, blip Zelo Djynk for me." she commanded.

"Yes Novawynd?" his voice resounded in her ear.

"We're dealing with Kirkazet. Don't take the usual steps. I'll deliver the pod directly to them myself. We'll just need to hold them off until the virus takes hold."

"Very well." came Djynk's usual response to her orders.

Novawynd ran to the missile bay and commanded one of the droids to fetch a Kirkazet pod for her. After what seemed like an eternity, although it was only a couple of minutes, the droid returned with the basket-ball sized pod.

Pirates, once they had a ship in a flux inhibitor lock, would use their battleots to affix to the side of a ship and penetrate the hull. Although Isotarin was impervious to ballistic strikes, lasers, axon beams, or Quanton particle beams, it could be penetrated by slow burn. This meant it would have to be subjected to very high temperatures for an extended period of time, until it melted. Battleots had the ability to focus a circle of concentrated heat on a hull. Once the hole was melted into the hull, intruders could attach a docking umbilical and get in through the breach.

That was only the first layer though. There was then the interior hull of the living spheres that were encircled by continually revolving magnetic rings, which gave the occupied portion of the ship gravity. The intruders needed to get through the interior hull as well. There were sections in between the spheres where joists connected the interior portion to the exterior hull. This was also the joint where the magnetic rings pivoted. There were access doors in these sections and these doors were the most vulnerable points in the ship. There was no need to secure them too much. The point was moot once intruders got past the exterior hull. Allowing intruders easy access at that juncture served two purposes: first, the ship suffered less damage, and second, the pirates were funneled into specific points where they could be easily picked off.

With all odds seemingly against pirates successfully invading a ship, one would wonder why they do it. The answer is: with persistence, cleverness and skill, they sometimes achieved their goal and the pay-off was usually worth it. In this case, the Kirkazet needed blood. Stunner authorized the use of the newest addition to the Xaxon arsenal, the drone scanners. These were battleots that were not controlled by anyone, but sat idly on the hull of the ship waiting for a signal from the ship that a foreign battleot had adhered to the hull. They then flew into action to destroy the invader. This doubled the Zenith's chance at keeping the pirate battleots off altogether.

Trevor entered battleot command, looking to be of some help, but was sternly ordered out by Stunner. Trevor's presence was not to be allowed during actual battle. Trevor left angrily and went to find where Novawynd had disappeared to.

Novawynd had made her way to the decontamination center with the pod. She planned to flux back to that same spot after returning from the Kirkazet ship. She would have to be tested and observed after being on their ship, just to make sure she hadn't been infected, but she felt pretty confident there was nothing she needed to be concerned about. It was really for everyone else's piece of mind.

Novawynd concentrated, reaching out to the Omniaural. She could envision the Kirkazet ship and where the greatest concentration of vampires congregated. They were in the external docking area readied with space suits on. They were not preparing themselves so much for the inhospitable atmosphere that waited between the outer and inner hulls of their opponent's ship; but rather, preparing for being gassed by the virus once they got on the ship. Luckily, none of them had their helmets on yet.

Novawynd opened the manual release hatch for the pod and readied her hand on the lever she would need to pull, in order to detonate the pod. "Here I go." she said to herself and took a deep breath. She fluxed to the place on the Kirkazet ship she had seen through the Omniaural. The vampires were shocked at her appearance. They lunged at her and they were fast, but she was faster. She pulled the lever and fluxed out of the ship in the blink of an eye. The pod detonated and the virus filled the ship through the ventilation. This virus worked faster even than the virus that expunged Terran DNA. Within minutes, the vampires were all but dust. Their battleots, loosing guidance, drifted. The space-guard directed their battleots to retrieve the defunct pirate droids. They could be reprogrammed and used by the Zenith.

The problem of the Kirkazet's flux inhibitor still remained. The Zenith needed to be released from its hold and that could not be done remotely. Also, a salvage crew from the Xaxony would come to retrieve the pirate ship, so someone needed to go aboard, release the flux inhibitor and make sure there were no survivors. That someone would obviously be Novawynd as well as Zefram. Zefram met Novawynd in the shuttle bay. It didn't matter that Novawynd hadn't gone through the decontamination process yet. Zefram was about to potentially be exposed also, so the both of them would go through it when they returned.

Trevor had reached the comcen in his search for Novawynd. She was obviously not there, but Zelo Djynk was. Trevor should not have been allowed in the CC either, but Zelo Djynk was more afraid of what Novawynd would do to him if he didn't allow it. Trevor was relieved to see that Novawynd was fine. She was with Zefram and on her way to the ship that, Trevor gathered, had apparently just attacked them. The shuttle pulled up close to the pirate's shuttle bay door and a servo-arm extended out to an access panel next to the door. The robotic appendage at the end of the servo-arm opened the access panel door and a plug extended from the tip of one of the robotic digits. This plug inserted into the appropriate receptacle in the access panel. The ship had been Xaxon built and the code for opening the docking bay door was easily accessible.

The door opened leisurely, and the shuttle moved into the bay. As it gently set down, Novawynd turned to Zefram, "I don't sense any life here, do you?"

"No." he concurred. "But, that doesn't mean there isn't a very faint life-force we aren't picking up. This is a case where we can't afford not to be sure."

"Well I'm pretty certain, but I know what you're saying, so let's go."

They exited the shuttle and proceeded vigilantly. They readied their axon guns, because their DESSes had no effect on the Kirkazets. They checked every nook of every floor, and there was nothing left. Until they got to the scientific section, their hackles rose as they sensed faint life signs. They quickened their pace to the section they felt the life-force coming from. The two of them flanked the door to a laboratory, and when the door opened, Novawynd peeked inside. This motion was supposed to be a quick glance, just to scope for enemies, but there were no enemies. Instead there were several tanks full of humanoid specimens. Novawynd gawked at the sight, and then moved into the room, followed by Zefram.

The humanoids were in stasis, their vital signs barely detectable. They were being nourished and their waste was being disposed, just as anyone who has ever been in stasis had been maintained. But, there was something else; there was a pic-line leading out of each subject, and out of the tank and at the end of each line, there were bags of blood. This was the blood farming Novawynd had learned about.

"Disturbing!" she said out loud, not fully aware that she had. "What do we do about this?"

"Ask the Superior Council." Zefram stated blandly.

Novawynd closed her eyes and reached out to the Superior Council. She was not drawing them out; she just needed to connect with them in their realm. She felt them and projected the scene of the tanks containing the humanoid specimens.

"Destroy them!" came the definitive answer.

Novawynd's eyes snapped open. "They say we are supposed to destroy them." Novawynd relayed softly in dismay.

"You connected with the Superior Council just now…outside of a chambers?" Zefram was obviously jealous. "I've never been able to do that." he added almost under his breath, then, "Let's do it then." He walked to the center of the lab and set a Quanton particle grenade in the center. He jogged out of the lab and together he and Novawynd ran down the hall. The lab exploded with a blue flash. Large projectiles of glass from the tanks blew out the door, smashing against the wall outside the lab. Then it was over. Zefram and Novawynd went back to the lab to survey the damage. It was done. Novawynd hadn't approved, but there wasn't much she could do about it now. The beings that had been maintained in those tanks were dead now.

At last, Novawynd and Zefram found the comcen and released the flux inhibitor. The Zenith was now free and the Xaxon salvage team had also arrived already. They left the ship to go back through the decontamination process with each other yet again. And, yet again, in the decon showers, Novawynd snuck peeks at Zefram's perfect physique. It was ridiculous that she was so turned on. She had already had sex with two men that day. However, she hadn't been with this man. She might as well put it out of her mind, because it couldn't ever happen. Then again, she thought it wouldn't happen with Stunner either, and it did. Perhaps it was the ultimate challenge to seduce Zefram; to make him go against his Ephilderone, but moreover, his principles.

Novawynd looked back at Zefram again and was surprised to catch him stealing a look at her. Her eyes met his sage-colored eyes and she thought for a moment that he had been enjoying looking at her, and wasn't afraid to let her know it. He looked away quickly then and left the shower. Novawynd lingered, wondering what had just transpired.

The two of them still needed to give blood samples, to check for signs of the Kirkazet virus. They sat in a holding cell, which was really more like a lounge. Zefram reclined on a sofa, running his hand through his wet blond hair, as he read logs from other Leluminali. Novawynd sat on the floor, cross-legged.

"Zefram," she began, "what happened back there? I thought I felt you…" she paused. "Never mind. It couldn't be."

Zefram sat up and leaned forward, toward her. "You thought you caught a glimmer of my attraction to you."

"Maybe?" she was confused.

"When someone is on Ephilderone, they can still appreciate beauty in things. They can still find someone beautiful, physically or otherwise, and they can come to care for someone. They just can't act on it in a sexual way. Imagine being in love with someone, but take away all the sexual urges that go along with loving someone. People on Ephilderone can feel that."

Novawynd was stunned. "You're not saying you're in love with me too?" she exclaimed.

"What do you mean 'too'?" he wondered. "Are you in love with me?"

"I meant…it's just that… someone else told me that today. It was someone I didn't think would, but that doesn't matter. What are you trying to say?"

"Was it Stunner?" he asked firmly. Novawynd turned her face away. "I knew it." he seemed to seethe.

"Listen Zefram. It's not about the Ephilderone anyway. You're *Zefram*. You're a clone. Moreover, you're a Leluminali. You're supposed to suppress feelings like that. Your conditioning dictates it. So, how could this be?"

"Despite all that, I'm not a robot. I'm human. I've been around for a long time Novawynd. Perhaps I'm evolving as a human."

They were interrupted at that point by Zacharieth, who informed them their blood tests were clear. Zefram looked Novawynd intently in the eye. "Besides Novawynd, you seem to have that effect even on men who shouldn't feel it. Why are you surprised?"

"Zefram, I just think what you're feeling isn't love. You don't really act like a guy who is in love."

"What is love? How does a man act like he's in love? You're right. I've never known it. I never even imagined what it might be like." he paused, stood up and shook his head. "I guess I can't be sure." With that comment he walked out of the detention center. Novawynd sat in stunned silence for a moment. She longed for the time when men didn't have this supernatural attraction to her; a time when men really didn't notice her at all. This revelation was really too much. The worst part was that she had this underlying feeling that she couldn't trust him. Novawynd could see no reason why she shouldn't. Besides, what purpose could it serve Zefram to confess to her he had developed some sort of feelings for her, whether it was love or not? It was just that he was still blocking her. Why block her? There was something not right about that.

CHAPTER 3

Novawynd needed to be alone for a while. She locked herself in her room and instructed Zacharieth to tell anyone looking for her that she was not accessible. Novawynd went to her bed and drifted into a lucid dream. Again she would attempt to find Star. She wanted answers. In the many times before she had willingly attempted to reach out to him, she had failed. This time she entered a dream where she could see a tree with weeping branches filled with pink flowers like cherry blossoms. Pink petals floated down in a gentle breeze. Novawynd could smell the sweet scent of the blossoms.

She felt his presence there. She parted the weeping branches and saw him sitting, leaned against the trunk with one knee up. His head was down and he was seemingly asleep. Novawynd's heart leapt at the sight of him. She found the other men she was involved with attractive, for certain, but none of them gave her this feeling. It was a feeling as if she was looking at her soul-mate. She felt ecstatic and content, all at the same time.

His sword was lying on the ground next to him and his hand was on the handle. As Novawynd crept into the flowery cave the branches had created, he awoke and the tip of his sword was at her neck in a flash. He recognized her then, "It's you, Lee-lee. I haven't seen you in some time." he smiled, then lowered his sword and put it to one side.

"I know. I've been trying to find you, but I haven't been able to." Novawynd crept close to him and knelt beside him. "I need to know what you meant when you said, 'Find me, you'll find the truth.' What is this truth?"

He looked down, silent for a moment as he pondered her question, then answered "I don't know. But, I know we'll have to find it together."

"Star, do you feel the same way I do?" Novawynd implored.

"Yes." he assured without hesitation.

Novawynd leaned over to kiss him on the lips. She hesitated for a moment, expecting him to resist, but he didn't. She opened her eyes and saw his were closed in expectation. Then they opened and his gloved hand went to her face. He stroked her face with his thumb and leaned forward to meet her lips. The second their lips met, there was body-enveloping shockwave of pleasure Novawynd had never experienced with any man she had ever kissed before. She felt so warm, as if she was melting into Star. Novawynd suddenly felt complete for the first time in her life.

They separated, both sighing heavily. "How do I find you?" she asked under her breath.

"Trust and follow the orange eyes." he answered cryptically. Then fear crossed his face. "You're in trouble. His eyes flashed to a point past her, "Look out!" he cried out. Novawynd whirled to see a member of the Superior Council behind her, reaching out to grab her. As it clamped on to her she awoke with a faint scream that was lost in her throat, or possibly only in her mind.

Novawynd sat up. She was more eager than ever to find Star. It was now the primary goal in her mind. All the duties she had as the alleged Lajiachine were not important any more. She would even use her influence as the Lajiachine to find Star if she had to. This dream confirmed what she had suspected; the Superior Council was not to be trusted and the Talosians (orange eyes) were her friends. Danalian would lead her to Star after all.

*   *   *

After a deep and dreamless sleep, Novawynd emerged from her unit more rested than she had been in a long time. She learned from Zacharieth that Trevor had tried to contact her three times, Stunner two times and Zefram once. Zefram had left a message that info was recovered from the Kirkazet ship about the people that were in stasis, and he needed to see her about it ASAP.

She decided to focus on business, so she went to see Zefram. He was in the cafeteria eating his breakfast. She got something to eat and took a seat across from him at his table. It was a little awkward, in light of what he had told her the dialo before. She tried to forget about that, but Zefram wasn't about to allow that. "So, I know you weren't with Stunner or Trevor the last six tecrons. Is there someone I don't know about?" he probed jealously.

Novawynd was shocked. Then she composed herself. "Not that it's any of your business, but I was alone. Sometimes I just need 'me time' in order to recharge."

Zefram leaned forward and put his elbows on the table. "You still don't trust me?" he said in an accusatory tone.

Novawynd leaned in toward him. "No Zefram, I don't. I'm your rival. I believe you would do anything to get me out of the way."

"So, then what? The Superior Council would be so angry, they'd scrap me. Besides, even if that were true, I wouldn't take this route. I'm a 2B on Ephilderone for enti's sake."

"Then stop blocking me."

"You're blocking me."

"Yes, but I'm not the one asking you to trust me."

"Are you saying I shouldn't trust you?"

"Like I said, I'm your rival, which makes you my rival. Perhaps I'm scheming to get rid of you. And, if I did it, the Superior Council wouldn't even notice." she practically hissed. Zefram recoiled and looked at her, obviously cut by her icy words. Then the emotionless mask he used to wear suddenly covered his face again.

"Anyway," he changed the subject, "A band of slave trading pirates was supplying those people to the Kirkazet, in exchange for immunity. The Kirkazet ship had information on how to find the suppliers. The Xaxony has been looking for these slave traders for some time, now we have been given a key to locating them and taking the ring out." "Okay. So, we call in a lower level Leluminalia to take care of it."

"No, we're going to take care of this one. We're going to get our hands dirty. I could tell how much you want to jump in and get some more excitement, and this is your chance."

"But, the Superior Council hasn't sanctioned this." Novawynd objected.

"I'm supposed to be your mentor, and I'm teaching you right now, that you don't have to sit around waiting for orders from the Superior Council. We can be self-sufficient too."

"In light of the conversation we just had, I feel like you're setting me up for something." Novawynd confessed. Zefram was infuriated by this comment.

"Don't trust me then." he was trying to hold back anger unsuccessfully. Novawynd found it interesting, all these new feelings he had been emoting, even though he was trying to block her from feeling them. "Ask the Superior Council if you must. Not only will they tell you to do it, they'll also tell you not to bother them about such things ever again." With that, Zefram stood up abruptly and left the cafeteria. He didn't bother to hide his anger.

Outside the cafeteria, he stopped and took a few deep breaths. The cool and unshakeable façade he usually fronted came back. His Lelumin conditioning was unbreakable, except when it came to Novawynd. She was the only one who could affect him that way. He began walking back to his unit. As he did so, he thought about how it would only be two more corona until his last dose of Ephilderone wore off. He felt pretty confident that he was on track to have her wrapped around his finger by then. The one thing that concerned him, however, was her comment about doing him in. She might not have been bluffing. Even so, if she was bluffing, why would she? Did she see through him? She couldn't. She wouldn't have been stupid enough to let on that she knew; unless, that's what she wanted him to think. "For enti's sake, she's going to drive me crazy." he said out loud, then thought "What if that's what she wants?" he put his hands to his temples, "Ugggh!"

The worst part was that Zefram's emotion was genuine. It obviously started as a mission, but as the last two-and-a-half aera passed with him trying to devise ways to worm his way into her heart, he lost track of himself and really started to care about her. He really was jealous when he knew she was giving her affections to Trevor or Stunner. When she made the comment about scheming to do away with him, he was genuinely hurt. None of that had been an act. That was what was really driving him crazy. He was torn between possibly truly being in love with her, and his duty to the Xaxony and the Superior Council.

What choice would he make, Novawynd or the Xaxony? His Lelumin conditioning was unraveling and he both hated and loved the feeling of loosing control. Was Novawynd shrewd enough to have plotted his undoing in this way?

Novawynd made her way to the council chambers to get the daily assignments. She also intended to ask about this side mission Zefram mentioned. Half of her wanted to believe he was in love with her because he was so damn hot, but half of her threw up red flags warning her of the improbability of that being the case. Since she also no longer trusted the Superior Council, she would have to be careful there too. If the Superior Council told her to do it, she would have to, but she would go along, always looking over her shoulder for any danger or treachery. She would have to go back to doing what Earthlings had done for thousands of years, trusting her instinct.

Trevor happened to find her as she was making her way to the council chambers. "Hey Novie!" Novie was his nick-name for her. "There you are, I haven't seen you for quite a while." he sidled up to her, wrapping his arms around her, his hands resting on her rear-end. "I've missed you." Trevor attempted to kiss her, but she denied him.

"Trevor, I have something I think I should tell you." she sounded tentative.

"Uh-oh, what?" he sensed the negative vibe.

"Stunner and I have been... You know." she confessed. Trevor let go of her and backed off. "When you first thought we were, it wasn't happening. Our first time was yesterday, actually. He knows about you obviously, but I thought you should know about him. It seems unfair to go about it behind your back." she looked at him searchingly. She could see the fury crossing his face. "I'm not saying that you and I can't be together." she interceded. "You are the only one I have anything in common with on an Earthling level. I need you. But, I also need you to be okay with sharing me with Stunner."

Trevor paused and choked on what he wanted to say, then he finally got it out "Well, you were clear that this was an open relationship, that you would be with other men, and I could be with other women too, but I'm a little freaked out that it's the one guy I never thought…I mean what about all that pheromone stuff?"

"I know. I'm as perplexed about the 'how' as you are, but obviously, I'm not like normal women."

Trevor looked down and snorted "I know…I have no choice but to accept this." he turned, without looking at Novawynd he added. "I just need some time." and then he walked away. Novawynd watched him go, knowing he would come around soon enough.

In the council chambers, after the usual update as to the various happenings in the universe and the missions to be doled out to various Leluminalia, Novawynd asked about Zefram's suggestion that they follow up on the flesh-peddlers. The Superior Council's response was exactly as Zefram had predicted it would be. They told her to feel free to follow any side-mission she saw fit, as long as it didn't interfere with any mission they had given her. There it was, she would have to do this with Zefram, and she would have to be on heightened alert for any treachery on his part.

*　　　*　　　*

Trevor went straight away to Stunner's unit. Stunner was surprised to see Trevor at his door, but felt a little suspicious that it meant Trevor knew about his and Novawynd's relationship. Stunner invited Trevor inside. Trevor dispersed with formalities and cut to the chase, "I'm here because Novawynd just told me about you and her." He waited to gauge Stunner's response. Stunner didn't seem surprised, so

Trevor continued. "I knew Novawynd would sleep with other men, if she wanted to, I just never thought it would be so soon, plus I never thought she would have a real relationship with someone she really cared about. I always thought it would be a fling here and there and it would mean nothing. I was okay with that idea, but this is something else." He paused again, waiting for Stunner to say anything.

Stunner did speak "Novawynd and I have cared for each other deeply since before you came into the picture. It's not normal for an Eron to fall in love, but it seems a natural progression, in light of the way we felt."

"Are you saying you're in love with her?" Trevor seethed.

"Undoubtedly." was all Stunner would say.

"Is she… in love with you?" Trevor asked more tentatively.

"She hasn't said as much." Stunner admitted.

There was an awkward silence for a moment, and then Trevor spoke again, "She's like a drug to me. I have to have her, when I have to have her." he confessed.

"I know what you mean." Stunner empathized.

Then Trevor made a radical suggestion, "If I come over to see her, and you're with her, would you be willing to let me join in?"

Stunner seemed appalled. "I've heard of Earth men that like to be with other men, but I'm not like that. I couldn't do anything with you."

"No," Trevor laughed, "I mean, we wouldn't even touch each other, we would just both make love to Novawynd. I think she would really like that. Most Earth women fantasize about two men making love to them at the same time."

"I guess I've seen the Earth sex-movies where multiple men are with one woman. The women seem to like it. I can only say, if Novawynd is okay with it, then I am. But, the same goes if you are with her, and I have a yearning. The thing is, because of my duties, if I come to her, it might be the only time I'll be able to be with her for a while."

"She asked me to be okay with sharing her with you, so I'd do it for her." Trevor assured. "Do we have a deal?" Trevor put his hand out for Stunner to shake. Stunner took Trevor's hand in his azure hand and shook it vigorously. "We have a deal then." Trevor confirmed.

*   *   *

Novawynd got back to her unit and spent the next two tecrons doling out the missions to the various Leluminali. Then she spent the next tecron catching up on the universal news. Then she spent the next two tecrons analyzing logs of zelos, intins and Leluminali for the last dialo. She was just about to make herself some dinner when her door chimed. It was Trevor. She allowed him in and offered to make him dinner. He accepted "Although I feel like I should be making you dinner, with the way I acted like a spoiled little boy earlier." he semi-apologized. Then he approached Novawynd in her kitchenette and hugged her. It was a long, warm, apologetic hug. Novawynd welcomed it.

They never did get around to dinner, because before either of them knew it, they were kissing passionately. Trevor lifted Novawynd onto the counter and they began pulling each other's clothes off. Trevor took her there on the counter. Once they came, they stripped completely and moved to Novawynd's bed. They cuddled for a little while before Trevor's staff became engorged again. Novawynd couldn't help but think about Stunner. She hadn't seen him since the dialo before, and she was craving him, even though she was with Trevor in that moment. Stunner's juices kept her aroused for several tecron after their initial coupling, and it made her feel like he was there, inside of her that whole time.

Just then the door chimed and Novawynd knew it was Stunner, as if he had felt her desire for him. When Zacharieth announced that it was Stunner, it was Trevor who told the computer to let Stunner in. At first Novawynd was appalled, because she thought Trevor wanted Stunner to see them together. But, she was surprised when Stunner didn't even flinch, but instead, took his clothes off immediately and crawled right into bed with her and Trevor. His penises erect.

"Boy that doesn't make a regular guy self-conscious at all." Trevor laughed. Stunner laughed too. Novawynd was perplexed that Trevor was accepting this. She started to realize, this might have been a set-up. There was obviously some sort of accord between the two of them. Well, if that was the case, she intended to take full advantage.

Stunner flipped Novawynd over, with little effort. Trevor positioned himself under Novawynd. She began to lick and suckle his balls and prick as Stunner pushed into her from behind. His minora pushed into her anus, so she was being dually penetrated from behind. She gasped from both pleasure and a little pain, but went back to working Trevor's shaft. Up and down she pumped in the same rhythm Stunner pumped her with from behind. Trevor groaned and she glanced at him His eyes were closed, and he was blissful. Novawynd realized she would have to use her empathic abilities to connect with both of them, so the threesome could come together.

She concentrated on her pleasure, and then she reached out to Trevor and Stunner. She connected with their ecstasy. It was odd that they were both feeling different sorts of pleasure; Trevor, a more physical and Stunner, an almost spiritual joy at coupling with Novawynd again. Novawynd knew Stunner would come first, because Erons were pre-programmed to finish quickly. She waited until she felt Stunner coming to climax, his pace and groans quickening and his thrusts getting harder and deeper. She concentrated on projecting her pleasure and Stunner's impending orgasm to Trevor. Once Trevor felt the intensity of both Novawynd's and Stunner's climax, he couldn't hold out either. The three of them melted into a burning rush like a boiling flood washing over them.

Novawynd felt the hot juices of the men injecting into her womb and throat all at once. After the men spent, Novawynd gladly swallowed Trevor's sweet semen and Stunner pulled his long rod out of her sheath. She looked down between her legs to see his spunk pouring out; that precious liquid that would cause a scintillating reaction in her love canal for the next few tecrons.

The three of them lay down, Novawynd sandwiched between Stunner and Trevor. She could hardly believe the two of them would have concocted this scenario. Nothing was said. They just lay in awkward silence as they recovered. After about a half-a-tecron, Trevor started kissing Novawynd's shoulder and neck. She was laying with her back to him and he lifted her leg, so he could insert his hardness into her warm, moist crevice of pleasure. The effort the two were making aroused Stunner immediately and he began to kiss Novawynd passionately on the lips. Novawynd reached down and began fellatio on Stunner. She felt a little sorry that she couldn't fellate the smaller of the two penises at the same time.

Stunner's larger penis exuded a substantial amount of lube, so Novawynd could easily continue the stroking motion as long as was needed. Trevor's stiffness was nothing to be disregarded by it self, but it seemed small to Novawynd after having just been rooted out by Stunner's massive phallus. It still felt quite pleasurable, as he knew how to hit her "G-spot" quite well.

Trevor was now enveloped in the juices Stunner had left behind in Novawynd. He also was affected by the chemical reaction the Eron's fluids caused on Earthling tissue. Trevor's sensitive penile flesh felt a sensation like it was being tickled by a million feathers. Even his balls tingled like this. It was hard to concentrate on what he was doing, because he was being driven delirious.

Soon, like the last time, Novawynd used her empathic abilities to bring them all to climax at the same time. Stunner's juices spraying all over her belly. After they lay back, exhausted, Novawynd told them she needed them to leave. She needed to rest. Reluctantly, they dressed. Trevor was the first to leave, Stunner the last. Trevor only had to go to his unit next door, but Stunner had a lot further to go. Novawynd waited until she felt Trevor had entered his room, and then she asked Zacharieth to blip Stunner. "Yes Novawynd?" Stunner's voice came back to her in her ear.

"Come back. Stay the night with me." she commanded, bordering on begging. It was obvious that although she related to Trevor on an Earthling level. She still preferred Stunner. It was the effect his fluids had on her. It was like the sensation made her continually horny. She felt like only his swollen rods could bring her relief. But, ironically the more she took him inside, the longer the sensation would last. She knew it, but didn't care.

"I'll be right there." he urgently responded. He was back in her unit in what seemed like seconds. He practically tore off his clothes and crawled right up in-between her legs. They laughed, kissed caressed and cuddled each other for a short while. When Novawynd felt his staff was fully stiff, she wrapped her legs around his waist and rhythmically ground her labia against his hardnesses. He reached down to insert the larger of the two phalluses into her. He tore into her with a strong thrust and continued to repeatedly tear into her even harder than he had before. She screamed out in delight. Stunner was able to hold out much longer this time, but eventually this coupling came to an end like all the other times.

Novawynd and Stunner made love, experimenting with different positions throughout the night. They were addicted to each other. They got little, if any sleep, and when Zacharieth blipped Novawynd in the morning for her wake-up call, she realized it was going to be hard to keep away from Stunner or to keep from thinking about being with him during her day to day dealings. This is where she would need to apply her Leluminali training. She would have to use it to suppress her physical desires. At least she had that. Stunner wasn't as lucky. She decided to apply Junatiel to Stunner, so he wouldn't be preoccupied by her either.

"Stunner? When you leave my unit today, I don't want you to think about me in a sexual way. Not until I call you to come over, okay?"

He looked at her blankly for a moment, and then responded, "Okay." he nodded slowly in acknowledgement.

"Good" she smiled and gave him a quick kiss on the lips. He knew he needed to get to his work also, so he left, with no intention of coming back, until she called for him.

CHAPTER 9

Novawynd had been called to Zefram's quarters. He had to confer with her on his plan. Being his superior, she needed to okay it before they could proceed. He was casual again when she entered his unit, with his jacket and boots off. Novawynd didn't intend to stay long, so she remained in full uniform. "Come, please." Zefram cheerily called out to her from the sofa. He seemed in good spirits for some reason. She half expected him to make some comment about her tryst with both Stunner and Trevor, but he seemed unaware of that incident.

"So, Zefram, what's the plan?" she inquired. She had decided to stand in order to give the impression she wanted him to make this quick.

"We'll use the former Kirkazet ship to put out a call to the flesh peddlers. I'll use Junatiel to convince them I'm the Kirkazet leader. Then we set a meeting and when they meet up with us, we've got them." Zefram laid it out.

"A simple plan." Novawynd commented. "It seems too simple." she voiced her concern.

"We have data from the ship on how they contacted the flesh peddlers and how the exchanges were usually set up. We won't deviate from the set parameters, so it won't be likely that they will be suspicious. If we can get our hands on just one living-being trafficking ship, we can get info on the whole ring."

"That is precisely why I think they would have a contingency plan in place to destroy any data that could undo the ring, in the event they are discovered."

"Of course they would. That's where you come in. Once we converge on the meeting place. I will stall them long enough for you to flux aboard and download the data. We'll have it before they know what's-up."

"Ah-ha! I was beginning to wonder where I came in." she confessed. "But, what if they figure it out and self-destruct the ship before I'm out of there?" That would have normally been a ridiculous question, because it would only take her zecrons to download the data, unless Zefram gave them a hint. Normally, Zefram wouldn't think of doing something that would put a fellow Leluminalia in harm's way, but she just didn't trust him entirely.

"You'd sense the danger and get out before there's any possibility of that happening." Zefram stood up. He was right. He walked over to her. "You would need to abort if you sense things have gone awry. You are more important than the data." He stepped close to her and gently stroked her arm. She withdrew, a little, but then relaxed. She was able to sense his action was a sincere act of friendliness, nothing more, but nothing less. He was starting to open up, to let her into his feelings. He withdrew his hand when he saw she was slightly unnerved by his touch, and then he continued, "We can't afford to lose you." then he paused and looked at her hard and seriously. "I don't want to lose you."

Novawynd gave him a look indicating she didn't believe it. He turned away and walked over to a pitcher of water on a table nearby. "And," he continued as he poured himself a glass, "if you're still thinking I'd benefit by taking you out, let me point out one thing. Even if something were to happen to you, I still will never be Lajiachine. They have your DNA, and are probably cloning you as we speak. Those clones may never achieve your fluxing ability, but they have a better chance than I ever will."

"Zefram, it's not about what benefits you." Novawynd couldn't keep quiet any longer. "You live to serve the Superior Council and the Xaxony. You do what benefits them, because that's what benefits you. If they told you to assassinate me, you would do as ordered without a second thought." she argued, but then realized she had said too much. She had just let on that she didn't trust the Superior Council and that was a bad move.

Zefram smirked, set down his water and looked judgmentally at Novawynd. "Are you saying you suspect a conspiracy by the Superior Council to assassinate you?" He approached Novawynd again. He scrutinized her, his eyes narrowing. Novawynd shifted on her feet, suddenly feeling very uneasy.

"All I'm saying is that if I am the Lajiachine, the Superior Council won't risk me fulfilling the prophesy. Anyone in my position can't afford to trust anyone."

Zefram folded his arms and regarded her for a moment. "So, when did your conditioning break?" He asked so matter-of-fact, it surprised Novawynd.

"What?" she scoffed, as if she was surprised he would think such a thing; but she had never been "conditioned" to begin with, and she had convincingly acted otherwise. She had dropped her guard and slipped up. "My conditioning is quite in tact, thank you." she lied.

"You wouldn't question the Superior Council if you were properly conditioned." Zefram stated flatly. "You would never mistrust them if you served them loyally, and without questioning their motives. Even if they intended to scrap you at some point, you should accept your scrapping as what is best for the Xaxony, and you would go into the Omniaural with honor and without fear." He just stared into her eyes at that point waiting for her to say something, but she said nothing. He could kill her right now and all he had to say was that he suspected her conditioning had failed. The data retrieved from his CI would support that. It was best for her to keep silent.

Instead, Zefram said, "Okay." his eyes and everything about him seemed to relax. That response was perplexing to Novawynd. That's not what she had expected. He added, "I should go to the Superior Council with this, but I won't. This remains a secret between you and me." He opened up to her so she could sense how serious he was about that.

Novawynd was shocked. That response could only mean that Zefram had a lapse in his conditioning as well, because there was no way the great Zefram would just let that slide. The two just stood looking into each other's eyes for a few zecrons. It was a moment of mutual understanding.

"Thanks." Novawynd finally said sincerely and humbly. "When are we going to go through with this mission?" she asked in an attempt to change the subject.

"That's up to you. When will you be able to lend yourself to the task?"

"We should just get it done. Will everything be ready to go in two tecrons?"

"Easily." Zefram assured.

"Good, then I will meet you in the docking bay in two tecrons." She affirmed officially, and then left Zefram's quarters. As she was leaving, she ran into Trevor in the hallway.

"Oh my God! Now it's Zefram?" he tittered. He was joking, but his comment made it clear to Novawynd that he was a bit hurt by her being with other men. Novawynd continued walking and Trevor followed.

"Trevor, you know that's not even a possibility. Even if he wasn't on Ephilderone, I still would never…and, he would never."

"That's good. That guy gives me the creeps. When we're together anytime he's around, he's always watching us." Trevor stopped Novawynd and put his hands on her waist. He started kissing her, but she rejected his advances yet again.

"T, I have to go do my work, and then after that, I have another mission to deal with.

"How long will the mission take?" Trevor was concerned that Novawynd would be gone an extended amount of time.

"Not long. From start to finalization of the decontamination process, it'll only a few tecrons."

"Oh, that all?" he seemed relieved. "Well, can we cuddle when you get done with all that?" He pulled her close again and gave her that gorgeous smile. Novawynd melted in his arms.

"It's a date." She whispered. They lingered in a kiss for a moment, and then Novawynd was off again to her work.

*   *   *

At the appointed time, Novawynd met up with Zefram in the docking bay. A shuttle had been prepared for their departure to the Kirkazet ship. Once the shuttle landed in the docking bay of the enemy ship, Novawynd and Zefram disembarked and proceeded immediately to the Commcen. The shuttle automatically left Novawynd and Zefram on the Kirkazet ship. As soon as it returned to the Zenith, the Zenith fluxed to a point where they could monitor the situation, but wouldn't be detected by the flesh peddlers.

Zefram had studied the logs of the Kirkazet ship, memorizing the protocol for the previous meetings between the pirates. That way, he could be sure he wasn't making a wrong move, which would definitely alert the enemy to a trap. Novawynd was to monitor the pirate ship. The main computer would identify the type of ship and what location onboard she could both download data and plant a bomb. Zefram looked at Novawynd and gave her a nod. She nodded back, indicating it was "go time".

"Computer, open communication frequency to XVB1295." Zefram commanded. A four-dimensional display projected in front of him. It showed a symbol. Usually a symbol like this showed up in a comm attempt when the receivers were screening communications, and it was expected. Beings in their line of work would screen for security purposes. It this instance one had to basically leave a message. Zefram proceeded to do so, mustering all of his Junatiel powers to cloak the minds of the pirates, so they would see the former zelo. "This is Quazar, requesting more requisitions. Please respond with availability and terms." Quazar was the code name the Kirkazet Zelo used. The pirates were watching and Zefram knew it. Shortly an image crackled within the display.

It was a Placsuni. The Placsuni were another genetic construct of the Xaxony. They had dark green, spotted leathery skin and were small in stature. They were well-known for the fact that they had no legs, but instead had two sets of arms and hands. One set of arms and hands replaced the legs and feet. The Placsuni could walk on either set of hands, but preferred to walk on all four. They were adept at balancing on their well-formed glutei and using all four hands to function. The Placsuni also had Green blood, which was also not digestible by the Kirkazet. The Placsuni could do business with the Kirkazet without fear that they would become dinner. However, the Placsuni were typically allies of the Xaxony, so these Placsuni were pirates for personal gain and the mastermind of the living-being trafficking might not be Placsuni.

"Quazar, you are going through the requisitions too quickly. But, we happen to have more on hand, as long as you have compensation."

"We have the compensation you require. At least, enough for four."

"Four!" The Placsuni zelo scoffed. "Well, it's a good thing you aren't particular. You at least buy up everyone else's cast-offs. So, yes, we can do four." The Placsuni was obviously oblivious to the fact he was speaking to a Leluminali.

"Where and when?" Zefram asked for specifications.

"Expect we'll be knocking at your back door in thirty zecrons. End transmission." the Placsuni was abrupt.

As expected, the ship's sensors began to alarm and the central computer announced there was a ship nearing. They would be scanning the Kirkazet ship at that moment, but they would scan to determine if they held the desired currency, not to determine if there were life forms. The currency was flux-gas. Among pirates, it was the most valuable of currencies and the booty most desired. Most pirates retrofitted their ships with extra tanks to make sure they never ran out, but also to use as payment to others. The Xaxon salvage ship filled the tanks to make sure the pirates would be satisfied. They would only make the exchange if they were certain they would get paid.

This was Novawynd's cue. The central computer identified the ship as a two-hundred-year-old Xaxon freighter. It calculated the most logical place to access a data port, plant a destructive device, all with least likely being discovered, was the initial access room to the engine compartment. Living or mechanical beings virtually never went there.

Novawynd had a computer about the size of a cell phone that had been programmed to communicate with the enemy ship's mainframe in a friendly manner, thus the mainframe would hand over the data without alarming anyone. The process of connecting with the mainframe and downloading the data would take only a couple of mecrons. It was imperative that the pirates not know they had been infiltrated, or the primary cell in control of all the flesh traders would pack up, move and lay low for a while; thus, the data would become instantly useless. That was the purpose for blowing the ship too. A non-existent ship could not warn its sister ships.

Zefram had gone to the docking bay to greet the Placsuni. It would take them a few mecrons to prepare their cargo and transport it to the Kirkazet ship. Novawynd was not to flux to the Placsuni ship until their cargo shuttle arrived in the Kirkazet docking bay. This way, the Xaxony would also get their hands on a couple of the flesh peddlers too. They would be interrogated, as long as they didn't self destruct in some way.

Novawynd watched the 4D monitor as the pirate shuttle left the ship. As the doors to the Kirkazet ship's bay opened to allow the pirates in, Novawynd took stock. She had her computer and she had the bomb. She was ready to go. She concentrated on the point on the schematics the computer showed as the room she should enter. She fluxed to that room in the enemy ship and immediately took a defensive position, in case someone or something was there. She was alone. Immediately she located the port on the wall she was to access. She plugged the computer into it and while it communicated with the mainframe, she readied the bomb.

The bomb was small, but very powerful. She walked over to the engine room access panel and put her hand on it. She didn't know why she was compelled to do so. She expected it to feel hot or something, but the engine was actually some distance away at the end of a long tube still beyond another monitoring station. She wouldn't feel heat from here, even though she also didn't think about the fact that there'd be no heat emitted by the engine, just powerful EMFs, and so it was kept in an area of the ship that had no gravity. Instead of heat, she was immediately hit by a flurry of visions, having forgotten her purpose for being there, she held fast to the door and reeled as the visions entered her brain.

She saw a giant blue glowing ball with long wispy tendrils like solar-flares. Novawynd ascertained it was the engine. It was locked into a harness of some sort. It reached out to her and grabbed her with its flare-like tentacles. She felt fear and pain. She sensed the blue ball was asking for her to help it. She didn't know how. She had a vision of a button on the console behind her and if she hit it would release the engine. Then the visions changed tracks completely. They showed her Star again, but he was not like he was the other times she saw him in dreams. He was sad and angry. He was standing over a grave and he held a drawing of a young woman. It definitely wasn't Novawynd. She sensed he had loved this woman, and she was now dead. She felt his despair. She then saw another man and he was naked with this same woman in the throes of passion.

Zefram yelled out through the Omniaural for Novawynd to set off the bomb. She snapped back to reality. Her computer was beeping that it had finished the download. She ripped it out of the port and stuck the bomb to the door but hesitated.

"What are you waiting for?" yelled Zefram in her head.

Instead, Novawynd hit the button on the console she had been shown. The engine harness released. Then she hit the button on the bomb that would detonate it. It would wait three zecrons then blow. That gave her enough time to flux out of the ship, back to the Kirkazet ship. Once back on the Kirkazet ship, she ordered the computer to flux to the position of the Zenith. In the blink of an eye, the pirate ship imploded as the Kirkazet ship disappeared from sight.

Zefram had lured the Placsuni, with the cargo, out of the docking bay and luckily, one of the pirates was the zelo, or at least the one he had been speaking to. He would be a valuable prisoner. Zefram sensed the zelo would normally not have come along, but wanted to negotiate for more. His greed would be his undoing. Zefram was still using Junatiel on them, so they did not believe anything was abnormal. Even the complete absence of other crew members did not seem odd to them. Zefram pulled out his DESS. Only then did they become concerned. He swung at their heads before they could react and they each fell, unconscious. He had his DESS set to the slightest setting, so it would not kill. That was how he subdued them, and then he yelled out to Novawynd to set the bomb if she hadn't already. He jettisoned the pirate shuttle and watched as it floated out into space like jetsam.

Zefram became nervous when the ship hadn't begun to blow. They would see the jettisoning of the shuttle and alarms would be raised. He had yelled out to her again, then shortly the enemy ship began to go, but he did not see it blow. Novawynd had returned to the ship and commanded it to flux, just as planned. Zefram was a little concerned as to what took so long for her to execute the first part. He checked the prisoners and removed any devices they might use to communicate with someone else. They were unconscious, but breathing without labor. He set a gas grenade next to them and walked away. It would anesthetize them until the Space guard from the Zenith collected them and the ship's doctor removed their CIs.

Zefram found Novawynd in the Commcen. As he walked in, she was standing as if talking to someone, "Star, what is your deal? What did you do?" she was saying, but there was no one there.

"Who is Star?" Zefram interrogated.

Novawynd flinched, obviously startled. She must have been intently distracted, or there's no way Zefram could have snuck up on her. "I don't know. I'm trying to figure that out." She responded, but she could see that was not the answer Zefram was looking for so she offered more, "I think he might be the Lajiachine. He's come to me in my dreams. *He came to me.*" she wanted to give him something, so he would not suspect she was hiding something, but she only told him what she knew, and that wasn't much. "I just had a vision of him, and apparently some things going on in his life. That's why I hesitated, I wanted to know more. I wanted to see as much as the vision would show me so I could figure something out."

Zefram was interested. He stepped forward. "How long has he been visiting you in your dreams?"

"Since I first woke up from my coma back on Earth, a little over two anios ago." She speculated.

"How often does he visit you?"

"It's only been three times, so far."

"Where is he from? Is he from Earth?" This was a dicey question. Novawynd didn't know where he was. That's what she'd been trying to figure out. It was a good thing she didn't know. She felt sure it wouldn't be a good idea to let Zefram know.

"He hasn't told me and I can't tell from what I've seen. He's definitely not Earthling."

"What makes you so sure he's not Earthling?"

"His facial features. The way he dresses and the fact that he carries a huge sword that no normal man should be able to use."

"A sword? A lot of planets still use swords, even a lot of civilized planets, because they hold onto a notion that skilled swordsmanship is as beautiful as music or dancing; so that doesn't really help. What about his face, what about it was different?"

"His eyes were larger than normal and he had high cheekbones and his nose and chin were pointy, but not in a severe way, in a…perfect way. Oh yeah, his ears were a little pointy too."

"Was he Aritrean?"

"His ears weren't even as pointy as an Aritrean's; just a hint of a point. Besides, if he was on Florencia when I was there, I would have felt him as surely as I felt you."

"And, you're sure he's real, not an enti of some sort."

Novawynd shot Zefram a glare, as if to say "Give me some credit."

"Okay!" Zefram acknowledged defensively. Then he added in a relaxed tone "What do you two do when he visits you?"

"Zefram! I'm getting tired of this interrogation now." She cautioned sternly. "If I haven't figured him out yet, you won't."

"I'm sorry, but I'm concerned why you would think he's the Lajiachine. If he is, we need to find him. You and I both would be free of some pressure then."

"Zefram, if we find him and turn him over to the Superior Council, you and I could be scrapped. Well, maybe not so much you, but I would definitely be."

"They wouldn't. They still need us as Leluminali. We are the most superior Leluminali in the universe. Valuable weapons."

"Right, that is until he goes to the Analida and obliterates both our scores."

"So, then he becomes Superior Council's ambassador and you get to do missions like this one." he nodded to their surroundings "Besides, you'd get to be his mentor for a while." Zefram was implying that Novawynd would then get to spend some quality time with this Star.

"That's not even a fun thought. He'd be on Ephilderone anyway." Novawynd complained.

"You're not. What if they don't make him either?"

The corners of Novawynd's lips curled slightly. Now that was a nice thought.

"I don't believe you." Zefram snorted. "You're really considering that aren't you?" Novawynd just continued smiling as she was now lost in the daydream of her and the exotically beautiful Star standing side by side in a CC somewhere. Her daydream was interrupted by the space-guard who had come from the Zenith to recover the prisoners. Their communication tore through her vision like old film slipping from its reel and melting on the projector.

Zefram responded before she could. He allowed them access to the docking bay. Novawynd and Zefram returned to the Zenith with the space-guard and the prisoners. They all had to go through decontamination because of the exposure to the Kirkazet ship. Although it was not likely anyone was contaminated, in the event the virus had mutated and could be passed by airborne methods, it was still imperative to test their blood for the contagion. They all had to wait until everyone's blood came back clean.

As far as the Superior Council would be concerned, it had been a productive day for Zefram. He was able to get enough evidence on Novawynd's lack of conditioning to have her scrapped without question. Simultaneously, he developed a stronger trust-bond with Novawynd. She was that much closer to falling for him, he was sure of it. The icing on the cake was Novawynd's information about this 'Star' person. As soon as Zefram's mission was complete, Novawynd would be scrapped, and then he would be sent out to find this 'Star' Novawynd spoke of, and kill him. But, as far as Zefram was concerned, this was not good. He had his qualms about letting her come to harm now. She was the first person he had ever come to have feelings of any kind for.

The other thing he considered was 'what if the Superior Council was playing him and Novawynd against each other?' "When did I start feeling so paranoid?" he thought to himself. His conditioning hadn't been irreparably broken, just dented a little, but it was enough for him to start questioning the Superior Council "I used to always know that whatever the Superior Council dictated was truth. I never questioned it. Now I don't know. But, Novawynd was right. What choice do I have? If I wasn't working for the Xaxony, what would I do, where could I go?" the conclusion he had come to was disheartening. "I don't want to harm Novawynd, but I have to. It's her or me." He was hit by a fist of fear that melted into sadness and then reignited into fury. He sat motionless, meditating. He controlled his emotions, because that's what he was trained to do, but he didn't want to control it anymore. He wanted to turn over furniture and ransack the room. No one knew the turmoil that was tearing him apart inside.

"Zefram?" Novawynd's voice sprung into his mind like a refreshing mist. He looked at her. She looked at the others. The prisoner's were unconscious in another holding cell, but the two space-guards were involved in a heated game of Ruckus. They were not paying attention. She pointed to her eyes with her fore and middle fingers and drew lines down her cheeks. He realized she was trying to covertly indicate to him he had been crying. He slowly wiped his cheeks, so as not to draw attention. He looked at the wetness on his hand with wonder. He had never cried. Novawynd gave him a side-long glance as if to say

"What's that about?" He knew she wouldn't press him with others in the room.

He changed the subject "Hey, we should go to the science lab when we get out of here. We'll put the retinatrodes on you. You can re-imagine this Star guy and the computer will render a 4D image of him. From that, the computer will surely be able to ascertain his origin."

Once everyone came back clear of the Kirkazet virus, they were allowed to leave the decon area. The prisoners, still sedated were taken to the med-lab for CI extraction. Novawynd initially thought it was odd that Stunner wasn't waiting for her, but then she remembered she had given him a Junatiel command to not think about her until she summoned him. It was for his own good, really. She and Zefram headed to the sci-lab, but she was not crazy about this idea Zefram had. "Why did I tell him?" she was silently kicking herself. "I guess I was still a bit stunned by the vision experience and my tongue was easily loosened. How do I get out of this? I want to know where Star is, but Zefram can't know." Novawynd's compassion had been piqued by Zefram's tears. She didn't know what was behind it, but she knew it was true. He had started to evolve emotionally as a human. She was impressed, but she still had a feeling that Zefram could not be trusted. In fact he may be more dangerous than ever if he was capable of emotionally manipulating her. Where Star was concerned, she was certain Zefram was a danger to Star. She tried to work through this. "However, now that Zefram knows about Star, I can stall, but he'll eventually find him. It's better that I cooperate and figure out a way to protect Star in the mean time."

Novawynd and Zefram arrived at the sci-lab. A lab tech was present, but he abruptly exited once they entered the lab. Zefram went straight to the compartment containing the retinatrodes. Novawynd was always amazed at how Zefram always knew exactly where everything was. She was detail oriented, but she still didn't know where everything was. Zefram, on the other hand, made a point of memorizing the schematics of every ship or city he would ever set foot in or maps of any world he would ever set foot on. Novawynd now knew why the Ephilderone was so useful to the Xaxony. How much more thought Zefram put into things since he wasn't wasting time thinking about sex?

"By the way, Zefram, now that we're alone, what was that all about back in the decon?" she was referring to his crying. He gave her a terse look, and then his eyes diverted to the ground. He looked back up at her with a look of apology and pointed to the area behind his left ear where his CI would be located just under the skull. He was implying that he couldn't tell her or it would be imprinted in the memory of his CI. He tried to hand the retinatrodes to her. Novawynd pushed them back at him. "I'm not dong this until you tell me. Earlier today I told you things that could be deadly to me, and you assured me no one would ever know. No one will know about this either, unless you choose to tell them." She was right. His effort to deflect the issue was feeble and she called him on it.

Zefram struggled with the right thing to say, so she wouldn't sense he was lying, but so he wasn't telling her the whole truth either. He began slowly, "I…was… thinking… about… the possibility that we are being played against each other." That was true and it was a good start. He continued, "I realized it will have to come down to… you… or me." He took a deep breath. "I feel sad and angry about that. I don't want to see it come down to that. That's why we have to find this Star guy."

Zefram thought he had come up with a pretty compelling explanation, but Novawynd immediately saw the flaw. "What do you mean 'played against each other'? I thought you were just supposed to be my mentor. You're supposed to be helping me. If you're helping me, how is that *against* me?"

Zefram needed to do some back-pedaling. "My mission is to be your mentor, so when you accuse me of having an ulterior motive toward your end, I'm shocked. It makes me wonder if you think that because the Superior Council told *you* to scrap *me*. I've never felt like this before. I've never questioned the Superior Council before. Your paranoia is rubbing off on me."

"I see." Novawynd responded flatly. Zefram couldn't read what that meant. "Let's do this then." She took the retinatrodes from Zefram and put them into her eyes, under the lids. Zefram asked Zacharieth to scan Novawynd's retinal image. Soon a fuzzy image of a man appeared before them. The face was the last detail to fill in and after a moment the figure filled in completely in detail, from the weave in his sleeveless, thread-bare black sweater, to the silver, star emblem on his leather shoulder shield.

"All the enti in the Omniaural!" Zefram scoffed. Novawynd pulled the retinatrodes out of her eyes.

"What? Who is he, do you know him? He's not the first Zefram is he?"

"No. I don't recognize him. I was just amazed by the size of that sword. You were right. It is a bit outrageous."

Novawynd looked at the image of Star. It was a static image, no motion or life, but here he was, life-size and very real looking, in front of her. His large, ocean-blue eyes were so expressive, they seemed to contain all the knowledge of the universe. He was staring at the floor with a contemplative look on his face. Novawynd was suddenly overcome with emotion. She wasn't sure which emotion, but she wanted so badly to embrace him, or to at least just touch him. She impulsively stepped up to the image and put her hand up to Star's face.

"He's not there Novawynd." Zefram stated the obvious. Novawynd knew it, but it didn't matter. She closed her eyes and could almost feel the smooth, hairless skin of his cheek. "Zacharieth," Zefram interrupted Novawynd's reverie. "Cross-reference this man's features and structure against other known living-beings. Go back as far as possible and consider races that are now extinct as well."

Novawynd held her breath. After only a few mecrons, Zacharieth responded, "I have cross-referenced this man with over 120 known humanoid species, living or extinct, and can find no match. I suggest he is either a cross-breed, a genetic mutation or from a seeded planet the Xaxony has left alone for long enough that the inhabitants have evolved to a different appearance, and our records are no longer accurate."

"Thank you Zacharieth. Save the image in case one of us needs to recall it later." Zefram instructed. He turned to Novawynd "Well, that was a dead end after all." Novawynd wasn't disappointed. At least Zefram wasn't any closer to finding Star's home-world. And now, whenever she wanted, she could recall the image of Star. She could gaze at it all day long and never get tired of it.

CHAPTER 10

Novawynd woke up in the morning next to Trevor. He was softly snoring. She smiled because she loved the comfort of a man's snore, as long as it wasn't loud and obnoxious. Then she felt suddenly guilty. The day before, when Trevor suggested they spend some time together, she wasn't sure how she'd feel after her mission was complete. She wasn't sure that she'd want to see him. However, after seeing the image of Star, so lifelike, she left the sci-lab and headed straight back to her unit, where she called Trevor to come over. The feeling she had upon seeing Star's image was one of needing to become one with him; but, not in a sexual way. That was even too superficial. She really wanted to meld atoms with him, absorb him. By the time she left the sci-lab, her feelings had become distorted a bit and she felt like she needed a sexual release. When Trevor made love to her, she had imagined he was Star.

It was time for her to get to work. She sat up and Trevor woke up and looked at her. Then he went back to doing what he did so well; looking good while sleeping in her bed. She smiled at the thought of that and she got up and got herself ready to face the Superior Council. When she was done getting ready, Trevor was waking up. He stretched and groaned. As Novawynd put her boots on, she looked at him. "What do you think about just staying in my bed all day today? We can pretend you're my sex slave, chained to the bed and I will come over there and use you as I see fit." She crossed the room to him and knelt on one knee next to him on the bed. He put his hand on her waist.

"That sounds like a dream. But, what if I have to go to the head or eat?" He asked for clarification.

"Well do all that, of course. Watch movies, or what ever you have to do to entertain yourself, because I won't be here all day, and when I am I won't necessarily be looking for your company; but when I am here, I want you naked in this bed and ready at a moment's notice." She commanded in a playful tone and bent down to kiss him. He chuckled and raised his eyebrow at her because he had gotten slightly aroused at the thought of that, but she just gave him a sly smile and left him there to go perform her duties.

As Novawynd was nearly to the Superior Council chambers, Zefram stepped out the council chambers door.

"Hey Zefram, what's up?" she inquired in reference to why he had been in with the Superior Council. She was concerned.

"A routine sweep was done on Earth to test for Terran DNA and the tests came back positive. Earth will need to be scoured."

"Why wasn't I informed before now?"

"The head of the genetics lab tried to contact you a few minutes ago, but you were unavailable, so he contacted me."

"Oh, I was in the shower. But, why didn't you bring it to me?"

"I didn't know why you were unavailable or how long you would be and I thought it would look good on my part if I dealt with it straight away. Novawynd..." He put his hands on her shoulders and looked at her sternly. "They are going to ask you to do the scouring of Earth, and you have to do it to prove your loyalty to them." She realized the weight of this problem immediately.

"How many people will die?" she asked solemnly.

"By estimates, probably only a little over a million. But, at current population rates, the Earth will recover quickly enough." he tried to assure her.

"What about my mother and sister and niece?"

"Your DNA was clear, so their's will be too. They won't be affected."

Novawynd shook her head in disbelief, but attempted brush it off before going in front of the Superior Council. She slid past Zefram in the doorway and entered the council chambers. The Superior Council appeared before Novawynd as they had every morning for the last two-and-a-half aera. This time, their priority mission for her would be a difficult one for her to accept graciously. She stood before them steadfast; ready for their instructions. They wasted no time getting down to the dirt.

"Zefram has informed us that Terran DNA has been detected on Earth. You will need to perform a scouring." The mutated voices of the eight ethereal council members seemed louder than usual in Novawynd's mind.

"That's unfortunate news." Novawynd stated aloofly. "But...of course I will carry out the scouring immediately." she guaranteed with a nod.

"Apparently," the council added, intensifying Novawynd's impatience with the situation, "the Earth-Terran DNA had been mutating for over ninety anios without our knowledge. A new strain of the scouring virus will need to be developed. It won't be ready for at least two aera." they notified.

"Very well then whenever it's ready." She kept her emotionless façade, but inside she was sweating. The new strain made her nervous. But, the geneticists knew what they were doing. They had dealt with this hundreds of times before. She knew she had to have faith in that.

Novawynd proceeded to do business with the Superior Council as usual. This time however, after her meeting with them, Novawynd felt drained. After leaving the council chambers, she slumped against the wall outside. She let out a huge sigh, and then straightened up and shook it off. As she started down the hall, a bright light suddenly rounded the corner. It was Stunner. She couldn't help the wide smile that crossed her face.

"Novawynd!" he called out to her excitedly.

"Stunner!" she called back. They approached each other, grinning.

"I haven't seen you in a while, I've been so busy and I knew you've been super busy, what with the Kirkazet mission and all." he tried to make an excuse, but Novawynd knew he had stayed away because she had asked him to, under the duress of Junatiel, so no excuse was necessary. None-the-less, she thought it was a bit cute.

"Don't worry about it. Like you said, I've been busy too." she enabled him.

"I was coming to see you though, because I have information about the data you got from the Placsuni ship. Also, the prisoners' CIs have been helpful, although the prisoners themselves have been a pain. What should we do with them?"

"Next time we need to refuel, we should go to the nearest remote refueling station and drop them off. Let the chips fall where they may."

Stunner gave an amused snort. "That is almost crueler than scrapping them."

"Is it crueler than kidnapping people, inducing them into a comatose state and selling them to vampires to become blood-banks?" Novawynd asked seriously.

"No." Stunner responded soberly.

"Well, perhaps we can devise something equal to that in the mean time." Novawynd smiled maniacally. "As far as the data you gathered, maybe we should get Zefram to meet us in the conference room and we'll go over it. Zacharieth?" she commanded the computer's attention. "Please blip Zefram and see if he can meet Stunner and me in the conference room in ten mecrons, to go over the Kirkazet data."

"Yes Novawynd." the computer responded dutifully. Novawynd and Stunner headed off to the conference room. They said nothing to each other on the way. They simply smiled 'knowing' smiles. When they got to the conference room, Novawynd took a seat and leaned forward, folding her hands on the table. Stunner took the chair next to her and mimicked her posture. Then he took her hand in his. She smiled and studied the back of his blue hand.

"Zacharieth, what is Zefram's ETA?" she was looking into Stunner's violet eyes as she asked.

"Approximately thirty zecrons." it responded. Novawynd released Stunner's hand.

"Sorry," she looked at him apologetically, "I can't have Zefram sending you to another ship." Just as she said that, Zefram entered. They both looked up at him.

Zefram had switched back to the "cold, calculating clone" version of himself again. Obviously, Zefram wasn't about to let others see how he was struggling with the slow unraveling of his conditioning. It was odd to Novawynd to see this. It was like watching someone going through a multiple identity crisis. But, she understood why he acted the way he did. She had done it enough times herself. Ironically, she was doing it at that moment, with the way she treated Stunner in front of Zefram.

Zefram sat down quickly and cut to the chase. "So, what do we know?"

"What we do know is that our suspicions are correct. Intelligence we previously gathered lead us to believe that initially there were several independent flesh-monger pirates and about fifty anio ago the most dominant faction cut a deal with the others to band together. By doing so, they were not competing with each other, thus driving each other's prices down. By becoming a cooperative monopoly, they can charge whatever prices they want and they all come out making more money than they did before they banded together. The data you gathered verified that.

There is no longer a dominant faction. It is run like a democracy. The slave-trader ship's zelos all vote on any changes, but there is one zelo who is voted in as the faction head. The head serves as the conduit for all the other zelos and has the power to swing a tie vote one way or the other because he is the last to vote and in the event of a tie, the others can present their case to persuade him. Then, his vote counts as two votes. Whoever is voted in as faction head, is only head for six anio, and can't be re-elected for consecutive terms. So, it seems there is not one dictator behind the flesh peddlers. They are actually an organized team."

"Fine, did we get information as to who is on the team?" Zefram seemed impatient.

"Yes. Zacharieth, please show us the slave-trader zelos and their ship data." Stunner requested, and then continued talking as the information appeared before them. "There are fifteen, including the one we have in the brig right now."

"So, we aren't going to be able to hit one zelo and bring the whole faction down?" Novawynd more stated, than asked.

"It would be just like cutting off a limb of a Scleropod. It would just grow back in no time." Stunner snorted, as he found his own analogy amusing.

"We'll have to send fourteen Leluminali out to find the fourteen remaining zelos." Novawynd schemed.

"Thirteen." Zefram corrected.

"What do you mean?" Novawynd didn't get it.

"We will find the head zelo and thirteen other Leluminali will find the rest." he clarified.

"We feel confident that the head is Zelo Annatippa, a Cirrilean. His ship is a commandeered Xaxon CV34 class freighter. He calls it the Quilexica. It was Angier 5 when it was in service for the Xaxony."

"Well it shouldn't be that difficult now that we know who they all are. We put their faces and ships, along with promises of rewards for info out on our snitch network and our snitches will report to us in no time." Novawynd decided.

"They were dealing pretty heavily in fuel; my guess is they may play it such that they would never cross paths with our snitches." Zefram hypothesized. Besides, snitches can't be trusted. They might give us useful information, but they wouldn't hesitate to tip off the people we're looking for too."

Novawynd turned her attention to Stunner, "Stunner?" she addressed him. "You would have told us if there was any data on whether the pirates met specific times and in regular locations wouldn't you?"

"Of course, but they were smart. Their meeting times were sporadic and they never met in the same place twice."

"We're chasing ghosts." There was a hint of hopelessness in Zefram's comment.

"That's why the Xaxony doesn't waste its time on pirates; so much brain-strain for so little return on time and investment." Novawynd commented. Then she seemed to have a bright idea. "Zacharieth, calculate the probability, that if the pirate ship we got this data from had continued on in its usual dealings, would it have come across one of our snitches within the next anio."

"Running data as requested." the computer acknowledged. Everyone sat silent for a moment. Then the computer returned "There is a ninety-three-point-eight percent probability."

"Okay Zacharieth, how about for only the next six aera?" she asked.

The computer came back quicker that time. "Fifty-seven-point-two percent probability."

"There you have it." she tossed her hands up. "We have a better chance at finding them if we sick the snitches on them, than if we what…sit back and hope they fall in our laps?"

"I realize that, but as soon as they find out they're wanted, they'll be that much more cautious and hard to find. Even so, if we tried a different method, they would get wise as soon as we started systematically taking them out. And, that's the other thing, if we don't move quickly enough, like Stunner said, the arms will re-grow…" Zefram drum-rolled his fingers on the table as he pondered the options. Then he got a bright expression on his face and leaned forward to Novawynd. "Couldn't you find them? Couldn't you reach out in the Omniaural to lock onto them, now that you know who they are? That way, it really wouldn't matter if they knew they were being hunted. They couldn't hide anyway. In fact, we could make it clear that it is us hunting them and that would really put the fear into them. "

"I don't know if I can do that. I mean, I know who Star is, but I can't find *him*." she made an excellent point. Zefram nodded.

"Who's Star?" Stunner asked.

Zefram spoke before Novawynd could, "That's classified." he qualified. It was a good thing he said so, Novawynd probably would've told Stunner about Star otherwise.

"Anyway, I'll certainly try." she assured. "However, as to how to deal with them once we've captured them. I think we definitely need to process their CI's. They might have useful info on exactly whose been keeping them in business. And I want to make sure that we capture the actual people behind the trafficking. No innocent people are to be scrapped. The first thing they will do, if they believe they have been captured, is let their captives go, and then they'll all claim they are captives."

"They can try whatever tactics they want. Once they realize they are dealing with Leluminali, they'll know their attempts were futile."Zefram seemed pretty self-assured. "See if you can lock onto the head zelo first."

"And, if I can't?" she asked for clarification.

"Then it'll have to be plan B, putting the info out to the snitches and waiting."

"I'll go back to my quarters and let you know if I was successful." she acknowledged. Zefram nodded. She stood and the men also stood. She gave a slight bow to them and they returned the gesture. Stunner gave her a longing look as her eyes lingered, locked on his for a moment. She remembered in that moment that Trevor was waiting for her back in her unit, and she had to exit quickly.

*   *   *

Trevor was waiting in her bed, just as she had suggested. "Hey, Novawynd! It's pretty boring waiting around in bed for you. I thought you'd be back sooner. What took you so long?"

Novawynd smirked. "Trevor, I'm sorry but we can't play today." She walked over to a chair in the corner and picked up his clothes the house-keeping droid had laid there. "I just got out of a meeting about the data we gleaned from the last mission and now I have some research to do before we finalize the details of the next mission relating to this." she tossed his clothes to him as he was now sitting up in her bed.

"You can do your research with me here can't you?" he almost begged.

"Not this research." she sat down next to him on the bed. He got up on his knees behind her and started to massage her shoulders.

"Why not?" he whispered in her ear and proceeded to kiss her neck.

"Because I need to dive into the Omniaural and I need complete silence and solitude."

Trevor sat back on his haunches. "Okay." He got out of bed and started dressing. "Later then?" He was obviously disappointed. Novawynd's heart ached a little at his dejected tone, but she had a mission to accomplish. She sat and watched as he slunk out of her room. She lay down and quieted her mind. She had been able to astrally project to find people on Earth, as she had done with Will Warner and Matt McClellan. But, she had tried many times to find Star this way and couldn't do it. Time was a factor. She couldn't be in her altered state for too long and the universe was a vast area to search. The Omniaural permeated the entire universe, and so it really helped her to know the general vicinity in which a target could be found.

Novawynd had better luck finding people in their sleep via her dream-walking abilities, but even then, it was difficult to get the targets to tell her where they were. It wasn't that they were reluctant to tell her, they just were dreaming; therefore, when asked where they were, they would almost always answer "I don't know". This was because they weren't familiar with their dream-world surroundings and didn't know where they were in the dream. Novawynd's efforts to get her subjects to focus on the real-world would almost always snap them to reality too fast, and they would awaken.

The only time it worked for her, was with Will Warner. She presumed that was because of the given scenario. But then, she didn't know if it was really his address he wrote on the blackboard, because she never got there. She smiled fondly at the memory of Will. She had visited him from time to time in his dreams, as well as Matt McClellan. She had become friends with them both on a bizarre level. Will was now a successful movie actor and Matt had given up on being a rock-star, but his connections in Hollywood gave him the tools he needed to become a successful, Internet, Hollywood gossip blogger. She sometimes secretly helped Matt out by visiting other stars, finding out their secrets and giving him the dirt.

Novawynd had tried to get Star to tell her where he was, but was obviously interrupted. She hadn't had the opportunity to try to reach him again since then. When she got an opportunity to sleep, she was just too exhausted to play around. This time, it wasn't play, it was work. Initially Novawynd thought she would project, but then decided on trying to find the head, slave-trade, pirate zelo in his sleep. Perhaps she would get lucky. Since this was for a mission, she would spend the next dialo trying to connect with the head zelo every half-a-tecron. She would have to catch him asleep at some point. She drifted off to a lucid sleep and found herself flying through space. This first attempt at trying to find the flesh-cartel head was unsuccessful. He was not asleep yet.

*   *   *

Trevor was back in his home away from home, the lounge where he was again drinking Timmian ale and watching the universal news. He should be shadowing Stunner instead of drinking, but he felt a little squeamish about the ménage a trios he had recently had with Stunner and Novawynd. He and Stunner had agreed to it, and it probably wouldn't be the last time, but he still needed to take some time getting used to the idea. As he concentrated on the display, Zefram entered the lounge. Trevor noticed him come in, but chose to ignore him. Zefram came straight over to Trevor, this time without Cirrilean brandy.

"How are you?" Zefram asked as he sat down next to Trevor.

"You haven't talked to me in the last aera, and now you want to be my mate." Trevor accused. "What is it you want this time?" Trevor was blunt.

"After our last conversation, I realized some questions were left unanswered. I'm interested in getting your feedback. That is, only if you're willing to give it."

"What questions?" Trevor's curiosity was piqued, but he really had nothing better to do anyway.

"You spoke very generally of the courtship process, but I would like to know, how do you actually convince a woman to mate with you? I need to know in specific terms."

"You mean, how do I convince a woman to make the final leap into bed with me?"

"Yes. What do you do to seduce her?"

Trevor paused, measuring up Zefram. Then he smirked "If I didn't know better, I'd think you were planning to seduce someone yourself."

He sat back and hooked his arm casually over the back of his chair, regarding Zefram.

"Even if it were possible, it wouldn't be probable. My interest is purely scientific."

"Okay then. The end result is obviously to get physical. You know if she's okay with you bringing it to that level, because she will flirt with you. She will make sexual innuendos. She will get close to you and touch you. She will look in your eyes and smile whenever possible. So, when you get those queues, you test her out by touching her in a suggestive, but non-aggressive way, like you might put your hand on hers. If she responds favorably, then you touch her in a sensual way, like you brush her cheek or stroke a strand of her hair. Make sure to make eye contact as much as possible, so she can read your sincerity. If she still responds favorably, then you take it to the next level, you kiss her. If she responds favorably to that, half the battle is already won.

Of course, it depends on where you are when this happens. The time and place that seems right to kiss a woman the first time, isn't always the time and place to go all the way to the sex. You may have to get alone with her, kiss and feel each other up several times before you get to that point. Most women don't like to be thought of as *easy*, so they will be difficult and try to find excuses not to get to the sex right away. But, in my experience, I like it when women play hard-to-get. The fun is in the chase, especially if the woman is very alluring. Delayed gratification can be very hot, because the sooner you do it with her, the sooner it's done.

Once she does allow you to be alone with her, you kiss and caress her as usual, to get her in the mood. Then you lay her down. If she allows you to do this, she's ready. She'll even be likely to help out the process in any way she can. But, there are other women who will let you get to this point and then stop you. I find it usually helps to confess to the woman the physical agony she has me in, and then she submits. Women love believing they have that power over a man. But, if she still protests, then it's a good idea to back off. I find then it works to retreat entirely. Leave her with the idea that if you can't have her, you can't be with her because of the state she has you in, and then be patient. After a time of personal reflection, they usually come to you, more than ready. The only way that doesn't happen is if fear of some consequence of the coupling is greater than their desire for you; such as, if they are married and don't want to cheat, or if they fear getting pregnant.

At that point, the mating ritual that you referred to as the 'clinical mating habits of Earthlings' takes over. I don't think you need me to describe." Trevor paused, and then added, "Any questions?"

"What about scents, music and appearance. How are those things used to attract a woman?"

"Well, if you think of birds, they have unique colors and songs to attract a mate of their own species. Humans are all the same species, but there are countless subcultures. Humans are like birds, in that they want to attract mates in the subculture they consider themselves a part of. We adopt dress and hairstyles and make-up, wear the scents and listen to the music that our subculture does. This way we hope to attract a woman who has more in common with us. And, if we do decide to settle down, she won't bore us to tears.

Honestly, I keep an open mind about women's culture preferences. I just need a beautiful woman who won't annoy me to death. So far, I haven't found one."

"You're saying Novawynd annoys you?" Zefram laughed a little.

"She doesn't annoy me. It's her position that annoys me. She's only available when it's convenient for her. I'm usually the one that has a woman when it's convenient for me. I'm not used to waiting around for someone's schedule to open up."

"I see." Zefram pushed himself back from the table. "You've been very helpful. I think I have all the info I need." He stood up. "This should be sufficient for the archives. I don't think I'll need to bother you about this subject again. Please excuse me." Zefram turned and exited the lounge. Trevor thought the departure somewhat abrupt, but he put it in the back of his mind and went back to watching the news.

∗   ∗   ∗

The man Novawynd was looking for, Zelo Annatippa was a Cirrilean. The Cirrileans were the very beings responsible for the delicious and potent Cirrilean brandy. They were humanoid and looked just like Earthlings; or more appropriately, like the majority of the Xaxon genetic constructs, such as Zefram. They had no unusual physical attributes to distinguish them. They did have an unnatural understanding of physics and mathematics and were generally employed by the Xaxony to be engineers. Their planet was technologically advanced, and yet steeped in tradition. The architecture, dress and customs were ancient, despite their advanced intelligence.

Novawynd had spent nearly one whole dialo trying to find Annatippa. She was just about to give up when she hit on him. She disguised herself with flaming red hair and blue eyes as she entered his dream. He wasn't an unattractive man and he was young in appearance, most likely a result of genetic manipulation. But the very thought of what he was, disgusted Novawynd. She would not lower herself to use her feminine wiles to seduce him. Instead, she allowed him to pursue her. "I want to know about you. What is your name?"

"Jhenya...Jhenya Annatippa"

Novawynd lead him to a window "Jhenya, look out this window and show me where you are at this moment." she directed. He was in a highly susceptible dream state. A landscape appeared out the window and she could see old, brightly painted, stone towers. She wasn't familiar with this scenery. "Are you on Cirrilea?" she guessed.

"Yes." he responded dreamily as he stared out at the landscape.

"Where on Cirrilea do you make your home?" Novawynd asked pleasantly. She was trying not to sound too interrogative. She began thinking about how she could take him out right now, in his dream, and he would never wake up. But then, no one would know it was the Xaxony that assassinated him, and that was necessary. The Xaxony was not adverse to some forms of piracy. Piracy did help the economy. Because pirates usually dealt in flux-drive gas, they usually stole it from others who legitimately purchased it. When those who legitimately purchased gas, which was stolen, need to purchase more, the Xaxony grows richer.

However, in the case of living-being trafficking, the Xaxony did not condone it. The reason was because there was a universal law put forth by the Superior Council that stated "All living beings across the universe have a right to free-life. It is unlawful for one race to oppress, enslave or tamper with another race. This was called the Scentian Proclamation and beings caught breaking the Scentian Proclamation were subject to immediate termination, without trial. In fact, vigilantism was encouraged to deal with those who were known proclamation breakers. Vigilantism made it very dangerous to deal in the slave-trade, but pirates usually found ways to keep would-be vigilantes under control. It was then when the flesh piracy went unchecked and began to spiral out of control. The Superior Council primarily put the Scentian Proclamation into force to have a reason to terminate the Terrans, who they knew were tampering with and abducting beings on the seeded planets. But, the law was the law and examples needed to be made of the pirates from time to time. The flesh piracy hey-days were cyclical. When they were at their most profitable, the Xaxony retaliated and culled the flesh pirates. Some time would pass, new pirates would emerge, and it began all over again. The Superior Council hoped eventually slavery would just become passé, and so there wouldn't be a market anymore.

Zelo Annatippa answered Novawynd "I have the largest house in Moav. I'm a wealthy merchant and very well respected in Moav." He offered that information to impress Novawynd, but she reviled him for referring to himself as a merchant, when she knew what he really was. She had to muster every once of her will, to fight back the urge to summon up her demonic alter-ego, Xilander, to keep from impaling him like she had done to the convict. Instead she just pushed him out the imaginary window. He would wake up before he hit the ground, and it was thus that she was free from his dream.

She blipped Zefram immediately.

"Yes, Novawynd? Did you have any luck?"

"I did. He's hunkered down on Cirrilea, in his own home in Moav. Apparently, it's the largest house in Moav. It should be easy to locate."

"Good work." Zefram affirmed.

Approaching Annatippa in his dream was a risky way to go about it. When people are in a dream state, they are always truthful, but in their dream state, what they believe to be true while dreaming, is not always what is true.

"He might not be at his house now, but he will be sometime." Novawynd clarified. "It's a place he is obviously fond of and he wouldn't maintain the residence if he didn't use it."

"Even so, we should go there, lay low and wait." Zefram suggested.

"Agreed."

CHAPTER 11

The Zenith arrived in a near planet orbit above Cirrilea. Novawynd and Zefram were to be dropped off by shuttle, in an outer city and travel from there to Moav. This was the best way to arrive in Moav without anyone knowing they were space travelers. The Zenith would not stay near Cirrilea, so no pirate ships would become aware of their presence and possibly alert Annatippa. Novawynd and Zefram were only to call the Zenith for retrieval if they had completed the mission, or were in trouble. Their mission would take several dialos, but could last up to several aera.

The mode of travel Zefram and Novawynd had to take to Moav was very low-tech, land traveling, bus-like vehicle. The trip would take them several days. This was perfect timing as far as Zefram was concerned. It was nearly time for his Ephilderone to wear off. He estimated he only had a few dialos remaining. In the mean time, he would be able to use what he learned from Trevor, to secure Novawynd's favor, and hopefully affections.

As they traveled, to kill the boredom of extended travel time, they talked. Zefram asked Novawynd many questions about herself and the things she liked. Novawynd was amused by his interest and kindly reciprocated by asking Zefram what he liked and asked him to tell her stories of some of his favorite missions. As it turned out, he was an entertaining story-teller. He seemed so excited about telling her of his adventures. She was easily caught up in his enthusiasm.

Three nights they had to stay in inns along the way. They didn't know how long they would be on the planet, so they needed to make their limited supply of Cirrilean currency last. They posed as newlyweds and always shared a room to save money. They laughed about the irony of that. The first night, it was Novawynd who slept on the floor, as Zefram took the bed. The second night, Zefram took the floor. The third and final night before they were to reach Moav, Zefram was to take the bed again, but insisted that Novawynd take it. She was impressed by his kindness, but she was more stubborn in not wanting to be the less nice of the two, and so she refused to make Zefram sleep on the floor again.

"Well," Zefram thought out-loud, "There's enough room for both of us on this bed. Why don't we both sleep on the bed? You know you're safe with me. I won't take advantage of you." He chuckled softly.

"I'm not worried about you taking advantage of me. I just thought you would be grossed out about being so close to me. I'm trying to respect your personal space."

"I don't want you to sleep on the floor when there is no need to, so if you won't come up here, I'm going to join you down there." he persuaded.

"Fine!" Novawynd got up and gingerly slid under the covers with him. Zefram really was still prohibited by the effects of the Ephilderone, but he knew he could win her trust this way. And, when the time was right…

In the morning, Novawynd woke to find herself being spooned by Zefram. She felt all at once content and yet, uncomfortable. She loved the feeling of a man holding her close, such as how she felt with Trevor or Stunner, but this was neither of them. It was then she realized, as a clone, Zefram had probably never spooned anyone before, but as a human, it seemed to him the natural thing to do. She sat up on the edge of the bed and stretched. Zefram woke up then and yawned. Novawynd crossed the room to her bag and started brushing her hair.

"Not long now." Zefram stated in reference to arriving in Moav. "I hope he's there, so we can make a short trip of this."

"Oh I don't know. It's kinda like a vacation."

"What's a vacation?" Zefram obviously had never had one.

Novawynd giggled. "It's where you take time off work, go somewhere you've never been, experience things you've never experienced, so your body and mind are replenished and ready to get back to work with a new attitude."

"I see. I suppose this is like that, even though we are working."

Zefram and Novawynd packed up and caught the next bus to Moav. During the ride, they continued chatting. After about two tecrons, Zefram experience something he never had before. For no apparent reason, he developed an erection. He used all his Leluminali training to suppress the fact that he was aroused from Novawynd. He shifted in his chair and crossed his leg, so she wouldn't see. "Not yet. Not yet." he said to himself. He relaxed and the stiffness went away as suddenly as it had come on. That happened three more times during the five tecron journey to Moav.

Moav was quite a large city. Novawynd estimated it was twice as large as New York City, as far as acreage, but there was probably one-quarter the population. The style of the architecture was ancient. There were no buildings over ten stories tall. It wasn't as if they didn't have the technology to build sky-scrapers, they simply didn't have the desire. Novawynd and Zefram hired a taxi-like vehicle to take them to the hotel they determined was closest to Annatippa's manor. They were able to move amongst the Cirrileans without raising suspicion, by using Junatiel. They couldn't take the chance that someone might recognize them.

After settling in their shared room, they took a walk, up four blocks to Annatippa's house. They strolled by slowly. Novawynd did not sense Annatippa was present in the home. "He's not here." she whispered.

"I know." Zefram whispered back.

"Let's head back." She continued on at a quicker pace and Zefram kept up. Novawynd sensed he had been unusually anxious all day. She was eager to get back to the hotel to bathe. Perhaps after she cleaned up, she would delve into what was on his mind.

After Novawynd returned to the room from the bathing chambers down the hall, she found Zefram in bed. His clothes were draped over a chair. Even his under-ware, which meant he was naked. Zefram hadn't gone to bed naked this entire trip. She was then slapped with a psychic pulse from Zefram, so strong it nearly took her breath away. It was as if he was reaching out to her for help. Something was very wrong with him. Novawynd approached him and could see that he was sweaty and seemingly in excruciating pain.

Novawynd thought he might have been poisoned. "What's wrong?" she asked frantically.

"My… Ephilderone… has… worn off" he said in between short breaths, "and I stupidly forgot to pack more."

"Oh Zefram!" Novawynd exclaimed her disappointment, followed by a deep sigh. "Are you in pain?"

"Yes." he shuddered. "Everything that touches my skin causes a sensation and I have an erection that won't go away."

Novawynd looked down and saw the prominence under the thin blanket. "I'll call the Zenith, they can come get us."

"No!" Zefram grabbed Novawynd's wrist. "We can't jeopardize the mission. And, we don't need the Ephilderone when you can help me." He pulled her to his side at the bed. "You have to have sex with me. It's the only way."

Novawynd was aghast, at first, but then she could feel his suffering, and she wanted to make it go away. She dropped her robe and whipped back the covers. Zefram sucked in air as the wind from the blanket's movement licked his skin. Novawynd climbed onto the bed. She knew, in his state, that he wouldn't last long. Because of that, this would not be a prolonged love making session. At that moment, her goal was just to get him off, so they both could find peace again. She sat astride him and gently took his stiffness in her hand. He grimaced and moaned. She began to position herself to slide him inside. He watched her and seemed to move his hands uncertainly, finally resting them on her legs. Novawynd paused and looked Zefram in the eyes. He was at last, completely open to her. She could sense his every emotion at that moment as they swirled around inside him like a cyclone.

Sensing her hesitation, he spoke. "I'm sorry Novawynd. I know this isn't something you want to do, but I thank you for being a kind enough person to do it."

"It's just that…I'm not used to going straight to this." she indicated to his penis. "I usually have some opportunity to get in the mood first. At least a kiss first." she smirked.

"I…want…to kiss you." Zefram meant it. There must be something about the act of kissing that is basically instinctual in the human mating ritual. Even Zefram, who had never kissed a woman before, wanted to taste Novawynd's lips. He had only seen Earth movies where people kissed, and he had an idea of how it should be done. He was ready to have Novawynd teach him.

Novawynd didn't insert Zefram's hardness, instead she leaned over him, pressing her body against his, sandwiching his projectile between them. Zefram moaned in obvious delight as winds of ecstasy blew through his body. Novawynd's face was close to his now. She looked intently into his eyes. He watched her lips and relaxed his. She tilted her head slightly and moved in to meet Zefram's eager, pouty lips. He met her kiss with enthusiasm and he was a surprisingly strong kisser. The joy this mingling caused Zefram was felt by both and Zefram came unexpectedly. The white juices flowed through the gaps between their bellies, seeking paths of least resistance.

Zefram gasped and relaxed. That was easier than Novawynd had expected. She didn't have to take him inside her after all. She pushed herself off Zefram and crossed the room to the wash basin. She wet a towel and brought it back over to the bed. She wiped her stomach off, and then proceeded to wash him as well. As she gently swabbed him down, she started to realize, she was not done. She sensed his immediate arousal at her caresses, and although he wasn't able to get an erection so soon after the last episode, he was intent to work on it.

"Novawynd," he put his hand on hers. "When someone goes off the Ephilderone, he or she goes through a detoxing process, which is a prolonged state of super-arousal that can last several days. We may need to stay here and do this for a while." He sucked air through his teeth and Novawynd glanced down at his cock to see it was growing thick again. It was a nice cock, after all. Back on Earth, she would have given anything to have one night with a man like Zefram, but now, she didn't know how to feel. Something just didn't feel right. He had opened himself to her. She could feel his attraction to her, and possibly even love, in the way only Zefram can love. All of that, she knew was genuine, but she felt there was something false behind it all.

"Come." He pulled her close to him. "Lay by me. I want to feel every inch of your body." Novawynd stretched out along side him and he began to trace her curves very lightly running his finger tips over her skin. This sent an icy tickle down Novawynd's spine and she actually liked the sensation. She looked into Zefram's wide, sage-green eyes and he was so hopeful. She realized she was not looking into the eyes of an android or a monster, but a man with feelings and desires; even though he'd been trained to suppress them. She decided to relax and let go. Finally she was losing herself in the moment. She began to enjoy it.

Zefram sensed her willingness and, this time, he kissed her. His soldier came to stand at full attention in no time. He moved to position himself between her legs as he continued kissing her. She wrapped her legs around him and tilted her hips up to him. Her attitude had completely changed. Now she wanted him inside of her. She needed his strong thighs and butt to strain between her legs, slamming his engorged staff deep into her. She reached down to part her labia, so he could maneuver it in more easily. He pressed up against the mouth of her vulva, and he had to stop. She buried her hands in his thick, ashen-blonde hair. He took deep breaths trying to hold back his welling orgasm. After a moment, with one determined thrust, he pushed it all the way in. It was then he came again, immediately, and to Novawynd's disappointment. It happened so fast, she didn't even get a chance to connect with him and share his orgasm. But, she knew as time progressed, he would hold out longer.

Zefram collapsed on top of Novawynd. He was shuddering. He began to chuckle softly.

"What?" Novawynd was curious.

Zefram rolled off of Novawynd, onto his side, and propped his head up on one hand. He put his other hand on her belly, just above the pubic bone. "I just thought about how I just left something of myself inside you."

Novawynd smirked. "You know. I used to think sperm was gross. Then I realized that a woman can't share her eggs with anyone else, they are her own, but a man can run around, ejaculating his life-creating liquid any where he wants. He can inject it into any hole he wants. I started to feel just a little jealous that I don't have that kind of power. I started thinking about sperm as a miraculous thing, and then I started loving it."

"I think I'll fill you up with my miraculous liquid, then I want to watch you come without me inside you, and when you come, perhaps you will ejaculate too."

"Oh my God!" she gasped. "Zefram, you're such a dirty talker, for someone who's never done this before." She grinned at him as she regarded him. He blushed. Novawynd didn't want to tell him about how a vagina is made to suck fluid toward the uterus, not to squirt it out. She'd heard legends of women that could ejaculate, but figured they were just flexing their diaphragms. That would put pressure on the vagina, squeezing the liquid out. Perhaps some women can make liquids squirt out of their vagina this way, but she doubted it would go very far. Novawynd decided to play along. She hated to dash his hopes, since he was so new to all this stuff and his desire to experiment is adorable. Anyhow, the fun was in the experimentation. "I guess we'd better keep at it then."

Novawynd and Zefram copulated several times over the course of the next few tecrons. After a few more times, Zefram was beginning to hold out longer, and was able to wait longer in-between sessions. Novawynd was then able to share in his climaxes. After going at it for several tecrons, Novawynd became sore and exhausted. "Can't you muster all your strength as a Leluminali to suppress these urges, just long enough for us to get a few tecrons of sleep?" she complained. She couldn't believe he could even have any more semen, with as much as he'd already pumped into her.

"I'll try." he promised. He laid back and began to meditate. Soon, he was asleep. Not long after, Novawynd also passed out from sheer exhaustion. She was awakened some time later by Zefram's kisses on her arm. She sat up, swung her feet over the edge of the bed and stretched as she yawned. Then she caught a whiff of herself. "Whew! Let's go take a bath." she suggested.

They snuck down the hall to steal into one of the public bath rooms. Novawynd prepared the hot water in the shallow tub. It was barely large enough for one person, let alone two, but they would make do. They stood in the tub, facing and as they sluiced each other with soap and wet rags, Zefram had a confession to make. "Novawynd, I didn't forget to take the Ephilderone. I didn't bring the dose on purpose. I knew when it would wear off and I wanted it to."

Novawynd stopped what she was doing and could only stare at Zefram in dismay. His words began to sink in. "You wanted to do this?" was all she could say.

"Yes. Once I realized I was in love with you, I started to wonder about it. What it would be like? I just wanted to experience it, but only with you. Now I think I don't want to go back on the Ephilderone."

"You're joking of course." Novawynd snorted in bewilderment.

"No, I'm not. Seriously, I've enjoyed this so much, I don't think I can go back to being celibate."

"Zefram, I already have my hands full enough with two men as my regular lovers. And now, you tell me you want me to try to accommodate you too."

"No. I think you should give them both up for me." Zefram was quite serious.

Novawynd smirked. "I wonder what the Superior Council would think of that?" she issued a subtle threat.

"I think they'd consider your lack of conditioning more serious than my conditioning's failure." He had her in a corner with that returned threat.

"Zefram, you can't blackmail me into cooperating with you. How can that feel to you if you know I'm doing it against my will?"

"You're doing this against your will? I thought you were really enjoying yourself."

"I was, until now." Novawynd began to pull away. She needed to get away from him right now. It wasn't so bad when she thought it would just be a temporary situation, but now she couldn't imagine having to add him to her bull-pen. What could she do? She couldn't lie to Trevor and Stunner, but she didn't think they would be receptive to sharing her with Zefram. If she chose Zefram, she would loose Stunner and Trevor. If she chose Stunner and Trevor, She would loose everything else anyway; including, possibly her life. Novawynd dried herself off slowly as she thought this through. "I'll have to think about this," She needed to buy herself some time.

Novawynd was almost dressed when Zefram returned to their room. Her sour mood soured his. His Ephilderone cold-turkey episode must have been over, because he wasn't aroused anymore. He actually felt disappointed. Her rejection was hurting him more deeply than he could have ever imagined. But, more importantly, he still had a mission to accomplish. He obviously failed to make her fall in love with him. He had underestimated her. She cared more about a man's depth, than his looks and he just wasn't deep enough, at least, not where she was concerned. They just didn't have enough in common. He could blackmail her into making love to him until he accomplished his goal, but he knew a different angle would be necessary.

Novawynd spoke as he was contemplating all of this. "I'm going back to Annatippa's house to see if he's home yet." she announced.

Zefram dressed quickly, because he was not about to let her go alone. She flew out the door before he was dressed. He picked up the pace and caught up to her just a block away from Annatippa's residence. Together they strolled past his house. They kept an awkward silence. Annatippa was not home. Novawynd turned and quickly headed off to a market a few blocks away, and Zefram followed. "Where are you going?" he insisted.

"I need to get some food. We haven't eaten for a day-and-a-half."

Zefram realized she was right. They did need sustenance after all. They haggled with some of the street vendors for some of the local fruit, bread and preserved meat. They commenced to carry a satchel of goods back to their hotel. At Novawynd's lead, they took a shortcut through an alley. They were approached by two large men and immediately felt the danger, but both Zefram and Novawynd turned, only to be met by two more men, who emerged from the building behind them. Zefram's hand went to his DESS hidden in his cloak. Novawynd put her hand on his wrist to stop him from making a rash decision. 'No' was the message she sent out to him and she shook her head. Then, faster than Zefram could react, Novawynd sent a pulse-wave out. It blasted the four men to the ground, unable to catch their breath. Novawynd ran, still clutching Zefram's wrist. They didn't stop, or look back, until they reached their hotel room door. Panting, more from excitement than from being winded, they fell into each other's arms and began to passionately kiss.

Zefram and Novawynd fumbled with each other as they made their way into the room. They made love again, this time, not because

Zefram needed it, but because they both wanted it. Afterwards, Zefram asked "Novawynd, if you don't love me, how can you do this?" He was referring to their passionate love-making session.

"Love and lust are two different things. You're the most beautiful man I have ever had the pleasure of commingling with. You make me really hot, but there needs to be a deeper connection for it to be love. Besides…why does it matter?"

"I've been around for over a hundred years and I have never loved anyone, until I met you. I want so badly for you to love me back."

Novawynd was touched, although she still suspected Zefram was only in lust with her, not in love. As a clone, he just couldn't know the difference. "Zefram, sometimes a person can start out with lust and grow to love the other person; perhaps if we give it some time."

They ate the food they had acquired at the market. Then they fell asleep. The next morning Novawynd woke with a start. Annatippa had arrived. She was sure of it. She could feel him. Novawynd shook Zefram awake and told him of Annatippa's arrival. They both threw on their clothes and hurried out to rendezvous with the head of the flesh peddlers.

They arrived at the pirate zelo's home just as he was getting out of the cab he took from the space port. Novawynd approached him confidently. "Zelo Jhenya Annatippa?" she queried.

"Yes." He responded curiously.

"You are under arrest for living-being trafficking. You need to come with us, now." Novawynd commanded.

Zelo Annatippa was a quick thinker, having been in many perilous situations before, and he was prepared when he pulled his Quanton particle gun and simultaneously fired it at Novawynd. Novawynd precognized his intention early enough to throw up a shield to block the beam, but it bounced off her shield and hit Zefram in the left, mid-abdomen. He winced and fell to one knee. Zelo Annatippa took advantage of that opportunity, and ran. Novawynd went down on her knees and braced Zefram.

"I'm fine. Go get him!" He yelled.

Novawynd released Zefram, jumped up and sprinted after Annatippa. There was no way he could out-run her. She flitted into semi-flux mode and over-ran him. She stopped just in front of him and drew her DESS. As Annatippa realized the Leluminalia had magically materialized in front of him, he attempted to evade, but Novawynd was already drawing down on him with her DESS. If he wasn't going to come quietly, she had every reason to terminate him right there. The sonic blade of the DESS sliced through his body, liquefying organs as it went. He dropped to his knees, breathless, and then fell over face-first in the dirt street. He had undoubtedly expired. She threw down an orb, which held a 4D message about how she had terminated Annatippa, and she would come for the rest of the pirates responsible for the flesh peddling.

She ran back to where she had left Zefram, hailing the Zenith as she did so. "Zelo Djynk, we need immediate evac." She didn't wait for a response. Zefram was standing, people had surrounded him and he was waving off their attempts at assistance. He was recovering seemingly well, thanks to the quick healing abilities Leluminali possessed. They stayed in their current location, despite the throng of curious onlookers. It didn't matter now. The message had been sent. Within a few mecrons, a shuttle from the Zenith settled in the middle of the street. Novawynd helped Zefram to the shuttle. Once inside, she breathed a sigh of relief. She was as good as home now.

*   *   *

Zefram was admitted to the med-lab. It was just a formality. The medic needed to run some tests on Zefram to make sure everything was healing up fine. Novawynd stayed with him through the procedures. She hadn't realized it at the time, but the wound was substantial. It was worse than Novawynd knew. Zefram, in his perfect Leluminali training, had kept up a good front, but he was wounded gravely, though not mortally. The medic suggested they put him in a state of semi-stasis, so he could sleep through the healing process without pain. Zefram agreed. The medic anesthetized him and as he began to lose consciousness, he pulled Novawynd to him. "You should know... I went off the Ephilderone because the Superior Council ordered me to. They wanted me to learn how to flux from you. They thought if I made love to you, I... could... learn." At that, Zefram lost consciousness.

Novawynd vehemently pulled away from him. She ran out of the med-lab and all the way to her quarters. Once inside, she half-sobbed, half struggled for breath as she was on the verge of hyperventilating. She stumbled to the bathroom, feeling nauseous. She couldn't bring herself to vomit. She paced around in a circle, like a caged tiger. Then she gave Zacharieth a command to make sure no one could access her until she said so. No exceptions. She stripped off her clothes and turned on the shower. She stood, dazed, as the steaming water flowed over her, cleansing her. She scrubbed her skin until she was raw. The water shut off after a while as the ship was programmed to conserve. She stood, shuddering, in the shower stall for a moment before she collapsed. She just about began to cry, but a voice spoke to her, reminding her that she saw this coming. She knew she couldn't trust the Superior Council and she knew she couldn't trust Zefram. But yet, it was Zefram who told her everything. What could his purpose be for betraying the Superior Council's plans?

She picked herself up off the hard, cold shower floor and wrapped herself in a robe. Still, somewhat in a daze, she lay down on her bed and thought things through. Never had she felt so trapped. She didn't want to be there, in her position anymore, but she had no where to go. She wanted to tell Stunner and Trevor, but she was so unsure if that was a good idea. It was enough that she would have to shoulder the burden of that truth, but she didn't think it was fair to ask them to share in the burden. Instead she would meditate, put it behind her and the solution would present itself. She meditated, and then fell into a deep restorative sleep like she hadn't had in dialos.

When she woke up in the morning, she went to meet with the Superior Council to update them on the termination of Zelo Annatippa, as well as other business as usual. They seemed not to be aware of any difference in her demeanor. She left feeling relieved. Just as she was leaving the council chambers, she got an urgent comm from Solin Balinar, the head of the genetics lab on Xaxon 2.

"What is it Balinar?" she was less than enthusiastic.

"We regret that the new scouring virus we were working on for your scouring of Earth has been stolen, along with all the data we needed to create the virus. It would seem your mission in that area will have to be postponed until we can produce more." he reported nervously.

"How long until you can produce more?" Novawynd asked flatly, not at all disappointed.

"Three aera, at least." he swallowed loudly.

"Does anyone have any idea who stole it?"

"We know for a fact that it was Tren Allexicixidou. But, he's no where to be found. He had outside help. We suspect Zefram 1 was behind it."

"Tren?" the same Tren who was her lab tech during her initial processing. He had been given a promotion after that. "Well, just get it done."

She was headed to the battleot control center, where Stunner would be running morning simulations. She needed to see him. She didn't know what she would say to him, but she just thought she would feel some comfort in seeing him again. But, her plans were thwarted when she sensed Zefram approaching from a side hall. She did an about-face and tried to retreat, but he turned the corner and found her. "Novawynd!" he called out to her urgently. She kept walking. He jogged to catch up to her.

"I wanted to talk to you, about what I said when I was going under." She kept walking. "Please stop." he begged.

Novawynd stopped. With her back still to him she hissed, "I don't want to hear what you have to say, but I'm curious as to what lies you can spin to get yourself out of this one."

"I deserve that, but… I didn't get a chance to finish what I wanted to say. I wanted to tell you that I was ordered to do it, but I never wanted to. At first, I couldn't stand the idea of having intercourse with you, but as I got to know you, I really did fall in love with you. It was then my reason for not wanting to do it switched over to…not wanting to hurt you. In the end, I went through with it because I thought I didn't have a choice. I'm telling you this now, because I realized I do have a choice. When you got angry with me on Cirrilea, because I told you I purposely went off Ephilderone, I realized I didn't want things to be this way. I need you as my lover, not as my enemy. He moved closer to Novawynd. She couldn't move back any further, her back was already to the wall.

"But, you're disobeying a direct order from the Superior Council. So, now I have to kill you. I have no choice."

Zefram shrunk back a little. His eyes narrowed as he regarded her. "If you could do it, you already would have." he said as a crooked smile crossed his face.

"I know, and I hate you for it!" She pounded on his chest with her fists. He pulled her to him and held her tight. She struggled against him, she was strong enough psychically to repel him, but she really lacked the fortitude at the moment.

"Novawynd and Zefram? Is everything all right?" Stunner's voice came from behind them. Zefram promptly released Novawynd and stood up straight. She hid her face from Stunner and ran back to her room. Zefram remained standing, glued to the spot.

"Zefram, you too?" Stunner was dismayed. "What about the Ephilderone?" he smirked.

"That's none of your concern." Zefram turned and walked away, opposite the direction in which Novawynd had exited. Stunner stood for a moment, tying to fathom what he had just witnessed, and then he hurried to Novawynd's quarters.

Novawynd allowed him entrance to her unit once he got there. He found her pacing the floor of her living room. "I was coming to tell you about it when he blindsided me. I'm sorry you had to find out that way." she apologized.

"Well," he attempted to be understanding. "I knew I was never going to be your one and only, especially with Trevor in the picture. I accept that. I'm not like an Earth man who expects loyalty and obedience. However, I never in my worst nightmares thought Zefram would be a factor." He walked over to the sofa and sat on the back, resigned. "What does this mean for Zefram? Is his conditioning broken?"

"It's gotten so complicated." Novawynd stopped and looked at Stunner seriously. "I can't answer that question. It's in your best interest not to know. But, I *can* tell you, I don't intend to let Zefram be a *factor* from this point forward."

"Are you going to tell Trevor?"

"I suppose I have to. Where the hell has he been anyway?"

"He's been shadowing Zelo Djynk. He's trying to learn everything he can about being a Zelo and Xaxon military history, etc."

"I'm glad he's taken a real interest in something; as long as it keeps him busy."

"Yeah! I'm glad also. It keeps him out of my way." They both chuckled, having briefly forgotten the Zefram issue. Then Novawynd remembered again and felt sad instantly. She walked over to Stunner and wrapped her arms around him. He returned her embrace and held her, rocking her and stroking her hair. That was all she needed.

*   *   *

In the unit next door, Trevor watched the 4D display of ancient space battles as Zacharieth explained the strategies which were employed to win the battles. He was aware that Novawynd had returned, but he was actually so engrossed in his new interest, he didn't care to go to her. Besides, she hadn't exactly come to him. In a way, he wanted to hold out until she did come to him. He made bets with himself as to how long it would take her.

Trevor's door chimed. It was both Novawynd and Stunner. He was happy Novawynd had come, but not happy that Stunner had also come. He wasn't really in the mood for a threesome. None-the-less, he allowed them in.

"Trevor." Novawynd's voice was serious. Trevor's hackles rose when he anticipated the bad news he was sure would come next.

"Sorry I didn't come over sooner Novie. I just got caught up in this."

"No problem. I just came over to tell you something important, so can you pause that for the moment?"

Trevor paused the action and gave her his attention. "What's up? Are you two getting married?" he was joking, but he half expected that to be the news. Novawynd and Stunner joined him in sitting.

"No." Novawynd responded, obviously not amused. "I need to tell you that while Zefram and I were on our mission, he missed his dose of Ephilderone, and…well…"

Trevor jumped up "God! No!" He wiped his face with one of his hands, in exasperation. "Not him. Anyone but him."

"Yeah. That's how I feel about it too. That's not the worst part." She paused and gauged his reaction. He put his hands on his hips and looked up at the ceiling. "Now that he's discovered the joy of sex, he won't go back on the Ephilderone. But, he just wants to have sex with me, and I won't have him. So, things have gotten dicey." Novawynd folded her hands and put them up to her lips. Trevor could see how worried she was at that moment and realized he had been very selfish.

"He isn't going to have you scrapped, is he?" Trevor sat down again, right next to her and put his hand on the back of the sofa, behind her. He didn't even realize this action gave Novawynd the subconscious cue that he was concerned and protective of her.

"I believe Zefram and I have an understanding, but I don't know what might happen." Novawynd sounded uncertain.

"He's not blackmailing you into having sex with him, is he?" Trevor was very serious then.

"Not yet, but let's hope he doesn't."

"Wait a minute. How could he even? Does he have something on you?" Trevor practically interrogated Novawynd. "You know, come to think of it, he was asking me all kinds of questions about the Earthling 'courting' habits. Could he have been planning this?" Novawynd looked at him sternly and moved her fingers across her lips in a zipper motion, and then pointed to her left ear. This was the indication that she couldn't say anymore because the information could be extracted from their CIs. The questions Trevor had just asked would have to go unanswered. Although disappointed, Trevor nodded in understanding anyway.

"Things will go back to business as usual. We will attempt to maintain our professional relationship. And, I expect you two to treat Zefram as if you didn't know about this." She looked at them both searchingly. They avoided her gaze. "Speaking of business, if you two will excuse me," Novawynd stood up, "I'm already late in getting to my morning business. Also, I don't want to be disturbed for a while. I really need some time to pat myself free of the dust before I can get back into the saddle again, if you know what I mean." Trevor understood.

"I don't understand that metaphor." Stunner commented. "But, I understand that you need some time."

"We will be having a short respite at XR234. It's a colonial refueling station. It won't take us that long to refuel, but we will spend a dialo there. The space guard will have an opportunity to unwind a bit, and so will you guys. Trevor, you may find a diversion for yourself." Novawynd insinuated, and then excused herself. After she left the unit, Trevor turned to Stunner. "Can we kill Zefram if we catch him off guard? You know, sneak up on him?"

"I doubt it. Novawynd is the only one who can take Zefram out. This will have to be between those two. I'm sure Novawynd will prevail. I have complete faith in her abilities." Stunner seemed so sure. Trevor realized Stunner was probably right.

CHAPTER 12

The Zenith had pulled into the colonial space-port. All the space guard would get a chance to take leave within the full dialo the Zenith would be at port. The aleph squad would go first while bet squad stayed aboard the Zenith on-duty. Cef squad slept until it was their turn to go on-duty, while bet squad took leave and aleph squad slept, etc. Even Zelo Djynk would take leave and Sub-zelo Kananga would be in command of the ship for that time. Stunner would get to take leave for the first shift, but would be back on the ship and on official duty for the rest of the time. As always, Novawynd and Zefram were free to come and go as they felt necessary.

Trevor was excited to have another opportunity to see more alien life forms, but he was hoping for some specifically of the female persuasion and preferably some who actually weren't prohibited by Ephilderone. As it turned out, Earth's oldest profession was also the universe's oldest profession and Trevor had been told there were females of all species at these space-ports that rented their reproductive organs out to whatever male of whatever species would pay the price. These females made an extravagant living on the space-stations, and the practice was not only legal, but deemed necessary.

Stunner took Trevor to the sex district, as it was blatantly called. And why not; that's what it was. Stunner thought he'd be safe there, but as it turned out, there were Eron prostitutes also. There was a whole avenue of Eron prostitutes that were just standing in front of "mating pods". Mating pods were the small rooms reserved for when the urge should strike an Eron male. They were as readily available on Eron as rest-rooms were on Earth. It wasn't as if an Eron male had to pay for sex. An Eron female never refused an Eron male if he was compelled to breed her, but here the women merely took advantage of the fact that Erons were numerous in the universe, and any that traveled through this thoroughfare, might be so compelled. Therefore, the lucky girl who had the right pheromones when an Eron male wandered into their midst, earned her money that night.

"Hey Stunner!" Trevor had to yell to him over the din of the men cavorting in the lane.

"Yeah?" Stunner acknowledged.

"Do Eron women have sex with non-Eron men?"

"Yes. In places like this they do. But…" He laughed. "You wouldn't get much pleasure from one. You would get lost inside one."

"Thanks!" Trevor was being sarcastic. Just then, Stunner stopped. He looked directly at a woman about ten paces away. Her skin was grape colored and hair and eyes seemed to match.

"Stay here." Stunner commanded Trevor, and then headed straight over to the Eron woman. She smiled at him and he put his arm around her shoulder and guided her into the mating pod. Trevor stood bewildered. Stunner was getting laid already, and they had only arrived. Trevor loitered uneasily. Some of the avenues they had meandered had women that came up to Trevor asking if he had ever been with whatever type of alien they had been. He had a hard time finding any of them attractive enough to go for it. It was just such a surreal experience. Here, however, the women let the men come to them.

Soon, Stunner emerged from the mating pod fastening his pants. Trevor had to laugh, that was too quick. "My god, you're fast!" he teased.

"I'm Eron... I don't need to take my time." Stunner shrugged. "Come on. Let's find you someone."

Had Novawynd been under different circumstances, she might have taken advantage of some of the male companionship to be had at the station. Instead, she hung out with Zelo Djynk and the Squad Aleph space-guard, because they were not in the market for the sex form of entertainment. They just wanted to play games and gamble. She had been watching a heated levi-ball game. Levi-ball was a game in which two people would sit at opposite ends of a long table. The table had magnetic forces that a player would manipulate with the controls at his end of the table. There was a line drawn about an arm's length in front of each person. The two players used their controls to lift, hold and push the ball at their opponent. The object was to get the ball across the line in front of one's opponent. This was hugely popular and some people made a living playing it. Those watching bet on who would win.

After her player won, and she collected her money, she excused herself to find a restroom. As she was relieving herself, she sensed a distant presence. She hadn't felt it in over four aera, but she recognized it as the Talosian that she had faced on Vilijia. His presence was getting nearer. He was on the station at that moment. She strained to finish, sanitized her hands and hurriedly left the rest room. She wanted to find the Talosian, so she headed down the hallway that lead out to the back alley. As she stepped out the door, she ran into a tall man wearing a cape with a hood. It was, in fact, the Talosian. His orange eyes flashed under his hood.

"Ahh! Your Supremacy, I came to find you." He kneeled in front of her. "I have some important information for you." He said quickly as he stood up again.

"I'm glad you're here. I have so many questions." she blurted out.

"I know, but I can't answer here and now. There is a more pressing issue you will need to deal with. Some day, I can answer all your questions." He handed her yet another manuscript. "Read this as soon as you can. The good of your home-world depends on it." He bowed again and turned on his heel. He left quickly, his cape billowing out behind him left a powerful impression in her mind. Novawynd wanted to yell at him to stop, but could not utter words, as if a spell had been cast on her to freeze until he had gone. Without doubt, he had used Junatiel on her, his abilities so powerful, he was able to affect her without her even knowing it.

After his presence had diminished completely, Novawynd could move again. She looked at the pages she was clutching and tucked them under her jacket. Holding them against her chest, as if they were precious, she ran back to the ship.

*   *   *

After a couple tecrons, Trevor still had not discovered an alien female he could do the deed with. In that time, Stunner had two Eron females. After the second, he quickly ushered Trevor out of that area to get away from the Erons. He had had enough. They turned a corner and Stunner froze. "Uh…you go ahead. I'll meet you at the end of the next street over."

"What's the matter?" Trevor had never seen Stunner like this.

"This is where the Cornithons hang out. I don't ever go where I'm outnumbered by Cornithons." Stunner informed. Then he pushed Trevor into the lane. As Trevor turned back, Stunner was already gone. Trevor was about to turn and follow Stunner. If Stunner didn't like Cornithons, he didn't need to hang out here. But, someone grabbed his arm from behind and spun him around. It was a Cornithon woman with violet skin, black hair and red cat-eyes.

"What's a Xaxon doing in a place like this?" she asked sweetly. Trevor's handle of the Xaxon language was improved, but not perfect and he felt he had to pick his words carefully here.

"I'm not a Xaxon. I'm an Earthling." Was the only thing he could think to say.

"Are you nature born?" she seemed to be dismayed.

"Yes." he affirmed in a cautious tone.

"Me too. Are you Ephilderone free?"

"Yes."

"And so you are here looking for a little relief." she supposed.

"Yes."

"Have you found any yet?"

"No. Not yet."

"You're so pretty, for a nature born. Are all men from your planet as pretty?"

Trevor was a bit put-down by the term "pretty", but he realized their words didn't necessarily translate the same way, and it was a compliment after all.

"Unfortunately not. I'm probably one of the prettier ones." He smiled.

"I've never heard of Earthling. Are there many of you out here?" She was leading him slowly back to her lair.

"No, there are actually only two. Myself and Novawynd."

She flinched. "That's right, Earth. I have heard of Earth. And of course, who hasn't heard of Novawynd. Do you know Novawynd?

"Of course. I'm her… good friend."

"Hmmm. I would like to experience an Earthling man." she informed. Then she whispered "Since you're so rare, and since you are Novawynd's special friend, I would even waive the fee."

Now that was something that interested Trevor. "Okay." he agreed and she rushed him into her place.

Trevor was nervous about what exactly was going to happen. How did Cornithon women have sex, exactly? She was dominating and guided him to an oversized, overstuffed cushion on the floor, piled with pillows. She directed him to lay back and she proceeded to undo his pants. Quickly, she began to suckle his semi-erect penis. It felt as good to Trevor as any woman, but he was fascinated by his hardness sliding in and out of her violet lips. He was thrilled by the flicking of her purple tongue on his throbbing tip.

Once she had gotten him thoroughly hardened and moist, she straddled him and he slipped in easily. Cornithons had physical builds like Erons, but the Cornithon males did not have two penises. None-the-less, Cornithon females were built to accommodate much larger male organs, and Trevor could feel it, but it still was good. She was tight enough and her juices tingled like he had remembered Stunner's had inside Novawynd. That feeling alone was almost enough to make Trevor come, but he didn't.

The prostitute's red eyes sort of unnerved him, so Trevor asked if he could take her from behind. She obliged and got on her hands and knees. He plunged into her from behind and delighted at the view of his cock tearing into her glistening purple vulva. In this position, he was able to come. It was a relief, but in that moment he realized how extraordinary sex with Novawynd was. When he was with Novawynd, he felt at one with her. Nothing could compare to that.

As Trevor was putting his pants back on, he felt a blazing hot pain in the back of his head. His hand instinctively went up to the point of the pain. He turned with a grimace and saw a dark blue Cornithon man, with white hair and yellow eyes, standing over him as he lost consciousness.

*   *   *

Novawynd had just returned to her unit and put the report, or whatever it was, down on her dining table when she sensed Trevor's distress. She saw through his eyes, the Cornithon man that accosted him. She shook her head. She had never had that happen to her before; seeing something thorough someone else's eyes. "Zacharieth, patch me into the zelos, Stunner, Zefram and all the space-guard on the station." she urgently commanded as she ran out her door.

"You are connected." the computer affirmed.

"All space-guard, attention! This is Novawynd. I need your immediate response. I need aleph squad to split into two teams. I need one team to cover the quadrant sec ports and the second team to cover the quadrant teo ports. Bet squad also, split up into two teams. One team covers quadrant uae and team two covers quadrant veta. I need squad cef to wake up. I need half of squad cef to cover shuttle-bay wan and half of you cover shuttle-bay xan. All teams make sure no Cornithons board their ships. Sub-zelo Kananga, you're in charge of the Zenith. Make sure no ships leave the station. Intin Stunner, Zelo Djynk, and Zefram, meet me at the Zenith's port. Something has happened to Trevor. Keep your eyes peeled. I'm out." she ended the comm. She was nearly to the port when Zefram caught up with her.

"I felt it. What happened." he inquired. She was too concerned about Trevor to be mad at Zefram at this moment. He followed her as she jogged along.

"Someone attacked Trevor. I think it was a flesh-peddling pirate, a Cornithon by the name of Tion Ex Glaberon."

"How do you know that?" he asked in disbelief.

Novawynd entered the docking umbilical. "I caught a glimpse of him through Trevor's eyes as he was attacked and I recognized him."

Zefram smirked, amazed again by Novawynd's evolving abilities.

Stunner blipped into Novawynd's CI. "I was just with Trevor. He's on the next street over, in Cornithon territory. I can go in and get him." Novawynd sensed the desperation in his voice. He obviously left Trevor alone with the Cornithons and felt responsible.

"No Stunner! I won't have you leaping into the lion's den on your own. You need to retreat and meet me here at the port. We'll deal with it from here." she instructed as the squad cef space-guard ran past her and Zefram hastening to their posts.

"I'll be there in two zecrons." Stunner acknowledged.

Novawynd and Zefram stepped out of the port and Zelo Djynk was approaching with two space-guards. Stunner came around the corner at a full-run, and slowed as he neared them.

"Alright," Novawynd started as they all came to attention, "they've probably already gotten word that we're mobilizing and they won't get out. So, they'll do one of two things. Take Trevor and lay low, or they'll dump him somewhere and lay low. If they don't know we're mobilizing, they'll move him." she paused. "However, I do sense that he's moving, so they opted to take him. That's unfortunate."

"What do you want us to do?" Stunner asked.

Novawynd's eyes were closed. She was homing in on where she felt Trevor. "They are moving toward shuttle-bay wan. Zacarieth, patch me through to the space-guard."

"You are connected." the computer's voice sounded in her ear.

"Space-guard, attention! The Cornithons are moving toward shuttle-bay wan. Squad cef, team one prepare. I need one other space-guard from each other team to move toward shuttle-bay wan as well, but keep a leisurely pace. I'm looking to have you close in on them from behind. You are looking for a dark-blue Cornithon man with medium-length white hair and yellow eyes. He will be accompanied by others and they will not have Trevor in plain sight. He will be in a container of some sort. Keep your eyes open for Cornithons moving large containers in the direction of shuttle-bay wan. Keep your distance. However, squad cef, if the Cornithons enter the shuttle-bay, you need to stop them to inspect their containers. Be assured that back-up is on the way." She looked at all the others who were anxiously watching her. "Okay. I want Zefram and the Djynk to come with me. Stunner, stay here with your men. You two men, Leveler and Rush, come with me also. Zacharieth, keep the comms open."

"All CI's are open for free transmission." Zacharieth confirmed.

"We have free comm, so that means silence everybody, unless it's business."

Novawynd didn't know why Stunner left Trevor alone with Cornithons, but she didn't have time to find out. Instead she punished him by making him hang around waiting for some action, instead of accompanying her to where the action surely would be. It would serve him right if he saw no action at all.

"Okay," the leader of the Squad Cef, team one, who's name was Zoomer, blipped in their ears, "the Cornithons have entered the shuttle-bay. We are going to commence with search." Novawynd, Zefram and Djynk quickened their pace.

"Hey there." everyone heard the Zoomer's voice speaking flawless Cornithon. He was obviously speaking to the Cornithons. "We apologize for bothering you, but we have to detain you for a moment. We have information that slave traders may be moving contraband in and out of this station and we've been instructed to search all containers. So, if you'll just open your containers for us, we'll take a look."

Faintly in the background everyone could hear, "This is outrageous! You're singling us out because we're Cornithons. See that ship, it's a Cornithon ambassadorial ship; my ship. I assure you I am no pirate."

"We're searching everyone, not just Cornithons. But, if we did single you out, you would have your brothers who are pirates to blame for giving you a bad reputation. And, if you are truly not a pirate, then when we search your containers, everything should check out and you can quickly be on your way."

Novawynd cringed when she heard this. Zoomer's response was a little too cocky and might just incense the ambassador, or whatever he was. She, Zefram and Djynk met up with the other five space-guards who were waiting outside the shuttle-bay, keeping anyone else from entering. Then, suddenly they heard what seemed like a scuffle over their CIs; men's and women's voices yelling,

"Zoomer!"

"Look out!"

"Take cover!"

"We are under attack, need back up."

Novawynd waved them into motion and the group waiting outside entered the shuttle-bay. The Cornithons had drawn their swords and it was well known that they were skilled enough to deflect axon beams with their blades. Novawynd saw Zoomer lying on the floor, decapitated. A Cornithon had gotten the drop on him. The Cornithons stood with their backs to each other, swords held in defensive shielding stance. The space-guard had taken cover. At this point, it would be impossible to get an axon shot off. They could only do damage with a more powerful Quanton gun or a DESS.

The Cornithons had left their contraband unguarded. When they saw Novawynd and Zefram, fear seeped into their hearts. Novawynd went straight to the container in which Trevor was stowed. She used her metaband to detect whether or not the lock was booby-trapped. There was nothing unusual about the lock. She kicked the lock open and dumped Trevor out. He was bound and gagged, but conscious and unharmed. "Well, Tion Ex Glaberon," she stood up and slowly sauntered over to the man known by that name. She kept a safe distance; however, "it would seem you are a pirate after all. Therefore, I have justification to terminate you immediately."

"Hah!" He threw his head up triumphantly guffawing. "I'd like to see you try, Lelumin koopak." A koopak was a Cornithon dog, but it was much more of a creature of burden than any dog ever was. Calling someone a koopak was a horrible insult amongst Cornithons, but it just made Novawynd smile, because koopak was kind of a silly word anyway.

"Okay." Novawynd obliged. She used her kinetic abilities to rip their swords from their hands. In a flash, too fast to react, the swords returned to their owners, blades first. The Cornithons found themselves impaled by their own weapons before they could react. The swords had penetrated their abdomens, cutting clean through their descending aortas, with the exception of Tion Ex Glaberon. His blade narrowly missed his aorta. Glaberon's entourage stared at Novawynd in disbelief through their glazing eyes. Glaberon pulled his sword out of his abdomen and charged at Novawynd with a howl. However, he had lost more stamina than he thought. His strength ebbed from him and the tip of his sword dropped to the ground just in front of Novawynd. She used the sword as a springboard, launching off it into a backwards flip and kicking him in the chin. His head snapped backwards and he flew back with a pain-induced groan. When Novawynd recovered her stance, she found him lying flat on his back. She picked up his sword, swirled it around deftly in her hand, gripped the hilt with both hands and brought it down where his neck met his chin. His head detached from his body. "That's for Zoomer!" Novawynd announced.

Novawynd looked around at this point and saw the mixture of fear and amazement on the faces of those who were watching. She didn't need to use her empathic abilities to read that. Even Zefram seemed to be concerned. Novawynd dropped the sword and walked past her comrades, out the door. "Come on." She ordered as she left the shuttle-bay. A handful of station police were arriving at that moment. "Sorry about the mess," she addressed the police, "but I have strict orders to take out all the slave traders in the universe. I just had to scrap a few more. Please deliver the space-guard's body to the Zenith." The police nodded and their lead began shouting orders to get things cleaned up.

"Attention all Zenith crew-members, the situation has been resolved. In addition, the first shift is now over. You can stand down, but those you on the bet squad who will be taking leave, make sure you never go anywhere alone. Remember, 'safety in numbers'. Zacarieth, close free comm and end transmission." Novawynd headed back to the Zenith with Zefram, Djynk, Trevor and the space-guard from the aleph and cef squads tailing behind. She did not look back. As they approached the Zenith, Stunner was waiting by the port.

"Thank the enti!" Stunner expressed his relief. "Trevor, I'm sorry. I was just having fun with you. I didn't think you'd stay there. That was really a stupid decision on my part, to put you in that situation."

Trevor seemed more chagrinned than angry. "Don't mention it. I tried to leave, but got waylaid by a woman. I should have left anyway, but decided to stay. The stupid decision was really mine."

Novawynd watched this interaction with interest. There was her explanation. For the sake of both men's pride, she decided not to press it. "Isn't that special?" she teased. "Why don't you two hug and make up." she said glibly. Trevor and Stunner shot her a look like "Are you serious?" and she felt that question behind their expression. She just crinkled up her face like "No, I'm not serious." Then she looked around and realized the only people still present were Stunner, Trevor and Zefram. The three men she was involved in a love-triangle with. Or, more like, a love-polygonal. She could feel the awkwardness and tension between the four of them. That was weird to Novawynd, but she couldn't let her personal feelings get in the way of the business she needed to attend to.

Novawynd spoke again, "Trevor, we've lost someone today, one of our beloved space-guard. Because of that, I'm giving you the position of honorary space-guard. You will have to fill Zoomer's position, which means you will have to follow the cef squad's schedule. You sleep when they sleep. You're on duty when they're on duty. You have free-time when they do. You're not a military person, so you don't have to sleep in their dorm or wear a uniform, but you do have to take orders from Stunner when you're on-duty. Stunner knows what he's doing and failure on your part to do as he says can be detrimental to the team. Also, it's a sure way to get me to remove you from this honorary position. Don't forget to refer to Stunner as Intin Stunner from now on." She paused and looked sternly at Trevor waiting for affirmation.

"Okay. I got it. I'm really sorry about Zoomer. I'll do my best, for his sake."

"All that being said, let's get back to the ship." Novawynd suggested. "I feel like we aren't out of the woods yet. The Cornithons on Glaberon's ship may choose to take action. If so, we'll have to prepare to defend the Zenith, possibly the whole station."

They started up the umbilical to the ship. Novawynd knew they were in a precarious position. If they were to try to leave, they would need to detach and move away from the station in auxiliary power, which was a slow process. While they were at port, they might be sitting ducks, but if they moved away from the port, they were still sitting ducks until they could flux.

"Novawynd?" Zefram cut in. "Don't you think we should recall our teams and leave?"

"I'm not afraid of the Cornithons, and I hope the fact that I'm going back to business as usual will show them that. Perhaps they'll turn tail and run. Besides, they're less likely to attack us while we're docked. Granted, they may just wait until we try to leave, so I intend to allow all our people to get their rest and recreation first."

It would seem that the Cornithons did not want to wait until the Zenith left port to strike. The umbilical shook violently, nearly throwing the foursome down. Everyone grasped at whatever they could to hold themselves up.

"You're on duty now Trevor. We need to get to the battleot center ASAP." Stunner commanded. They ran the rest of the way up the umbilical and out of sight. Zefram and Novawynd quickened their pace, but neither was too concerned. That was a warning shot. The Cornithons knew full well that a fully armored Xaxon battleship would not succumb to such blasts.

"Novawynd?" Zelo Djynk's voice blipped in her head. "The station wants us to disembark."

"Tell them I said 'no'. We'll have the situation under control shortly." She ordered.

"Very well. End." he acknowledged. She and Zefram made their way to the CC, where they joined Zelo Djynk. They watched as the cef squad took their places at their controls, the empty position filled by Trevor. The Leluminali and the commanding officers watched as the Cornithon ship pulled up next to the Zenith, blocking any exit they may have had.

"I was wondering why you didn't immediately go after their ship." Djynk smirked. "Now I realize you knew they would take this action all along, didn't you?" Novawynd and Zefram looked at the zelo in wonderment. That was the most they had ever heard Djynk say at one time.

"Damn fools." Novawynd scoffed. "Cornithons are so caught up in pride, honor and glory, that they will always make the most deadly decision. They know it's certain death, and they do it anyway. They just don't care. There's so many of them, and so little room for them all, it's almost like they do it as a means to population control or something."

Zefram chuckled at the truth of her comment.

"Go ahead Zelo Djynk. Do whatever you have to do." Novawynd gave him permission to command.

"Intin Stunner? Disable their ship." Djynk gave the order.

"Yes zelo." Stunner responded.

They watched as the battleots shot from their pods and surrounded the Cornithon ship. The Zenith's sentry robots emerged and took their positions on the hull of the Zenith. The battleots from the Cornithon ship flew out of their pods and headed straight for the Zenith. Half of the Zenith's battleots pursued the Cornithon battleots. The other half went about trying to penetrate the hull of the Cornithon ship. Between the sentries and the battleots, the Cornithon's battleots were dispatched quickly, and the Cornithon ship began to maneuver away. The Zenith's battleots continued to penetrate the enemy's hull even after the ship began to retreat. One battleot had just succeeded in getting through the outer hull, but Stunner gave the order to recall the battleots. They abandoned their target and even the lone battleot that had breached the hull, came flying out of the hole it had created just as the Cornithon ship initiated its flux.

A collective cheer went up from the space-guard, but Novawynd was only perplexed. Why had the Cornithons retreated? They never retreat once they engage. Perhaps there were no more Cornithons left on the ship. Novawynd would never know for sure now. She left the CC and proceeded to the battleot command center. Everyone was pouring out, reveling in their victory. It wasn't much of a victory, but they saw so little action, Novawynd understood their exaltation. Then Trevor emerged and a fellow Space-guard was slapping him on the back, giving him kudos. She was glad then that they were accepting of his replacing Zoomer.

"Novie!" Trevor exclaimed. He was high on adrenaline. He hugged her and swung her around. "Did you see me? I was awesome!"

"Well, I can't tell who's who when you're all out there, but you were all awesome, so it goes without saying. You did good."

Stunner remained in the command center backing up data, reviewing each space-guard's actions, and making comments on what was wrong and how it should be handled differently in the future. He also pointed out in what ways were handled very well. All battles, simulated or real were followed-up on this way. The constructive criticism helped the space-guard perform better each time. Novawynd went to speak to Stunner, Trevor followed.

Stunner spoke before Novawynd could. "Trevor did very well." he assured, not that Novawynd was looking for that assurance.

"The team did very well, considering their loss. But, then again, I never had a doubt. You are the best intin there is."

"Oh brother!" Trevor groaned. "I'm out of here. You two have fun."

Stunner and Novawynd looked at each other. "I have to finish my work here Novawynd." he seemed apologetic.

"Sure. If you'll excuse me, I'm going back to my unit." she informed "I could use some rest myself."

*   *   *

Back in her unit Novawynd saw the report the Talosian had given her sitting on the table where she had left it. With all the commotion of the day, she had forgotten about it. She was exhausted, but she couldn't help it, she had to read it. The first line read "As I'm sure you've already concluded, the man who delivered this report to you, as well as the last, is none other than Lord Danalian, Commander in Chief of the Planet Talos. That man is me." Novawynd nodded in satisfaction that her suspicion was confirmed.

> "I have come across some very important information that affects the welfare of the Earthling race. You were asked to perform a scouring of Earth to cleanse it of Terran genetics. This procedure meant nothing to you, since you have done it before and everything seemed to come out as expected. However, this new strain the Xaxon geneticists were working on was not just a strain to destroy a greatly mutated Terran gene, but to destroy all human life on Earth. The Superior Council intends to wipe out any chance that another Lajiachine could potentially emerge from Earth again. By restructuring the virus, if all life on Earth ceased as a result of the cleansing, they could just say the virus cleansed all the Terran

tampering and everyone would accept that, because no one likes the Terrans. Also, how you react after you learned that the virus killed everyone on Earth, would determine your loyalty to the Superior Council.

The Superior Council gave Zefram the specific secret mission to instruct the geneticists to produce the new virus. He carried out his orders and the virus was being developed. However, it would seem you had a friend in the genetics lab. Tren was involved in the development of the virus. Just as they were about to complete the effective virus, Tren got in contact with people I have on the inside who work to get people out. They contacted me about what was being done. I, in turn, instructed Tren to trash all the information, samples and product. He did so and we helped him to escape. They have suffered a great set-back, but they will re-develop the virus and the virus will definitely be unleashed on Earth eventually. I have no one else inside who can hinder the production of this virus and you can't stop it. If you try to stop it or if you don't perform the scouring, you will be scrapped and someone else, probably Zefram, will do it."

Novawynd stopped there for a moment. She realized she was so furious that she was mangling the edges of the pages by gripping them so tight, her finger-nails tearing into paper. She fought the urge to hyperventilate. Once she has collected herself, she continued.

"Your options at this point are few, but you have options. Right now, I suggest you defect. Your chance to stop this is better if you work from the outside. Your days are numbered if you stay with the Xaxony, knowing what you now know. If you decide to defect, and I hope you do, reach out to me in the Omniaural

and I'll pick you up at the XR234 station. Feel free to bring along whomever you can trust. Then you can begin to fulfill your destiny as the true Lajiachine."

Here the report ended. Novawynd didn't like his last sentence. It would seem fate was forcing her to fulfill the prophesy. She seemed to have no choice. She had been between a rock and a hard place for some time, she continued on in her position, because she didn't think she had anywhere else to go. Now the hand of friendship had been extended to pull her out of the mire she had found herself in. She would gladly take the assistance.

Novawynd got up and went to her closet. She opened the door to find Bianca hibernating. She picked up Bianca's hand and Bianca snapped to life. "Yes Novawynd? Can I be of assistance?" She stepped forward out of the closet.

"Yes Bianca. I have a very important mission for you to carry out." Novawynd put one of her uniforms on the bed. "Change into that. You need to be me for a little while."

"Good." Bianca acknowledged as she stripped and re-dressed in the Leluminali uniform. Novawynd used this moment to meditate, reaching out to Danalian, sending him an affirmative message. He connected with her and responded favorably. They cut off their communication and Novawynd turned to Bianca who was dressed and standing at attention. Her likeness impressed even Novawynd.

"Bianca, you are now Novawynd. I need you to pretend you are me. I need to leave to go on a secret mission. No one should know I'm gone. Wait here until I get back."

"Yes Novawynd."

*   *   *

Novawynd managed to leave the Zenith without any crew-members seeing her. Her mission was to find a weapons dealer. There was always one on every station. She found what she was looking for in a non-descript shack, discretely tucked away in a back alley. She entered the shack and a man, a Napojan of course, weapons experts that they were, scrutinized her from behind his counter.

"I need a fifty-five MJ Quanton bomb with a remote detonator." she blurted out.

"Well, well, the illustrious Novawynd in my little shop. This is a rare pleasure." He approached her. "I'm Vertigo." He offered her his hand for shaking, but she didn't take it.

"I'm sorry, I don't have time to make your acquaintance. I'm in a bit of a hurry." she insisted..

"Why do you need my Quanton bombs? Don't you have a supply of those on your ship?" he pried.

Novawynd was getting impatient. She used her Junatiel powers on him. "It shouldn't matter why I need your product as long as I'm paying you for it."

"Oh yeah, I should tell you…" he leaned in, "I'm one of those rare people that aren't susceptible to Junatiel." He grinned at her. "It's part of why I do so well as a business man. I can't be taken advantage of by every Leluminali who talks sweet to me. Besides, your money is no good here. You see, I understand you recently lost a space-guard. I used to be a space-guard a long time ago. I retired, but now I'd like to get out of this hole. I sure would like to get back into the action. I'll give you the bomb if you get me in as the replacement."

Novawynd thought about it. If she told him he could come aboard, it wouldn't matter, because she would be gone and the Zenith's crew would have to deal with him. But, then again, she needed to start thinking about making friends outside the Xaxony and he had valuable skills. Her intuition told her he was shrewd and skilled, but more over, he was a good man. His was the old story of a man who was in the action for so long, he wanted nothing but to get away from it. Once he got away from it, he was relieved and content, but after so long, he grew bored with contentment, and wanted nothing more than to get back into heat of things. Perhaps he could be useful to her.

"Zacharieth?" she blipped the computer.

"Yes?" came the answer in her CI.

"Do we have Napojan snitch by the name of Vertigo?"

"One moment…searching…no."

"Thank you Zacharieth. End." Novawynd turned her attention back to Vertigo. "Okay Vertigo, I can't get you on the Zenith. Besides, you wouldn't want to be there. However, if you want to get out of here, I can arrange that. Once I leave here, go to the shuttle-bay zeta. Go to the Talosian ship and tell them you were sent by Novawynd. Do everything they say."

"Sounds intriguing, but I don't have any idea what you're asking me to do, so I kinda feel like I can't give you this bomb without some sort of monetary compensation after all. I might need to buy myself out of a sticky situation."

Novawynd slapped the gambling chips she had won at the levi-ball table down on his counter. It was more than what he would have asked, but she didn't need it.

"Okay." he laughed, and then turned to fetch the bomb. He brought back a device about the size of a cereal box and handed it over. She took the device. "This will work right?" she searched his face for signs of falseness.

He looked her straight in the face, "Absolutely." he assured with one-hundred-percent confidence. With that she put it into her bag and ran back to the ship.

*   *   *

Stunner had finished his work and headed over to Novawynd's unit. He hit the door chime button and there was no response.

"Zacharieth? Blip Novawynd for me."

"You are connected." Zacharieth confirmed.

"Novawynd?"

"Yes, Stunner?"

"Where are you? I thought you were home."

"I'll be right there. Go inside and make yourself at home."

The door to her unit opened and he saw Novawynd standing in her bedroom. "Novawynd, what are you doing? I thought you weren't home." He laughed nervously, because he didn't know what she was up to.

"I'm not doing anything, Stunner. Welcome." she responded. That was an odd response from Novawynd.

"What's wrong with you? Are you feeling alright?" He moved closer to her.

"I'm fine." she claimed, but wouldn't move. Suddenly the door to her unit opened again and the real Novawynd walked in. Stunner saw her and immediately realized he had been talking to Bianca.

Novawynd moved swiftly to Bianca, pulled up her shirt a little and strapped a bag onto her, with the pack in the back. She pulled the AP's shirt down over the pack and made sure the jacket covered it. Bianca accepted this readily.

"I'm glad you're here Stunner. I have to go meet some important people and I need you and Trevor to back me up. Zacharieth, please blip Trevor for me."

"Yes, Novawynd, you are connected."

"Trevor, what are you doing right now?" she heard voices in the background. It seemed like a party going on.

"I'm at my official space-guard nick-naming party." he responded jovially.

"Well, sorry man to ruin your fun, but I need you to get to my unit right away."

"No worries. What you've got planned is way more fun, I'm sure."

"Just hurry. End" Novawynd got a bag and threw a couple of reams of paper, with something written on it, into the bag. "Alright." she exhaled deeply.

"Who are we meeting and why do you need Trevor? Wouldn't Zefram be a better option?" Stunner was confused.

"No. I want Trevor to come, because I want Trevor to come. Don't ask anymore questions. I can't tell you anything yet."

Zacharieth announced Trevor was at the door. "Let him in." Novawynd gave permission.

"Okay you two, I need you to come with me." she said referring to Stunner and Trevor. "You…" she referred to Bianca, "wait here until I give you your orders."

"Okay." Bianca affirmed.

Novawynd, Trevor and Stunner left the ship. "What is this all about?"

Trevor was inquisitive.

"I'm going to meet some people and you guys are going along as my body-guards." Novawynd lied.

"Oh. What kind of trouble have you gotten into this time, and how'd you do it so fast?" Trevor teased.

"I'm not in any trouble. I was, but not anymore. Someone else is in trouble, and I'm going to see what I can do to help. I really can't tell you more right now. Just trust me."

"Famous last words." Trevor said under his breath. They arrived at the Talosian cargo-shuttle in the shuttle-bay and Novawynd stopped.

"Zacharieth, blip Bianca please."

"You are connected."

"Bianca?"

"Yes Novawynd?"

"Go down to the mainframe room and tell me when you get there. If you see anyone on the way there, remember, you are Novawynd and I am Bianca."

"Yes Novawynd."

"Good. End."

Both Stunner and Trevor looked at each other, then at her. They were really curious at that point, but they did trust that she knew what she was doing and so, refrained from asking any more questions. The door of the Talosian shuttle opened in front of them. "Come on." Novawynd jerked her head toward the open door and walked in. Stunner and Trevor followed on her heels, wary of anything that resembled trouble. As they entered the empty cargo hold, two Talosian men stepped forward with Axon guns drawn and fired on Stunner and Trevor before they could even react. They were only stunned however.

The two Talosians rushed over to Stunner and Trevor who were lying incapacitated on the floor. They pulled out small tools with which, they drilled holes the size of lentils, into the skulls of the two prostrate men. They extracted the CIs, which came perfectly out the small holes. Finally they inserted tiny screws, into the small holes, and cauterized the incision. All this took a mere mecron to accomplish. Apparently, they were experts at CI removal. Novawynd watched with casual interest.

Danalian stepped out of the flight center after this scene had ended. "Your other friend already arrived."

Novawynd nodded, realizing Vertigo obviously decided to take her up on her offer.

"Are you ready?" Danalian asked her, referring to the removal of her own CI. Her CI was not as difficult to get out. One just needed to pull it out of her auditory canal with long tweezers. One of the CI removal specialists stood up, brandishing the long pointed tongs.

"Not yet. I need to communicate with my AP. Once I know she's accomplished her mission, I can." No sooner than she had said that, than Bianca blipped Novawynd.

"Bianca?" Bianca addressed Novawynd thus, per Novawynd's strict instructions.

"Yes, Novawynd. Are you at the mainframe room?" Novawynd asked.

"Yes" Bianca affirmed.

"Good. Open the access pad to the right of the door and hit the green button. That will switch the lock over to manual override. Then type in this code: 1, 7, D, R, 7, #."

"I'm entering the code now."

"Did anyone see you go down there?"

"I passed a couple people on the way, but they didn't seem to notice anything unusual."

"You didn't see Zefram did you?"

"No. The door is opening."

"Okay. Remove the pack I put on you and put it up against the central tower. Then you should leave the room and let me know when you have left."

"Okay. I'm doing that right now. Okay. I'm leaving. I'm out."

*   *   *

Aboard the Zenith, Zefram started to feel uneasy. There was something not right, and he felt Novawynd's presence had moved away from the ship for the second time that evening. He had been about to go talk to her about the issue they had left unresolved. He wanted to tell her that he wanted to run away with her, to escape the Superior Council's control. He just wanted to be with her whatever the cost. He obviously didn't know how she would respond to that, but he knew had to tell her. "Zacharieth, blip Novawynd for me please."

"You are connected Zefram." the computer affirmed.

"Novawynd, where are you?" Zefram probed.

The real Novawynd could hear this, but Bianca could not. Novawynd pulled the remote detonator out of her jacket pocket. "I'm on level ten, sector B."

"I sense that you are not on board." Zefram argued.

"Well, I assure you, I'm where I said I am."

"What are you doing down there?" Zefram was suspicious.

"I felt the need to check things out down here to make sure everything is up to snuff."

"Up to snuff?" many of Novawynd's metaphors were lost on Zefram, but he was too concerned about why he didn't feel her there. "I'll join you. We'll do a walk-through together."

"I'm done with my sweep anyway Zefram. I don't need your assistance." She deflected.

"No problem, really. I'm already on my way. End." he followed his intuition. "Zacharieth?"

"Yes, Zefram?"

"Is Novawynd on tenth level, sector B?"

"No. Bianca, her AP is, however."

On that information, Zefram's hackles rose. Without ending his comm, he ran out of his unit and sprinted to the central elevator, headed for Novawynd's or Bianca's alleged location.

*   *   *

Novawynd hit the detonation button. She expected to hear an explosion, followed by alarms, but nothing happened. She was too far away from the Zenith for the remote to work.

"Zacharieth?" she hoped he would not respond.

A Zecron passed, then "Yes, Novawynd?"

"Patch me through to Bianca."

"You are connected."

"Novawynd, go back into the Mainframe room." Novawynd ordered Bianca.

"Yes. I'm typing the code. I'm entering. Now what?"

"Go to the pack and open it." the real Novawynd instructed.

"Okay, I see a mechanism. It has lights and buttons."

"Are the lights on?"

"Yes."

"Okay. I need you to press the small yellow button on the side." Novawynd instructed. That button was the manual detonator and when pressed, the device would explode immediately. Novawynd didn't want Bianca to go, but she had to remind herself that Bianca was only an artificial person, not a real person. Some zecrons passed.

"Novawynd?" the real Novawynd sought affirmation.

"I can't. It will explode." Bianca protested. She was downloaded with Novawynd's knowledge, which meant she had knowledge of weapons as well; therefore, she knew what that device was for.

"I know, but you won't be irreparably damaged. The blast will only be severe enough to take out the mainframe for a short time. Consider this, you will only be disabling the Zenith, but you will be helping me save many, many lives elsewhere in the universe. Trust me." Novawynd assured.

"I understand." Bianca acknowledged. Then Novawynd heard it, the explosion she had been waiting for.

*   *   *

Zefram had just stepped off the elevator on the tenth level when the explosion rocked the ship. He was thrown to the side of the hallway. All lights went off and back-up power immediately flickered to life. Zacharieth was off line. Confusion would ensue.

"Damn it, Novawynd, what are you up to?" he could only yell to the walls, because he was no longer connected to anyone.

*   *   *

The man with the tweezers approached Novawynd. She pulled her hair to the side and tilted her head so he could see. Trevor and Stunner were just regaining function and Stunner sat up, just in time to see the Talosian pulling Novawynd's CI out of her ear. He kept it, as the data would prove useful later.

"Novawynd?" Stunner was uncertain of what was going on and needed her to explain, but wasn't at full mental capacity, and so he couldn't ask straight out.

"I'll explain everything, but first we need to strap in. Stunner was still unable to function fully, so the Talosians strapped him, as well as Trevor into their seats. Novawynd secured herself. The Talosian shuttle was on its way to the Talosian ship that waited just outside the station. Once they had set down safely, the Talosian ship fluxed.

CHAPTER 13

Somewhere out in the middle of space, well out of the reach of the Xaxony, The Talosian ship sat comfortably in a Caesura interval. Inside the ship, however, things were a little more hectic. Trevor and Stunner were dazed and allowed themselves to be lugged along by the orange-eyed aliens, as long as Novawynd was there, assuring them everything would be alright. They were brought into a med-lab where they were laid out and sedated again. When they awoke, they had new Talosian construct CIs. The reason the Xaxon CIs had to be removed was because the old CIs would record all information the bearer experienced. This could include military secrets, and if that CI fell into the wrong hands, there was no telling what could be done. The new Talosian CIs also recorded information, but in a different code that the Xaxony could not interpret. If the Xaxony got their hands on one of these CIs, they would only interpret gibberish that even their most sophisticated computer couldn't crack.

Their ID chips had also been removed. These were the tiny chips buried under the soft skin of their left wrists, usually beneath the metaband. The mainframe computers scanned these chips regularly to determine a being's identification, location and credit. The Talosians would not put new ID chips in. They had a way of dealing with the Xaxon computer's scanning.

As they were recovering, a green skinned alien, a Napojan, was also in the med-lab recovering from something. When Trevor woke up, the alien immediately got his attention. "Hey, aren't you with Novawynd?" he probed.

"Yeah." Trevor answered groggily.

"We will be comrades then. She saved me from that enti forsaken space station. I suspect we will be working together."

"She saved you?"

"Yes."

"That girl was busy." Trevor said under his breath.

"Sorry?" the Napojan sought clarification.

"Oh, nothing. I just was wondering why she saved you. How did she know you?"

"She was looking for a bomb and I had a few. I negotiated with her. She gets the bomb if she gets me out of there and back into the action."

"That's how it is, huh?"

"I am still a little perplexed as to what is going on here. I have to wonder what she is doing getting involved with Talosians. They took our CIs you know, and gave us new ones? This can only mean she has defected from the Xaxony altogether." He folded his arms behind his head satisfactorily.

"I'm sorry!" Trevor expressed his consternation. "Who are you?" He didn't mean to be rude, but this guy's revelations were a bit too much for him to fathom right now.

"I'm Vertigo." the Napojan answered. Not at all put out by Trevor's rude inquiry. "I used to be a space-guard for the Xaxony about fifty anio ago, but I retired and I've been making a living selling weapons on XR234 since then. And what is your name?"

"I'm Trevor. And, our sleeping blue friend over there is Stunner. He was the Intin of the Zenith, Novawynd's ship. I am just a companion to her, but I've done some space-guard work myself. I just was made an honorary space-guard to replace someone we lost, and I got my first battle under my belt back there at XR234. Novawynd interrupted my official nick-naming party to bring me here."

"Oh, so you're the replacement." Vertigo looked up at the ceiling thoughtfully. "What name did they give you?" he wondered.

"Patch." Trevor admitted almost ashamed.

"Patch? What was the reason for that?"

"Because, I was a temporary patch until a real space-guard replaced Zoomer." Trevor confessed.

"Oooo, that sounds almost mean-spirited." Vertigo empathized.

"It was completely mean. They didn't like Novawynd putting her 'companion' in the place of one of the better space-guards on the ship. They made it quite clear that I didn't belong, and I wouldn't be accepted. I was happy to get called away from that party, actually."

Stunner began to wake up, moaning. Trevor and Vertigo sniggered at his effort to awaken.

"Good morning beautiful!" Trevor called out to Stunner.

"Ughhhh!" Stunner groaned. "I've never experienced this thing Novawynd calls a hang-over, but now I think I know what she means." he complained.

"Stunner, we have a new companion." Trevor informed. "Meet Vertigo. He was a space-guard once and it would seem Novawynd intends to bring him back into his old occupation."

Stunner rolled over onto his side a bit to look at both Trevor and the person of whom he was speaking. "I see you're a Napojan." Stunner acknowledged. "I knew a Napojan space-guard by the name of Vertigo, or at least I knew *of* him. Are you the Vertigo that had worked for the Xaxony as a space-guard for two-hundred-fifty anios, had eight-hundred-sixty-three kills, and retired after serving on Zefram's ship for eight anios?"

"That would be me." Vertigo admitted.

"You were a legend."

"I *was* a legend." Vertigo claimed wistfully.

"You were the best there ever was." Stunner declared. "I have one question though. Why didn't you ever take an intin position? You could have been a zelo a hundred times over."

"I liked being a space-guard because I liked being in the action. I would make ata of the aleph-squad, and then they would tell me I was getting a promotion to intin. Each time, I would tell them I preferred to wait until the aleph-squad ata position opened on the highest ranked Leluminalia's ship and I would accept that as a promotion. For the first two-hundred-forty anio I bounced around from one Leluminalia ship to another as new, better Leluminalia emerged. Then Zefram came along and his ship, the Tauron, was my final home for the last eight anios of my career."

"Why did you retire?" Stunner asked, maybe a bit too personal a question.

"Truth be told, I had become quite attached to a woman space-guard I worked with, and although we weren't sexually involved, with Ephilderone and all, I still cared for her quite a lot. I made a grave miscalculation during one of our ground battles, as a result... she died. I was profoundly distraught and couldn't continue, so I retired. And, that's the story."

"I'm sorry to hear that. None-the-less, I'm honored to meet the legendary Vertigo. What are you doing here...wait a minute...what are we doing here? What is this?" Stunner just began to come awake enough realize the situation.

"Apparently this is a Talosian ship." Trevor answered. "And, I understand Novawynd has defected from the Xaxony." he calmly ascertained.

"What?" Stunner cried out. "She dragged us with her? Ughhhh!"

"If she asked you, would you have come or stayed on the Zenith?" Trevor posed the philosophical question.

"I would have come, as long as I knew the reason was a good one."

"We know things were not good between her and Zefram. I want to believe she fled because she feared for her life." Trevor hypothesized.

"Knowing Zefram, I wouldn't doubt that." Vertigo interjected. "I can't stand the bastard. When I heard he was on XR234, I prayed we wouldn't cross paths. Then again, he probably would have just pretended he didn't know me. I'm not worthy of his acknowledgement now. Well, I wasn't then either."

Just then the med-lab doors opened and it was Novawynd. "Hello boys." she seemed cheery. "Good to see you all recovering so well. Of course, the procedure was pretty minor. You'll be back on your feet in a few mecrons, which is good, because in a few moments, guides will come to bring you to your quarters. I wanted to take this moment, while I have you all here together, to explain everything to you, now that we are free of the ever vigilant eye of the Superior Council."

"Did you defect, Novawynd?" Stunner was the first to ask.

"Yes." Novawynd explained everything that happened to lead up to her defection. She explained the overbearing mistrust between Zefram and her. She explained the mistrust she had for the Superior Council and the plot against her, instigated by the Superior Council and carried out by Zefram, which solidified her mistrust. Finally, she told them about the Xaxony's plan to annihilate all intelligent life on Earth. With that, they were all dumb-struck.

"They're gonna kill everyone on Earth?" Trevor slowly verbalized his disbelief.

"Yes. The Talosians are basically the secret underground for anyone who needs to escape the Xaxony. They have helped thousands of beings who have been in trouble with the Xaxony, escape. Lord Danalian is a Leluminalia and he scored only fractions of a point below me, but he graduated the Analida hundreds of years before me. He's ancient and his wisdom is unparalleled. I trust him implicitly. I believe he is more likely to be the Lajiachine, than me. But, he seems to be convinced that I'm the Lajiachine, and he is willing to do anything to help me and my people...your people. I have every confidence that they've been working on a way to solve this problem." Novawynd smiled and stroked Trevor's cheek. He pulled away from her a little.

"What's wrong?" she asked him.

"I'm kinda pissed off that I didn't get to get all my stuff, and Swizel. You made me give up my real dog, and just when I was really loving the artificial one..."

"We'll be going back to Earth, so you can see the real Swizel again." Novawynd assured him.

"I hope so."

"Novawynd?" Vertigo interrupted. "I want you to know, I worked for Zefram for a long time and I think he is the universe's biggest sphincter. I will be happy to do anything I can, to tighten the bolts on him. Anything you ask." he assured.

"Thanks Vertigo. That's reassuring." she smiled. The med-lab doors opened again and the medics entered. They placed the clothing of the three men, along with new metabands, on their beds. The men were instructed to get dressed and await their guide, whom would take them to their quarters for the remainder of their recovery. Novawynd parted company with them as they dressed.

As she began to leave, she mentioned, "There is going to be a summit on this Earth Scouring issue and you'll all need to be there. You'll get word once you've gotten to your quarters as to time and location. Don't be late." she jokingly commanded and winked at them as she made her exit.

*   *   *

Zefram's own ship, the Tauron, arrived at Station XR234. He disembarked from the Zenith for the last time and boarded his own ship with his old zelo and his old crew, leaving Zelo Djynk to deal with the mess Novawynd created on the Zenith. He was furious, and unusually, a little nervous. His first order of business was to get his Ephilderone injection. There was no need to go without now. Novawynd had betrayed him. She had betrayed the Superior Council and the Xaxony. She was his enemy now, and never did he feel more hatred for someone. If he were to meet his former nemesis, Zefram 1, he would embrace him, for Zefram 1 couldn't be half as evil as Novawynd. Zefram didn't understand the feelings he had at that moment, but basically he had just experienced what it was like to fall in love, and then have his heart broken inside of one corona.

Once the injection of Ephilderone was complete, he could feel the numbness overtake his libido, and he welcomed the relief. Then he was off to the Superior Council chambers to speak with the Superior Council and await his fate. He fully expected he might be scrapped for his failure, but he was fully prepared to offer himself up solely to the location and eradication of Novawynd as his penance. Earthling poets wrote of how "hell hath no fury like a woman scorned", but the Omniaural hath no fury like a Zefram scorned. Zefram laughed at this analogy. He would use it as his mantra. He would find Novawynd, as he had before, and this time, he would kill her.

*   *   *

Novawynd finally made herself comfortable in her new, temporary, VIP quarters. She admired herself in her new outfit in the mirror. She now wore white tight pants, sporty, knee-high white boots and a high-necked, sleeveless, white tunic. A drastic difference from the Black Leluminali uniform she'd been wearing. As a point of rebellion, she resolved to always wear white from this point forward. She sat back on the edge of the bed and turned the events of the last few dialos over in her head. She was certain she had made the best choice. She had never felt more certain, or more free, but she was concerned about Earth. She was to meet with Danalian and some other ancient and wise Talosians on the welfare of Earth and what could be done. Trevor, Stunner and Vertigo would be present at the meeting.

The meeting was a quarter of a tecron away, but Novawynd decided to leave to find the conference room anyway. She thought she'd like to hang out and calm her nerves before anyone else arrived anyway. However, when she arrived at the conference room, she found Danalian already there. Danalian was a diamond in the rough. For some reason, he was not the slightest bit attracted to Novawynd, and he was not on Ephilderone. He simply seemed to be uninterested in her sexually. As far as Novawynd could tell, he was not homosexual or even bisexual. In actuality, he seemed to be purely non-sexual. It wasn't just her. Novawynd sensed he had no attraction to anyone. The most important thing she sensed was that he held a deep seeded respect for her. Frankly, he thought of her as a sacred being and would never even dare to imagine touching her. To Danalian, that would be something close to blasphemy. As one of the most highly ranked

Leluminali ever, he was well able to control any inhibitions he might have had. Novawynd welcomed the respect. She needed him to be her true mentor. She felt a trust in him she had never felt with Zefram.

"As long as we're both here, alone, I'd like to ask you about something." Novawynd broke the awkward silence.

"Anything you have to ask, I will do my best to answer."

"I've been having these dreams about a man named Star. We tried to identify his origins, but even Zacharieth, the computer on the Zenith, couldn't identify where he might have been from."

"What does he look like?" Danalian was intrigued. Novawynd pulled out the chip with the image of Star on it. She kept it always in the breast pocket of whatever Leluminali uniform she happened to be wearing, close to her heart. She inserted it into the slot on the table. The 4D image of Star sprang to life in front of them.

Danalian didn't seem surprised. He nodded. "He's Lozian, without a doubt."

"I knew it!" She blurted out excitedly. "Good thing I never told Zefram I suspected that. But, why couldn't Zacharieth identify him?"

"The Xaxony erased all knowledge of Lozia from general access after the Lozian incident."

The door to the conference room opened and Novawynd pulled the chip out. The image of Star dissolved. Danalian leaned across to Novawynd. "You'll have to tell me of those dreams later."

✳　　　✳　　　✳

Everyone had assembled. Stunner sat to Novawynd's left and Trevor sat to Novawynd's right. Vertigo sat to the left of Stunner. Then there were a handful of Talosians besides Danalian and one Vaget present. Trevor leaned over to Novawynd and whispered, "I like your new outfit. It's nice to see you in something other than that uniform."

"Thanks. I think I'll stick with white from now on. I think it looks good with my hair." Novawynd joked.

Danalian stood up and the room fell deathly silent.

"We have entered a new age, the age of the Lajiachine." Danalian began. "We Talosians pledged our loyalty to the Lajiachine where ever, and when ever he or she emerged. This is a great day, because Novawynd, whom I believe with all my heart to be the Lajiachine, has begun down the path of her destiny. This path will lead to the destruction of the universe's *oppressors*, the Superior Council." Polite applause erupted from the Talosians, but Novawynd remained stoic and Stunner, Trevor and Vertigo were still confused. "We gather today, because the home-world of the Lajiachine is in great peril. We have a witness who can explain." Danalian informed. "Tren, would you tell this assembly what you know?" With that, Danalian sat.

Tren, the tall, lithe, golden-skinned Vaget stood and explained how the Xaxony intended to wipe out all life on Earth with the new virus. They wanted to make sure not one soul survived. He explained how he got in touch with the underground and he destroyed any chance the Xaxon geneticists would be able to re-grow the virus. "We have bought Earth approximately three aera. We need to act fast if we are to save Novawynd and Trevor's people." That is how he finished, and then he resumed his seat.

"So," Novawynd began. "How do we stop them? I trust you guys have ideas."

"We had our best people on it and we couldn't think of any way to stop them, exactly." Danalian seemed ashamed to admit it. "Any way we thought of, we realized the Xaxons would just keep coming until they succeeded. We could hold them off for a time, but they would succeed eventually. So, we turned our concentration on how to perpetuate the Earthling race despite a Xaxon scouring. We thought of ways to evacuate the Earthlings, but we don't have enough time to build ships that could evacuate the majority. However, we have already begun working on a ship that can take at least one hundred evacuees. We are assembling parts on Talos right now. The actual ship can be assembled on Earth. After the scouring, the Xaxon ships will leave, and you can escape the Earth, with your chosen survivors."

"Why do we have to build a ship and leave the planet?" Novawynd probed "The other viruses only lived a couple of days after release. Why don't we just go into hiding and emerge when the virus is dead."

"Because, the Xaxony will send ships back to do probes. They will come back maybe every half anio, maybe more frequently, and send down millions of hunter-probes to seek out human life. They will kill any human they find. They do this to make sure they have eliminated everyone, and to make sure pirates aren't using the planet. We believe you stand a better chance if you just leave the planet and disappear into the endless void of space for a while. We believe they won't keep up the probing for more than fifteen anios. You could return to Earth after that."

Novawynd was furious at what she was hearing. "Can't we put out propaganda about the Xaxony waging genocide against yet another innocent planet? Can't you threaten the allies with an embargo of Isotarin if they don't come together to defend Earth?"

"Propaganda works too slowly. As far as an embargo… the only reason we can force an embargo against the Xaxony proper, is because we still supply the allies. But, cut off the allies and what is to stop them from full on occupation of Talos. I said we support the Lajiachine. I would give up my life and sacrifice the lives of my people for you Novawynd. But, I can't put my people and my planet in peril for your people, your planet. If the Xaxony knew we were behind preventing them from scouring Earth, all free life on Talos as we know it would be finished. I can't make that trade-off. We can help you, but only as long as Talos' involvement isn't obvious. Because of that, I can't save all life on your planet. As much as it pains me to say, I can only save you and a handful of your people. At least that way, you can repopulate your planet after the scouring. That's the best chance you have right now."

Silence blanketed the room. Novawynd considered what he had said. She didn't like it, but what he said seemed to make sense. Danalian had been aware of this situation long before she became aware of it and she was sure he had thought out every possible solution. She trusted that if there was a way to save everyone on Earth, Danalian would have figured it out. He was over six-hundred-years-old and infinitely wiser than Novawynd; even though he looked not a day over twenty-eight, which caused Novawynd to forget his wisdom. "Alright," she relented, "I want to hear your proposal."

"The main problem is time. We could do more if we had more time, but we will only have three aera to put this plan into action. We would need to complete the assembly of the rescue ship on Earth. You need to do some research and select one hundred of your people with superior genetics to perpetuate the race, and then they need to be collected. The rescue ship's pieces will be brought to Earth discretely in sections. It will somehow have to be well camouflaged. The reason for this is because the Xaxony may send scouts, so it can't be built off planet, or it will be seen for sure. If it isn't camouflaged on Earth, the scouts may pick up on it also. We suggest it be built underground in a type of chute, so that it is covered, but easy to assemble and easy to launch from the chute when the time is right. We suggest this chute is dug into solid rock of some sort."

"Wait a minute." Novawynd interrupted. "That feat alone would take several months to complete."

"With Earthling equipment, yes. But, with Talosian mining equipment, it should take only a couple dialos. It would take about an aera to complete the engine compartment, another aera to complete the biospheres and gravity generators and the last aera, we would complete the hull. We suggest you begin to collect your chosen ones only a corona before the zero hour."

Trevor scoffed and everyone looked at him. "I like how he says 'collect'. You mean 'abduct'. I can't believe you're considering this Novawynd. There has to be other options."

Novawynd looked calmly at him "Do you have any ideas, Trevor?"

"Yes," he stated confidently. "Why don't you just use your abilities to flux into the Xaxon genetics lab and destroy the virus, and keep doing it until they realize they're defeated and give up on Earth? At some point they must realize, it's not worth it."

Tren was the one to interject at this point. "They will have changed the location of the main lab, in which they are producing this virus. They'll have anticipated someone re-attempting to sabotage their work."

"That means," Danalian jumped in. "Novawynd could flux in, but she wouldn't know the location of the new lab. She would have to find it, and since the Superior Council is hyper-sensitive to her fluxes, they would know immediately that she had fluxed to the Xaxon. They would send out people to hunt her down. She might be able to accomplish her mission, but the Xaxony could act against her, faster than she can act to find and destroy the virus. The risk is too great. We have to always keep in mind that Novawynd, of all people, is not expendable, but the rest of us definitely are."

Novawynd looked over at Trevor. Having made the promise to him that she wouldn't try to read his feelings, she knew she had to honor that, but she didn't need empathic abilities to sense that he was struggling with a mixture of emotions. He was obviously not accepting the fate of his home planet as well as Novawynd seemed to be. In actuality, Novawynd was even less accepting. She felt somewhat responsible for all of this, and wanted to do whatever necessary to stop it. Surely, a way to save all people on Earth would present itself.

*   *   *

Zefram stood before the Superior Council. "After my Ephilderone wore off, I fear I went too far in trying to win her trust. Her suspicions were only piqued. I lost control. I failed the Superior Council. I am willing to take whatever punishment you choose for me, but first I would like to volunteer myself to the dedication of finding Novawynd wherever she might be, and destroying her."

"That is a very noble offer," the distorted, bisexual voices of the Superior Council accepted, "and we will hold you to it, because we feel you did not fail. You were succeeding in your mission; however, there were other forces at work that took her away from you before you could complete the mission. That is not your fault. We cannot punish you for circumstances that were beyond your control. Novawynd is dead to us, so bear in mind that now that you are once again our number one Leluminalia. You are once again our right hand. But, as your first and only mission, until you complete it, you will find Novawynd and destroy her, as well as any memory of her. The first thing you will do is to scour the Earth. This particular virus we are developing, which you were not initially aware of, will extinguish all life on Earth. We can't have another Lajiachine emerging from that planet."

"Whatever you command, I shall carry it out." he said intently as he bowed to them.

"Very well. We are putting our faith in your unfailing abilities." This was the hint that they didn't trust him entirely after all this, and the Earth scouring mission would prove his mettle and get him back into their good graces. That was a contradiction and a definite warning sign. If they believed in Zefram's Lelumin conditioning, they would not mistrust him. The very fact that they mistrusted him, lead him to believe they suspected, or knew, his conditioning had broken. He bowed to them and left as their energy dissipated.

Outside the council chambers and breathed a sigh of relief. That had been a close call. He had prevailed. The only thing keeping him alive was his desire to find Novawynd again. As to whether he would actually terminate her or something else, truly remained to be seen. He, himself, didn't know what he would truly do when he found her. He hated her. He loved her. He wanted to end his pain. He wanted to kill her and he didn't care if he died in the process.

*   *   *

The decision had been made. Novawynd had agreed to be on-board with the Talosian's proposal. Trevor was not at all happy with this. Outside the conference room he expressed his disapproval to her. "What are you thinking? Have you been a Xaxon so long you have no love for your own people anymore Novawynd?" He pleaded passionately.

She squeezed his shoulder. "I'm going along with it in hopes that a better solution will come along Trevor, but we haven't a lot of time, so we're going with 'plan A' for now." she assured. Lord Danalian, whom Trevor expected to be really old, given Novawynd's assertion that he was "Ancient", exited the conference room.

Vertigo bowed to Danalian. "Lord Danalian, allow me to say that we were not allowed to know about you in the Xaxony, but everything

I've heard about you and everything I have seen today, leads me to believe that you are a great man. Your generosity is inspiring." he finished his bow and stood up straight.

"Thank you friend of Novawynd..." Danalian looked at Novawynd at a loss for the Napojan's name.

"Vertigo." Novawynd answered. If the universe was to be compared with Earth, one could say Talos was like the Vatican and Danalian was like the Pope. Only, trading Isotarin was the Talosian's religion. And so, it was often that Danalian experienced responses to his presence like Vertigo's. Trevor was clueless. The first time he had even heard of Danalian was only a tecron ago when Novawynd first apprised him in the med-lab.

"Yes, Lord Danalian, you are truly generous, and I'll thank you on behalf of the Earthling race for your kind actions." Novawynd bowed to him. Trevor couldn't believe she would kowtow to him too.

"No Novawynd, It is you I should be thanking. You are the Lajiachine and you are where you belong now, among friends. Now you are free to follow your true course. You are free and you will save us all." Danalian's response surprised Trevor. Never before had he been so aware of Novawynd's place in the universal scheme. He had never felt so confused. All at once he felt repulsed by this strange new religious significance Novawynd seemed to now hold, but he needed and wanted her more than ever. He scowled. It had been a long time since the two of them had experienced a private moment and he wanted that more than anything at that moment. It was his way of feeling comforted.

Trevor leaned in to Novawynd and whispered in her ear, "Let's go back to your room and cuddle." Novawynd turned to him, smiled and nodded. Trevor was ecstatic. His eyebrows raised impetuously in anticipation. The only person that could comfort him was the only other Earthling he knew in the whole universe. They turned to leave, hand in hand.

"Novawynd?" Danalian called after her. Trevor's shoulders slumped. He wondered if yet another guy would be competing for Novawynd's attention.

Novawynd turned to Danalian. "Yes?" she responded as he approached her and Trevor.

"We need to talk…later. Visit me when you have a free moment." Danalian smiled at the both of them in understanding. Trevor was a little perplexed. He didn't know what to think of Danalian's response. Was he using the passive technique? Trevor had seen it before. A man pretends not to care about a woman already involved with another man, all the while scheming to weasel his way into her heart. Trevor had used the technique himself.

Back at Novawynd's quarters, the couple found themselves too distraught to make love after all. They tried, but both of them just broke down crying. They cried for their families, their former friends and all fellow Earthlings. Instead, they cried themselves to sleep. Tecrons later, Trevor woke up and had to relieve himself. Afterward, he crawled back into bed with Novawynd and felt amorous. He began kissing her neck and his prick hardened immediately. He pressed it up against the smooth folds of her buttocks. She stirred. Novawynd turned her face to Trevor and they kissed. He pushed her over onto her belly and straddled her with her legs together. He slipped his hardness between her thighs where they met her pubic area. This way he slid along her labia and pushed against her clit. He pulled her hips up to him and this gave him the angle he needed to push into her love canal. He slid easily into her and it was a welcomed, pleasurable relief. They finally made love, but it was not an extended session as both of them were exhausted anyway, but what little they accomplished didn't matter.

The important thing was that they were two Earthlings experiencing an important bond.

*   *   *

Zefram woke up in his comfortable quarters on the Tauron. He was sweating profusely and he didn't know why. He got up and splashed cold water on his face. He was wide awake then, and so he went out to his living area and sat down. He leaned back and thought about how he was supposed to find Novawynd. Where in the wide, wide universe could she be hiding? Who had helped her? He had attempted to track her escape on video from the XR234 station, but it seemed to be corrupt from several tecrons before the moment he felt her missing. Obviously someone scrambled the transmission. Zefram watched the station video of all the times Novawynd was off the Zenith on her own. In several scenes, she seemed to know where the cameras were and where their field of view stopped, because she moved within the camera's blind-spots when it seemed to be convenient for her. Such as the time she left the levi-ball table. Also, there was the first time she left the Zenith after the Cornithon attack. Novawynd seemed to disappear off the cameras at that point. She couldn't use Junatiel to make herself invisible. That was only a power one could use to play tricks on people's minds, such as making one believe you are invisible, but it doesn't work on machinery.

Zefram had checked the logs of all ships docking and all shuttles entering or leaving the shuttle bays. He had been curious about Talosian shuttles docking and departing twice in one day. The second departure precisely the moment of the Zenith's incident. That might not have seemed suspicious, except that even though the first was a luxury shuttle and the second was a cargo shuttle, it was a little suspicious that they came from the same ship. Zefram had a feeling about that situation and the only way to know for sure was to find that ship. Since it was a Talosian ship, Zefram wouldn't be able to communicate directly with it, because Talosian ships weren't online with the Xaxon communication system. However, they were online with the allies. Zefram would put the notice out to the allies to inform him if they encountered this ship. He suspected it wouldn't be long before he received information.

* * *

Novawynd and Trevor were cuddling comfortably as Trevor gently snored away. Novawynd found it somewhat comforting. Her door chimed. "Who is it?" she asked, groggily.

The ship's computer responded, "Lord Danalian is here to see you."

Novawynd got up and put a wrap on. Trevor stirred. Novawynd made herself presentable and gave permission, "Let Lord Danalian in please." The door opened and Danalian stepped in. He bowed to her and upon resuming his stance, noticed Trevor sleeping on the bed. He approached Novawynd, put his hand on her shoulder and steered her to the kitchenette table. He sat down and Novawynd followed suit.

Danalian spoke in a low voice so as not to disturb Trevor. "We are at a pirate out-station. We're going to ditch this ship and move to a different one. We knew we would have to register this ship with the XR234 station, so we took one of our oldest ships. That way, we could give it up with little concern. Since this is a pirate station, we don't have to register and there will be no record of having switched ships. We're just going to leave the ship at the station with the computer dismantled and hope some idiots take it. We're doing this to throw Zefram off our tail. By now he would know that Talosians were present at the station and he would naturally suspect us first. He'll be looking for this ship."

"Danalian, if you ditch the ship, won't that be like an admission of guilt? He would see that action as obvious attempt to throw him off. What if you just moved us to another ship and faced up to him when he finally did catch up to you? You could deny you had any involvement and he would be hard pressed to prove you did. He can't prove you were there right?"

"I had the Xaxon identification chip which used to identify me as Danalian removed a long time ago. Just as yours and your friend's chips were removed once you came aboard." Novawynd rubbed the spot on her wrist where her chip used to be. The sore had already healed. "When I go into Xaxon territory I always carry a new chip with me. I don't bother implanting it, I just carry it here." He showed Novawynd his metaband, which had special slot to insert the chip. "The one I have now is someone who is called Gaddard Celenavae. I change it from time to time so I can move in the Xaxon territories without being positively identified. You and your friends will get new chips as necessary. As far as the Xaxony is concerned, you'll all have new identities, but from now on, you'll do well to avoid anyplace the Xaxony controls. You can be identified easily enough by sight. I can be identified that way too, so I made sure to mess with the cameras in all the areas I traveled on the station. Zefram wouldn't see anything but static. As for the ship, I certainly can't let him confront me and if he confronted the zelo he would still get no admissions, but he could tap into the computer. He would find that information was erased, which doesn't prove anything, but it's just as suspicious as a ditched ship. Then this ship would be monitored and it would be that much more difficult to do the business we need to attend to in the next three aera. It's just better to cut off any connection to us whatsoever. So, Your Supremacy," with that he stood, "if you'll get your friends together, we're moving to the new ship in a few mecrons." He bowed to Novawynd again. Novawynd stood and gave a slight bow back to him, and then saw him out.

Novawynd went back to the bed and sat down. Trevor awoke and ran his hand up her back in a comforting manner. "You okay sugar?" he asked.

"Yeah. Danalian was just here and he told me we have to transfer ships. So we need to get up, clean up and get out of here." she turned her face toward Trevor. "That means right now." she got up again and went into the shower. Shortly, she was joined by Trevor. They didn't make love this time, they just washed each other. Soon they were dried off, dressed and out the door.

People were scrambling in the hallways. There was obviously an exodus occurring. "Trev, go get Stunner up and I'll get Vertigo moving." Novawynd suggested. Trevor nodded and went to Stunner's door. Novawynd went to Vertigo's. She chimed his door and after a couple of chimes, the door opened.

"Novawynd! What a wonderful surprise to wake up to." he seemed cheery in a sarcastic way. "What brings you by?" he added more seriously, followed by a yawn.

"Get dressed, we're changing ships. Trevor and I will be waiting in the hall outside." Vertigo looked at her with his head cocked to one side. He took that stance often, as his dark green hair was buzzed in the back, but his long bangs were cut at a sharp angle, covering one eye. "Affirmative." he mocked as he stood up straight. He had a sarcastic sense of humor, but she liked that about him. She exited Vertigo's unit and met Trevor in the hall. They waited and soon Vertigo nearly leaped out of his room to join them. Not long after, Stunner also joined them. They joined the exodus and followed the ship's crew members out into the station and back into a new, larger ship. A lower ranked crew member met them at the entrance and informed them he would need to show them to their new rooms. When they got to their own rooms, each was relieved to see their units were slightly larger than their quarters on the last ship. Danalian must have sensed Novawynd's presence, because as soon as she sat down on the sofa in her new room, he blipped her.

"Your Supremacy, I need to talk to you further about what is going to happen from this point forward. Will you meet me in my quarters in ten mecrons?"

"Certainly, Your Lordship." She looked around her new space and noticed there were a couple of new outfits on the bed. Like the one she was wearing, these were white, with some sort of color embellishments; one outfit had aqua-blue piping and the other had hot-pink trim. She knew Danalian heard her comment to Trevor about always wearing white, and he would seek to suit her tastes whatever they may be. "Computer, do you have a name?" Novawynd addressed the mainframe.

"I am called Kae." it answered matter-of-factly.

"Who was Kae? Was Kae an important Talosian?" Novawynd was curious.

There was a pause, and then the computer answered, "Kae is the thirteenth letter of the Talosian alphabet."

"Oh, I see. So are all main-frames called by letters?"

"On the ships, yes."

"And how many letters in the Talosian alphabet?"

"Thirty-five."

"Are there only thirty-five ships in the Talosian fleet?"

"Yes, never more, never less."

"Really? That doesn't seem like a lot."

"For one planet, it's enough."

The time had come for Novawynd to head over to Danalian's quarters. "Kae, will you show me how to get to Danalian's quarters?"

Kae showed Novawynd the 4D map to Danalian's quarters. She memorized it and headed out to meet with him.

At Danalian's room, he greeted her with the customary kowtow and then led her to his living area. He offered a comfortable looking chair to her, and then sat opposite her on a sofa.

"Well," he began as he sat, "To get down to business. We are bringing you, Trevor, Stunner and Vertigo to Earth. I will give you twenty-nine men and women, Talosians, to be your space-guard. Vertigo will take the thirtieth position, but he will be ata of aleph squad, where he feels most comfortable, of course. These people I am giving you will help you locate and procure the people you indicate as those you will have upgraded. So you need to work diligently on finding the best, the brightest, the strongest and most beautiful of your Earthling race. I suggest you find three each of the most gifted doctors, surgeons, psychologists, robotics people, physicists, mathematicians, biologists, chemists, botanists and zoologists. After that, anyone else you choose."

"Okay, I can find those people easily when I get back to Earth. I can access the Internet, which is a world-wide database and everyone who has done anything can be found on the Internet."

"Very well, more importantly, you need to find land that would support the undertaking I spoke of earlier. That would be the first task."

"I think I know the perfect area. There is a place in the northern mid-western region of the United States where they used to mine iron ore. The rock is so rich with iron, it confuses compasses. My thought is, it would be great cover for our silo. Xaxon scanners wouldn't be able to see through it. Do you think your machines can cut through iron-rich rock as easily as you thought?"

"I have some experience with the element, iron. Our machines will cut through it with no problem. You just need to get us the land. We will produce whatever currency you need to get the transaction done."

"I think I might have enough." Novawynd thought of her lottery winnings and knew she would only need a fraction of what she had won to buy a few acres. She could spend it all, apparently it really didn't matter at this point. That thought brought her back to Kat, Ana and Maris. She had been so busy with her Xaxon life, she hadn't thought much about them recently. Not that she had ceased caring. That could never happen, but she hadn't been worried about them. They knew the truth of where she was and what she was. She was certain they were living happy, healthy lives. But, this new threat on the Earth had her worrying about her family once again.

"What about my family? I'd like to upgrade them. I'm sure Trevor will want to save his family too."

"Then you should. We'll build one small biosphere of the ship, just to hold you and your family and anything you want to have in it. One biosphere will hold the Earthling's living quarters and one biosphere will hold everyone and everything else. It will be a great ship; the most unique we have ever built. It will be built such that it can sit erect in the launch-chute while on Earth, and all biospheres will be level, but once the ship launches and evens out, the spheres will also change level. Once in space, the gravity generators will go to work. It's a feat of engineering that I'm quite proud of."

"It sound's fascinating. Do you have plans I can look at?"

"Yes of course. Kae, pull up the schematics for the new Earthling ship." Danalian ordered excitedly.

Novawynd was amazed at the design she saw before her. It looked like a trilobite, multi-segmented and armored, but far more aerodynamic.

"I have a suggestion. I want it to be red, because I have never seen another ship that was red and I want people who see it to say 'my god, what is that?' I want the space-guard's uniforms to be red also. I'm going to name the ship The Phoenix. The Phoenix is a legendary bird on our world. The legend says that the bird is reborn from its own ashes. In a way, I feel like this ship will rise out of the ashes of Earth and we will live again. It seems appropriate."

Danalian nodded. "Now you're getting into the spirit. So the symbol would be a flaming bird? We can do a nice emblem to signify the Phoenix bird."

"Yes, and I think," added Novawynd, "it should be black on a blue background."

"Anything you say." chuckled Danalian. "But, let's be serious for a moment. About your captives…you shouldn't tell them what's going on until it happens. They won't believe it anyway. We'll set up a system so they can see it first hand; that way they'll believe it when they see it. You'll need to keep them locked up well until the zero hour, so none escape. This is why it's best to wait as long as possible before acquiring your chosen ones. The shorter they are in captivity the better. Not to mention that you'll only have fifty, small holding capsules, which would comfortably hold fifty captives at one per capsule; but, you'll have to put two per capsule and that will be uncomfortable for them. The longer they are together, the more uncomfortable."

"About my 'chosen ones' believing what they see…we have Hollywood and Hollywood can make fake things seem real." Novawynd explained. "They won't believe it until they see the actual devastation with their own eyes. Is there any way I can bring them out to see it?"

"The virus will only live a couple days. You could bring a handful of the chosen ones out after the virus has died off. They can see the devastation and relay it to the others that it is a fact. You know how this goes, because you've done it yourself. The Xaxony will release the virus, wait a dialo and do a sweep. When they are satisfied the number of life signs are minimal, they will leave. They will not detect the Phoenix, or those who populate it. You will be quite safe.

In the mean time, Xaxon demolition robots will be dismantling the nuclear plants. They will load the waste onto barges, which will be sent into your sun. Other demolition robots will come down to clean up other scrap. This will all be done so the Xaxony can repopulate the planet with another Xaxon creation. They will wait, however, several thousands of years before re-populating, to allow nature to overtake the former man-made things. After the Xaxon ships leave you will have time to escape the planet. The demolition robots will not take note of your departure, because they are programmed to do demolition and not recognize a departing ship as unusual.

Once you get into space, you might have a lot of people who won't take it well. There might even be suicides. That's why I said take three of the essential intellectual types. If any of them end their lives, there will be two others or, hopefully, at least one other."

"Danalian, I still hold out hope that things won't end this way. We still need to think about other ways to save all life on Earth." Novawynd sounded desperate.

"Novawynd, I don't want to tell you that there is no hope, but I wish you would believe me when I say we have thought through every possible scenario, and nothing could defeat the Xaxony. This is a slow route to take, and there will be casualties, but in a way you are defeating the Xaxony without having to fight them. When the Earthling race comes back, and it will, it will be even smarter, stronger, healthier, faster, more talented, more beautiful, etc. Yes, it will be unfortunate for those who aren't chosen ones. If you look at it from a different angle, you know for sure, the bad elements will definitely be eliminated. War, famine, pestilence, oppression, exploitation, poverty, crime, ignorance, over-consumption of natural resources and pollution would all end. I could go on about how this scouring could be beneficial to the planet on so many levels, but I know you are still concerned about the human aspect. May I suggest that you use the next three aera to concentrate on what may be positive about this? You can teach the chosen ones to pass along to their children and their grandchildren the importance of respecting the Earth and fellow Earthlings, and never letting your world get in that state ever again."

Novawynd was silent for a moment as she considered this. "I know there is a lot of bad in the world, but there are so many more good people who don't deserve this. How can I choose only a handful?"

"Your Supremacy, I am so relieved that you only see the good in your people. I find that very admirable. But, please understand, that as an alien to your world, I see a lot of bad. In fact, I see mostly bad. I see very little beauty worth saving. The things that are beautiful will be saved by this scouring. I'm certain of it." Danalian looked at her intensely. He squinted his eyes at her, as if he was trying to squeeze a response out of her. "You know, Your Supremacy," he continued, since she had no comment, "once you get out in the universe, you need to make it your mission to find allies. You need to build an anti-Xaxony, so-to-speak. You carry more weight than you know as the Lajiachine. People will get on-board with you when they realize it isn't in their best interest to stay with the Xaxony. Some will gladly help you out, but with a modicum of discretion. They'll sneak around behind the Xaxony's back, but never overtly damage their image in the eyes of the Xaxony. Then there are those who hate the Xaxony and will join with you immediately. Those are the ones you should seek out first. You should also seek out any non-upgraded civilizations of the Xaxony. If you think they are civilized enough to handle the space race, then they are good enough to upgrade. Finally, those who will always support the Xaxony; you may as well avoid them all together. I've been doing business across the universe for over six hundred anios. I've learned who you can and can't trust. I'll guide you in this."

"Danalian." Novawynd interrupted. "I don't have the heart to destroy the Xaxony. It would be detrimental to the allies too, and I can't do that to all those people. I can't be the Lajiachine."

"Whom the Lajiachine is, will not truly be known until he or she fulfills the prophesy. But, I believe you are. As far as how you feel about acting against the Xaxony…right now you're in denial, but after they unleash the virus on your people, we'll see how you feel about the Xaxony."

CHAPTER 14

Danalian's shuttle had brought Trevor and Novawynd back to Earth. Novawynd went immediately to visit her mother again. Trevor went to visit his parents. Kat was happy to see Novawynd. She looked a little older, but well. They called Ana and soon Ana and Maris joined them. Maris was easily a foot taller than the last time Novawynd saw her.

"Let's go down to the houseboat." Novawynd suggested. "I'd like to take a cruise today. Maybe we should prepare a little picnic?" The other's agreed eagerly. They tore through Kat's garden and the cupboards and the refrigerator, looking for items they could put together for a nice lunch. They had all they would need for a nice meal and possibly two, if time slipped away from them. They trudged down to the houseboat, situated themselves, Ana unmoored the lashings and Novawynd maneuvered the boat out into the canal. She took the vessel along at a leisurely pace, while the others sat, surveying the scenery, feeling the wind on their faces. It was such a beautiful day, and it had been so long since Novawynd saw the rivers, trees, grass, birds, etc. of her home planet. Seeing the pleasure and carefree attitude of her family, she found herself fighting back tears. They didn't know what was about to happen. Maris came up to Novawynd's side.

"Can I call you Aunt Leelee, or do I have to call you Novawynd?" Novawynd was amazed that she remembered her Xaxon name, but Maris always had been bright.

"Novawynd is my Xaxon name, and although I'm not a Xaxon anymore, the rest of the universe knows me as Novawynd. However, you are my family and you should can me Leelee, as you always have."

"What do you mean you're not a Xaxon anymore? Have you come back to stay with us?" Kat asked hopefully.

"Not exactly." Novawynd pulled the boat up to an island in the middle of the river. She beached the vessel there, so they could have their lunch and talk. "Let's eat. I'm starving for Earth food." she rubbed her hands together. They sat out on the deck and said little as they ate. It was a little awkward. Novawynd knew her family wanted to ask so many questions, but sensed they should hold off until lunch was over, to be polite. It was Novawynd who spoke first.

"I defected from the Xaxony because the Superior Council was plotting with Zefram to glean my fluxing ability, and then kill me. But, that wasn't the worst of it. In about three months, Zefram will unleash a virus on this planet that will destroy all human life. They don't want to take the chance that someone with my abilities will emerge from this planet again." There was silence. Ana swallowed her food, but no one took another bite.

"Zefram, you mean the breath-takingly handsome man who was with you the last time you were here?" Kat seemed disappointed to hear it.

"They are going to kill us all?" Ana asked for clarification. "Because of you." That almost sounded accusatory.

"Ana, I didn't ask for these abilities I developed. If I had known I was going to gain the attention of a superior space race, and ultimately bring doom to my planet, I would have killed myself. As it stands, it's too late. It can't be undone. Earth, it seems, unfortunately can't be saved now. But, there are some very nice aliens called the Talosians who are helping us. They are building us a ship and we have enough time and space on the ship to evacuate a handful of people. You guys get to go, naturally. You're not in any danger." Novawynd looked at their reticent faces. Maris pushed her food around her plate, pouting as she did so. "Of course, you can choose to stay here. I understand if you don't want to go live in a box in outer space for the rest of your lives. You can stay here and pass on under this beauty." Novawynd spread her arm out and leaned back in her chair, face up to the sky. She closed her eyes and never felt so alive.

"I want to live on the space ship." Maris demanded.

Being a former nurse, Kat's first question was obvious, "How long does this virus remain active without a host?"

"A couple of days…and I know what you're thinking. We can't come back after the virus is dead. In fact, we can't come back here for at least fifteen years, they tell me, because the Xaxony will send down robot probes to hunt down anyone still living here. For us to be safe, we need to stay away until the Xaxony is satisfied that there is no one here. And consider this. After the virus, there will be no television, radio, Internet, because there will be no electricity. You will have to go back to living a hard life. At your age, do you want to live so hard when you can come aboard and live life like everyday is a luxury cruise? You can get pedicures and manicures and facials and massages and hairdos when ever you want, and not have to pay for it. Also there are four floors devoted solely to a park. I've seen the plans. It will have trees and bushes and streams and artificial peacocks and artificial koi fish and artificial lizards running up the trees. You'll love it. You can even have your own garden there.

You'll never want for anything to do. There are so many life-forms and civilizations and religions and philosophies to learn about. I know how much you love learning all you can about everything. That will keep you busy for ten life-times. I can even give you a job with the biologist or botanist or whomever you want to work with so you can study alien life-forms in a hands-on manner." Novawynd stopped for a moment to catch a breath.

"What about me? What can I do?" Ana asked.

"Anything you want. You love cooking. You could be in charge of helping our kitchen workers come up with interesting, nutritious and flavorful meals for the cafeteria. Maybe you could also have your own little shop where you purvey not-so-healthy, but incredibly delicious treats. All of you can do whatever interests you."

"Does that mean I don't have to go to school?" Maris bounced up and down in her seat excitedly.

"No. You still have to go to school, but it will be more fun than your usual school. We'll be your teachers. "

Maris pursed her lips and tilted her head back and forth, without comment.

"Anyway, I would rather that you come with me. I'm concerned that Zefram will come here and abduct you guys to use you against me. I'm actually surprised he hasn't already come. As long as I have time, I need to hurry up and get you out of here. We'll need to pack up what ever you think you want to take with and head out of here as soon as possible. A Talosian ship is waiting in orbit and will let me know if a Xaxon ship approaches.

With that, the lunch cruise was over. They headed back up river to Kat's house and Ana left hurriedly. She was to go back to her place and pull together anything she couldn't live without and help Maris do the same. Kat and Novawynd were to go to town and buy the biggest RV they could find, for both storage and short-term living. The RV would be their home during the construction of the new ship.

When the RV salesman asked Novawynd if she was licensed to drive the vehicle, she lied and told him "yes". When she and Kat were going through the purchase process, he asked to see Novawynd's license. Not only did she not have a license, she didn't even have a purse or wallet with her, so she used Junatiel. She pretended she had the license in her back pocket. She pulled out an imaginary card and threw it down in front of him. He picked up the non-existent card and scrutinized it. Then he handed it back to her acknowledging that she was indeed qualified to drive the rig. Kat watched the exchange with wonder. She didn't see any license, but she knew it was best not to say anything.

As they walked back to the RV to take it home. Novawynd had the keys in hand. Kat leaned over to her and whispered, "Are you sure you can drive this thing?"

"I can do anything mom, remember." Novawynd chuckled. "Besides, it can't be that hard, as long as I only go forward."

As it turned out, Novawynd thought it was easier than driving a car. It had huge, multiple, side-view mirrors and rear cameras. She could see everything around her. They cruised back to Kat's house and Novawynd helped Kat collect some important things. She should have been nervous about Zefram coming, but she felt no immediate danger. "Zefram," she thought to herself, "You dropped the ball this time. Why didn't you predict I'd come back here immediately to save my family?" She wasn't unhappy about his miscalculation, but it bothered her that he would have made such a grievous oversight. What if it wasn't an oversight? What if it was calculated for some reason? What if they had been tampered with? The Xaxony could have done anything to her family members in the time she was away. They could have implanted monitoring devices, or worse, bombs. Novawynd focused her attention on Kat as she moved a box of books she wanted to save. Novawynd closed her eyes and connected with the Omniaural. Through the Omniaural she connected with Kat's life-force and searched her fibers for foreign objects within her body. There was nothing to be found. Novawynd was relieved, but she would have to scan Ana and Maris too, before she could be completely relieved.

Kat had too many things, which she wanted to bring, so Novawynd had to stop her. "Mom, the physical things aren't going to be destroyed. We can always come back for other things, but right now, let's just take things you can't live without for a few months." Novawynd helped her mother narrow down her selections, and then they were on their way. When they reached Ana's house, Ana also had too many things collected to bring along. Novawynd went through the same process of elimination with Ana. It was a little more difficult getting Maris to let go of some of her things. She believed that she needed all her toys. Novawynd let her bring them. There would be no toys on the ship and anything that kept Maris entertained was welcomed.

They were off on their excursion. They needed to drive hundreds of miles to the Iron Range of northern Minnesota. There, Novawynd could buy Taconite rich land into which the Talosian machines could drill the shaft where the Phoenix would find its new, but temporary home.

*   *   *

Trevor was on the opposite side of the globe from Novawynd, and where he was, it was the middle of the night again. He found his parents sleeping again, like he had when he first said goodbye. This time he made sure they were well awake before he started talking to them.

"Trevor!" His mother, Carol, sat bolt upright. "Where have you been for God's sake?"

"Good Lord boy!" his father, John, cried out in his thick Australian accent. Even Trevor almost didn't understand it. "You've had us all worried stiff. Where the hell have you been?" he scolded the way a father would.

"I have something important to tell you, but I want to tell everyone, I need to have Troy and Trent here too." Trevor's parents called their other two sons and told them Trevor was back, and ordered them to come over immediately. Trent, the youngest, was still single, but Troy was married with a little boy and a little girl had come since Trevor last saw him. He made small talk with his parents while they waited for the brothers, but Trevor would not answer any questions about what this was all about or where he had been. He did not want to tell it twice.

After a while, Trent showed up and after a lot of hugging and mutual roughing-up between the two, Troy also arrived with his family in tow. The oldest child rubbed his tired eyes. The baby slept peacefully in Troy's wife Lori's arms. Trevor tried to keep the greetings short, because he knew he was pressed for time.

"I'm sorry I had to get you all out of bed tonight, but there is something very big about to go down and you'll all think I'm crazy, but the good news is I have proof of everything I'm about to tell you." Trevor explained everything from when Novawynd first came to him to the Xaxony's scouring plan, and the plan the Talosians devised. "And, you all have places aboard the Phoenix, if you want to come." There was an uncomfortable silence then. No one had spoken while Trevor told his story. They merely listened in disbelief. Now they still weren't sure if this was for real.

"Well," Trent broke the silence, "I want to see this ship. It would be awesome living on a space ship. And, you're telling me I could get busy with an actress or model or some super-smart broad, or an alien chick? Well, hell…why not?"

"Trevor?" his mother began. "What would we do to pass the time onboard a spaceship?"

"Consider it like an early retirement. Instead of just traveling and seeing the world, you'll see the world, from a distance, and then you'll see the rest of the universe. But, in the mean time, everyone will take a test and Novawynd will give everyone duties that best match their interests. That way, everyone contributes and keeps busy. She doesn't want anyone going stir-crazy. It can be very confining in a ship. I know."

There were many more questions. After all questions were answered, the obvious choice was for the lot of them to come aboard the ship. Even if they could eek out a living on the planet after the virus was finished, and if they could avoid the probes, there would be nobody left on the planet. Without other people, they would simply exist to exist and the point of that was ridiculous. At least on the ship, they would contribute to the greater good. Not to mention, the children would have other children to grow up with and possibly have children of their own with, etc. After they were satisfied, Trevor had a question for them.

"Where's Swizel?"

They were all silent. Trevor's mother looked down at the floor.

Trevor's father answered. "I'm sorry son. A croc got her."

Trevor was silent then too, while that sunk in. He had already previously dealt with having to let her go, so he wasn't as sad as he should be, but he was disappointed. Then suddenly, he was glad. "Oh well, I would've just had to say goodbye to her all over again. At least this way she died with honor.

"With honor!" Trent laughed as if that was the most ridiculous thing he'd ever heard. Everyone looked at him sternly, and he cut his laughter short.

"Well, let's get busy."

Trevor explained the next thing they had to do was collect their special belongings, as Novawynd and her family were doing on the other side of the globe at the time. When they were finished, Trevor used his metaband to hail the ship's computer, Kae, to blip Novawynd.

"Yes Trevor?" she cheerfully replied.

"We're ready on this side." He informed.

"Okay, we just took off and are heading up to the property I'm looking at. We haven't even bought it yet. I'll have the ship send a cargo shuttle. Load all your stuff on the shuttle. You can bring your family to the Talosian ship to see what its like. Leave your belongings on the shuttle in that time. Showing them around the ship will kill time and that'll be interesting for them too. Then I'll let you know when you can come back down and meet us here."

"Gotcha." Trevor acknowledged.

"End." Novawynd ended transmission.

*   *   *

Novawynd had used Kat's cell phone to arrange a meeting with the realtor who had the listing for the property she was interested in. It was two hundred acres of wooded property, formerly someone's hunting grounds, and ten miles south of the Mesabi Iron Range. The price was incredibly reasonable at about one-thousand-forty-dollars per acre. Even so, Novawynd intended to negotiate for a straight thousand per acre. Novawynd felt two-hundred-acres in the middle of nowhere would be sufficient to keep people from seeing crafts coming and going. They would set up an infra-red fence around the perimeter that would be monitored, and if a human tripped the sensors, he would be disintegrated by a Quanton particle beam. It would be unfortunate if that should happen, but Novawynd's crew couldn't have some wayward hunter trespass on the land and accidentally come across their project, and considering the fate that awaited human-kind, it was probably a more humane way to go.

Several hours later, it was well past dark and late. They pulled into an RV park that happened to be present outside one of the towns they passed through. They paid for their one night. Novawynd hooked up the sewage, water and power and they proceeded to get ready for bed. The next morning, the foursome met the realtor at the property. He seemed a bit concerned that they were arriving in a massive rig. Novawynd, Kat, Ana and Maris walked around the property a bit. Maris chased butterflies and Novawynd took mental photographs of the moment, because she wouldn't see Maris chase butterflies for a long time to come, if ever again. Luckily the seller was motivated and willing to close as soon as the realtor's agency had an available time when everyone could come together. After making a few calls, the realtor was able to pull some strings and get a closing set for the next day at one o'clock in the afternoon.

After the deal was done, they went over to the local car dealer and purchased a used four-wheel drive SUV, and then they drove the SUV to the motor sports dealer and bought two ATVs, for running around on the property, and a trailer for them. Ana drove the SUV and Novawynd drove the RV back to the new property. Novawynd pulled the RV as far down the access road as possible. They took the SUV back into town and bought five of the largest RVs they could find there, using the same trick they had used on the first RV salesman.

Novawynd told him they were gifts for her family, because they all liked camping together, and now they would camp in luxury.

He was shocked that they could afford such a generous purchase, but they did have the money. Averaging around three-hundred-thousand-dollars apiece, they could have bought two hundred RVs before they ran out of the lottery money. However, even if they had run out of funds, Novawynd only needed to access an ATM, and she could transfer as much money as she wanted into her mother's bank. They drove away in one of the RVs with a promise to come back for the other four the following day. Novawynd pulled the second RV up next to the first one and they were set for phase two.

*   *   *

Trevor had shown his family around the Talosian ship and they were, in fact, amazed that Trevor wasn't crazy, and the life he had told them he had been leading was reality. They were interested in the orange eyed aliens, but these aliens were so much like Earthlings, they didn't think too much of it. Then, at length, they came across Stunner. This looming, handsome, sky-blue colored man was awesome to them. They stood speechless and agape at the sight of him.

Stunner walked up to Trevor to address him and his family. "That guy's blue!" Trent tittered in excitement. Stunner stopped and gave Trent an amused look.

"Yes," Trevor affirmed, "he has the implant I told you about, that translates alien languages. He can understand you. They can all understand you quite well, so please be polite and watch what you say." Trevor warned.

"I have also made a point of learning Novawynd's native language, and I speak it quite fluently as well." Stunner informed.

"Right," Trevor acknowledged facetiously, and then added in Xaxon, "Because you're always kissing Novawynd's ass."

Stunner seemed unmoved by that comment. "I have good news for you Trevor." he began in English, as he smiled at Trevor's family. Then he continued in Eron, "Novawynd feels you put enough time in with me in the battleot operations center back on the Zenith and she feels you studied tactics diligently and are skilled with the battleots. Because of this, Novawynd is giving you the position of intin, or what she is calling the 'commander' of the Phoenix's space-guard. Normally, you would need many anios of training to be qualified for that position, but because we don't have a lot of options and with Vertigo under your wing, you should be fine. However, you should know that Novawynd has made me the zelo, or what she refers to as 'captain'. That means I will be your commanding officer and you can no longer speak to me like you just did." Stunner grinned.

"I see." Trevor answered in English, stifling his emotional reaction. He was both ecstatic that he would become the commander of the space-guard, but he was also slightly chagrined that he would have to be under Stunner's command. The truth was, he liked Stunner and was only mildly jealous that Stunner was also an object of Novawynd's affections. He acted more jealous than he was, just because he had always been overly dramatic anyway. Trevor believed Novawynd didn't necessarily favor Stunner; he was merely an apple, where Trevor was an orange. Whom Novawynd preferred really depended on her mood.

Trevor forced a smile and spoke to his family. "Captain Stunner here, just informed me that I will be the commander of the space-guard on our new ship. This is a great honor, and I'm very excited about it. Come on, I'll show you what I'm talking about." He led his family to the space-guard command center. Stunner tagged along. He had nothing better to do, and perhaps he could answer some questions. In the SGCC, the bet squad was going through simulations, which was perfect, because his family members could see first hand how things were done. Trevor pointed out the space-guard and their controls. He explained how fighting with the drones worked. He pointed out the intin and explained what she did. Trevor mentioned that's what he would be doing.

"This is awesome!" Trent, who seemed to be unshy of expressing his thoughts, blurted out. "Can I be a space-guard? I totally could do it. It looks like video game controls, and I rock at video games."

Stunner responded to that, "Initially, Talosians will be the space-guard, but we will train chosen Earthlings to fill the positions. In time there may be no Talosians left on board, so the possibility is good that you could be a space-guard."

"What about Vertigo? How come he didn't get the commander position if he's so good?" Trevor questioned Stunner.

"He was offered, but of course, he didn't want it. He just wanted the ata, or what word did Novawynd use, 'major', position on the Aleph squad. He prefers it that way."

Trevor turned to his family, "If you were astounded by the looks of Stunner, you'll love Vertigo. He's your classic green alien." The family made a collective "Ahhh." in understanding.

As they left the SGCC, Danalian approached them. Stunner bowed to Danalian and Trevor did so also, reflexively. Danalian just seemed the type one should bow to, considering he had a strong presence and he was the Commander in Chief of a whole planet. Trevor admired Danalian, because he viewed Danalian as a savior. The only time Trevor didn't admire Danalian, was in the presence of Novawynd. He hated the way Danalian acted diminished, how he genuflected and took a knee to greet Novawynd as if she were a goddess. But, Danalian truly believed Novawynd was this religious figure called the Lajiachine.

Maybe he wasn't wrong. Trevor introduced Danalian and explained his position to his family. They seemed to have an understanding of the seriousness of his position.

"I hope you have all decided to stay on board the Phoenix and help fight against the oppression of the Xaxony." Danalian encouraged.

"Fight?" Trevor's mom piped up.

"Well, not actually, physically." Danalian explained. "By defecting you all help throw another chink in the Xaxon armor. And, we need all the chinks we can get." Danalian nodded, gave a small bow and was on his way again. His lanky legs carrying him down the hall as swiftly as he had come. After that, Stunner showed the Eams family to their temporary quarters. They would spend two nights on the ship before leaving to go back to Earth.

*   *   *

Zefram, having information that the ship involved in Novawynd's disappearance was Talosian, went straight to Talos. He was guardedly welcomed by the President of Talos. Zefram insisted on speaking to Danalian, but the President assured Zefram that Danalian was gone on matters of state and would not be able to be called back just then. Because Danalian hadn't mentioned any of this to the President, he truly had no knowledge of the defection, and so when Zefram probed him, he could tell the man knew nothing of Novawynd's disappearance. But, where was Danalian? It was frustrating that the President didn't know where he was, but apparently it was common that the President of Talos didn't know where Danalian was or what he was up to.

While Zefram dilly-dallied on Talos, one of his snitches reported on the ship Zefram was looking for. Zefram had learned that ship was at a pirate out-station undergoing repairs. Zefram was gleeful. He had his zelo bring the Tauron straight to the pirate station. Several ships docked there, made a hasty retreat upon the appearance of a Xaxon war-ship. However, the ship in question did not move. Zefram took a team of his space-guard to check out the situation. There were beings moving things onto the ship, and they were shocked when they noticed him coming. They realized they were caught, so they didn't attempt to flee; besides they didn't think they were doing anything wrong. The ship had clearly been abandoned and they were entitled to claim it. Zefram didn't know that though. He calmly approached a Mikonade whom calmly stood outside the umbilical entrance to the ship. The Mikonade looked like large grass-hoppers, but were still only half-the size of a man. They also did not hop, or fly for that matter. They lacked wings that Earth grass-hoppers possessed and they walked upright on spindly legs. They did however have two sets of arms, besides their two legs. Their exoskeleton gave them an excellent natural armor and it was a mottled, grayish-green color. Although they stood out in space vehicles, their coloration was excellent camouflage on their own planet of Mikona. On Mikona, they were the superior intellect, but there were larger predators, very much like pterodactyls, which found them quite tasty. They developed their camouflage to avoid the flying reptiles.

"What you want, Leluminalia?" He asked in his language, which consisted of a series of clicks, buzzes, whistles and titters. His obstinate manner toward Zefram told him this Mikonade couldn't know who he was.

"Is this your ship?" Zefram knew the answer almost as soon as he asked it.

"It is now. It was abandoned here and we have rightfully claimed it."

"I see. I suppose the mainframe was gone too?" Zefram asked for clarification.

"That's right."

"Of course." Zefram turned and left the Mikonade pirate to his business. The ship was merely an empty shell now. Novawynd was not there, nor was any information as to who was behind this and why. It was a Talosian ship, but it was an extremely old model and it could just as easily have been a pirated ship. The Talosians would undoubtedly deny that they had anything to do with Novawynd's defection, even though they swore they would support the Lajiachine to spite the Xaxony. This trail had gone stone-cold, and so Zefram's only choice was to go to Earth to wait for Novawynd. She would show up there eventually, and he hoped she would show up after he released the virus. He wanted her to see the devastation and know it was he who unleashed it on her people. However, even though Novawynd couldn't know about the impending doom of her people, she was shrewd and she would realize Zefram would go after her family. Therefore, she would get to them as soon as she could.

Zefram headed back to the Tauron. "Let's go." he ordered his space-guard detail. "We're going to Earth, now."

*   *   *

Trevor got the call that it was time to gather his family and return to Earth. He rousted everyone up and they quickly headed down to the shuttle. Also on the shuttle, were Stunner, Vertigo and a handful of Talosians; as they were to assist with the preparations. Several other cargo shuttles had already begun descending to the location. They housed the mining machinery that was needed to drill the massive hole, as well as the perimeter defense systems. In all, five shuttles would descend to Earth. It was night in the northern woods, but all Earthlings would see were five meteorites falling to earth.

No sooner had the shuttles landed, than Novawynd got a transmission from Danalian. "Xaxon ship entered orbit, must flux."

and that was all. He had come at last. Zefram had arrived, and they were left alone on Earth until who knows when. They would go about their business with the Xaxon ship overhead, but the Talosians couldn't bring any parts of the ship back to Earth until Zefram left. And, would he leave? They moved fast to cover the shuttles with branches and debris to hide them from the prying eyes of Earth satellites and Xaxon probes.

Novawynd would need to apply one-hundred-percent of her Lelumin training to cloak herself from the supernatural senses of Zefram. She could not have him sensing her after all this, everything would be jeopardized. Novawynd let the others know what had happened. They pondered it silently for a minute, and then the Talosians began to move the machinery out and went about their business, they were on a time frame after all, and they couldn't worry about it. They had been briefed on this and knew it may happen. "They set a good example." Novawynd encouraged. "We all need to continue on and everything will work out. Danalian has things under control up there."

*   *   *

"Zefram, the ship's sensors locked onto an alien ship orbiting the planet. It fluxed as soon as it sensed us. The computer was unable to identify the ship. It had its interference shields up, but it's shape was unique." the Tauron's zelo informed Zefram.

Zefram was furious. "Fornix!" he cursed the Xaxon word that was equivalent to the exclamation *fuck*. "Novawynd was on that ship. I know it." He didn't really know it, he just assumed. "Make my shuttle ready, I'm leaving immediately."

Zefram headed down to the point on the planet where Novawynd's mother was supposed to live. He had been there before with Novawynd, when she initially came back to see her family, after she got command of the Zenith. The lights were on in the house, but he had a bad feeling as he approached it. The door was open a bit. He pushed the door open and there was a stack of stuff in the hallway, the type of stuff an Earthling might cherish and want to bring with if leaving. He quickly moved through the house, he felt no human life there at all. Novawynd had been here, for sure, and had gotten her mother out before he arrived. Zefram knew Novawynd had a sister too, but he didn't know where she lived. At this point, it didn't matter. He knew she would have gotten to the sister too. No doubt the ship that had left the Earth's orbit upon their arrival was the mysterious ship that carried Novawynd. He had missed out on his opportunity to get the mother. He kicked himself for not having made that his first priority. He reached out to feel for Novawynd. "Where are you?" he asked in his mind. He could not feel her. She was far away by now. She had won again, but wait until he released the virus on her home world, then who would have the last laugh.

*   *   *

The ground crew located the point Danalian's ship had indicated would be the best place to dig the shaft. Robots ran around the perimeter, precisely placing poles in the ground with interference-shield emitters on them. The multitude of emitters interlaced and created an interference-shield blanket over a twenty-thousand-square-foot area to hide it from anyone who might see the hole from above. The shuttles and machines would also have their interference-shields up while operating, so they would be invisible to the human eye, and no devices of observation would see them; but while they weren't functioning, the shields weren't on, so they needed to be covered the old fashioned way. The machines would dig the hole and carry the waste taconite to the shuttles, which would then carry it to the taconite dumps located only a few miles away. No one could see the shuttles as they did this, but the shuttles would still need to dump in the most remote location. It was imperative that no one witnessed taconite pouring out of the air from seemingly nothing. There would be a lot of strange things going on in the three months that the aliens would be here. People would disbelieve one unusual occurrence, labeling the witness a "crack-pot". But, if several people experienced odd happenings, there could be trouble. It was bad enough that Zefram was interfering, but Novawynd certainly didn't need any National Security Agency officials poking around.

The robots swiftly assembled the mining machines and they were soon at work. By daylight, there was a crater about one-hundred-twenty-feet in diameter, and ten feet deep. It had taken the miners only an hour to get that far. The shaft would have to be six-hundred-fifty-feet deep. At ten feet every hour, it would take the mining machines sixty-five hours to dig it. That was only a little under three days, just as Danalian had predicted. Hopefully Zefram would be gone by then, because if he wasn't, Danalian would have to take action. Novawynd was unsure of what action he could take. It would have to be some sort of decoy, to draw Zefram away, because there would be no way to win a full on attack of a Xaxon ship; especially the top Leluminalia's ship. Only the best of the best space-guard worked on Zefram's ship. Besides, Danalian couldn't run the risk of the Xaxony realizing Talosians were attacking them. He hadn't discussed this possibility with Novawynd, but she was certain the decoy method would be Danalian's tool.

In the morning, Novawynd took Trevor, his father and his two brothers to town to claim the other four RVs. After driving them off the lot, they headed to the local big-box store to stock up on cooking utensils and toiletries. Then the convoy went to each Grocery store in town and bought up each store's supply of jugged and bottled water. At the final store, they each grabbed two shopping carts. They filled one with frozen meat, one with frozen vegetables and the rest with canned, boxed and preserved items. The cashier was shocked at the amount of food and other goods they were buying.

Trevor turned to Novawynd and jokingly asked, "Do you think we have enough?" The young cashier girl laughed at his joke flirtingly. No doubt she had never seen a man as handsome as Trevor in her life.

"We'll come back after...you know what, to get the rest." she answered.

After loading the last of the goods into the rigs, they drove them to the RV park to fill the water tanks, and then headed back to the property. They parked the behemoths along the access road so there was a line of six RVs lined up end to end. One rig, the most luxurious one, was to be for Novawynd alone. One was for Kat, Ana and Maris. One was for Trevor, Stunner and Vertigo to share. One was for the three Talosians, who were assisting them, to share. One was for Trevor's brother Troy and his wife and children. The last rig was for Trevor's parents and his brother Troy to share. The previous owner of the property had parked a significantly smaller RV on the site when he went hunting, so he had electricity running to the site. This would keep them set with running refrigerators, freezers, washers, dryers, televisions and multi-media players.

Novawynd went back to survey the progress of the miners. They were now down twenty feet. Lately everything had been so surreal. She had been in denial, obviously. Now the reality of this situation seemed very real to her. Danalian had given her the transcript chip for the brain-storming meeting he had with the other great minds of Talos. They literally had conceived every possible scenario in an attempt to save Earth, and there truly was no solution. This was the only way and she was beginning to accept that. Novawynd also started to experience a profound guilt. She felt responsible for all of this, even though she knew she had no control over the events. "Why me?" she asked aloud to no one. There was no one there to hear her.

Novawynd went to Stunner, Trevor and Vertigo's new home on wheels. They were arguing over who got to sleep where. Stunner was pulling rank "As your captain…" he was saying as Novawynd entered. They all stopped and looked at her.

"Listen, you're all gonna sleep in the back bedroom. We got all the extra twin-sized mattresses so you could pull out the king sized ones in the bed rooms and make enough bunks to accommodate everyone. You'll have to get it done before bed-time, so you'd better get moving." she ordered. They darted to get to work, but Novawynd stopped Stunner. "Captain Stunner?"

"Yes, Novawynd?"

"I need to talk to you back at my place, if you don't mind."

"Of course." he was happy to oblige. They walked back to her RV, which was a few yards away, and went inside. Novawynd asked Stunner to take a seat on the sofa. He did so, and she continued standing. She paced and wrung her hands for a couple of minutes.

"What is it that you want to talk to me about, Novawynd?" Stunner could see her obvious tension and attempted to pry something out of her.

She sat down next to him. "Stunner," She put her hand on his leg, "I'm so sorry I got you into this. I should have asked you if you wanted to come."

He put his arms around her and held her then. "I'm sorry all this is happening. This is terrible for you and your people. Don't feel sorry for bringing me along. You wouldn't have had time to ask me, because you would have had to explain everything to me, and I know you had no time to explain. Besides, from the day I met you, I was devoted to you. I would have followed you anywhere." He rubbed her back to comfort her. It was amazing how an alien who had no natural inclination towards intimacy, could be her best confidant because he empathized and he gave advice and comforted her, but most importantly, he listened. Trevor, on the other hand, always turned the conversation back around to him. He didn't know how to comfort her, but Stunner never failed.

"I couldn't leave you there. I couldn't stand the thought of Zefram torturing you or using you to get to me. He knew we were involved."

Stunner pulled her onto his lap. "I wouldn't ever want you to worry about me." He stroked her face and Novawynd couldn't help herself. She kissed him. They continued kissing passionately.

She pulled away after a little while. "I suppose this is inappropriate considering the circumstances, but I just need to have my mind taken off of what's happening right now."

"I'm happy to help, anytime. I'm so glad you didn't leave me behind and I'm glad you came to me now." they continued kissing then, and soon they were in the bedroom on the king-sized bed, writhing around as they feverishly stripped off their modesties. Novawynd loved the heft of Stunners long, blue body. It felt so nice as he pressed down on her. She had been in such a dreamlike trance these past few days, she felt as if she would float away. His weight made her feel planted. It was the middle of the day, but there was really nothing else they could be doing. They took their time and stayed in bed. Then they fell asleep after they both had enough.

Vertigo had programmed one of the robots to build the bunks for them, so he and Trevor sat outside catching sun on the beautiful late summer day.

"I thought Novawynd was *your* woman." Vertigo stated matter-of-factly.

"Sometimes she is, and sometimes she's Stunner's." He took a drink of his beer.

"I didn't even know an Eron could get into anyone other than an Eron woman." Vertigo also drank one of Trevor's ales. Trevor had explained to him that it was made of fermented plant material. Napojans and Erons were vegetarian. But, only on Earth, because they couldn't ingest any Earth animal meat or fat. The chemical composition of the meat didn't sit well with their delicate alien systems.

"Apparently, Stunner has no problem. Novawynd trained him." Trevor laughed. Then he looked at Vertigo, sitting in the Earth's sunlight. "I wonder if you can tan?" he laughed again at the thought of Vertigo turning dark green.

"If I can what?"

"If your skin will get darker in the sun."

"Why would it?"

"Our skin does."

*   *   *

Zefram stood in front of the eight blobs of light that made up the Superior Council. "I have discovered that Novawynd has been here and collected her family. A ship fluxed out of Earth's orbit as we came out of our flux near the Earth. We couldn't identify the ship. Now that Novawynd has what is most important to her, she won't go back to the planet. However, if she knows about the scouring, and the results it will have, she may attempt to stop it. My guess is, she is with pirates now, so they can't do too much to stop us and she'll know this. None-the-less, she may be sitting at a safe distance from the Earth right now, monitoring when Xaxon ships come and go. She may, in desperation, attempt to attack my ship when I return to deliver the virus. I will make sure it is launched as the ship comes out of flux, so there won't be any time for her to act. Until the virus is done, I intend to go back to following my leads and putting feelers out on our spy network. She'll turn up somewhere. Even if it isn't until after I scour Earth. I believe, after that, she'll come to me."

The Superior Council spoke. "We are concerned about your suspicion that the Talosians are helping her. Do you think the mystery ship at Earth may have been Talosian?"

"Hard to say, but I doubt it. The Talosians certainly could build their own ships, but any ship that can flux is retrofitted at Xaxon 3. All ships fitted with a flux engine are catalogued. We would have identified it. I'm sure it was a modification of some sort."

"Very well Zefram. Keep on as you were, but we have other work for you to do as well. The allies are nervous now. They believe the Prophesy is coming to fruition. We need you to do damage control on this. You need to be the one to quell their fears about Novawynd. Make sure to make it quite clear that anyone found aiding Novawynd, will be deemed traitors, and subject to immediate scrapping."

"Yes Your Excellencies. It shall be done." he bowed to them as they disappeared. He left the room and headed back to his own quarters. On the way he blipped his zelo. "Take us back to the pirate out-station where we found the abandoned Talosian ship." He intended to do some detective work there.

*   *   *

Novawynd woke up from her cat nap with a start. Stunner was nestled up next to her, spooning her. He stirred as she sat up. She felt as if the vice-grip that had been clamped on her brain had suddenly been loosened. She knew immediately what that meant. "He's gone!" she cried out.

"Who is?" Stunner asked sleepily.

"Zefram. He's left. We're clear, and hopefully for a while." She hailed Danalian with her meta-band.

"Yes Novawynd, we tracked him leaving." Danalian already knew. "I have some business to attend to, but we'll return in two days with the first parts of the ship." That was all Novawynd needed to know. She felt a little better. She sat up on the edge of the bed. "Stunner, there is a night and day difference between when Zefram is around and when he's not. No one can ever know how exhausting it is to constantly block him. Even when we were on the ship together, I was always blocking him and he was always blocking me." she sighed heavily. "It was just…exhausting. I'm so happy to be rid of him." Stunner sat up and put his arms around her from behind.

"I can only imagine what it must be like."

"Well let's get moving. I want to have a bar-b-cue for everyone so we all get to know each other. Let's take a shower and meet the world.

*   *   *

Two days later, Danalian's ship was back and the shaft was complete. The mining machines were broken down, and packed on the shuttles they came in. They went back up to the ship and returned with new fabrication robots and parts for the Phoenix. The first part to be built would be the rockets. These would propel them out of the shaft and into outer-space like a missile. Once the ship escaped Earth's atmosphere and leveled out, the rockets would be jettisoned, and the auxiliary engines would push them out to a safe point in space from which to flux. Four new and much smaller mining machines also came. These would drill six shafts down to the base of the chute at forty-five degree angles, which would serve as ventilation shafts for the heat, steam and flames upon ignition.

Everyone in the landing party was pretty well acquainted with each other at this point. They were all curious about the various machines, robots, and parts and pieces coming and going. Except the Talosians; they had seen it all before. Within a few more days, the engine was being brought down. The Talosians had learned, if they took an existing ship already fitted with a flux engine, they could basically tear apart the former ship and modify the design. And as long as they kept the engine containment cell in tact and always powered, they could save the engine in pristine condition. If the power was ever cut, the engine simply disappeared. This was a phenomenon; one which Novawynd witnessed herself on the flesh-peddling pirate's ship.

The Phoenix's engine was from a new Xaxon ship that pirates had commandeered, and the Talosians bought it from them. Those on the ground watching the engine's arrival, only saw the outer walls of the former ship's engine-containment cell. It was a huge box, thirty feet tall, wide and deep. It was cautiously lowered into the shaft. Novawynd got an extremely uneasy feeling that seemed to come from the box itself. She felt drawn to it. She moved closer as it was lowered. Stunner grabbed her arm to stop her just inches from the edge of the deep shaft. That snapped her out of the trance she had been in. She had just been compelled to go to it and touch the box, just as she had touched the door to the compartment on the pirate ship.

Within a few more weeks, Novawynd and her group could move into the livable areas of the ship. They would have to say goodbye to the RV's, but everyone was happy to do so. They needed to use a stairway that lead down into the shaft a ways. Then they took a working elevator that slid along the wall of the shaft. The ship, when finished, would consist of six, life-supporting spheres called "biospheres", plus the engine compartment, the battleot containment braces and the auxiliary boosters. All covered by layers of Isotarin armor as its protective hull. There was only one stop on the elevator, as it went directly down to biosphere two. From Biosphere two, the occupants could take an interior, magnetic elevator, up and down through biospheres two through six.

Biosphere one was the shuttle bay and not necessary for them to access at that point. Biosphere two was for Novawynd and her family alone. Biosphere three was basically the entertainment center. All things for amusement would be located there, from places to eat and drink to gaming and sporting facilities. Biosphere four contained one-hundred-twenty-eight condos for everyone except the space-guard. Biosphere five housed the space-guard dormitories, the defense and command centers, as well as the brig and the med and sci-labs.

Biospheres one and six were the smallest at forty-eight-feet in diameter. Biosphere one had only one floor. Shuttles were tucked away under the floor and up against the ceiling. It would house two thirty-foot cargo shuttles, two twenty-two-foot personnel shuttles, and one twenty-foot and one fourteen-foot, luxury shuttle. Biospheres two and five were the second smallest at fifty-six feet in diameter and seven floors. Biospheres three and four were the largest at eighty-eight feet in diameter and eleven floors. The first and second floors on biospheres two and three were dedicated to parks. Finally, biosphere six was purely for storage, but even with all that, there wasn't enough storage to keep enough goods for 144 people to subsist for long. They would need to make regular trips back to Earth to pillage, but that food would soon perish or become infested. They would need to produce their own food. That was the true purpose for the parks. They were actually gardens, more than parks; a place where fruits, vegetables and grains would be cultivated. The Earthlings would become vegetarians simply because it would be too difficult to sustain animals onboard.

Water stores were contained within the top floor of each sphere and waste was contained at the bottom of each. The Xaxons had used a system of waste recycling that worked very well. They had a waste treatment system that super-compressed any waste that contained liquid. This squeezed every last drop of liquid out, the liquids were allowed to leach through fine silt, and then it was filtered several times over, boiled and chemically treated. The left-over solids were incinerated. All dry waste was compacted and incinerated. It would be difficult for some people to deal with the fact that the water coming out of the tap, although it would be ninety-seven percent cleaner than Earth water, came from rotten banana peels, or old coffee grounds; not-to-mention the bodily fluids. But, once they have no other option, they will adopt it. Even so, the waste recyclers took some time to work, so water would still need to be rationed.

As the ship sat upright at the moment, all the spheres were level. The ship had been designed such that all the spheres would pivot as the ship left the earth's atmosphere and evened out in space. That way, they would always be level. There were four more elevator cars stacked in the shuttle bay, and once the ship prepared for take off, they would all descend to their respective spheres. The now, long, singular elevator shaft would become four shorter ones, once the spheres repositioned. Once the ship was in space, robots would cap off the elevator shafts in the rooms they currently moved through, but wouldn't be welcomed in later, such as the shaft that currently penetrated straight through the middle of Novawynd's quarters.

*   *   *

Novawynd needed to start thinking about who would be her chosen ones. She left the ship with her laptop and drove into town. She found the local coffee shop and sat in the corner. She tapped into the wi-fi and started searching for people that filled the slots on her list. She had done as Danalian suggested, and thought of doctors, scientists and technical wizards of all types, whose intellect and skills would serve the fledgling Earthlings well. She had thirty slots designated for the intellectuals. The other seventy slots would be filled by the beautiful people; actors, models and athletes. Other people who had miscellaneous skills would be considered also. The Earthling race needed culture too, and so musicians, artists, writers, poets were also selected.

It would be a long process. There was a lot of data on the internet to wade through. The celebrities were the easy ones, but the intellectuals who had information out on the net, didn't necessarily have pictures, or any information about their personal lives. "This is going to take a while." she thought to herself. But she had a month to figure it all out, even if she had to work at it full time.

CHAPTER 15

Novawynd found the search for intellectuals over the internet more difficult than she had thought. She finally had to resort to going on field trips to the best colleges the Earth had to offer. That way she could see students, teachers and student-teachers with her own eyes. She hung around where they hung around and asked questions. Finally, after a month, she had her thirty intellectuals picked out. It would only be another month before what they expected to be the zero-hour would arrive. Novawynd felt, since they couldn't be sure exactly when it would happen, that they should start collecting the chosen ones within one week. They would spend two weeks collecting.

In the mean time, Danalian had brought the AP workers and a slew of artificial animals. For the most part, the artificial animals were to be kept in the parks, but there were a few exceptions. Danalian also brought six kittens, which would never mature into cats, and two dogs. Novawynd, Ana and Kat would each get two kittens. Kat would also get one of the dogs, a faux Jack Russell terrier. The last dog was a second version of Swizel, for Trevor. Trevor was ecstatic when he saw the new Swizel. If other people wanted artificial pets, they could put their orders in later, but the goods needed to be ordered, produced and delivered discretely. The very fact that Danalian had gotten the exact replica of Swizel, told Novawynd that the Uinalons now knew that Danalian was aiding Novawynd. Novawynd had told Danalian about the Uinalon premier's comment, and how she felt sure he would support her. Danalian was not surprised.

"We have had a strong relationship with the Uinalons for ages and I know they feel quite the same about the Lajiachine as we Talosians do." he affirmed her suspicions. "They would fly in the face of the Xaxony to support the Lajiachine, but, under the radar. You'll find most Xaxon allies who will support you, will not do so openly. But, that's to our advantage. Soon the network of those who support you will be stronger than the Xaxony itself, all-the-while gaining strength right under the Xaxony's nose."

Other items of importance Danalian brought were the uniforms for the space-guard and the commanding officers. Novawynd had decided on red uniforms. Trevor looked very fetching in his uniform, but she hadn't figured on the hue of Stunner and Vertigo's skin tones clashing against the red of the uniforms. She wondered if she should have chosen a more neutral color. But, the uniforms were done and they looked great, besides, Stunner and Vertigo didn't seem to mind. They actually seemed to be relieved to wear something other than the grey of the Xaxon uniforms.

*   *   *

Zefram gleaned no information from the people who worked at the pirate out-station. They admitted to seeing the mystery ship, but swore they never saw anyone boarding it. Zefram knew they had to have seen someone, but they honestly didn't think they did. This told Zefram that Junatiel was used on them. Novawynd must have blocked them from seeing the crew that exited the old ship and proceeded onto the new ship. As for the new ship, the station's workers testified that there were no markings and the design was unlike anything they had seen before. That, Zefram already knew. He seemed to hit another dead-end at the pirate out-station.

One dialo, Zefram received a comm-link. It was from Lord Danalian.

"Zefram, I just returned to Talos and President Inata told me you had been looking for me. What is it you want?" Danalian was only slightly lower than Zefram as a Leluminalia; however, being Talosian, his psychic skills were unrivaled. Zefram could out-fight Danalian in a physical battle, but he couldn't outwit Danalian. He knew, whenever speaking to Danalian, he must use extreme caution.

"I trust, by now you've heard of Novawynd's defection?" Zefram chose his words carefully.

"Yes." Danalian admitted without emotion. "What of it?"

"It was a Talosian ship that she escaped on."

"So? A lot of our cast-off ships are used by pirates. We aren't in control of what they do with our ships."

Zefram didn't feel that Danalian was blocking him, but he also wasn't picking up on whether Danalian had any involvement or not. "Lord Danalian, I need to know what sort of business you were attending to at the time Novawynd defected." Zefram got to the point.

At this, Danalian finally showed a little emotion. He smirked, "No Zefram, you may need to know, but you have no right to ask and you are not entitled to the answer. I'm sure you haven't forgotten that Talos is not your ally. My business is just that…mine. However, since you obviously are accusing me of helping her, I'll tell you this; I didn't help her, but if I ever come across her in the future, I will not hesitate to help her. I believe she is the Lajiachine, and as you know, Talos has pledged allegiance to the Lajiachine."

"I'm not accusing you of anything, but it is precisely because of that pledge that you are *at least* suspected." Zefram defended.

"Yes, well everyone knows about the Talosian pledge. A shrewd person would have capitalized on that by using a Talosian ship to cast suspicion in our direction."

Zefram snorted. "Funny you should say that, because I would think a truly shrewd person would use their own ship. Say an older one, and then try to tell me they wouldn't be stupid enough to use their own ship."

"Well," Danalian calmly responded, "I can't help you Zefram. Not just because I don't have any information, but because that would go against my principles. I knew what you were going to ask, and I knew I had nothing to offer. I could have just as easily not contacted you, but I couldn't resist the opportunity to make something clear. You see, we are now in a race, Zefram. I want to find her too. I want to make sure I'm on the right side when it all goes down. I feel confident that I will find her before you do."

*   *   *

Novawynd laughed when Danalian told her about his interaction with Zefram. "Danalian, you'll have to teach me how you block without it being obvious that you're blocking. That's a useful skill."

"It took me several hundreds of anios to develop it. I'm not sure how to teach you how to do it."

"Quite simply, actually." Novawynd assured, "Give me your hand." She put her hand out to him, palm up. He hesitated for a moment, but then put his hand in hers. He felt nothing, but Novawynd felt all the knowledge and skills of Danalian pour into her. It actually made her a bit dizzy, but in seconds it was over. She suddenly felt significantly wiser. Novawynd let go of his hand. "There, it's done." She smiled at him.

"You can absorb knowledge from people, just like that, in zecrons?" Danalian was amazed. "That's a skill I'd like to learn from you, if you don't mind."

"Well, that's the problem. I know how to absorb, but not how to exude. I would love to be able to bestow my abilities on others, especially the ability to flux. I would bestow that on everyone, if I could. That is my goal, to figure out how to do that."

*　　*　　*

Trevor, and three of the Talosians designated as space-guard, had begun to find and collect the people on Novawynd's list of chosen ones. Not in any particular order. This was it. No other solutions had presented themselves to Novawynd after all. The truth of it began to sink in as people began to fill the cells in the brig. There was no going back now. The ship was nearly complete. The hull was the last thing needing to be assembled, and the final pieces were nearly in place.

The chosen ones were usually unconscious when they were brought in. There were only ten cells in the ships brig, so fifty temporary cells were set up in the cafeteria. It was decided that temporary cells were preferable to cramming people into the ten cells in the brig. Even though only two people would need to eventually share each cell, the accommodations were still uncomfortable. Each cell was only seven feet wide, deep and tall. The cells were made of Isotarin and the walls facing out were clear, and riddled with air holes the size of quarters. At the bottom of the front panel there was a slot where the captives' food, water or other accoutrements could be put through to the people inside. The captives could not go to showers, so they were given hot water, soap and washcloths to wash themselves in the morning. As for a toilet, in each cell, there was a hole in the floor with a catch basin beneath. There were robots that collected the basins as often as needed.

Every time a new captive was brought in, Novawynd would go and introduce herself as soon as he or she woke up.

"I'm very sorry for the situation you now find yourself in." She would say. "The arrangements are only temporary. You will be moved as soon as possible, but this might be your home for a couple of weeks."

People were obviously not comforted by this. They were angry and confused and had a lot of questions, primarily "Who are you?" and "Why are you doing this?" and "Why me?" and "What kind of place is this?" Novawynd wished she could tell them, but the time would come when she could.

"I can't tell you right now. When everyone has been gathered, I will tell you all; but really, this is for your immediate, personal safety, and you will see soon enough, it's also for the greater good."

There was a lot of hollering and futile pounding on Isotarin cell walls and whining and crying. Novawynd frequently monitored the goings-on in the detention center, and she listened to the conversations. She tried to walk through a couple times a day, just to make sure the detainees saw a human face. She would talk to them about the frustration they were feeling. She used her Junatiel powers to force them to talk about it, so they could vent. She would do her best to ease their fears.

Then the day came when *he* was brought. The one man she had anticipated more than any other…Will Warner. Of course she selected him as one of her chosen ones. He was too perfect to leave behind. Once he awoke, he put up a fuss, like everyone else had. However, as soon as he saw Novawynd, he recognized her. His face softened into a smile. His eyes twinkled. He pressed up against the clear Isotarin and jutted his fingers out through the holes. "Ms. Smith? It's you isn't it?" he grinned. "You are real." he whispered in a relieved manner.

"Yes Will." she approached the façade of the cell to within inches of Will. She admired the sheen of his black wavy hair and the clearness of his blue eyes "I did tell you someday we would meet. Although, I never would have imagined it would be under these circumstances."

"Yeah, what's up with this? Are you really going to keep me locked up in here?"

"Afraid so. I don't like having anyone locked up, but it is necessary. Also, it's quite temporary."

All the usual questions came out of Will's mouth, pertaining to the situation. Novawynd answered the same as she had for everyone else.

"Your name is Lilil, right?"

"My name was Lilil then. Now I'm known as Novawynd."

"Novawynd." He repeated thoughtfully. "I won't run away from you if you let me out. I'd stay right by your side, all the time, and you could keep a close eye on me." He grinned at her. "You can trust me."

Novawynd knew he wasn't lying. He probably would stick close to her. "Tell me something Will. I read on the Internet, that you were recently divorced. I didn't even know you had been married. When I came to you in your dreams, I didn't even get a hint that there was a wife. Tell me about that."

"The studios kept our relationship under wraps. I was a sex-symbol for both women and men, and they were afraid if people knew I was married, that would turn a large market sect off. Aleesha and I met when I was twenty-one. We were both models, but my career took off, and hers didn't. I started acting in TV first, then movies. All while she was kept practically locked away. She couldn't even go to functions with me, which isn't the way she wanted it. She liked being in the public eye, but she stayed out of it for me. She never got anywhere with her modeling career and she never found anything else that she could really get into for a career. She decided to try being a career mother, but we had so much trouble trying to have a baby. That put a huge strain on us. I just didn't have enough time to deal with the fertility thing. Finally we both realized it wasn't working anymore."

"What about the bondage thing? I thought I never saw you with any women because you were into some sort of alternative sexual lifestyle."

"That was just fantasy. Aleesha never even did any of that stuff with me, and I never asked her, but I thought about it a lot and you helped me act it out. Thanks for that, but you left me wanting more. In a way, I feel that was partially responsible for the trouble between Aleesha and me. I wasn't attracted to her in the traditional sense anymore. I wanted her to be more like you were in my dreams."

"Do you think if you were with me now, I would do those things for you?"

"Would you?" he face lit up with hope.

"Like you said, it was just fantasy. I did those things for you in your dreams because you wanted it, but in real life, I'm not like that either." Novawynd thought Will was even better looking in person. However, she wasn't attracted to him the way she had been nearly two years ago. So much had happened since then. She had her hands full with men at the moment anyway, and didn't need to take on another lover. "I can't let you out yet, for the same reason I can't let anyone else out. But soon…soon." She turned to leave, but turned back to him and added as an after thought, "If it makes it any easier for you, pretend like you're on a reality show."

Novawynd left abruptly, ignoring his pleading. Outside the cafeteria, she ran into Trevor. "I know that last guy we just brought in."

he informed Novawynd. "We worked for the same modeling agency. He was on his way out when I was just coming in. I started working for the same studios as him, but my TV show didn't make it and his took off. We had chances to talk from time to time. I liked him. He was like me you know, down to Earth and not typical Hollywood type."

"Trevor, you'll probably run into a couple people you knew, that is, among the beautiful people I chose. A lot of them were actors and models."

"It just seemed weird, kidnapping a guy I knew. Back in the day, I looked up to him, and now he's like some stud in a stall that will be used for breeding purposes, and that's his only purpose. But, I now serve a greater purpose and I kinda feel like I'm looking down on him, you know, pitying him."

"None of those people should be pitied. It's the people we can't save who should be pitied."

"I know. Can I at least go talk to him?"

"No. Soon enough though."

"Novawynd, why do they have to be locked up in cells like that? Why can't we just put them in their rooms and lock the doors behind them?"

"I love that you're always thinking of ways to do things better. You'll make a great captain some day. But, they are contained together like that for two main reasons. Logistically, when the zero hour approaches, we will show them what is happening outside on large screens. We want them all to be together when this happens, to make sure they have all seen it, and we want to monitor their reaction. Keeping them contained together is the best way to achieve that. The other reason, and more important, is that they are going through a tough time, and keeping them together allows them to bond with each other. When the scouring occurs and they see what has happened, they'll be able to turn to those they have bonded with for support. Their chances for survival are greater with that support. If they're isolated, they don't have those bonds, and things would be tougher for them. I've been monitoring them. I see and hear them talking and getting to know each other and commiserating. You see, they are already bonding."

"I get it." Trevor conceded.

The day after that conversation, Trevor had to put Will's cell mate in with him. Will recognized Trevor. "Hey! I know you." Will seemed amused.

"Yeah, I'm Trevor Eams. We worked for the same modeling agency, and then the same studio. We ran into each other a couple of times before."

"What are you doing here? How come you get to be out there and the rest of us have to be in here? You seem to be working for Novawynd. Is that how we get out of here, we have to offer to work for her or something?"

"I do work for Novawynd, but I have been for nearly a year now. So that's why I'm out here."

"A year? How long has she been doing this? Wait a minute…you went missing about a year ago. It was a big deal. That was all they talked about on all the entertainment news programs for a while. Your disappearance was a real mystery. After a while, your mystery wasn't solved, and some other popular celebrity died an early and unexpected death, so the focus shifted off your disappearance. I almost forgot about that. Is that what I have to look forward to? Stories about going missing."

"Novawynd asked me to come with her. She gave me the choice and I wanted to go. You guys don't have a choice. But, I think when you find out what she's up to, you'll be happier that you're here."

"If she gave me the choice, I'd choose to stay with her too."

"Really? Why would you give up your successful career and your fame and everything, for a life you don't even know what's in store for you?"

"I don't know. I just feel like I need to follow Novawynd, where ever she goes."

"Yeah. I had that same feeling. I think everyone has that feeling around her."

"So, why are we here Trevor?" Will tried to wrench the truth out of Trevor.

"I can't tell you that. But, we anticipate it should be only a few days now before you all know the truth. I shouldn't say more, but I'll just say this...prepare yourself for the truth to be the worst possible thing that you can ever imagine."

"Is she going to kill us?" Will seemed afraid suddenly.

"No, the opposite actually. You've been saved." With that, Trevor turned reluctantly and left.

Soon after that, all the chosen ones had been collected. Luckily the scouring hadn't taken place yet and the Phoenix was complete, ahead of schedule. The Talosian ship left the Earth's orbit for the final time and the fledglings were on their own. All they had to do was wait, and the wait was excruciating. Novawynd started making passes through the containment area three times daily, instead of the former two times. The detainees were getting to know her and they would stop her and talk to her. They learned to stop asking questions about what was going on. They instead asked about what was happening on the outside. In a sense, Novawynd became their news-caster.

Novawynd provided them with games and books and news papers. She regularly gave them various tests and surveys. She applied two different personality profiles, an IQ test, an aptitude test, two psychological profiles and a survey that determined interests and capabilities of each. The main-frame would be fed this information and determine a vocation that would be most fitting for each person.

Another familiar face to Novawynd was the, saucy, happy-go-lucky rocker, Matt McClellan. He recognized her from his dreams also. Of course she had selected him as one of her chosen ones.

"Hey Frosty!" he would call to Novawynd as she came near his cell. He called her frosty because of her snow-white hair, not because she was in any way frigid. In fact, he thought she was as hot as a pistol, so he tacked the nick-name on her as a display of the typical ironic brand of humor he had.

Novawynd would sidle up to the cell. "What can I tell you today, Matt?"

"I was wondering about the babe I hear overhead who gives the time on the hour; the one with the hot Brit accent? Where is she?" He was referring to the Phoenix's main-frame computer. Novawynd laughed, but of course, he couldn't have known that voice was a computer. Novawynd had wanted the main-frame to have a sexy, female voice, with an English accent. She just thought it sounded soothing, yet intellectual, attention grabbing, and worthy of respect. Novawynd named it Ariel, which wasn't an angel name, but it didn't have to be. This ship was not a Xaxon ship. None-the-less, because the ship was named for a bird, albeit a mythical bird, she wanted everything to be named for avian and airy things. The space-guard were not to be referred to as space-guard, they were now "avians". The battleots were now "talons" and the shuttles were named, Eagle, Condor, Red-tail, Osprey, Kestrel and Peregrine.

"Actually Matt, that isn't a real woman. It's a computer." Novawynd was sorry to have to tell him that. "But, over on the other side of these cells, there are some British babes. You'll meet them later." she assured him.

Novawynd made friends with the captives this way, some she got to know better than others. Needless to say, she became quite close to Matt and Will, but also with another actor who was in the cell next to Will. He was Scottish and his name was Gerrard Tanner. He referred to himself as Tanner and so everyone else began to call him by that name too. He had sandy brown hair and hazel eyes; he was just under six-feet-tall and nicely fit. He was muscular, not in a bulky way, but in a perfectly cut way. He was ruggedly handsome, not pretty. He was the oldest of all Novawynd's chosen ones at a ripe thirty-six-years-old.

"So, Frosty," he had heard Matt calling Novawynd that and he glommed on to it, because he also found it humorous. "How many men and how many women?"

"There are now fifty men and fifty women of all races, religions and lifestyles here; a real broad mix. The most intelligent, talented and beautiful the world has to offer." Novawynd stated proudly.

"Sounds kinda like Noah's Ark." Tanner suggested in his Scottish brogue. Novawynd did not respond to that. She just gave him a knowing look and left the containment area promptly. She was impressed with Tanner, he was smarter than she thought he'd be. Although he had been an actor for the last eight years of his life, he had graduated from Princeton, quite high in his class. He had pursued a career in teaching literature just out of college, and taught for two years. He knew within that short amount of time that he hated teaching. He quit and got a job as a construction worker. He did that for four years before being discovered by a casting agent in London. He didn't think he would be interested in acting, but he thought he would give it a try anyway, just for the experience. As it turned out, he was a natural, and acting was a good fit for him. Once he appeared in his first movie, casting agents were clamoring for him. He was just one of those brilliant but restless people who always strove for something better, and happened to get exactly what he wanted handed to him on a silver platter. Novawynd thought he could be a good commander some day.

*   *   *

Zefram was called to return to Xaxon 2. The scouring virus for Earth had been completed. It was a particularly lethal bug and would damage any humans with iron-based blood, who may come in contact with it; not just earthlings. Several pods were loaded with the agent and carefully crated. The crates were loaded onto the Tauron. Zefram oversaw the loading of the cargo personally, even though that would normally be beneath him. Everyone who had worked with Zefram for many anios thought it was strange that he would lower himself to such duty, but no one would ever question the mighty Zefram. If he was taking time to personally oversee the cargo loading, it was probably because the Superior Council told him to.

Zefram felt an odd stirring in the Omniaural. He hoped it was Novawynd. He hoped she now knew of this plan and realized there was nothing she could do to stop him. He hoped she would try. He looked forward to an opportunity to face Novawynd as a true rival and to pit his skills against hers. Who would win in such a fight? It surely would be a fight to the death. If he couldn't take Novawynd out, he would be glad to die trying. However, the stirring wasn't Novawynd, it was the Omniaural itself. It knew of the plan to destroy all life on Earth, and it pulsed with negative energy, but it couldn't stop Zefram.

Once the virus was loaded safely onboard, Zefram didn't feel that there was any reason to delay in delivering the goods to Earth. The more swiftly he moved, the better. The Tauron came out of its flux, some light years from Earth. The robots uncrated the virus pods and loaded them into the pod-launchers. This would normally be done in orbit around the planet, but Zefram intended to move in on Earth, launching the probes as the Tauron came out of flux. This way, there would be no time for interference from another ship. Such as, a ship that Novawynd might be on. The robots signaled when they were done, and once the final pod was locked in its launch chute, Zefram commanded the Tauron to continue on to Earth. "Ready the pod launch chutes and hold for my signal." he ordered the main-frame.

The Tauron came out of flux near the Moon and moved in auxiliary power toward Earth. As the ship bore down on the Earth's stratosphere, Zefram was somewhat shocked that he met no resistance. There was no Novawynd, and no ships to meet him. She was not there to witness what he would bring on her people, nor was she there to stop him. It was just as well. He would be able to complete this mission more quickly without the interference. "Release the pods." he gave the command. The pods shot out of their tubes, hurtling toward the Earth surface like meteorites.

*　　　　*　　　　*

On the Earth surface, the Earthlings went about their business, completely unaware of the danger hurtling toward them. Some people noticed the meteorites, but most thought nothing of it. Thirty-three thousand pods had been released and once they reached the Earth's troposphere, they stopped and hovered in mid air. They set up a perimeter around the planet. Each pod would release enough of the viral agent into the atmosphere to cover a one hundred mile radius. Some people would probably not be exposed to the virus. Danalian had predicted that out of six billion people on the planet, about half of a million would probably survive. However, anyone left alive would be hunted down by the hunter-probes that would be inevitably sent down to the planet from time to time.

Novawynd had probes too. They were located in seven of the Earth's largest cities. Their primary function was to alert Novawynd to when the virus hit and return digital imagery of the ensuing tumult. She felt Zefram before the probes alerted her, but she was shocked at how quickly she received the alert, once she sensed Zefram's presence. Novawynd in turn notified her family, Trevor, Stunner, Vertigo and the Talosians of the arrival of the zero hour. Trevor ran to the quarters of his family and told them all to turn their monitors. They sat huddled together on the sofas in Trevor's parents' living room and watched in horror. Novawynd's family did the same in Kat's quarters. The Talosians, Stunner and Vertigo watched in the avian's dormitory lounge.

Novawynd was in the command center. Arial turned on the large screens in the temporary containment area. Novawynd appeared on the screens. She had knots in her stomach. She had prayed to the Omniaural to not allow what was happening. She had hoped that she would not have to say what she was about to say. "Hello, everyone! You have wondered what this place, in which you find yourselves, is. You have wondered why you are here. You have wondered who I am and why I am doing this. I am going to answer all those questions right now." Novawynd explained her history of how she came to have her abilities. She relayed how she came upon the Xaxony in this way. She explained about the Superior Council and the prophesy of the Lajiachine and how that scared the Superior Council. She told the story of Zefram and of the Leluminalia. She explained about how she defected and the people that were out there who are helping them. Finally she explained how the Xaxony had unleashed the virus and what was currently happening on the Earth's surface. "But, don't take my word for it. I will let you see for yourself. Only, be warned that this is not Hollywood magic. What you are about to see is very graphic and very real."

The screens cut to the views from the probes. The cameras were looking down streets and one could see people running frantically down the middle of the streets, clawing at their skin. Some people dragged themselves, some vomited blood, in several instances there were bloody pools congealed here and there. Novawynd cut in with her voice, but allowed the video to keep running. "This is happening right now. The virus works fast. In a matter of moments, it causes the tissues to liquefy. Notice the pool of blood. Those were people only moments ago. What you are looking at is a street in New York. But, it's happening everywhere. I'm switching to my probe in Tokyo." they could see the same thing happening there. "Now Sydney." Novawynd switched the view again. "This is London." the scene switched again.

Sounds of yelling, screaming, wailing and retching came back to her from the containment center.

A man with a strong voice yelled, as if to calm the others. "It's not real. This is not real, people." It was Will.

Novawynd cut to a scene of a mountain pasture. It was serene and starkly juxtaposed to what they had just seen. Light ambient music played low to calm them. "I'm afraid it is really happening Will." Novawynd assured. In a couple of days, when we are sure the virus is dead and the Xaxon ship is gone, I will take ten of you out to survey the damage with your own eyes. This will prove to you the truth of it."

*   *   *

Zefram watched the 4D display of the globe and the hotspots for the viral activity. He never ceased to be amazed by how quickly the scouring viruses spread. The computer showed the virus as hot pink and Zefram watched as the putrid color as it engulfed all the populated areas. He watched the death toll rise and the population count fall. He watched for nearly a whole dialo without sleeping, but the strength of the virus had dwindled with the lack of living beings to spread it along. He then only checked its progress every once and a while for the next couple of dialos. There were approximately six-hundred-thirty-seven thousand people still alive on the planet and they were sparse. "Send down the drones." Zefram gave the order at last. They would spend another dialo sweeping the planet free of the stragglers.

In the mean time, the demo robots had already set off to the planet surface to shutdown and dismantle the nuclear reactors that had popped up all over the Earth's face like boils. The demo robots would also do away with any other nasty toxic waste immediately. After a while, different demo robots would return to the Earth's surface to obliterate the physical structures the Earthlings worked so hard to build. That would actually be a long and expensive process, but it was worth it to the Xaxony to reclaim a viable planet.

*   *   *

Novawynd left her captives alone for the next couple of days. She wanted them to have some time to deal with what had happened before she showed her face again. She sensed that Zefram was still out there and they couldn't go out just yet. She couldn't send her new probes, which would test the air, soil and water for the presence of the virus, until the Xaxon ship was gone. Another day would pass, and then suddenly the pressure of Zefram's presence was gone.

Novawynd sent out her drones to do the testing. They sent back data showing the results, in hundreds of samples taken, were all negative. It was safe to assume the virus had run its course and was now dead. "Ariel?" Novawynd hailed the computer.

"Yes, Novawynd?"

"Announce that the probes have verified the virus has terminated its lifecycle."

"At once, Novawynd." it affirmed. Novawynd heard the computer making the announcement, and then she blipped Stunner, Vertigo, Tren and Tracker, who was the Talosian lead of the B squad. She summoned them to meet her in the temporary containment area. She went to meet the aliens just outside of the cafeteria. She had them follow her in and she slowly walked down the aisles with them, observing the detainees. But really, letting the detainees get a good look at the aliens. When the detainees saw the aliens, they were either confused, or in awe. Novawynd had four aisles to walk down, and in the middle of each she stopped and introduced the four alien men with her. After introducing them and making sure to point out that they were friends who were there to help. She asked if anyone wanted to go outside to be a witness to the damage.

"I need ten people. I would prefer five women and five men." To Novawynd's surprise, many of the captives volunteered. She did not select any she felt were only volunteering because they planned to escape. One who was sincerely volunteering was Will. Not to be outdone, Tanner also volunteered. She smiled to think they were using healthy competition to put the horrible occurrences of the past seventy-two hours behind them. Finally, Novawynd had her away-team selected. Novawynd and Stunner took one of the shuttles with a Talosian avian by the name of Chase to give the Earthlings a tour of the devastation. Meanwhile a different army was to go out from the ship. Trevor, his family, Novawynd's family, Vertigo, the Talosians and the AP were to take the remaining shuttles and RVs and spend the rest of the day scrounging up all the provisions they could muster. They would continue collecting food until they had the entire biosphere six stocked wall to wall and ceiling to floor. Ariel had computed this would take three more days, given the locations of available food sources and their proximity to the ship. Some grocery stores along the lines fed by the nuclear power plant would possibly still have power. The shuttles were to go along the lines to check on those grocery stores. The reason for this was because they may still have refrigerated and frozen foods. Otherwise the Earthlings would have to resort to preserved and dried goods. Not the healthiest options necessarily.

Novawynd's away party was brought to the nearest large city so they could see with their own eyes the devastation. When they saw the cars abandoned in the middle of the streets and the papers blowing along the abandoned side walks, and the dried pools of blood everywhere, they were convinced. They begged to return.

Will pleaded, "Do we have to go back to the cells though Novawynd? I mean, now that that the virus has run its course, do we really need to continue to be imprisoned?"

"Yes, but only for a short while longer. The only way you can get out of your cells is if you want to help with the duty of collecting our provisions."

"Why don't you let us all help?" The woman who spoke was a surgeon of Eastern Indian descent. Her name was Padema and she was stunning. "All of us in captivity? It would give us something to do and it would go that much faster?"

Novawynd sensed the motive behind her request. Such a move would give the captives opportunity to escape. Novawynd shrewdly responded, "Currently, all of our available shuttles and other vehicles are already being utilized and this shuttle is the only one that isn't being used for that purpose. We would only need a couple more bodies to assist. We couldn't accommodate all our chosen ones, nor could we keep an eye on all of them. What if someone was foolish enough to try to escape? They might get away from us, but their attempt would be fruitless, because probes will be back in a while to do another sweep. The Xaxony will continue to sweep until they have wiped all human life from Earth. It would be sad to see a promising human who could offer so much to our flock, go astray, only to be cut down by a cold, calculating machine." Novawynd looked at Padema intently, as if to say "Don't even think about it." Then Novawynd finished, "If you would like to help Padema, you may."

"But Frosty," Tanner interrupted, "I think we all realize that there's nothing out there for us now. We would all stay close to other humans. I don't think anyone would run off."

"I know what you're saying and I agree, but you don't know what is going to happen, and I do, and I can't tell you. Let me put it this way. You are not so much in captivity as you are in containment. Another event is to occur, and until it occurs, you need to be contained. I can't set you all free yet. But, I *will* let you all out of your cells, and soon. Very soon." Novawynd assured them.

"I want to help with the provision collecting." Will stated, somewhat off the subject.

"Me too." Tanner declared. Then everyone started to pipe up, offering their help.

"I can only take two." Novawynd informed reluctantly. "Tanner and Padema. You two can help. The rest of you will go back to your cells. I'm sorry.

*   *   *

Two and three quarters of a day later, the crew, AP, robots and captive helpers had accumulated enough food to fill the stocks. The shuttles had found some grocery stores that still had frozen goods, but the frozen goods would not last long. They would become freezer-burned in a matter of time. When that happened, the Phoenix could come back to Earth to have a hunting party, to get fresh meat, if necessary.

The helper robots organized all the goods in biosphere six. They made sure everything was secure for the take-off, which would commence soon, now that the final phase was complete. Novawynd called all her officers together in the auditorium. "In two tecrons, we will commence launch sequence. All systems are optimal and Ariel affirms there are no anomalies in the structure or engine components that would delay launch. We have a green light. I need the officers to decide how to get all our chosen ones from their containment cells, in a peaceful and orderly fashion, to this auditorium within one tecron, thirty mecrons. With that, she turned on her heel and left.

The captive moving process went along steadily, and soon the temporary cells were empty and the robots began to dismantle them and stow them away immediately. Novawynd and Stunner arrived with Kat, Ana, Maris and Trevor's family. They took the seats that were left open in the front rows. Novawynd stood and faced the people. She was torn between tingling with excitement, and feeling utterly sad for the substantial loss of human life that had occurred. She did not like what she had to say, but this was to be the pep-talk to rally the spirits of the chosen ones.

"By now, you all know that the events you witnessed on the screens were not a falsity. You have probably guessed that you were brought here to be saved from that fate. I want you all to know, if there was a way that I could have saved everyone, I would have. We have powerful alien friends helping us. Their civilizations are many, many millennia older than that of Earth and they are advanced beyond anything you could imagine. They had their best minds working on it and even they could not find a solution; at least, not one that could be accomplished in three months. The best we could do was to select a handful of the best and brightest Earth had to offer. You were all selected because you had the very best genetics to offer to a new Earthling civilization. Everyone here is indispensable from that stand-point. I'm sorry I couldn't save your families, but... there was only so much space.

I had hoped that the greater spiritual force in the universe, whatever you call it; God, Allah, the Omniaural, or whatever, would present us with a solution, even if it was in the eleventh hour. Obviously, no solution was offered. This leads me to believe that this destiny was mandated, because the human race had bred too much negative energy and God felt it was necessary to wipe it clean. The annihilation of most people on Earth is not an easy reality to accept, but it may be easier to accept it if we think about all the bad things about our civilization and tell ourselves, based on that, 'we asked for it'.

You'll need to grieve, of course, but I want everyone to look to the future and to do everything you can to make sure something like this doesn't happen again. You all will build a new civilization. You will have children and grandchildren and you will teach them to be better people.

From this point forward, I don't want to hear another word about what happened. We have counselors, and if you need to vent, go to see a counselor. I only want to hear positive things, about the future, and how you plan to make it brighter."

Ariel blipped in Novawynd's ear "Twenty zecrons until lift-off."

"Very good." Novawynd responded to Ariel, and then addressed the group again. "You all will need to remain seated for the next five minutes. You will feel the ground shake, but don't be alarmed, you are perfectly safe here and if you remain in your seats, no one will get hurt."

The ground did begin to shake and a distant roar could be heard. It intensified as the floor shook even more violently. The boosters were at full ignition, pushing the Phoenix out of its launch chute. Some in the audience grabbed the arms of their chairs and others shifted nervously in their seats. "What's happening?" a man yelled.

"Just a little movement, it'll be over very quickly." Novawynd didn't want to say too much right now."

Ariel updated Novawynd and the commanding officers as to the progress. "The Phoenix has cleared the launch chute. Initializing Novawynd's launch sound-track." Music came on overhead and would be heard all over the ship, if everyone wasn't already in the auditorium. The first song was the first part of the *Winter* movement of Vivaldi's *The Four Seasons.*

"The Phoenix has broken through the troposphere. Ship's biosphere leveling system is fully operational." At that point, the Earthlings could feel the G-Forces pressing them into their seats. "Breaking through the Earth's Stratosphere. Ship's gravity systems are operational and all life-support and propulsion systems are optimal. Flux engine is optimal." Ariel informed. At that point the music changed to a heavy goth-rock song about the Earth being wiped clean of all evil. The ship had leveled out and was now in near Earth orbit. Novawynd jumped up out of her seat. "Ariel, flux protocol Z-Y-one-two." This was an order given to the ship that told it to flux immediately to any random point in space. Ariel did as commanded and the flux engine worked flawlessly.

"Okay everyone. Avians, you are excused. Eams and Novawynd families, you are also excused. The rest of you, I will explain what has just happened and what will happen. This rather space-age looking structure we are in right now, is actually a giant space-ship, and the tremors you felt moments ago was us taking off. We've left the Earth and are now light-years away."

A buzz began among the Earthlings. A woman spoke up "Are we never going back to the Earth?" she asked, and it was the question on everyone else's minds.

"We'll go back to Earth, from time to time, but when it's safe. In the mean time you should all think of some personal items you'd like to collect the next time we go back."

"But, we aren't going back to live there, we have to stay on board this ship?" one of the men asked.

"Yes. Because of the probes the Xaxony will send down from time to time, it won't be safe for about fifteen to twenty years. Then we can go back to stay. So, we have to make ourselves scarce and untraceable out here in the wide expanse of space until then. This will be our new home for a while. Your focus now is to attempt to repopulate and *my focus* is to make the beings responsible for this *pay*."

"Are you telling us we have to *mate* with each other and have babies?" Another woman asked, as if the thought of that was horrifying.

"We will produce offspring, even if we have to genetically engineer clones in test tubes. However, I would think in time you will all warm up to the idea of doing it the old fashioned way. I mean it's really more fun that way anyway, right?"

There was a collective, but nervous laugh.

"We don't have to go back to living in those cells do we?"

"No, the ship is really quite large. The designers tried to make it as comfortable as possible. However, your units are not as large as you're used to a home being. For some of you, it will seem like you're still in prison, but try your best to stay positive and to make it a home for yourself as soon as possible. The units were actually designed so you aren't too comfortable in it. The point was to get you all out of your units to seek entertainment and socialize. You are completely free to move around the ship at your whim. There are only certain areas that are off limits.

I'm afraid those are all the questions I can answer for now. I will answer any you may have later on, but now you will now be given a tour, and then brought to your units. Captain Stunner, Please take half our guests and start at the back of the ship, working toward the front. I'll take the other half and start at the front. Answer any questions they might have." she commanded.

The tour took an hour because of all the questions, but Novawynd was happy to answer them. She felt the more people knew, and the more she could allay people's fears, the healthier they all would be mentally. During the tour, she also showed them the 4D displays and trained them on how to ask the computer anything. They seemed to be very interested in the alien technology, and eager to use it. But, the overwhelming question was, "When do we get to see our new homes." Because of the trauma of the past events, they were all exhausted and needed to rest. Not to mention, so did Novawynd.

After showing them all to their units, Novawynd returned to her own. It was an expansive unit that took up the whole of the uppermost livable floor in biosphere two. The tech robots had already dismantled the elevator tube that had been running through her unit. She instructed Ariel to lock her in for the whole next half dialo. This meant that no one would be able to visit her or even to blip her. Ariel was the only one who could, and that was only in a dire emergency. She stripped down and curled up in her bed. She thought about Star again. "So, Star, you are on Lozia after all. It seems we are destined to meet, sooner than I expected. I'm making a point to visit your world as soon as I can." she announced, to no one but the Omniaural. Then she fell asleep with the image of Star imprinted fresh in her mind.